Rose Alley

AUDREY HOWARD

Rose Alley

HODDER &
STOUGHTON

Copyright © 2006 by Audrey Howard

First published in Great Britain in 2006 by Hodder and Stoughton
A division of Hodder Headline

The right of Audrey Howard to be identified as the Author
of the Work has been asserted by her in accordance
with the Copyright, Designs and Patents Act 1988.

A Hodder & Stoughton Book

1

A CIP catalogue record for this title
is available from the British Library

Hardback ISBN 0 340 89533 0
Trade Paperback ISBN 0 340 89534 9

Typeset in Plantin by Hewer Text UK Ltd, Edinburgh
Printed and bound by Mackays of Chatham Ltd, Chatham, Kent

Hodder Headline's policy is to use papers that are natural, renewable
and recyclable products and made from wood grown in sustainable
forests. The logging and manufacturing processes are expected to
conform to the environmental regulations of the country of origin.

Hodder and Stoughton Ltd
A division of Hodder Headline
338 Euston Road
London NW1 3BH

I would like to dedicate this book to my three grandchildren, Daniel, Adam and Natalie Pitt because Adam requested it. He wanted to see his name in print!

I

Queenie stopped, bringing the handcart she was pushing to a standstill, and placing her hands on her broad hips straightened her aching back. Her feet were inches deep in the rutted dust of the track which was really no more than a sheep trod and she wondered if she had made a mistake in taking this short cut across Oswaldtwistle Moor. Her hands, which were hardened after years of pushing the cart along every path and track of the South Pennines, were rubbed sore, for she had forced herself and the child to the limit these last few days. Winter was coming on. Sleeping out of doors under the handcart would be out of the question before long and the sooner they reached Liverpool and home the better.

She looked about her at the endless rolling moorland, wild and uninhabited except by the wavering dots of sheep which wandered in what seemed to be an aimless manner from one small heathery shrub to another. A group stopped to stare at her, lifting their tangled heads in a supercilious way, then scattered as the child, as children will, clapped her hands and shouted 'Boo', laughing with delight. Queenie wondered, as she had done for years now, where the child got her natural exuberance from given the hardship of her life. Probably from that red-haired scamp who was her father and whom Queenie had not clapped eyes on since the day she had told him she was with child.

'Come on, chuck, don't dawdle . . .' Which was unfair, for the child never failed to keep up. Her little legs would go ten to the dozen, almost running to keep pace with her mother, and if she wasn't running she was hopping or skipping, probably singing as she did so, which again was an inheritance from her merry Irish father.

'Look, Mam, what's them on those bushes?' she asked, pointing a finger at the spreading carpet of vegetation that lay about them for mile after mile, broken only by enormous misshapen boulders, some looming silently alone, others in companionable groups, scattered as though by some mischievous giant child. Queenie followed the child's pointing finger, scanning the variety of plants among which only the sheep moved. There was cowberry creeping across the landscape, its white flowers beginning to die as autumn progressed; mosses of all shades of green, for the ground was boggy and wet; moor grass; the massed and lovely purple of heather which was at its peak; but the plant the girl pointed out had black fruit growing on it, deep and luscious.

'Why, them's bilberry, our kid, an' if I can find that old basket nobody wanted ter buy in't market-place we'll pick us some to mash up wi' our oats. That'll mekk a right nice finish fer us dinner when we gerr 'ome which I 'ope'll be by th'end o't week. That's if they keep. Should do, picked fresh terday. But we'll 'ave ter look sharp, fer we've still over thirty miles ter tramp. Are yer mothetten, lass, 'cos if ya are yer can 'op up on't cart when we've picked bilberries. Yer a good lass an' we've come a fair way terday.'

'No, Mam,' the child said stoutly. 'I'm not tired.' And to prove it she skipped a step or two.

'Right, well, let's gerron. 'Appen we can get by Over Darwen, on ter Darwen Moor an' set down under't cart fer't night there. Them big stones mekk a good shelter. We should know, shouldn't we, chuck. We've done it a few times.' She chuckled and the child laughed with her, then the mother turned in a complete circle, putting her hand to her forehead and studying the sky. 'It don't look like rain.'

The child copied her mother's action. 'No, Mam, it don't,' she said solemnly.

Queenie smiled, her heart bursting with love for this gift she had been given so late in her life, this precious girl who not only had her father's merry ways but her own good common sense. And she was so lovely that Queenie had begun to worry, for she had noticed men looking at her with that certain expression Queenie had come to recognise. She was only seven years old but there were perverted chaps who liked a bit of young flesh; indeed there was a flourishing market in the cities for innocent virgins and plenty of greedy, unscrupulous women to provide it for the right price.

The sun moved slowly across the deep blue bowl of the sky, skirting a cloud or two as the woman and child moved deep into the clutching embrace of the bilberry bushes, their ragged skirts catching on the ground-covering branches. They picked steadily, staining their already dirt-engrained fingers, Queenie holding up her skirt to catch the luscious fruit, the little girl placing those she picked in the basket that had failed to sell at the market in Accrington. She was careful not to crush the fruit, though now and again she popped one of the berries into her mouth, staining her lips to an even more rosy red, and she sang as she moved from bush to bush.

> *I know where I'm going,*
> *And I know who's going with me*
> *I know who I love,*
> *But the dear knows who I'll marry.*

Queenie smiled, creasing the honey-coloured skin of her face into deep wrinkles. It was said that Queenie came from gypsy stock and her sun-browned face seemed to prove it. She walked like a queen, which was probably where she got her name, some thought, straight-backed, her dark head held high, swaying

gracefully with long strides, looking neither to left nor right as
though those who passed by her were beneath her. She was tall,
full-breasted with generous hips and it was a mystery to those
who lived about her why some man had not moved in with her.
Of course, someone must have had his way with her, for where
had she got the kid, but none had ever seen him and Queenie
was not a woman to question or to pass on confidences, even to
her neighbour Jess Wilson who was the closest Queenie had to a
friend.

It was Jess's son Jem who had taught the child the song she
was singing now and not just this one but many others he had
learned in his work about the shipyard. 'I Saw Three Ships
Come Sailing By', 'Greensleeves', 'It Was a Lover and His
Lass' and the one Queenie herself used to sing to the child
when she was a baby, 'Golden slumbers kiss your eyes, smiles
awake you when you rise . . .' which was exactly what happened as soon as the child woke in the morning. Smiles,
laughter, beauty, joy, as though it were an enchantment just
to be alive with the ability to pass on all these wonders to those
in her world, despite their desperately poor lives.

'I think we've gorr enough now, luv. We'd best gerr a move
on or it'll be dark before we get ter Darwen Moor.'

Instantly obedient, the little girl turned and made her way
behind her mother to the handcart. The bilberries Queenie had
picked were tipped into the basket and placed carefully on top
of the tottering pile of goods that Queenie had failed to get rid of
in the market at Accrington but which she hoped to sell in the
markets of the several towns and villages they would pass
through on their way to Liverpool. There was Over Darwen,
Chorley, Wigan, St Helens and Prescot, all fair-sized places
with a market in each. She and the child had spent many weeks
in the cotton towns of the South Pennines, going from factory
to factory buying, as cheaply as they could, the cotton goods
that were surplus to requirements. They had even gone over

the tops and into Yorkshire, to Keighley and Halifax, where woollen goods might be on sale, then back into Lancashire to Colne, Barnoldswick, Burnley and yesterday Accrington. They had set up their cart on the edge of the market, erecting the wide banner Queenie had made years ago which proclaimed that woollen and cotton goods were for sale along with donkey stones, brass fire irons, a coal scuttle, a battered bird cage, an enamel frying pan, a golden syrup can, a mouse trap, all what the rest of the world would call rubbish and which were rusted and in a poor condition. She had picked up innumerable household goods for next to nothing, which were all that the desperately poor who had bought them could afford. Cleaned up, they would make a decent profit, even as much as a penny on each item! And this winter she and the child would scour Liverpool, knocking on back doors asking if the household had any old rubbish it wished to get rid of. There were many markets in the city, starting with the magnificence of St John's Market where the upper classes – or at least their housekeepers – shopped. But Queenie favoured the Pedlars' Market in Deane Street where the kind of goods she had to offer might be displayed for the benefit of those less well off: baskets, earthenware, glass, toys, bonnets – second or even third- or fourth-hand goods. And there was St Martin's Market in Scotland Road; Pownall Square, which was held in the open air; the Pig Market and Gill Street Market where, at the rear of the market proper, in the yard there was space for market dealers like herself selling hardware, woollen and cotton goods, cheap stuff that was within the financial range of the inhabitants of the tenement houses in which she herself lived.

Since she had been a small child Queenie Logan had been practical, sensible, clear-headed, but it all deserted her seven years ago when it came to the naming of her newly born daughter.

'*Gillyflower!* What sorta name's tha' fer Christ's sake? Poor kid'll get six bells o' shit knocked out of 'er by them in't street.' Jess, who had just delivered the child, was open-mouthed with amazed horror.

'I don't care, Jess. That's wharr I'm callin' 'er.' She didn't explain why to Jess. That was *her* secret. 'She'll 'ave ter learn ter stick up fer 'erself, same as I did. Anyroad, I like Gillyflower,' she said, wincing sharply as Jess dealt with the afterbirth.

Jess swabbed carelessly with a none too clean cloth at the tear between Queenie's thighs from where the baby, a strong, lusty girl, had just yelled her way into the world. The afterbirth, which she had dropped into one of Queenie's chipped basins, was carried to the door which opened on to a small basement area with steps leading to the street. Climbing the steps, she flung the mess into the foetid gutter where it was pounced upon by two scrawny dogs who immediately began to fight over it. It was a raw February night and Jess shut the door hurriedly to keep in the warmth of Queenie's cellar room. Coal was expensive and the fire in the grate was no more than a smouldering ember or two but the hard labour the two women had just gone through had brought both out in a sweat, giving the impression that the temperature was warmer than it actually was. Jess wanted to keep it that way. She would have to get off soon or her own children would be howling for her, but none more so than that fat arse of a husband who had given them to her. Of course he wasn't actually her husband in the eyes of the law, for none round here had the cash to purchase a marriage licence, but at least she had a chap, which was more than could be said for poor Queenie.

She looked round the dingy room, still littered with the debris of the conflict they had just fought, rags slopped on the floor, a spilled basin of water, a small pool of Queenie's blood, the knife with which she had cut the cord and the remains of a dish she had dropped and broken. Not that she had the time or the inclination, if the truth were told, to tidy it up a bit; in fact she wanted to do no more than make a cup of weak tea, one for each of them, which she would drink while she rested in Queenie's sagging old rocking-chair before the sulky fire. The baby had been wiped round with the same cloth that had tidied Queenie up 'down there', wrapped in an old blanket Queenie had brought from the market in preparation for this day and put to her mother's breast where she was suckling heartily. Jess watched approvingly.

'That un'll survive, lass. Look at way she's slurpin' it down. A good sign, Queenie. An' she's a good weight. Seven pounds, I'd say. But yer'll be wantin' some more water fetchin', ter clean up a bit and bath 'er like.' Not that Jess would bother with such a thing herself, for she was indifferent to the state of her home and her children's hygiene, or lack of it, the last born only three months ago but still surviving, since water was a scarce commodity in the alley, but she knew Queenie was a bugger for it. 'Shall I send our Jem round ter fill yer bucket?'

'Thanks, Jess, that's kind. I'll be up termorrer ter see ter messen but I'd be glad of Jem ternight. When this un's 'ad 'er fill I'll get some sleep. I'm off ter't Saturday market at Aintree Racecourse an' I could do wi' a birrof a rest first. An' 'appen your Jem could give me a 'and wi't handcart. Gerrin it up them steps is tricky at the best o' times.'

'Course, lass.' Jess eyed the handcart which was Queenie's livelihood and which took up a fair space in the corner of the dingy cellar. It was a dilapidated thing made up of odd bits of wood tacked together, rusted nails holding them in place and the two leaning wheels giving the distinct impression that they were about to fall off at any moment. But Queenie, with the help of Jem who was glad of the ha'pence he earned, kept the thing on the road despite its unsafe appearance. It should be said that Tommy Wilson, Jem's father, was the beneficiary of the money Jem earned, for it went straight into his pocket, finding its way across the bar counter of the Crown and Anchor at the corner of Pumpfields and Vauxhall Road right next to the coal yard, which was handy of a cold night. Jess was glad of the lump or two her Tommy often fetched home in his pocket and the only loser was poor Jem. But he was a good lad and Jess didn't know what she would do without him! And neither did Queenie. He would help her to load up the handcart in the morning from the neat piles of what looked like decomposing rubbish that was stacked in every corner of the room and if she gave him a few pence would come with her to Aintree and help her set up her stall, which would be a help with the baby to see to. But she'd manage. She always had, hadn't she?

There was quiet in the room but for the sucking of the child, which was becoming slower as satiation and sleep overtook her, and the hissing of the kettle which sat on the bars across the front of the fire. As Jess rocked the rockers tapped gently on the bare floor and for a moment she almost fell into a doze, then she shook herself awake and stood up. She smoothed down the stained apron she wore, stained with the blood of the woman who had just given birth and other matter which did not bear looking into! A small ginger cat twined round her feet, mewing piteously. She pushed it irritably aside with her foot as she made her way to the door.

'An 'yer'd best watch this bugger wi't baby, chuck. Cats is known ter lie on their face an' smother 'em. One o' Mrs Berry's went that way, poor soul. Eight weeks old, it were, an'—'

'Aye, thanks, Jess, I'll keep Gillyflower in bed wi' me.' Queenie's eyes were drooping and the baby lay peacefully at her side.

Jess raised her eyes to the stained ceiling and tutted exasperatedly, feeling sorry for the poor little beggar and wondering how she would survive in Rose Alley with a name like *Gillyflower*. 'Right then, chuck, I'll send our Jem wi' a bucket o' water right away otherwise stand pipe'll be turned off before we know where we're at.'

'Thanks, Jess, yer a pal.'

'Nay, we 'elp each other in this bloody world, Queenie. I'll pop in later termorrer, lass. See 'ow yer gorron at market.'

Queenie was more than half asleep when a tentative knock on the door brought her from the rest her body craved. For a moment she was startled then she remembered young Jem and as she struggled to sit up he put his tousled head round the door, his freckled face beaming from ear to ear, for he liked Queenie and was always glad to give her a hand. She often slipped him a farthing or two, some of which he managed to keep secret from his pa, when he helped her with the handcart. Well, it had to be bumped down the steps of the basement area and into her cellar at night since it could hardly be left outside where not only its contents but the handcart itself would have vanished by morning. Then it needed two of them to get it up the steps the next day before Queenie set off for market.

'I brought yer water, Mrs Logan,' he whispered. 'Me mam ses yer want ter wash baby,' his face as perplexed as his mam's, for none of the Wilson family were much acquainted with cleanliness.

'Thanks, lad, purrit down by't fire. 'Appen yer could fill kettle fer me an' leave it on't fire then I can see ter't baby first thing.'

'Right you are, Mrs Logan.' He did as he was told then crept closer to the bed and peered down at the swaddled bundle beside her mother. 'This 'er?' He studied the sleeping baby with little interest but something about her caught his attention and he leaned closer. She was still mucky with dried blood and the stuff newborn babies were coated with, but it was her eyelashes that fascinated him. They were the longest he had ever seen, resting in a fan on her rounded cheek, and they were the colour of copper, as were her delicate eyebrows which arched above her swollen, tightly shut eyes. Her pursed lips sucked hopefully and then were still and Jem Wilson, who had seen many newborns, since he was the eldest of his mam's seven, felt something inside him move, melt, become warm.

'She's right pretty, missis,' he said hesitantly, surprising himself and the baby's mother. 'Look at colour of 'er 'air.'

They both studied the infant's hair which even under its smear of damp birth traces could only be called red. It lay flat in waves on her delicately formed skull with a short curl sticking up here and there. Jem reached out a tentative finger and touched one and it was then that he fell in love with the woman the baby would become, though he was not yet old enough to recognise the emotion. He turned to smile at Queenie. It was clear he was lost for words which was surprising, for Jem's life was made up of a definite need to speak up and *stick up* for himself in the rough and ready world he inhabited. Among the noisy family of which he was a part he fought for his place in it and amid the scores of street urchins who lived and died in the multitude of tall and tottering houses that lined Rose Alley and the neighbouring streets that jostled against one another, their occupants numbering thousands. They lived in filth and squalor in the tenements which rose out of a sea of stench in dense, dirty masses built by landlords who cared only for the profit they made from the rents. From cellar to attic, three storeys high, the structures were so rotten they were in grave danger of simply tumbling into the courts around which they were built. In the space of one square mile, should any of them have cared to count, lived 66,000 inhabitants, sometimes a family of nine, such as Jess Wilson's, in one room.

'Right, missis, I'd best be off then if there's nowt else yer need. I'll be in first thing ter give yer a 'and wi't barrow.' The boy grinned engagingly, took one last puzzled look at the sleeping baby then scuttled off up the area steps to the cellar next door where the bit of straw and sacking that he shared with his siblings awaited him.

Queenie would have liked another cup of the weak tea Jess

had made but was too weary to climb out of the sagging bed where she and her new daughter lay. Her new daughter. Her first child and undoubtedly the offspring of that red-haired scamp who had caught her eye at the Aintree Market ten months ago. Irish and impish and as handsome as the day with bright red hair which curled riotously from beneath his rakish cap. Thirty years old she had been and a virgin, for she had never met a man who was worth a second look but he had been and for a month she had become, in her own words, as daft as a bloody brush on her bed of gillyflowers, losing her normal good sense along with her virginity in the delights of the flesh. For fifteen years she had avoided the attentions of the many men who had attempted to get into her drawers but somehow 'Red' O'Hara, as he said he was called, with his impudent Irish smile and his ability to make her laugh in a world where such a commodity was scarce, had got past her defences and the result snuffled beside her.

Still, she supposed she was better off than poor Jess who was the same age as herself but had seven children, having lost five, and a lazy-arsed husband to look after. Tommy Wilson, like the rest of the denizens of Rose Alley, was unskilled without a regular trade, working when he could or when he felt like it, which was not often, on the docks, in a factory, as a general labourer, leaving Jess to earn what came her way as a midwife and layer out of the dead, depending on the soup kitchens set up by the worthy ladies of Liverpool to feed his children.

Now with her old handcart she was better off than any of her neighbours, even those with husbands, for sewn about her person in small, unobtrusive bags were the profits of the business she had dealt in since she was fifteen years old and had been thrown out on the street by her father when she had refused to submit to his attentions. Aye, she had done well, had Queenie Logan and now, as she snuggled down beside her sleeping small daughter by the old handcart beneath the tattered blankets and the bit of old tarpaulin, she allowed herself a small thrill of pride. Above her the stars shone like diamonds flung across velvet, not that Queenie had ever known either, but she meant her child, her Gilly, to have more than she had. Not diamonds or velvet, of course, but a decent start in life and that meant education. This winter, while they were stuck in Liverpool, trapped by the weather from moving more than a few miles from Rose Alley, she again intended to send the child to Sunday school. During the winter months in the past years Gilly had gone with Jem to Sunday school where she had learned the rudiments of what were called the three 'R's but from April to October while they were out on the road she got behind with her learning and Queenie meant to change that. She had no idea what this would produce or where it would lead her daughter or even how she was to manage it, since they were away from Liverpool for much of the time, but surely it could be done and with the ability to read and write she and Gilly would have the chance to . . . well, perhaps open a shop somewhere, a haberdasher's shop catering to respectable persons such as the lower middle classes of Liverpool. In Bold Street or one of the decent streets that led off it with rooms above so that they might get out of Rose Alley.

The child murmured and turned in her sleep and at once Queenie pulled her gently into her arms. It was not often she and Gilly embraced, for Queenie came from a family that did not show affection, nor, indeed, felt any. Her old dad was always trying to get his arms about her or one of her sisters while his hand crept up her skirts but that was not the same. Now, while Gilly slept, Queenie held her gently, her heart overcome with her good fortune, not only financially, which she kept very private, but in having this beautiful child for her very own. She had not loved the child's father but she had enjoyed him, his laughter and joyous ways, his handsome face and virile, eager body and though he had deserted her she knew he would never have made her a good husband even if he had been willing. No, she and Gilly were grand as they were. Underneath the ragged clothes they wore, as did the rest of Rose Alley, they were well fed and clean, and neither of them had ailed a day, even when some of the terrible diseases that roamed the streets made inroads into other families. It had been hard at times with a young baby but Gilly had seemed to recognise and accept that she must be no trouble to her mother when she stood behind the old handcart which had done them proud. A good baby, placid and content, and now, at the age of seven, able to help her mother in the search for and the selling of the goods on the handcart. She was, in fact, as asset, for with her vivid loveliness and her sunny disposition she attracted women – and men – to the handcart and they invariably bought something!

Queenie sighed with deep content, her cheek resting on the bright curls of her sleeping child. There was a chill in the air, despite the sunny day that had just gone and she knew 'back-end' would soon be upon them and they would no longer be able to sleep out of doors. But as they had done for years they would spend the winter in their cellar home in Rose Alley. They were luckier than most of their neighbours in as much as Queenie had no man to pester her, to get her with child every year and to take what she earned, pitiful as it might be, as Tommy Wilson did from poor Jess. Since Gilly was born Jess had been pregnant four more times, two of the babies surviving somehow in the festering conditions in which they lived. There were fevers of unknown origin on every street corner in the teeming population of Liverpool, fevers that carried off the malnourished offspring of women like Jess. And though the month or two Queenie had spent with Red O'Hara, travelling with him from town to town, following the path of the markets, had been very sweet and the result, her lovely child, well worth it, Queenie wouldn't swop her life with anyone. At least in the same station of life as herself. She didn't know any other!

2

It was November, the winter which the poor dreaded upon them. Jem and Gilly turned the corner into Maguire Street before her hand slipped into his. It was an unspoken agreement between them that those who were screaming and fighting in Rose Alley in what they called 'playing out' should not see them hand in hand, since the pair knew it would create calls of derision, sneers and now and again more nasty innuendos which Gilly, even at the age of seven, understood. She skipped along beside him taking two steps to his one, the long thick plait that hung down her back bobbing in time to her stride. Her eyes, the exact shade of her hair, shone with anticipation. They were the colour of beech leaves in autumn, Jem said, though her hair, as the winter sunshine struck it, had a glint of gold in it, a streak of cinnamon and amber, as glossy as the fruit from the horse chestnut tree, the 'conkers' that country children used in the game originally known as 'conquerors'. The plait of hair was as thick as Jem's strong young wrist.

Jem did his best to keep his long stride to the short, almost hopping progress of his companion. His face, from which his boyhood freckles were beginning to fade, beamed his pleasure. He was a tall, lanky lad with an easy gait. He was of the world in which he had been dragged up but gentle, warm-hearted, his mouth tender and ready with an unrestrained smile. His hair was the colour of ripe wheat, thick and unruly, falling about the collar of his shirt, and his eyes were a brilliant blue. He was quick to anger but after a bit of shouting it left him easily.

Though his life was hard and he rarely had enough to eat, hence his leanness, he bore no grudge. He worked over the water in Birkenhead at the Barrie and Hughes Shipyard, running here and there at the direction of the men who were called 'Royals' because they were the best paid. Blacksmiths, brassfinishers, boilermakers and welders, joiners and crane drivers and plate-layers, to one of whom he was apprenticed, which earned him three and sixpence a week. He was cheerful, willing and well liked in the yard and they told him he would do well when he had learned his trade. Any would do as long as it was around ships, for next to Gilly Logan, Jem Wilson loved ships.

From Maguire Street Jem and Gilly turned into Limekiln Lane, crossing the dozens of narrow streets all leading to alleyways and courts exactly like the one in which they lived. It was Sunday and since it was a pleasant day, fine and sunny, there were scores of people idling about the streets, not exactly taking a walk since exercise was not something they relished, being already overworked in their hard lives, but ready to enjoy the street entertainment that was taking place. Along the buildings that lined the streets was a mark on the exterior of the houses. The mark, a broad dirty streak, was about on a level with the men's hips where they and the lads who were not at work were in the habit of standing, leaning a bit forward as they smoked their pipes and from where they watched whatever was going on in the street. Today there was a rumour that at the back of the Crown and Anchor there was to be a bull baiting where a bull, tethered by the horns to a post in the middle of the yard, would be worried to death by relays of bulldogs. It was illegal but that made it more exciting.

A group of musicians had set up in preparation for the day's business, though the hope of any financial gain in this poor quarter was not great. Trundling along the narrow street was an organ grinder, its monkey chattering wildly on the man's shoulder, and following him was a man with a great shambling bear which he prodded cruelly in an effort to make the beast give a show of dancing.

The men who watched apathetically were stunted of physique, pale and bowed from malnutrition and yet it was known that poverty was harder on women than men. The man stayed at home only to eat, sleep and get another child on his wife, his only pleasure spending what money he earned on himself in the beer houses that stood on every corner of every street. The lowest of the working men had very hazy ideas of the marriage bond and took his pleasures where he could and it had been known for men to exchange wives on the way home from the public house. It was the women who tried to keep their children fed and clothed, who worked until, at twenty-five, they looked fifty, as was the case with Jem's poor mother; who bore the brunt of their 'husband's' ill temper and the unwanted babies they had foisted on them, but whom, when they died, they sincerely mourned.

Along Limekiln Street, moving towards St Martin's-in-the-Field, the church where the Sunday school was held and where they were headed, Jem and Gilly strode out, Gilly almost running now to keep up with Jem and escape the street scene, for neither of them approved of the cruelty to the animals on display. It was not exactly disapproval, because they lived in a world which was itself cruel to them who were of the lowest poor, but unconsciously they cringed at the thought of the pain that the animals, meant to entertain, were made to suffer. The bull could be heard bellowing its fear and anger from the back of the public house and Gilly clung tighter to Jem's hand as they left behind the crowds and the noise, though they were still boxed in by narrow, filthy streets, each one subdivided into vile-smelling lanes and dark back alleys. Along these passages ran the drains, in the pattern of all the slum streets like the one they themselves inhabited. There were open gullies carrying their filth to the river but Jem and Gilly jumped them blithely until they reached the arched gateway of the church that led into the churchyard.

They joined others at the stone-built building that stood next to the church, going to the class where lessons were held for young people up to the age of fourteen when it was agreed they had learned all the Sunday school could teach them. Prayers would be said to some Being Gilly could not even imagine, for religion played no part in her or her mam's life. Her mam sent her here for one reason only and that was to learn her letters and numbers, as Jem had done. When the lessons were over she and Jem would go, as they always did, on what Jem called an outing, though they were very familiar to Gilly by now as she had been accompanying Jem ever since she could walk.

Gilly could not remember a time in her life when Jem had not been there and though he was a man of fourteen doing a man's job in the shipyard in Birkenhead and she half his age they shared a closeness of which perhaps only Queenie was aware. The two of them, of all the shrieking hordes of half-naked children in Rose Alley, were making an effort to better themselves, Jem thanks to his own ambitions and Gilly because of her mam's.

As they left the church hall where they had completed their lessons they turned towards the delights of the river, making their way across Gerard Bridge, which spanned the Leeds and Liverpool Canal, stepping over the railway lines of the Lancashire and Yorkshire Railway towards Great Howard Street and Stanley Dock. They could already see the flying sails of the ships moving up and down the River Mersey, its waters gunmetal grey even in the sunshine, although under the hulls of the hundreds of ships that sped on the great highway, coming into or leaving the dockland, was a glint of gold.

Waiting for a break in the brisk traffic they darted across Regent Road, skirting Collingwood Gate and Clarence Graving Dock until they reached their goal: the Marine Parade.

Clarence Dock was exclusively the destination and home of steamships and had been built to accommodate the ready ingress and egress of such vessels. Glasgow packets lay crammed there, of particular interest to Jem, for the shipyard where he was apprenticed to a plate-layer built only steamships.

Simultaneously they both sighed contentedly, moving to lean on the railing that separated them from the mighty river and look over the beautifully designed packets in the dock. Gilly rested her bright head against Jem's arm then they turned to one another and smiled.

'I know,' he said, 'one day yer gonner gerron a boat an' sail ter the other side o' the world an' if yer do I suppose I'll 'ave ter come wi' yer.'

'I couldn't go wi'out yer, Jem,' she said solemnly.

'I wouldn't let yer, Lovedy,' his pet name for her. They turned, leaned their elbows on the railing and narrowed their eyes as they stared across the water. The River Mersey was as broad as a channel of the sea, opening outwards to the west, bearing ships of all sizes and nations. Along its banks were canals and stone-walled basins, a complicated warren in which to load and unload goods. Furled masts seemed like a wintry forest, enclosing the horizon from north to south. Each dock entrance was fitted with massive lock gates fashioned from long-lasting tropical timbers such as greenheart. The gates penned the water inside as the tides fell and over them were moveable walkways. Iron posts linked each one with steel chains for safety because it had happened that men had fallen in the heaving waters and been crushed between quay and ship. There were pillars a hundred feet high to indicate the entrance to the port by the Rock Channel. Jem and Gilly scanned the wide outer estuary of Liverpool Bay and the narrow middle section where Liverpool itself stood, leading on to the wider, shallower estuary that finished twenty miles inland at Warrington. Twenty-seven miles of quays, the dock area six and a half miles in length, beginning with the Canada Dock to the north, progressing through Wellington, Clarence, Trafalgar, Victoria, Princes, Albert and many others until the waters lapped at Garston Dock where the tide swept through at seven or eight miles an hour, the difference between high and low tide a remarkable thirty feet.

Exchange flags drooped behind the Town Hall, for there was very little wind, and since it was Sunday the usual hurrying groups of top-hatted and tail-coated cotton brokers, merchants and shipowners who crowded there during the week to do deals and exchange gossip were nowhere to be seen, being at home with their families.

But despite the day of the week the Dock Road was in continuous motion, for ships and the tides they sailed on were no respecter of the Lord's Day. There were horse buses, carts and team wagons shifting goods to and from the quaysides, from warehouses to ships' holds, and ships tied up along low transit sheds. The entrance to the Gorée warehouse swarmed with stevedores, tally clerks, porters and casual labourers intent on loading and discharging ships, one of whom was Tommy Wilson, Jem's pa, who had been persuaded by his Jess that unless he brought in a few bob she would take to the streets and earn them herself. She'd probably bring back the clap, she had screamed, which she would pass on to him. Their Rosie, eighteen months old though scarcely bigger than an eight-month-old, needed some 'medicine' for her cough which clogged her chest so that she could barely breathe and the old hag at the bottom of Rose Alley who made up her vile potions, mostly containing gin which put the child to sleep, doing little good but allowing the mother a respite, would not give credit!

Still hand in hand, the child leaning on the young man's arm, Jem and Gilly sauntered along the Marine Parade, saying little, for they were both enchanted by the bustle, the smells, the slow dip and rise of the ships at anchor even though they had seen it all a hundred times before. A vast range of packages, barrels, boxes and bales lay about on the dock, closely watched by the tally clerk because they all had to be accounted for and loaded in the correct position in a ship's hold. Barrels were the universal container in shipping as no matter whether the goods were liquid or dry they could be packed in such for transport abroad.

Jem and Gilly stood for several moments watching some men with huge hammers, wearing cloth caps and aprons of sacking, rippling their sweated muscles as they struck with a deafening clang on an iron post, while men in half hose and knee-length trousers, carrying oil lamps in readiness for the dark, hurried towards the doorway of a warehouse. A substantially built wagon pulled by enormous dray horses lumbered slowly past them towards a crane which was ready to lift iron bars on to it. A coastal schooner carrying coal from the Lancashire mines, salt from Cheshire, china clay from Cornwall, moved off slowly, her sails filling with what little wind there was. She would call at Runcorn with materials for the potteries in Staffordshire, iron ore and pig iron from the mines and blast furnaces of Furness and stone from North Wales, trading to all the ports round the Irish Sea. Liverpool was the second port after London in the British Empire, a great crossroads of sea and land. Tea from China, grain from North America, nitrates and guano from South America, cattle from Ireland, bales of raw cotton from the southern states of America, grain and wool from Australia, timber from America, Canada, Newfoundland and spices from the orient. The smell of brimstone, coffee, cowhides, ginger, jute, molasses, palm oil, pepper, rice, rum, saltpetre, sugar, tallow, tobacco and turpentine drifted on the fragrance of the sea, swirling together to make an intoxicating aroma which was the breath of life to the two Liverpool-born youngsters and they sniffed it in deeply, almost lovingly.

A woman with a basket on her head, her hips swaying gracefully, sang a song in a language they did not know and when she turned they saw that she was a deep brown colour. She had a bandana round her frizzing hair and her teeth were incredibly white in her brown face. A sailor spoke to her, his hand going to her round breasts which were like watermelons beneath the flimsy material of her blouse, but she laughed and pushed him away.

'I'se sellin' wet nellies, man, an' nuffin' else.' 'Wet nellies' were stale bunloaf soaked in treacle, as hard as rock but as they warmed the treacle melted and ran down inside the bunloaf, softening it.

The sailor said something that made the woman laugh again but he moved on good-naturedly. Jem tightened his grip on Gilly's hand and hurried her on, for though he was aware that she knew all there was to know about the 'doings' of men and women – how could she not living cheek by jowl with all the other Rose Alley dwellers? – he knew she was still at heart as innocent as a baby.

They turned at St Nicholas' Churchyard, the sailors' church as it was called, inspecting the forest of masts from which pennants of all colours were gaily fluttering, measuring with their young eyes the distance between the river and the spot where they stood, scarcely able to believe it possible that in the span of a man's lifetime this mighty encroachment upon the stream could have been effected.

'Just ter think all these docks below the churchyard wasn't 'ere a century ago, Lovedy.'

'What were 'ere then, Jem?' Gilly asked breathlessly, clinging more firmly to his strong hand just as though it might all be swept away again before her very eyes, and her with it.

'Angry waves boiled an' bristled up river an' the ragin'

current swep' along from't sea. I read that in a book, our Gilly. Two 'undred years ago a great wave damaged church an' broke winders an' threw great stones a distance where no man could carry them.' Jem spoke in an awed voice, for it was hard to believe that in place of all this vitality, this energy, the vast ships, the cranes, the busying men, there had been nothing but a small harbour where ships struggled to survive.

Gilly leaned even closer to Jem, never questioning his knowledge because Jem was the fount of all wisdom to her. Without him she would know nothing, about the city and port, the world as far away as Australia, China and the east. She learned about the royal family, important people who lived in London, for Jem, whenever he had a free hour, made his way to the William Brown Library where there were books and newspapers available to all. Though they were not aware of it, she and Jem were probably the most erudite young persons in Liverpool, though the word erudite had not yet come into Jem's vocabulary. For instance last year there had been a terrible slaughter in India when native soldiers had turned on the white people who lived there and killed them. The Indian Mutiny it was called, and Jem said that the British people were filled with horror, that was how he had described it, and that more troops had been sent over to quell the rebel black man.

This year he had told her all about the marriage of the Queen's daughter, the Princess Royal, Victoria Adelaide Mary Louisa – such a pretty name – to the Emperor of Prussia. He knew the names of all the high and mighty men in Parliament and spoke admiringly of Lord Palmerston who had suppressed the Indian Mutiny. When she was a little older, and could read more fluently – he used words like that – he would take her to the library and she would find out for herself all that transpired in this great world of theirs.

She relied on her mother for her comfort, her food, the clothes on her back and the relatively easy life she led – at least compared to others in Rose Alley – but it was this boy who held her heart and filled her receptive mind, who taught her, cared for her, protected her and took her on these wondrous journeys.

They continued to stroll along the docks, standing to watch as great American liners, beautiful sailing vessels, floated serenely on the still water.

'One day you an' me'll go on board and 'ave us a look,' Jem told her.

'Will they lerrus, Jem?' Gilly asked him dubiously, for the folk who were making their way on board were what her mam called 'gentlefolk'.

'Oh aye,' Jem assured her. 'Folks can go over 'em when they're moored, so one o't chaps in't yard told me. Strangers is allus welcome, 'tis said. They're right fine, Lovedy, the fittings made from lovely woods, costly, they say, luxurious an' clean, an' a sea voyage in one of 'em would be a marvel. One day,' he boasted as young men will, 'when I've medd me fortune, us'll go across the seas ter New York in one of 'em.' And so sincerely did she believe him she knew quite positively that they would.

They came at last to Queens Dock which was given up to Baltic, Russian and Dutch trades, and since the day was fine and clear they could see, outlined against the November sky, the Cheshire woods, the whole line of the Cheshire coast including New Brighton, Egremont, Seacombe, Woodside, Birkenhead, Tranmere Rock and the ferry boats which chugged regularly across the waters from Princes Dock. They sighed simultaneously, for this was all theirs for the asking and cost them nothing.

'D'yer feel up ter walking ter't Zoological Gardens or are yer ready fer 'ome?' Jem asked her, bending down to look into her eager face and was not surprised when she tugged at his hand and began to pull him towards Parliament Street which led to Upper Parliament Street. 'The Zoological Gardens it is then?'

He grinned, for he knew she loved the animals that were quartered there. She was always ready to go anywhere with him, though they had been a dozen times before, this lovely child whom he loved and cherished more than any other soul in the world. He had loved her on the night she had been born and from that day onwards had visited her and her mam every day during the months they were at home. He missed her during the summer months when she was travelling with Queenie, helping her mother in her trade, and when she came home he could not contain his joy and exhilaration though he did his best to hide it from his family. Queenie, for the sake of security though God knows there was nothing worth stealing from her damp cellar, allowed him to live there while she was absent, which suited him down to the ground for his ma would keep producing a child every year. He knew it was not her fault. He had heard her protests in the night when his pa came fumbling round her, and the cellar in which they all huddled was jammed so tight with nine children and two adults there was scarcely room to move. Jem meant to ask Queenie if she would consider him as a lodger full time. He was quick and adept with his hands and with a bit of conjuring a screen of sorts could be put up so that the ladies – as he respectfully called Queenie and Gilly – could have some privacy.

She kept up with his long stride, her hand still curled in his and all the time they talked, he telling her what he had read in yesterday's newspaper at the William Brown Library. At the beginning of the month Her Majesty had been proclaimed Empress of India and from now on that country would be ruled by their very own Queen. The William Brown was a free library built by the great philanthropist for the educated poor who could not afford to buy books of their own. Jem told her about the book he was reading at the moment, bringing her up to date on the activities of the characters in *Westward Ho!* by an author called Charles Kingsley and which was the inspiration for Jem's determination to travel some day, taking Gilly with him, of course.

They moved quickly through the maze of poor streets inhabited by the working classes, where children shouted and screamed and played their elaborate games as they did in Rose Alley and women gossiped on doorsteps, until they reached the road that led to the village of Prescot. Branching off, they climbed a fence and waded through the tall dying grasses of several meadows where cows grazed, all of them turning curiously as the two youngsters passed by. Each meadow was surrounded by trees which were in the full glory of their autumn colours. At the far side of the third meadow they came across the stumps of two old trees perched on the bank. They were completely covered with masses of flat toadstools, orange brown above and scarcely any stem. Under some beech and pine trees in the same field were toadstools that actually grew up the trunks but Jem said she was not to touch them. She had put out a hand thinking them to be mushrooms which were a rare delicacy and would make a fine meal for her and Mam but Jem shook his head saying they were poisonous. Jem knew everything, Gilly decided. The oak trees, which he recognised, still had their foliage and were all shades of bronze and brown and the hedges glowed with golden tints of nut leaves. And everywhere there were trees was the delicious autumn scent of fallen leaves. Blackbirds sang, and thrushes darted here and there and when they climbed the far fence into Love Lane there was the entrance to the Zoological Gardens.

As though to welcome them a lion roared and while both of them had shuddered away from the organ grinder's monkey and the pathetic sight of the shambling bear they did not consider the cruelty of keeping a fine animal, a wild animal shut up in a cage in the same light.

They wandered from cage to cage peering through the bars at chattering monkeys, at zebras and elephants that swayed from side to side, at the Deer House where the timid creatures pressed themselves against a fence, and last of all peered longingly through the window of the tea house where those who had larders overflowing with good food at home sat and drank tea and ate rich cream cakes. They were both hungry, for they had walked a long way and had an even longer walk home to the other side of Liverpool. It was getting dark and the narrow back streets could be dangerous with thugs who would steal the boots off your feet or even worse if you were female.

He was ready to carry her as they reached Scotland Road because she was beginning to hang on to his arm but she shook her bright curls and it was then that he hunkered down and gazed into her face.

'Yer a great little lass, our Gilly,' he said gently, using the possessive kept for one's own family or a dear one. 'I love the bones of yer, d'yer know that?'

'Aye, I'm't same.'

'One day, when I've a good job an' yer a bit older, we'll be tergether.'

'Yes, Jem.'

'Come on then, let's gct yer home. Yer mam'll wonder where yer've got to,' knowing as he said it that Queenie Logan would wonder no such thing, for it was understood between them that Gilly was to be his and that he would guard her with his life.

3

It was on a bright, sunny day in August five years later that Jem Wilson's life changed dramatically, and as a consequence so did that of Gilly Logan. It was the day that the ship was launched and there were hundreds there because everyone, from those who had built her, those who had watched her being built, to the public, loved a launch!

The sheer vitality of the scene at the launching of the ship, an ocean-going liner, a twin-screw steamship by the name of *Rose Marie* after the wives of the two owners, brought an intoxication to the young man that stirred his blood and filled him with a nervous energy. He had helped to build her as he had helped to build scores of others since he began work at the Barrie and Hughes Shipyard seven years ago and now, with hundreds of others, he was to watch her go down the ways to her element – the waters of the Mersey and thence to the sea. To the Atlantic Ocean, as she was to sail to New York on her first voyage. Of course that would be a few weeks off yet since she still had to be fitted out. It was rumoured that she was to be the most luxurious liner ever built by Barrie and Hughes and Jem could believe it, for he had seen the glowing wood, bird's eye maple, walnut and rosewood, the deep carpets and the rich materials that were to be fitted into the dining rooms, the state rooms, the library, the drawing room and the music room, the first-class smoking room and what was known as the Grand Entrance. She would do the crossing in eight days and carry 126 passengers on two decks. Even men from the Laird Brothers

Shipyard further along the river had come to gaze in admiration at the competition!

They were all there, Mr Barrie and Mr Hughes, the owners of the shipyard, with their wives and families, and Jem marvelled at the fineness of the ladies' attire, making special note of their dresses so that he could describe them to Gilly, as best he could, being a male, the colours and even the styles. Their bonnets had wide brims and were tied under the chin forming a circular frame round their faces. They were lavishly trimmed with blond lace, tulle, ribbons and flowers, and though they were very smart Jem thought both ladies were overdressed for their age as he supposed them to be in their thirties. He was not aware that the wives of gentlemen needed to show off their husbands' wealth, both in the way they dressed, which was expensively and up to date, and in the jewels that flashed from ear and bosom and fingers. Their dresses, which were called 'day dresses' though Jem was not aware of it, had a jacket bodice, pagoda sleeves with *engageantes* and a single skirt with broad zigzag trimmings. The skirts were very full, supported with a cage crinoline, and each lady carried a dainty parasol to protect her complexion from the sunshine.

Mrs Rose Barrie was to launch the ship since Mr Barrie was the senior partner. Mrs Hughes would launch the next one, her husband had promised her, so she did her best to smile and keep her eye on her children, five in all, the youngest a little lad of three years old who was in to everything. The new nursemaid had her hands full, shepherding him and the rest, the eldest seven years old – Mr Hughes being a lusty man – away from what she considered the danger that lurked behind every coil of rope, every anchor, every wagon pulled by horses with huge hooves the size of buckets which could squash an unwary child like a fly; the chains over which any one of her charges might trip and the wrath of Mrs Hughes should the slightest accident occur.

In the enormous crush the men who had helped to build the ship crowded at the back of the main party and down each side of the building slip, which was a forest of scaffolding, shoving and shouting and ready to stand beside Mrs Barrie and Mrs Hughes in their excitement. There were men actually standing on the deck of the ship where a Union Jack stood out from a flagpole in the stiff breeze that blew from the river. Thick ropes bound the straining vessel to the land and towering over the enormity of it all were four great cranes on to which men had climbed and where they clung like monkeys in a tree.

The crowds were huge on both sides of the ship, tiny dwarf figures waving and cheering, gazing with awe up to the pinnacle of the great vessel, for no matter how many times they had watched a launch it never failed to amaze and delight them.

Jem steadied himself on the extreme edge of the dock, clinging to a bollard, for he was in grave danger of being pushed into the gently lapping waters of the river. He had a fine view of the small platform from where Mrs Barrie was to christen the ship and send her on her way. Among the party was Frank Webb, the designer of the fine ship that lay waiting on her bed of keel blocks, ready to start her journey.

'A fine day for a launch, Mrs Barrie,' Jem heard him say courteously to the owner's wife.

'Indeed, and will the ship be ready soon, Mr Webb?' Mrs Barrie answered, as she was eager to get on. There would be a reception afterwards attended by all the important dignitaries of Liverpool and Birkenhead and even some from as far away as a shipyard in the Clyde where Mr Barrie had business connections. A coming man was her husband and she felt it only right that she, as his wife, should be the centre of attention.

The bottle of champagne was ready. There was a great deal of shouting from the men on the deck to those who stood far below where the ship's frame curved under her keel and Jem leaned even further forward as though he could see where he had 'brightened the lines'. In building the hull the steel plates would be marked by platers using a chalk line and a marker, making lines on the steel like ruling lines on paper. Over time these chalked lines would fade and would need 'brightening' by re-chalking. He had been trusted to do this important job since he was known to be conscientious and he was one of those who had helped to shape her. He had been at work now for four years as plate-layer and would, when he finished his apprenticeship in two years, be a journeyman and then a fully qualified plate-layer. Most of the apprentices who could not find the five pounds towards their Certificate of Indenture had one shilling a week deducted from their wages until the sum of five pounds had been accumulated. This was usually for the term of six years or until they were twenty-one whichever be the longer, as it said in the certificate. But Queenie had given him the money needed to pay for his indentures and he would be for ever grateful to her for her help, not only financial, but for her quiet support in allowing him to share the cellar where she still lived with Gilly and where, while Gilly was reading one of the books she brought from the William Brown Lending Library, he would study ships, marine engineering, the history of shipbuilding and indeed anything and everything to do with ships and the sea. Gilly and Queenie had both been away on their travels for most of the summer, moving from fair to fair, from market to market and it was Jem, from his research in the library, which he haunted whenever he had free time, who had shown Queenie how to invest her money.

He vividly remembered the day he had taken her to the Royal Bank in Dale Street, both of them dressed in their respectable best, where a clerk who had looked down his nose at them – until he learned the amount of money Queenie had to invest – had shown them into the office of the deputy manager.

The first problem had arisen when it was realised that

Queenie could neither read nor write so someone must be found who could do these for her; and who else was there to lead her through the complexities but himself and Gilly? So Gilly had been brought to the bank, dressed in the clean but plain dress and bonnet Queenie put her in and the account had been opened in Queenie's name. Whenever Queenie wished to deposit a small sum of money, or withdraw the same, Gilly accompanied her and though she was too young to make the transactions herself, she could read whatever was needed to her mother and check the amounts put in or withdrawn against the passbook which was Queenie's proudest possession. The staff at the bank were charmed with the pretty, polite little girl who clung to her mother's hand, but Queenie, despite her lack of education, was not in the least overawed by either the bank clerks or the customers. Jem's help and constant overseeing of her financial affairs, as he called them, had enabled her to give him the money needed for his indentures.

She and Gilly were doing so well in their small business and, as Queenie was careful with her growing account, she was beginning to look about her, saying nothing to either Jem or Gilly, with the intention of moving out of Rose Alley into a more salubrious neighbourhood.

Suddenly there was a great shout as some signal was given. Mrs Barrie's voice came faintly over the noise of the crowd: '. . . this ship *Rose Marie* . . . bless all who sail in her . . .' He could hear no more, not even the crack of the champagne bottle which Mrs Barrie aimed with great dexterity. A pair of men smashed the blocks that supported the keel, and the blocks were knocked away; the weight of the hull was thrown on to the cradles, piles of beams built up along the hull's underbelly. The interface between two layers of cradle beams had been greased and the weight of the ship settled into the cradles. The top layer began to slip, allowing the ship to move down the incline towards the water. Stern first, she started to go with the eyes of every person present on her, all except those of Willy Hughes who, bored with the whole thing, spoiled by his doting parents and accustomed to doing whatever he pleased, had squirmed between the legs of those about him and darted towards the edge of the dock overlooking the river. Men whose legs he brushed against looked down at him in bewilderment but, not wishing to miss the graceful descent of the ship, the tremendous splash as she entered the water, looked away again. All those apart from Jem who watched in horror as the child, dressed in a sailor suit as was the fashion, laughed up at him, leaned over the water and fell in.

His small body seemed to take an age to hit the water which was heaving and tossing as the launching vessel displaced it and when it did he disappeared, unnoticed, it seemed, by the crowds of cheering, hat-waving men.

Jem and Gilly had wandered one day to the sands at Bootle where there were bathing machines and horses to draw ladies who desired to preserve their modesty into the waters.

Neither Jem nor Gilly cared about such things since modesty and decency did not exist in Rose Alley and they simply stripped off their outer clothing behind a sand dune, revealing what passed for a swimming costume on the stalls Queenie frequented. They had learned to swim splashing about at the water's edge to both their delight and satisfaction. Jem being the stronger was the better swimmer and though he had never attempted to dive in the shallow waters off Bootle sands, he did so now into the turbulence that surrounded the just launched vessel. Not a dive really but a jump in which his arms and legs flapped erratically, bobbing to the surface like a cork, for the waters were still heaving in undulating waves.

Others had noticed now, standing with their mouths agape at the dock edge wondering what the devil was wrong with the struggling bugger in the water. Had he overbalanced and fallen? Was he mad? Did he have a death wish, for it was unlikely he would survive in the undertow of the ship. Her propellers were still and would not suck him under, but just the same it was mad to be so close to the slowly bobbing vessel. She was still fastened to the land by lines that held her but it was a bloody dangerous position to be in. Nobody recognised him and it was not until a woman's screams began to tear the warm air that they realised there was more to this than some madman taking a dip in the deep waters of the river.

Jem had taken in a great deal of murky water as he landed in it. He had gone down a long way before striking up again and when he reached the surface, though he desperately trod the water, he could see nothing of the boy, and his saturated clothing was beginning to drag him down. Men were starting to shout and the woman was still screaming as he searched round for a glimpse of the small white-clad figure of the little lad. He could feel the pull of the ship and wondered how long he could stay afloat because he was almost under the keel and his clothes were heavy as lead.

And then a miracle happened: floating just below his pumping legs a small body appeared. The sailor's hat was gone and the child's bright curly hair hung limply round his face which was as pale as death. His eyes were closed, his mouth open and from between his lips ran a dribble of mucky water. Grabbing at his clothing, Jem hung on to the small, limp body, accompanied by shouts of encouragement, for by now the realisation of what had happened had dawned on the watching crowd – indeed one or two of the men had jumped over the edge of the dock and were flapping around in the water in an effort to help him. The child was not heavy and Jem began to pull him towards the steps that led from the water up to the dock. He could hear the mother shrieking now and the hoarse bellow of a man's voice, then strong hands grabbed him, pulling him upwards, taking the boy from him, all talking at once, some women weeping as it could easily have been one of theirs. The child lay limply on the planking of the dock, beginning to cough and splutter, a great rush of dirty water coming from his pale mouth. He himself lay sprawled, vomiting up not only the water but the butties he had eaten before the ceremony began, his jacket and trousers holding him down to the dock with the weight of water, though he noticed vaguely that he'd lost his boots and his cap. That would cost him money he could ill afford but perhaps Queenie could find him a cheap pair, was his drifting thought.

He had never spoken to either Mr Barrie or Mr Hughes – indeed they were vague figures seen on the edge of his world – but now they were both at his side, their hands lifting him while beside him the child's mother, he supposed she was, knelt on the dock, the boy in her arms, rocking him, weeping noisily while another woman held her, also crying. One of the men who lifted him to his feet, Mr Hughes, he thought, had tears in his eyes and was ready to clasp Jem to his breast.

'Dear God, man, how can we ever thank you. My son, a little demon he is, his nursemaid never even saw him slip away and we were all watching Mrs Barrie . . . We'll never be able to repay you . . . never . . . He is dear to us, the scamp. Ah . . .' He turned to another man. 'Doctor, check on the lad and then see that this young man is unhurt. You must come with us. No, I insist that you be checked over by Doctor Grayson. Now then, Marie, stop weeping,' though he was sniffing himself. He began to lead a stunned Jem through the pressing crowds, all the men patting Jem on the back, smiling, wanting to shake his hand, the excitement of the day heightened by the drama. The newly launched ship was quite put in the shade as Jem, beginning to shake now in reaction, was led away. The boy in his mother's arms was crying weakly and the nursemaid who stood within the circle of the Hugheses' other children, doing her best to keep any of them from straying further, waited stiffly for the axe to fall, which she knew it would. In a way it was hardly her fault, for Willy was a little devil and to expect one young girl to watch over five lively youngsters at an event like this was really too much. She bent her head and wept pitifully.

That afternoon Queenie and Gilly as they were between trips had been to the Corporation Baths in Upper Frederick Street which had been opened in 1842 for the use of the working classes. When they were at home they went once a week, though the rest of the time when they were on the tramp they made do with a dip in a convenient pond or stream. Inside the baths were apartments in which warm, cold and shower baths might be obtained, and attached to the side of the building were large reservoirs for the supply of the baths and washhouses where a woman could bring her family's washing. There were tubs and facilities for drying a load at a penny a time though women had to bring their own soap as it was not provided.

There were vapour baths which cost a shilling but a warm bath could be had for sixpence and it was one of these that Gilly and Queenie shared, men having access to the baths on alternate days. They had made an afternoon of it, mother and daughter, first bathing themselves and then hiring a tub to wash their underclothes.

They were just turning into Rose Alley from Maguire Street, the basket of clean clothing between them, when the carriage drew up to the entrance. There was not enough room for it to turn the corner between the scabby walls into the narrow courtyard lined by the tenements on either side, but it stood for a moment, all shining and splendid and the sight of it silenced every man, woman and child in the vicinity. It was pulled by two matching grey horses, their coats gleaming, their heads moving nervously, their hooves pawing the slimy cobbles, for they did not like this stinking place to which they had been driven.

'Glory be ter God,' Peg O'Dowd whispered, crossing herself as though at the sight of some devilish thing and when the carriage door opened and Jem Wilson, a shawl about his shoulders, emerged, the silence fell even deeper.

'Now don't forget, Jem,' a voice from inside the carriage said, 'first thing tomorrow in my office, that's if you feel up to it. Perhaps a day off might be in order. After all . . .'

Jem turned to speak to whoever was in the carriage and the inhabitants of Rose Alley strained to hear what he had to say.

'No, sir, I'm fine. A bi' wet is all. I'll be there, thank yer, sir,' putting a hand to his head where his missing cap should have been.

'Very well, lad, tomorrow it is. Right, Saunders, drive on.' And with great difficulty and a fair bit of manoeuvring Saunders drove on along Maguire Street. Children, come suddenly to life, ran after it in their bare feet and tattered rags that passed for clothing, shouting and screaming, following it towards Vauxhall Road, while Jem hesitated in the gutter, quite dazed, it seemed, as though not sure where to go.

'Nay, son,' a female voice said, 'wharrever 'ave yer bin up to?'

'Well, nutten really,' Jem stammered, overcome with some strong emotion that was robbing him of speech. 'This little lad fell inter't water . . . anyroad I must gerrout o' these wet things.' But still he stood undecided until Queenie bustled up, dragging a bewildered Gilly, the basket between them. Like the rest of the gaping crowd, who had not yet got over the fantastic sight of the splendid carriage from which Jem had stepped, wet, cold and shivering despite the warmth of the day, she was mystified as to what had happened to him but she could see he needed to get away from the pressing crowds.

'Inside, son, an' get yerself changed. Yer need ter get warm an' 'appen summat inside yer,' for reaction was making Jem's teeth chatter even more.

The crowd parted reluctantly. Like most Liverpool folk they liked a good drama and the chance to gossip about it. The sun, which was moving westwards in its descent towards evening, managed to throw a stray beam of light into the courtyard, revealing even more clearly the foetid state of the area. It was paved with uneven cobbles and in the centre was a hollow filled with water on which unspeakable matter floated. The water, it seemed, was unable to drain away towards the river where sewage was dumped. Standing in the centre of the hollow was a small, decrepit building with a doorway from which the door was missing. From this broken-down structure came an appalling stench, an eruption that in the unlikely chance that any stranger should venture into the courtyard would bring stinging tears to their eyes and make them retch. Everywhere there was filth, mud, rotting carcases of what must once have been a living cat or dog, and in it the pallid, scrawny children, having lost sight of the carriage, screamed in play. Men and women returned to their lolling and gossiping in the bit of sunshine. Slime ran down every wall, which did not prevent the pipe-smoking men from leaning against them.

Putting down her basket, Queenie produced a key from her apron pocket which seemed startlingly clean in comparison with the filth about her. She moved down the area steps and unlocked the solid door into her basement room and with a grim nod at her neighbours signalled to Jem to enter, then moved up the steps again to help Gilly with the basket. She closed the door with a sharp thump.

'Stuck-up cow,' one woman muttered, then turned to shriek at the children, many of whom were hers.

Once inside, Queenie crossed the room to the smouldering fire on which a kettle steamed and, with what seemed careless abandon, reached into the coal scuttle with a shovel and threw a generous pile of coal on to the fire. In a minute or two it caught and a bright, warm glow filled the room, reflecting off the white walls which Jem frequently whitewashed in an attempt to cover the green stains of damp that grew despite his efforts.

Gilly and Jem watched Queenie, Gilly with her mouth still open but Queenie soon had them on the move.

'Right, son, get yer be'ind that curtain an' strip off. Aye, everything or yer'll catch yer death and then give yerself a good rub down wi' this,' throwing a bit of rough towelling from the basket to Jem who dropped the shawl to catch it. He still had bits of flotsam from the river clinging to his sopping wet and foul-smelling clothes. A shiver shook his tall frame but he moved obediently behind the curtain that hid his rolled-up mattress.

'An' you, my lass,' turning to Gilly, 'mekk us a cuppa, will yer and then Jem can tell us what 'appened ter gerrim in such a mess. It looks ter me 'e's bin in't river an' I don't suppose it were fer't sake of 'is 'ealth.'

When Jem emerged from behind the curtain he had on a clean shirt, for Queenie did his washing along with hers and Gilly's, and his working trousers. His hair stood about his head in a mass of curly spikes, like a beam of sunlight in the glow of the fire. His face had some colour in it now and his blue eyes were clear where they had been confused. He had not yet recovered from his ducking in the murky waters of the Mersey and his tender heart was still concerned with the plight of the little lad he had plucked from it, but he gratefully took the cup of tea Queenie put in his hand and managed a smile into the face of the girl who knelt waiting at his feet.

'Are yer gonner tell us, Jem,' she asked, 'or must we clout it outer yer?'

'Leave lad alone, our Gilly.' But it was obvious Queenie was as keen to hear his tale as her daughter. She sank down in the chair opposite Jem as he told them of the events of the afternoon.

'An' termorrer I'm ter go an' see Mr Hughes in 'is office,' he finished raptly.

'Well, I never did,' Queenie murmured, wondering why this wonderful news put a feather of apprehension down her straight spine.

4

Queenie had sent him down first thing to the baths, it being men's day, since he could hardly turn up at Mr Hughes's office stinking of the river, could he, she asked sharply. She'd found him another clean shirt, one that fitted him somewhat loosely, flapping about his rangy body, but it was in good condition. She had dried his jacket and trousers before the lively fire she had built up, brushed them, then watched carefully as he polished the boots she had retrieved from her 'stall' basket. She always had spare clothing, stuff she hadn't got rid of at the last market and as he couldn't go barefoot to see Mr Hughes he must make do with what she had. They were a snug fit, for he had big feet, but were better than nothing.

Gilly fussed about him, pulling down his jacket which had shrunk a bit, fiddling with the top button of his collarless shirt and doing her best with a broken comb to curb his wheaten curls from rioting over his head.

'Eeh, I'll look like bloody Prince o' Wales at his weddin' way you two're goin' on,' he complained good-naturedly. 'Give over, our Gilly. We can do nowt more wi' me hair unless I shave me head. It's always bin't same an' wi'out me cap . . .'

''Old on, son, I might 'ave summat as'll suit.' Beneath his exasperated gaze Queenie rummaged in the basket and produced what was known as a 'wideawake' hat of straw, a fashion from the last decade.

Jem backed away, a look of alarm on his face. 'Nay, I can't

wear tha', Queenie. Lads'll be laughin' an' callin' me names. 'Ave'nt yer gorr owt else, like?'

'That's a gentleman's 'at, that is.'

'I know that, Queenie, an' I'm no gent.' He stood with his back to the door that led out to the area basement, turning to Gilly for support.

'I think it's grand, Jem. Try it, go on,' she begged, but he shook his head.

At last, from her basket Queenie produced a country cap with a covered button on top, what the gentry might wear but also a cap that a working man might get away with. She placed it on his bright curls and pressed it down firmly.

'There,' she said triumphantly. 'Yer look right bonny, dun't he, our Gilly?'

'Bonny,' spluttered Jem.

Gilly studied him, her eyes running up and down his tall frame and though he was no more than a rough working lad, in her eyes he was perfect. He always had been. He was her only friend and her expression said so. Her tawny eyes in which golden flecks glowed, tilted as she smiled and as it always did, his heart turned over. His tender mouth curled up in the wide smile that was peculiarly his and he held out his hand, which she took. She was only twelve years old and his deep, enduring love for her had as yet no sexuality in it but in a couple of years' time or perhaps a bit more he meant to marry her. He was doing well at the shipyard and with the help of the books he borrowed from the library he would get on. He wasn't quite sure how but he had overheard the minister at St Martin's-in-the-Field tell another scholar that the only way was through education.

He stood before Queenie and Gilly, waiting for their approval, turning in an exaggerated circle to make them laugh, his cap thrown to the back of his curls, but Queenie tutted and moved forward to straighten it again on his head.

'Now listen 'ere, lad, yer did a good thing yesterday savin' that little nipper from drownin'. It made a big impression on 'is pa an 'e wants ter thank yer, an' rightly so. See yer mekk most of it.'

Gilly nodded her head encouragingly as though to tell Jem he must be on his best behaviour, for who knew where this might lead. Perhaps a rise in his pay and even a promotion to some grand job in the building of a ship.

'So speak polite,' Queenie continued – as if Jem would do anything else – 'an' lerrim see wharr a good lad you are. Mind, 'e'll know that fer there's not many'd jump in that there mucky water, even ter save a little lad.'

'Nay, Queenie,' he protested honestly, for that was his nature, 'a few did.'

'Right then, 'appen I'm wrong. Anyroad, mekk most of it an' me an't lass'll be waiting fer yer ter come 'ome an' tell us all about it.'

Queenie was not a great one for hugging but Gilly was and now she flung her arms about Jem's waist, her cheek pressed against his chest. His rose to enfold her and his own cheek rested on her bright hair.

'Right then,' Queenie said briskly. 'Ta-ra, son, an' see yer ternight. We've a bit ter do, me an' our Gilly, seein' as 'ow we're off ter St Helens first thing termorrer. Summer'll be over soon an' we'd best mekk the most of it afore winter comes and we settle in 'ere. I've a lorra stuff ter sort out an' it'll need ter be packed onter't cart.'

With that she hustled Jem roughly through the door and up the steps as though he had deeply offended her, which was far from the truth for she thought the world of him and had often thanked the fates that had sent him to her. Only from next door, true, but what a godsend he had been to her in her business and especially with Gilly as lovely as she was. She and Gilly stood at the top of the steps and watched him lope off across the courtyard, his long legs leaping the pools of stagnant water. He turned to wave and as he did so Tommy and Jess Wilson flung open their rotting door and with more alacrity than he had shown since he was himself one of the shrieking children who swarmed about the place, Tommy Wilson ran shouting after his son followed by his wife.

'Aye, lad, what's bloody 'urry? Aven't yer time ter say "ow do" ter yer old pa?' His voice was ingratiating and Jem and Queenie knew what he was about. Once Tommy Wilson had been as straight and supple as his son. He had suffered from a lack of nutritious food as they all did, but working on the docks among the ships that brought food into Liverpool he had managed extra victuals which he had not shared with his family. But lack of exercise, vast amounts of ale and a diet of bread and lard and oatmeal had made him slack-faced, fleshy in the wrong places, squat and pot-bellied. Like most of the men not yet risen from their greasy beds but who would soon be leaning or squatting about the courtyard, he was unskilled and without a regular trade. When there was work to be had they were all dockers, factory hands and general labourers, street sellers and pedlars. They sent their children out to be chimney sweeps, street sweepers, little piecers crawling under whirling machinery to collect cotton waste in the cotton mills. Many of them were Irish who would take a job even the poorest of the poor would not accept. They could not save for their old age, should it occur to them to do so. There were charities like Doctor Barnardo's Home and the Waifs and Strays Society but many went into the poorhouse. There were soup kitchens where they sent their children. Bad water supplies, filth and overcrowding regularly produced typhoid, tuberculosis, diphtheria and 'fever'.

Those who lived alongside Queenie Logan and her daughter could never understand why she and the lass were not struck down as they themselves were, for the Logans were as poor as they. They knew nothing, of course, of Queenie's small nest egg and it did not occur to them that Queenie's defences against the ailments that afflicted them were cleanliness and the willingness to work, week in and week out, for the few bob she earned. She made nourishing meals, she boiled every drop of water, she, the lass and now the lad drank and the three of them bathed every week. They stayed healthy, thin, true, but healthy.

Jem turned to face his father. Had his mother not been at his pa's back he would have ignored him, for he was well aware that having heard of Jem's deed the day before, convinced the rescued boy's father was to reward him financially, Tommy was looking for a hand-out. His mother's pitiful face, sporting the usual black eye, and the annual bulge of her pregnancy stopped his tongue.

''Ow do, Pa,' he said patiently.

'We 'eard what yer did yesterday, son, yer mam an' me an' right brave it were an' all. I reckon old man Hughes'll be givin' yer summat fer yer troubles.' He licked his lips and tried a smile. 'Yer see, me an' yer mam're a bit be'ind wi't rent. Wi' nutten comin' in and all them mouths ter feed' – mouths that had just been sent off to the soup kitchen – 'we've norra brass farthin' in't house.' He smirked.

Jem could smell the stale beer on his breath. 'I'm only gonner see Mr Hughes, Pa,' he said mildly, 'not gerra bloody knighthood.'

His father hadn't the faintest notion what a knighthood was but he persisted in sidling alongside his son who had begun to walk quickly in the direction of Vauxhall Road and the docks where he would board the ferry to Birkenhead.

'Now listen, son, after what yer did fer 'is lad 'e's bound ter give yer summat an' yer mam an' me'd be—'

'Let's wait an' see, Pa,' Jem said, impatient now. He had parted with enough of his hardearned wages to help out his mam but knew full well that most of it disappeared over the bar counter of the Crown and Anchor. He had no idea what Mr Hughes would reward him with, if anything, but he was determined his pa wouldn't touch a penny of it.

'Ungrateful son of a bitch,' his father yelled after him, 'an' after everythin' me an' yer mam 've done fer yer, an' all.'

Gilly followed her mother inside after looking back over her shoulder, though Jem had by now vanished round the corner. She watched as Tommy Wilson slouched back to his place along the rotting wall, leaning his bum against it, one leg bent, the heel digging in to the mouldering bricks in the exact posture of every other man in the courtyard. He was grumbling loudly and obscenely about the ingratitude of children in general and his son in particular. She closed the door behind her and moved across the room, which was still warm from the fire that had been kept in to dry Jem's jacket and trousers. As though her hands were cold she held them out to the glowing embers, gazing sightlessly into their depths.

Queenie was emptying a basket of clothing ready to sort through the bundles in preparation for their journey to St Helens Market the next day. These worn bodices and skirts, bonnets, several pairs of boots, baby clothes and other garments were within the range of working-class women who had a decent and responsible husband, one who laboured hard and long to provide for his family. These families probably lived hardly any better than the inhabitants of Rose Alley but they were careful, abstemious and admired cleanliness, listening to the good ladies, those who worked for the poor and advised them on how to achieve a better standard of living. These were Queenie's customers. She sold many an object that still had a bit of wear in it, perhaps a teapot with a chip in the lid, a kettle that, with a careful patch, would again hold water, a saucepan with a dent in it but perfectly usable, plates, cups, saucers, all

damaged in some way and therefore useless to their previous
more affluent owners.

She watched Gilly from the corner of her eye, knowing the
child was restless and disturbed, concerned with something,
for normally she would be chattering about their coming
journey, her hands busy helping, her mind busy with what
might sell on the market. Her incredible mane of hair, rippling
down her back to her buttocks, had not yet been plaited into the
rather severe style Queenie favoured. She pretended to herself
that dragging the child's hair back from her face reduced her
attraction to men but she was fooling herself. Instead it ac-
centuated the perfection of her high cheekbones, her broad
brow, the firm set of her small chin, her full, peach-tinted lips,
the fine chiselling of her nose, the delicacy of her arched
eyebrows and revealed the enormity of her tawny, gold-flecked
eyes. Most people with her colouring had pure white skin but
Gilly had inherited her mother's honey-tinted flesh and the
result was stunning. Dainty she was. Her father had been tall,
brawny and she herself was no shrimp but here was this slender
little thing, perfectly proportioned and growing into a beautiful
young woman.

Many's the time in the last few years Queenie had been glad
of Jem's protection in their basement room, for the men in the
adjoining tenements ogled Gilly Logan with greedy lust. But it
was understood by them all that young Gilly was intended for
Jem Wilson and they kept their distance. Jem had taken up
boxing and wrestling, learning from the men in the shipyard
how to give as good as he got. He was wiry without an ounce of
fat on him, but strong as whipcord and many a puffed-up
buffoon had believed he could knock him into the middle of
next week. But he had found to his cost that though Jem Wilson
might look as though he'd go down with the first punch he
didn't stay in one place long enough to receive it! Like a gadfly,
he was, and his own fists were hard and accurate.

Queenie knew that she and Gilly were safe as long as Jem was around and she had learned at the markets to hide her lovely child under a drab shawl and in the background behind her own broad figure when men came to the stall. Her customers were in the main housewives and so far all had gone well. But the child was developing ripe little breasts which men would notice and as she matured the danger would increase. In Queenie's mind was the knowledge that the sooner Gilly was of marriageable age and she and Jem were wed the better it would be. She marvelled again as she had over the past twelve years how it was that she and Red O'Hara could have made between them this exquisite creature. Red had been attractive, true, and she herself was not exactly ugly but still it was a constant mystery where Gilly got her looks from.

'What's up, chuck?' she asked abruptly. 'Yer in a birrof a daydream. Mithered about Jem, are yer?'

'No, our Mam, not Jem. Me.'

'You?'

'Aye, I feel as though 'e were leaving me be'ind.'

'Leavin' yer be'ind? Wharrever d'yer mean?'

'This wi' Mr Hughes.'

'Mr Hughes?'

Gilly sighed heavily and moved to the table where the pile of clothing lay. She picked up a baby's dress which had seen much wear. It had evidently come from a home where such things as lace and delicate embroidery were commonplace, a pretty garment of what had once been white muslin threaded with faded ribbon. Who would buy such a thing among the clientele she and her mam dealt with? she wondered, but apparently Mam had liked it when she had bought the cast-offs from some home in the better part of Liverpool, Everton or Walton maybe, for the Logans cast their net wide in their search for unwanted items.

'I got this feelin', Mam, that things'll change from now on.

As though yesterday turned Jem about facin' another way, like.'

Queenie stared at her daughter with consternation. She remembered the small shiver of premonition that had slithered down her own spine yesterday when Jem had told them that Mr Hughes wanted to see him. But this thing with Gilly alarmed her. It was said that the Irish were 'fey', that they could 'see' and Gilly had Irish blood in her veins. She shook herself briskly and began to stir the garments on the table, holding up a threadbare pair of trousers, an ancient bonnet adorned with two feathered birds, throwing each to one side.

'Stuff an' nonsense, girl. Jem'll always be Jem. 'E . . .'e thinks the world o' you, of us. This is 'is 'ome. Any road, Mr Hughes'll probably give 'im a few bob, 'appen a sovereign, Jem bein' so brave.'

Gilly did not answer. Her mind was considering what Mr Hughes might be saying to her Jem. Yes, he was her Jem, the person she loved most in all the world, bar none. Even more than Mam who was very dear to her. They were two sides of one coin, her and Jem, impossible to split apart, as a coin could not be split. She had been raised, if that word could be used in Rose Alley, where children ran wild with no restraint put upon them by their parents, by two good people, Jem and her mam, but Jem was her rock, her anchor in the often stormy seas in which she swam, in the dangerous world of Rose Alley and its environs. She was still a child in years but her mind was mature and her body was moving from child to woman. She had seen the way men looked at her, even the eyes of the minister at Sunday school had a gleam, a softness in them when he spoke to her. Jem's eyes, though, were the only ones to which she responded, like blue flames in his suntanned face. She was already aware that he loved her as a man loves a woman and soon, when he thought she was ready, he would make her his in the truest sense, as Mr Darcy had claimed Miss Bennet in *Pride and Prejudice.* She was already his, even her mam understood that, but they all knew that they must wait for the marriage he intended.

But suddenly she was afraid. There seemed to be a darkness rolling in from the direction of the river and she could not understand why. She wanted Jem to come home with a sovereign in his pocket, a broad grin on his beloved face, with the good news that Mr Hughes was to promote him to . . . to . . . what? She didn't know. She only knew that something was telling her that everything was to change from this day on.

Jem stood in the empty office where the clerk had put him, turning his cap round and round in his work-callused hands. It was a magnificent room, the walls panelled in some sort of glowing wood, and on the walls hung pictures of stern, be-whiskered gentlemen who watched him reprovingly as though daring him to move from the bit of carpet where the clerk had left him. There was an enormous desk, again in wood you could see your face in it was so highly polished, and the chairs had dark red leather seats. On the desk were many papers and a silver pen and inkstand. There was a silver box which he later was to discover contained cigars. Not that Mr Hughes offered him one. Not then!

He turned when Mr Hughes flung open the door and noisily entered the room, shouting back some order to the clerk in the outer office. Mr Hughes was immaculately dressed in a dark frock coat and narrow pin-striped trousers with a diamond pin at his neck cloth.

'Well, lad, you've got here,' he boomed, the tearful, thankful, agonised man of yesterday totally evaporated. He was himself again now. He had calmed his hysterical wife, dismissed the irresponsible nursemaid at Marie's insistence though he himself was inclined to believe it was not really all her fault. His youngest son was a wilful child and with four others to watch over the poor girl had had her hands full but Marie had been determined. But now there was this lad to reward, for surely he deserved something, they had all agreed. Willy might be a little demon but he was much loved.

'Now then . . . er . . . I'm afraid your name . . .'

'Jem Wilson, sir.'

'Jem, of course.' Mr Hughes sat down behind his desk, carefully lifting the tails of his coat as he did so. He did not ask Jem to sit. He picked up his pen and pulled several documents towards him. He did not expect this to take long.

'My wife and I cannot begin to thank you for what you did for our boy yesterday . . . er, Jem. Had it not been for your swift action he surely would have drowned. Now Mrs Hughes and I think you deserve—'

'I want nowt, sir,' Jem said mildly. He stood calmly before his employer, one of the most wealthy and influential businessmen from either side of the river, the expression on his face saying he was not overawed as most men would be. He was not humble but neither was he what Mr Hughes might describe as 'cocky'. Dignified and modest were the two strange words that came to Mr Hughes's mind.

'But you must allow me to show you my . . . our gratitude,' he protested.

'No, sir. Little lad fell inter't water an' I fished 'im out.' It was said simply.

'Nevertheless, Jem Wilson, something will be done for you.' Mr Hughes found to his surprise that he had taken a great liking to this unpretentious young man. He took the unprecedented step of asking him to sit down.

Jem lowered himself into one of the splendid leather chairs, placing his cap on his knee.

'Now, my lad, tell me about yourself. How old are you? Where in my yard do you work? Where do you live? What does your father do, that sort of thing?'

He leaned back, steepling his hands beneath his chin, prepared to listen to this young chap flounder through his life story
as most from his social class would. Inarticulate, illiterate,
awkward, out of his depth, hesitant, all the characteristics of
the lower classes when faced with a higher.

'I'm a workin' man, Mr Hughes, a plate-layer apprentice.
I'm nineteen years old, I can read an' write. I love the novels of
Anthony Trollope.' He smiled engagingly.

Mr Hughes found himself responding to this astonishing
young man. He himself had barely read a book in his life since
business, commerce and shipbuilding were his world. In fact he
had to drag his memory to remember who the hell Anthony
Trollope was!

Jem continued, 'Eeh, that there Mr Slope in't *Barchester
Towers*! Wharra character! But most of all I love ships. One day
I want ter design ships, learn ter be an engineer, a marine
engineer, 'appen.' Jem's face lit up and the truth of his dream
shone from his eyes which sparkled like blue diamonds. He
leaned forward, his elbows on his knees and John Hughes
found himself doing the same on his desk.

'And how would you go about doing that, lad?'

Jem sat back in his chair and the light ebbed from him. 'Nay,
I dunno, Mr Hughes. The minister where I went ter Sunday
school, the man what taught me all I know says it's only wi' an
education yer can gerron, but . . .' He looked down, his hands
busy with the peak of his cap. It seemed he had nothing further
to say for could anyone born in Rose Alley have the slightest
chance of achieving the dream that Jem had kept locked in his
heart until now?

There was silence for perhaps a full minute, Jem busy with
his thoughts, those of Mr Hughes racing round in his head like a
flock of pigeons. He studied the lad who sat quietly before him
and had his wife been present she would have known at once
that he was 'up to something'. His face was quite without

expression and his eyes were unfocused. His left hand played with a letter opener and his right was stuffed in his pocket; otherwise he was perfectly still. Then suddenly he jumped to his feet, startling Jem who was beginning to wonder at Mr Hughes's fixed stare.

'Well, lad, we must do something to thank you for your courage. I shall speak to Mr Barrie. Perhaps some opening . . .' His tone was vague. He wanted to slip the boy a sovereign which would be a fortune to someone in his position in life but something stopped him. This was no ordinary young chap you could pay off with a few bob and then forget. No, he would go right now and have a word with Herbert and . . . well, discuss it with him, see what might be done with the idea that was growing in his mind.

He held out his hand across the desk and Jem stood up to take it.

'Thank you again, Jem,' he said sincerely, then he was all bustle, moving across the deep piled carpet to open the door as though Jem were an important client.

'You'll be hearing from me soon,' he added, then the door was closed and Jem found himself being stared at by the half a dozen clerks who worked there.

As he crossed the busy yard towards the skeleton of the ship on which he had been working the day of the launch, he sighed, then shook his head, smiling at his own foolishness. What had he expected? To be made a bloody director! Still. . . !

5

'But what did 'e say? I mean about yer job?' It was evident from Queenie's voice that *she* had had high hopes for him of at least a foreman's position. After all, it was not every day the life of a man's son was saved.

'Well, nowt really,' Jem said, spooning good broth into his mouth. Queenie had made the soup that day with carrots, onions, barley, potatoes and scraps of shin of beef which was cheap, tasty and, if cooked long enough, tender.

'Burr 'e muster said summat.'

'Well, I've ter see 'im again after 'e's 'ad a word wi' Mr Barrie.'

'There yer are then,' Queenie said triumphantly. ''E's gonner do summat, stands ter reason.'

'What does?'

'Well, 'e wouldn't say that unless 'e 'ad summat in mind, would 'e?'

'Well . . .' Jem continued to eat his meal, then, after another few mouthfuls, turned to Gilly. 'An' what der you think, Lovedy? D'yer reckon 'e's gonner mekk me a partner or—'

'Don't mekk fun, our Jem,' Gilly said reprovingly. 'Yer don't tekk things serious enough. Yer saved the life o' Mr Hughes's little lad, an' that's nowt ter joke about.'

'Nay, my lass.' Jem was aghast. 'I'm not jokin' about tha'. I'm just sayin' don't let's gerr our 'opes up. We must wait until Mr Hughes . . . well, I dunno what he's thinkin' of but . . .'

Gilly leaned forward across the small pine table, which stood in the centre of the crowded room, and peered into Jem's face. She, like Jem, had a bowl of broth in front of her. On the table stood a two-day-old loaf from which Queenie was hacking thick slices and beside the loaf was a dish of strawberries fetched that evening from the market along with the loaf. Food that was getting past its best at St John's Market, which was considered to be supreme in the city, was sold off late in the day to housewives who could only afford to pay a much lower price for goods that would not keep until tomorrow. There was always a scramble for the fruit and vegetables but Queenie was tall and strong and could hold her own in any free-for-all. The strawberries, only a few hours off being mouldy, had been mashed up with oatmeal and sprinkled with a spoonful of sugar, a rare treat. With the nourishing broth, a pan of which still kept hot in the oven next to the fire, ready for 'seconds', which Jem always had, it all made a satisfying meal. There were three somewhat bruised pears and a chunk of hard cheese to end with. They drank weak tea with a splash of milk.

'Tell us again wharr 'e said, Jem,' Gilly pleaded. Gilly had her dreams just as Jem did, dreams that concerned the garment trade she and her mother were involved in, but like Jem she kept them to herself. She knew her mother was eager to get them out of Rose Alley, as she was herself, but whereas Queenie merely had a desire to go somewhere better, anywhere really, Gilly knew exactly what her destination was to be. But she needed help, support, a chance at a better education, a trade, cash – most important – and if Jem was to get a better job and hence better wages at the shipyard, then it might give her a leg up, so to speak.

Patiently Jem went through the whole of his interview with Mr Hughes, doing his best to remember every syllable of every word, describing the magnificence of the office, the pictures on the walls, even the well-tailored frock coat and trousers his employer had worn. He had been surrounded by his workmates the moment he had emerged from the office block and crossed the yard, all dying to know what Mr Hughes had said, and, more importantly, what the owner was to do for the man who had saved his son's life. There was no doubt the nipper would not have survived had not Jem jumped into the water and pulled him out.

They had been disappointed, as were Gilly and Queenie, who were home between trips when Jem had nothing to tell them, ready to believe that Jem was keeping something back from them but Gilly knew he wasn't. Honest as the day was her Jem, so it seemed as though they were all to wait as patiently as their natures allowed for Mr Hughes to divulge to Jem what his reward was to be. Five bob? Ten bob? A guinea? Perhaps just a new cap and boots to replace the ones he had lost in the river?

They were all, including Jem, flabbergasted when it came out the following week what Mr Hughes was prepared to do for the young man who had saved his son from a watery grave.

He had run all the way home – even on the ferry, moving jerkily round and round the deck until the boat docked – and his face was flushed and sweated, his fair curls standing up in a halo about his head where he had thrust his hand dazedly through it. His pa, who had tried to accost him as he ran headlong through Rose Alley, still hoping for a hand-out since he was convinced his son must have received *something* for risking his life, was brushed aside. Jem jumped the four steps down to the basement area, flung open the door, badly startling Queenie and Gilly who were laying out their evening meal, and shut the door in Tommy Wilson's infuriated face.

'I'm ter go ter school,' he began, his face rapt.

'School . . . what school?' Queenie faltered, sitting down abruptly on the rickety cane chair beside the table.

'Mechanics Institution.' His eyes were enormous in his face.

'Mechanics . . ?'

'Aye, in Mount Street. I'm ter learn English, writin', mechanical philosophy, wharrever that is, navigation, astronomy, naval architecture, chemistry *and* engineerin'. Three days a week then three days in't shipyard learnin' all't jobs what go inter buildin' ships. Draughtsmanship in th'office an' all. They'll pay me ten bob a week an' I'll live at 'ome but when I'm qualified I'll gerra rise. I didn't tell 'em I lodge wi' you. An' if I shape . . . Dear God, I can 'ardly believe it, I'll be a designer o' ships. Iron ships, steamers, like what the shipyard builds. I'm ter 'ave a new suit paid for by 'im – well, I can't go ter school in these old things, can I? – an' I'm ter start on Monday. Mr Hughes 'as spoken ter't headmaster at school an—'

'What'll'e gerrout of it?' a quiet voice asked. Jem and Gilly turned to stare at Gilly.

'What?'

' 'E'll not be doin' this fer nowt, Jem Wilson. What does 'e want at the end of it?'

'Nay, Gilly, that's no way ter talk. This is 'is way o' thankin' me fer wharr I did.' Jem was not to know that Mr Hughes and Mr Barrie had seen the rarity of this lad who read Trollope and wanted nothing more than to design ships. What might he contribute to their business for the price of a new suit and the fee of five pounds per annum that the school charged? If at the end of the year he had not 'shaped' as Jem put it, they'd not lost much and still had the young man's labour. And they had the satisfaction of knowing that they had done their best for the man who'd saved Willy's life.

At once Gilly felt remorse. Jem's words had frightened her and she had spoken out of that fear. Hastily, without thinking, or at least only of herself. She had been right when she had seen darkness coming, a great change that would affect all their lives, but how could she spoil it for Jem, this wonderful opportunity that had come his way.

'Jem, I'm sorry . . . sorry, o' course it's wonderful, just what yer wanted an' what yer deserve. Yer clever, me an' Mam know that an' so does Mr Hughes. It's just . . .'

'What, Lovedy?' Jem knelt at her feet where she had sat in a chair by the fire.

'I . . . we . . . can't bear fer yer ter leave us, can we, Mam?'

'Leave yer! Who said I were ter leave yer?'

Queenie watched and said nothing, her own thoughts busily occupied. The old clock, one that had cost her nothing, broken but which Jem had mended, ticked melodiously. The flames of the fire crackled, drying their underclothes draped on a line in front of it. On the mantelpiece stood several chipped orna-ments dear to Queenie's heart: a gaudily painted shepherdess with a lamb at her feet; a Toby jug with its nose missing; two candles stuck in the neck of bottles. In one corner of the room was the iron bedstead she shared with Gilly and in the other the handcart ready to be loaded up for tomorrow's journey to the market in St Helens. Behind a long curtain of faded velvet which she had laboriously darned was the rolled-up mattress where Jem slept. There was even a picture on the stained wall of a purse-mouthed young woman with protuberant eyes. From beyond the walls on three sides came the sounds of their neighbours: Sean O'Dowd giving his wife, Peg, what for; a baby wailing; a crash from something being thrown, no doubt at some poor soul. For a moment Queenie's mind slipped, because Jem and Gilly were not the only ones with dreams. She did not speak.

' 'E might want yer ter go away,' Gilly was whispering.

'Gilly, I'll be 'ome each night same as usual so wha' put that idea in yer 'ead? Anyroad, in't summer you an' yer mam'll be away ter't markets.'

She put her arms about his neck and placed her forehead on his shoulder. 'Don't leave us, Jem,' just as though he was to be off in the morning for parts unknown. Both Jem and Queenie were amazed. Gilly had always been a sunny-natured child, as her father had been, bubbling with optimism and joyousness despite the life she led in Rose Alley but now this foreboding she appeared to have that Jem was to be taken from them had her in its grip. Perhaps she was not quite the sensible, well-adjusted girl they had believed her to be, for this was irrational.

'I'm never gonner leave yer, sweetheart,' he said emphatically. 'I'm goin' no further than Mount Street.'

'I didn't mean tha', our Jem. I . . . you'll be 'avin' a different life, not like ours, goin' ter school an' tha', an' I'm feared . . .'

'Lovedy, yer know what yer mean ter me. I'll never leave yer behind. No matter what I learn or where I go, you'll be wi' me. You an' Queenie,' smiling up at Gilly's mother who was watching closely. None of them really knew how to put into words what Gilly meant, but they each knew what was in the other's mind. With this splendid opportunity Jem had been given he had a chance to move into another world. He would acquire not just academic qualifications but, mixing with gentlemen and the sons of gentlemen, his manners, his speech, the way he dressed would surely change. He would no longer be one of the gang of plate-layers, anchor smiths, rope-makers, boilermakers and innumerable other tradesmen who helped build the ship, but a designer of ships, with his own office, a draughtsman who built the ship on paper for the guidance of the labourers who would put it together. He would be a craftsman, a professional man and would they, Gilly and Queenie, be able to keep up with him? For the time being he would remain one of the gang of working men who crossed the water to Birkenhead. Three days a week he would don his rough jacket and trousers, his jaunty cap, and stride to the yard with the others he worked beside now. He would come home to Queenie's cellar and eat her plain wholesome food, sleep on the mattress behind the curtain and would be as he had always been, a denizen of Rose Alley which once had been named 'Sickman's Lane', the rumour being that upwards of 200 people, who, carried off by the plague in 1651, were buried beneath the cobblestones. The landlord, having bought the properties, and having a sense of humour, had considered it politic to rename the yard.

But the other three days Jem was to attend the Mechanics Institution in his new suit, which he was to purchase on Saturday morning from Dawbarn and Davies, tailors and drapers in Bold Street who sold off-the-peg garments at a reasonable price. When he had mentioned that he knew some-one who could supply him with a second-hand suit for next to nothing, both Mr Barrie and Mr Hughes had thrown up their hands, saying that since they were to pay for the suit, they would choose the supplier. Mr Dawburn or Mr Davies would know exactly what was needed from the soles of his boots to the correct hat he should wear!

Gilly sat up straight and blinked back the tears that had begun to form at the back of her eyes. She must not cry. *She must not cry!* She must do nothing that would upset Jem or make him hesitate to take this step towards the wonderful future that beckoned him. She really did not know why she felt as she did: the dread that was ready to freeze the blood in her veins, the terrible premonition that things would never be the same again, which, of course, they wouldn't. And that was how it should be but it still awoke this irrational fear in her.

She rose from her chair and pulled Jem up with her. She was twelve years old, a child, a child who wanted to stamp her foot, shout that she didn't want this thing to happen. He must not go away from her. Others must not have him, he was hers, but that would be foolish, unforgivable and at that moment the child became a woman with a woman's instincts. She could stop him, she knew that, keep him here with her, by which she meant in the life and work he had done since he was a boy. He loved her and his heart needed to please her. But she knew as surely as the sun rose in the east and sank over the massed shipping in the west he would come to resent her for it. She must let him go gladly. Show him that she was pleased for him. Hide her feelings, her fear that with Mam and her continuing to live their lives in Rose Alley, their tramping life with the handcart, while Jem moved up the social and business ladder, mixing with a much higher rank of persons, they would drift apart. Perhaps he would come to look down on her and Mam . . . Oh, dear Lord, let him not leave us, addressing the dear Lord who lived at the church where she had learned to read and whom the minister seemed to think listened to everyone who spoke to Him.

'I dunno,' she said at last, 'anyone'd think yer were ter sail across the ocean on the mornin' tide, way I'm mopin'.' She managed to smile, standing on tiptoe to kiss his cheek, watching the relief on his face, then she put her cheek against his chest and hugged him.

He talked of nothing else all evening, forgetting to eat in his excitement, letting his stewed tripe, onion sauce and mashed potatoes go cold while Queenie kept pressing him to eat up. Repeating what Mr Hughes had told him, he spoke of the shipbuilding yards in Liverpool and of how on their side of the Mersey, the Liverpool side, it was only lack of land that prevented even more shipyards from opening up. Mr Hughes had said he needed experience in every aspect of building a ship. *Aspect!* That's how he talked. Words they had never heard before and didn't understand. Mr Hughes had said that iron shipbuilding was overtaking sails and wooden vessels. Mr Hughes had said that carpenters, because of the slowing down of ships built of wood, were to become known as *shipwrights*. Mr Hughes had said that wages in Cumberland where ships were built at Whitehaven were three shillings and sixpence but in Liverpool they were the incredible sum of five shillings. *A day!* So you see, Queenie, he exclaimed, there would be an enormous rise in what he could put in her hand each week. Mr

Hughes had said . . . Mr Hughes had said . . . Mr Hughes had said . . .!

And so it began. On Saturday he set off for town in the best outfit Queenie could devise for him but even so he was well aware that Mr Dawburn, or was it Mr Davies, was confounded by the appearance of the tall, rangy young man whom Mr Hughes had ordered them to 'fit out'. From the skin out, Mr Hughes had informed them. He was, it seemed, a protégé of Mr Hughes and so he was measured to be fitted into one of their business suits, one that a gentleman in an office would wear. He was prodded and turned this way and that until they were satisfied that they had done their best. They could not, of course, put him in a frock coat and narrow striped trousers but it seemed a lounge suit would do splendidly, one of subdued brown tweed with peg-top trousers in a plain wool of the same colour. They had a boot and shoe department, which displayed elastic-sided boots, button boots, short boots laced up the front, long boots meant for riding, shoes, galoshes and gaiters. They sold hats for every occasion, top hats, bowler hats, straw hats and felt hats, but when Jem asked wistfully for a cap there was general consternation. Mr Dawburn, or was it Mr Davies, twirled his moustaches which met his side whiskers in a luxuriant bush and placed a brown bowler on Jem's head, advising him politely but coolly that a haircut might be in order.

They wished to dispose of his old clothes, underwear, boots and cap, thinking that such garments could only be destined for charity.

'No, sir, I'll tekk 'em 'ome,' he told them firmly. 'In fact it might be better if I kept 'em on,' visualising the slack-jawed amazement followed by jeers and catcalls that would arise in Rose Alley should he emerge in his new finery. On Monday he would make his way to Mount Street and the Mechanics Institution where a place was awaiting him but until then, until he had revealed his new glory to Queenie and Gilly, he would wear what he thought of as his own clothes.

Tomorrow he was to take Gilly to Sunday school, later meeting her for their usual outing. If it was fine he intended to take her across the water on the ferry to Woodside – in view of his hope of improved wages – on the Cheshire shore and from there to Bidston Hill. He sensed that she was fearful that his new position in life might separate them and he meant to reassure her that this would not happen. For the next two years he would leave home at the same time and return as usual, the only difference being that on three of those days he would go to the Mechanics Institution and not the shipyard. He must be instructed in mathematics, Mr Hughes had told him, and draughtsmanship, if he was to become a marine engineer and design ships. The rest he would learn at the shipyard.

Instructing the shop assistant, to whom Mr Dawburn or Mr Davies had handed him, to wrap up his new outfit, he left the shop, a bulky parcel under his arm, turning left on the busy pavement, bustling with Saturday shoppers.

She was waiting for him in the churchyard of St Luke's Church at the end of Bold Street, her lovely face upturned to the sun. She sat on a bench opposite a vivid bed of phlox planted against the wall of the church. Behind the phlox were delphinium, tall and stately, and, in front, on the edge of the border, grew yellow, orange and velvety crimson-brown marigolds. She did not see him coming. He stood just inside the wrought-iron gateway, brought to a standstill by the girlish perfection of her. She wore no hat and the sunlight turned her copper-coloured hair to molten streaks of reddish gold and flame. It was plaited, a great thick plait wound round her head so that she appeared to be wearing a crown. She wore her usual clean, well-patched grey bodice and skirt, for Queenie always rescued the best of her collecting for her child, but she had threaded a bright, orange marigold through one of the buttonholes down the front of the bodice. Her boots were old, second or third hand, but even dressed as she was she caught the eye of every man who walked by. From Bold Street to Rodney Street the churchyard was a short cut and there were many men and women walking by who wondered at the beauty of the young girl in her working-class garments.

He walked towards her until she heard the crunch of his boots on the gravel. Her head turned as it had done a score of times while she waited for him and when she saw him her face lit up. Her eyes glowed as though the wick of a candle had been touched by a taper inside her head. She stood up and smiled and when he dropped his parcel and held out his arms she ran into them, much to the amazement of those on the path.

They had eaten their simple meal and were sitting round the bright fire when Queenie said, 'Well, son, when are yer goin' ter show us yer new duds? We're dyin' ter see 'em, aren't we, Gilly. Go on, purrem on an' let's 'ave a look at yer.'

He was reluctant. Like Gilly he had this feeling that as soon as he put on the garments the *toffs* wore, he might become a different person and that was the last thing he wanted. Now that he had this wondrous opportunity in front of him, the chance to become what he had always dreamed of, he was suddenly afraid, though he couldn't think why. Not only would he go up in the world, earn a decent wage and a decent place in life, he would take Gilly with him. His young imagination saw him buying her pretty, *new* dresses and bonnets, perhaps even a ring to show the world that she was really his, but then it changed to the thought that he might fail and . . . Give over, lad, he told himself, why should you fail when you have the promise of where you and Gilly might end up? Away from this muck heap on which they now lived . . .

'Please, Jem, let's see yer in yer new suit,' Gilly pleaded.

'Well, promise yer won't laugh.' He managed to grin.

'Why should we laugh? Now gerron with yer, yer daft 'alfporth.'

He slipped behind the curtain and slowly unwrapped the neat parcel the salesman had done up for him, shaking out the jacket and trousers and placing the boots and bowler on the mattress which had been put out ready for when he went to bed. Stripping completely, he drew on the long under-drawers and sleeved vest, the shirt and then the trousers, carefully tucking the shirt into the waistband. He had a bit of trouble with what the assistant had called a 'shoe-tie' which was worn under the stiff collar of the shirt, since he had no mirror, but at last he was dressed, his boots comfortable on his feet, the first time he had ever worn brand-new, and the bowler tipped forward on his unruly mop of hair.

He stepped out shyly from behind the curtain and was immediately disconcerted by the blank expressions on the faces of his audience. Their mouths had popped open and they sat as though pole-axed. Jem Wilson had no idea what an attractive man he was and the two women, one old – for forty-two was considered old – the other young, were quite overcome with admiration, and something else which neither recognised. This engaging young man, this endearing young man who had no idea of his own worth, would go far, at least Queenie realised that. The suit was nothing much as fashions go, decent and even quite smart, but Jem's tall figure, his broad shoulders, the narrowness of his waist and hips, his long, well-proportioned legs, gave it an elegance that was denied to most men, no matter how expensively they dressed.

'Well?' he said at last when the silence seemed as though it would go on for ever.

At last Gilly spoke and her voice was hushed as though she had been confronted by an enchanted being from some other world. 'Jem, you look beautiful,' she breathed.

' 'Ere, give over,' he laughed, embarrassed somehow.

'No, Jem, I mean it. Yer look . . . different.'

'Well, I should 'ope so, though what them in't courtyard are gonner say . . .'

'It doesn't matter, Jem.' Her voice was soft and loving and Queenie watched them from her corner by the fire and was satisfied that though Gilly had been initially afraid of Jem's elevation in the world, she had come to believe that he was not going to leave her behind in his climb to the top. Oh, yes, Jem Wilson was on his way up. Put him among the gentlemen who peopled Mr Barrie and Mr Hughes's world, and he would fit right in. Teach him to speak as they did and no one would know he had not been born into their world.

Now it was Gilly's turn!

6

The tall stately figure of a woman dressed completely in black climbed the broad steps of the Mrs Hunter's School for Girls in Williamson Square and pushed open the double doors into the entrance hall. She looked about her calmly, unmoved by the splendour or the stream of well-dressed young girls who moved in orderly lines across the wide hallway, some of them climbing the broad staircase that rose from its centre. It was all achingly clean, from the black and white tiled floor to the high, arched ceiling, the walls painted cream and adorned with framed pictures of bonneted ladies. The banisters, the shallow treads of the uncarpeted stairs, the doors and shelves, all the wood glowed with polish. There was a faint and not unpleasing smell of carbolic overlaid with what might have been beeswax.

A line of younger girls, probably no more than five or six years old and not quite so subdued as the older ones, came down the stairs in pairs, holding hands, inclined to giggle until hushed by the woman who led them.

She looked enquiringly at the visitor. 'May I help you?' she asked politely, halting her charges with a movement of her hand.

'Aye, yer can that. Where can I find Mrs 'Unter?'

Looking considerably taken aback, for only the Queen's best English used by those high in society was spoken here, the teacher hesitated.

'Is she norrin?' the visitor demanded to know. 'I'll not keep yer. Just tell me where ter go.'

'Well . . .'

'Nay, 'tis an easy enough question. If yer busy send one o' these little lasses ter tell 'er there's someone ter see 'er.'

The teacher recovered enough to ask, 'Have you an appointment?' Her voice was cool.

'I didn't know I wanted one. Now just—'

'Very well,' the teacher interrupted. 'Elizabeth, run to Miss Hunter's room and inform Miss Jones there there's a . . . a . . . person to see her.'

'A person, Miss Dunstan?'

'Yes, and then come straight back to the dancing class.'

'Yes, Miss Dunstan.' Full of her own importance, Elizabeth sped off in her dainty pink ballet slippers, going to the right down a corridor off the main hallway while the teacher and the rest of the little girls moved away, disappearing behind the staircase. Two minutes later Elizabeth returned and followed them, casting a curious glance in the visitor's direction.

Ten minutes went by. The message that a 'person' was waiting in the entrance hall was of no importance to Miss Hunter, it seemed, for she was of the class who dealt with 'ladies', being one herself. A 'person' was not a lady!

A tall, gaunt woman, past middle age, approached from the right-hand corridor. Her face was lined, parchment-coloured and her upper lip was decorated with one or two coarse hairs. She was dressed in a plain grey skirt and bodice devoid of any adornment or even a touch of white at the collar, her thin grey hair was scraped severely back and she had a lorgnette hanging by a chain on her flat bosom. She had a great sheaf of papers in her arms and a look of supercilious disdain on her face. She was very busy, her expression said, with no time to waste, particularly on a woman who should have gone to the back door of the school, the tradesmen's entrance where the domestic staff entered.

'Can I help you?' she asked icily.

'Are yer Miss 'Unter?' the visitor asked, not a bit intimidated by this woman's manner or the surroundings in which she found herself.

'No, Miss Hunter is extremely busy. I am her assistant.'

The bonneted ladies stared down disapprovingly from their frames but Queenie Logan had dealt with situations *and* people far more alarming than Miss Hunter's assistant, or the faces in the portraits.

'Is tha' right? Well, I'm sure yer must be a great 'elp to 'er burr I've business wi't 'eadmistress so if yer'd tekk me to 'er I'd be obliged.'

'You must—'

'I tekk it Miss 'Unter's the one what admits pupils to 'er school?'

'Indeed, and she—'

'Then show me to 'er room an' I'll waste no more o' yer time,' and mine, her attitude said. 'Yer look as though yer've a lot ter do,' nodding calmly at the sheaf of papers in the woman's arms.

Mrs Hunter's assistant, Miss Jones, was seriously affronted. She was not accustomed to people of this woman's class interrupting her, or even standing up to what she knew was her own superiority. She bristled and her face flushed.

'I'm sorry but Miss Hunter will be busy for a while and can see no one.' And definitely not the likes of you, she longed to add, but Queenie Logan was not easily put off. Ask any of the people she dealt with in what she was beginning to call her 'business'. In the last year she had quietly added to her small nest egg and with Gilly and Jem's help, and, of course, Mr Field at the bank, she had decided that she could now afford to extend to her daughter the education Jem was receiving. It was a foregone conclusion that some day Gilly and Jem would be married, that she was certain of, and Gilly must be able to stand beside him in his brand-new life, be equal to him and to those with whom he would mix.

It was just over twelve months since Jem had become Mr Hughes's protégé at the Barrie and Hughes Shipyard in Birkenhead and in that time there had been an imperceptible shift in his . . . well, she was not quite sure how to describe him, or the change in him. He was exactly as he had always been in his dealings, which was an odd way of describing it, with her and Gilly. Kind, loving, generous, caring, helpful about their cellar home. He took Gilly out every Sunday as usual in his fine new clothes. She no longer went to Sunday school, for every evening when Jem returned from the Mechanics Institution whatever he had learned during the day he passed on to Gilly. If it was suitable, of course. There was no need for her to know about navigation, chemistry, naval architecture or astronomy, though she could identify and name all the stars in the nightly heavens. She still read avidly and could do not just 'adding up' and 'take-aways' but multiplication and long division and could have held her own with any scholar at the Institution. Jem had taken them to the Institution and shown them round the splendid library, the theatre which could hold 1,500 people and to an exhibition last summer, which had attracted a great crowd of people, to see the paintings and the works of science; neither of them had understood them but they had been immensely impressed.

But despite this Gilly could not be mistaken for anything but what she was: a young, working-class girl. She was extremely pretty, of course, and from the piles of clothing she and Queenie collected she had a knack of picking out the less well worn, simple dresses which between them they altered to fit her. She was like a rose on a dunghill in the foetid alley that was so inappropriately named. Had Jem taken her to dine with the Hughes family, which, naturally, was out of the question, since he himself had not been invited, she would not have been out of

place until she opened her mouth. She spoke with the nasal
dialect of Liverpool which was a mixture of Irish, Welsh and
the language of the polyglot nationalities that had settled there.
She was bright and had a sense of humour which rose above her
upbringing but she was not, and, unless she was taught, would
never be, a lady. Queenie meant to remedy that.

There was nowhere to sit down as Miss Jones scurried off in
the direction from which she had come so Queenie strolled
about the hallway, examining the portraits on the walls, wondering who these ladies could be, turning when Miss Jones
glided silently back towards her. Her expression seemed to say,
'So you're still here then,' but Queenie followed where she
beckoned, moving in her slow and majestic way along the
hallway until they reached a door which the assistant opened.

'This is . . .' She looked enquiringly at Queenie as she held
the door open for her.

'Mrs Logan,' Queenie told her.

'Mrs Logan, Mrs Hunter.'

The room into which Queenie was shown was a mixture of
parlour and office. The fireplace was of cast iron, black and
shining, set at the sides with colourful tiles, and on the mantel-
shelf sat a large black marble clock with gilt scrollwork, marble
pillars and reliefs and bronze mounts. There was a sepia
picture of a bewhiskered gentleman, brass candlesticks and
several ornaments the nature of which Queenie could not
recognise. An enormous fire blazed cheerfully and the room
was warm. The long windows were dressed with snowy nets
and red velvet curtains, while a corner cupboard contained
dozens of ornaments, whether of china, porcelain or just plain
pot, Queenie could not tell. A firescreen, beautifully embroidered stood to one side of the fire, a great palm towered in one
corner and in front of the fire were grouped three velvet chairs
and a round, lace-covered table set with tea things. The only
concession to an office was an enormous desk behind which sat

a plump, round-faced woman, the exact opposite to her assistant in appearance. She was plainly but richly clad in a warm brown silk dress with a very pretty shawl in autumn colours draped about her shoulders.

Mrs Hunter glanced up as her assistant spoke, raking Queenie from head to foot with probing eyes behind the pince-nez perched on the end of her nose. She allowed them to drop to her plump breast where they dangled on the end of a ribbon. She did not get up, nor speak.

But again Queenie was not dismayed. She intended to pose as a widow, for it was her belief that Gilly's illegitimacy would be a mark against her, should she even be admitted. She was not to know that Mrs Hunter had several boarders at her well-regarded academy who had been born out of wedlock to persons of rank and who had been placed discreetly with her until they were of an age to marry. They were brought up as ladies, taught the refinement needed to attract gentlemen who hoped to gain some advancement from the alliance. Of course they came from good families where the daughter of the house had fallen from grace, gone on a long trip to Italy or France, and the result hidden in Mrs Hunter's respectable school for young ladies.

Queenie looked about her, then, with the casual aplomb of a lady of rank, sat down in the chair on the opposite side of the desk to Mrs Hunter. It was clear that Mrs Hunter was taken aback but for the past twenty years, like her visitor, she had dealt with people who thought themselves to be above the rules of ordinary mortals. She had girls from many classes, including the minor aristocracy of the northern counties, and courteously but firmly she had dealt with demanding parents who assumed that they could tell Emily Hunter how to run her school.

Emily came from a good family, the only girl among four boys, and to keep her content, since she was of a wilful nature, her indulgent father had allowed her to be taught with her brothers until they went to school, since there was no doubt she was the cleverest of the lot of them. She had been a pretty girl and, in a class where husbands were chosen by fathers, she had dutifully married a man who, though he was not rich, was well connected and *clever*, intelligent as she was. But they had had only a few contented years together when he died of a sudden fever, leaving her childless and almost penniless. Sooner than join the household of one of her married brothers where she would have become an unpaid governess to their children, she chose to open a small school, which quickly grew, in Liverpool. That had been twenty years ago and the remains of her youthful prettiness still showed in her face. But her brain was needle-sharp and she recognised in the woman who sat opposite her something of herself. She had made her own way in a man's world and this woman, so respectably but unfashionably dressed and with the speech of the lowest of the lower classes, was the same.

She lifted her head, which had once been a mass of bright blonde curls but was now grey, covered with a pretty frilly cap, and waited.

Queenie smiled, for as Emily Hunter had known Queenie's strength, she saw it in Emily.

'I 'ave a daughter, Mrs 'Unter. A good girl, a clever 'un an' all. She can read an' write an' do all manner o' sums but she don't speak right. Like me. I want 'er ter be a lady, or at least be able ter act like one. I want 'er ter gerron . . .' as you have, her unfinished sentence said.

From the back of the room, where Miss Jones sat at a small table going through the exercise books she had carried in her arms, came a sound that might have been derision but neither Mrs Hunter nor Queenie took any notice.

'I can pay't fees, Mrs 'Unter, there's no bother about tha'. I know it'll be 'ard fer't lass ter start wi', fer I'm sure all t'other girls speak proper an' will mekk fun of 'er but she's a sticker an' she'll soon learn. She's strong an'll not let anyone . . . any other girl, I mean, gerr 'er down. So, will yer tekk 'er?'

Queenie sat back calmly, her head in its old-fashioned bonnet as high and proud as Mrs Hunter's. She was so sure of her Gilly, her loveliness, her cleverness, her ability to assimilate with any of the girls at this school, which she was certain she would once she learned to speak as they did, that she had no conception of what was facing her daughter.

But Emily Hunter did. There are no more cruel creatures than young girls who at once see the difference between themselves and an outsider and that was what this woman's child would be. She didn't want to take her, for she wouldn't fit in but the woman opposite her was looking at her with that calm, frank, but self-confident attitude as though she could see no reason why her child, for whom she would pay the same fee as the others, should not have what they had. But it would be a feather in Emily Hunter's cap if she could shape this child into what her mother wanted. It would be an experiment that might be successful.

At times she became dissatisfied with trying to knock some learning into the pretty, mostly empty-headed girls who passed through her doors year after year. She sometimes felt like a nanny, a caretaker if you like, who was employed to watch over them until they were married which was usually at about seventeen or eighteen. They were taught reading, spelling, grammar, simple arithmetic, drawing, needlework and vocal music, along with dancing and a smattering of French. She had six assistant teachers who – her words – 'minded' the pupils sometimes for as long as ten years, since she had a small infant class. And in the twenty years she had run the school and the hundreds who had been in her care she could count on two hands the girls who had soaked up learning like sponges, responding to the dry facts of an education as plants, trans-ferred from a cellar, respond to the sun. Not that it had made any difference, for their families didn't want clever girls, they wanted accomplished young ladies who would make a good marriage. Ladies who could paint a little, draw a little, play a pretty tune on the piano and be an adornment in their husband's parlour and bed.

'Mrs Logan, you must realise that my school – and I mean no offence – takes in the daughters of gentlemen. From the nursery they have been taught to become what their position in life demands. They will marry gentlemen. I have not met your daughter . . .' She visualised some clodhopper dressed in the same kind of clothing that Mrs Logan wore. A girl who would speak as her mother did and whose table manners might be appalling. She could imagine that when they were collected in their splendid carriages at the end of the day, as many of her pupils were, they would inform their parents of the inferior creature who Mrs Hunter had admitted to the school and who, for all she and they knew, might be lousy and foul-mouthed. Looking at the neatly dressed, immaculately clean woman who sat before her she didn't think so and, strangely, she rather liked the woman. She was not cringing, cowed or in any way intimidated by herself, Emily Hunter, or by her surroundings, but at the same time she did not have that false, high-flown belief in herself that covered up lack of confidence. Where did she and her daughter live? And how did this woman earn her living?

'I mean no disrespect, Mrs Logan, but are you in . . . business?' She pictured a shop perhaps, or maybe she was a housekeeper who was allowed to keep her child, supposedly born in wedlock, in the house where she worked.

'Yes, I am, Mrs 'Unter, an' over the years I done well.' At the back of the room Miss Jones shuddered but there was worse to come. 'I deal in second-hand goods. Clothes, kitchen stuff, boots, anything that'll sell. I buy cheap an' sell at a profit. I've a stall, one we can push round from market ter market. An' if yer need ter know me financial state yer've me permission ter speak ter Mr Field at Royal Bank in Dale Street. My lass does it all fer me since I can neither read nor write but she's a 'ead on 'er 'as my Gilly. We 'ave a . . . a lodger 'oo's workin' fer Mr Hughes at Barrie an' Hughes Shipyard. He 'as lessons at Mechanics Institution. At moment we live in a . . . well, it's a poor sorta place but I've a mind ter move as soon as our Gilly's settled 'ere.'

There seemed to be no doubt in Queenie Logan's mind that that would happen and there was none in Emily Hunter's either, it appeared.

'Bring her to me.'

For the first time Gilly wore a dress that had never been worn by any other person. She and Queenie had, after much searching in shop windows along Bold Street, Regent Street, Church Street and Dale Street and reading the advertisements in the *Mercury*, decided on the establishment of E.S. Tuton of Lord Street where a splendid assortment of rich shawls, cloaks, mantlets and ready made clothing might be had. Despite her belief in herself and her capacity to deal with supercilious persons who thought themselves to be above her, Queenie's heart was straining and thumping against her breast as she and Gilly stepped over the threshold of the smart establishment. They were dressed in the best that could be found among the garments collected a few days ago from the back entrances of smart villas around the area of Everton Road. The dresses had been washed and mended and Gilly's bonnet had been sewn with a bunch of pale pink silk roses under the brim, filched from another garment. The pair of them were well known in many parts of Liverpool where, every winter when it was too cold to move to distant markets and sleep under their little handcart, they spent their days buying the discarded clothing of the middle classes, taking them to the markets that were within a day's travelling distance from Rose Alley.

They were sitting round the table after their evening meal, Jem explaining to Gilly, or trying to, some rule that must be applied to designing a ship when Queenie cleared her throat and held up her hand for silence. They both turned to her expectantly.

'I've summat ter tell the pair o' yer.' Jem raised his eyebrows and looked at Gilly. 'It's ter do with Gilly, really, an' it's this.' Queenie paused as though not sure how to continue, looking down for a moment at her empty plate, which had contained herrings bought that day at St John's Market. They had eaten them with a loaf of fresh bread and butter, and were now drinking a cup of tea each with a slab of fruit cake also bought at the market. They waited somewhat breathlessly.

'I bin ter see Mrs 'Unter at the girls' school in Williamson Square an' . . . well, she wants ter see yer, lass.'

'To see me?' Gilly was bewildered.

'Aye. I've gorra place there for yer.' Which was a bit premature but so sure was Queenie that Mrs Hunter wouldn't have bothered to see Gilly if she wasn't interested, that she felt it was right to tell the lass. 'Yer ter go ter school, chuck, learn all things what—'

'But I can already read an' write, Mam, an' Jem learns me all sorts o' things what 'e's learned at the Institution so there's no need ter—'

'D'yer wanter stop 'ere all yer life, my lass? Live in Rose Alley an' do what I've done fer't past twenty-odd years? We've worked 'ard, you an' me, an' we've a bit put by, burr I want more fer you, Gillyflower. Look at yer . . .'

And Jem looked, for he knew just what Queenie meant. He himself had spent a whole year working in different parts of the yard and just recently, when he was not at the Institution, he had taken his place at the drawing board in the department where designs were created for the ships Mr Barrie and Mr Hughes were to build. There was an order for several naval ships, frigates, in the offing and the yard was growing rapidly. Jem was accepted now as a coming man, one who would in the future be an important part of the business and when he married Gilly, which, naturally, he meant to do, she must be able to mix with the ladies and gentlemen who were, more and more, becoming Jem's new world. Not that as yet he mixed with them socially, but it would surely come as he moved imperceptibly upwards. His Gilly was beautiful and with the proper clothes would be an asset to him and put in the shade the ladies who occasionally visited their husbands in their offices, but clothes and beauty were not enough. She needed what he called *grooming* as he himself was being groomed and Queenie was offering it to her.

Gilly looked from one to the other. She was thirteen now, almost as tall as her mother and as graceful in the way she moved. Like a young queen she was, back straight, head high and had it not been for the second-hand clothes she wore might have been taken for one of the well-bred young ladies who sauntered, parasols aloft, along Bold Street where the most fashionable shops were.

It was clear that she was speechless and as yet Queenie could see no enthusiasm in her for the plan she had worked out and had already set in motion.

Jem approved, Gilly recognised that. He was smiling and ready to reach for Gilly's hand, to squeeze it encouragingly, for she must rise with him, his expression said. He had changed from his good suit into an old pair of corduroy breeches and an open-necked, collarless shirt, looking as he had done since he had first moved in with them years ago. His hair was ruffled and his vivid blue eyes shone into hers and for a moment she was tempted to snatch her hand away, to stand up and tell the pair of them to go to hell since she had her own life mapped out and had no intention of discarding it, but something stopped her. What she meant to do had been part of her for years but as what her mam had just told her sank into her swirling brain she realised with that quick, intelligent turn of her mind, probably inherited from her sharp, Irish father, that what her mam said made sense. She must learn to act, and *speak* as ladies did, for in the life she envisaged she would be mixing with them.

'D'yer not wanner go, lass?' her mother asked quietly. 'It'll be 'ard, I know but . . .'

Gilly reached for her mother's hand so that the three of them were linked, Gilly between Queenie and Jem, protected as she had always been by them all her life, but now she was to go out on her own. But she was not afraid.

'No, Mam, I'll go, but wharrin?' She looked down ruefully at the shabby black dress she wore as she pushed the handcart round the streets of Liverpool but her mother smiled and, leaving go of her daughter's hand, tapped her nose and winked.

And so Gilly Logan, like a butterfly emerging from its chrysalis, stepped from the emporium of E.S. Tuton, changing the drab grey of a dress once worn by the governess to the children of a wealthy merchant in Liverpool for one the very colour of a Chalkhill Blue, a butterfly that is on the wing between July and August. Not that Gilly would last so short a time as she lifted her pretty puff bonnet, small and decorated with white lace and blue velvet ribbons the exact colour of her gown. The assistants were open-mouthed with admiration, but none more so than her proud mother as she stepped out in the direction of Williamson Square and Mrs Hunter.

7

Emily Hunter stopped writing and stared in astonishment when Gilly and her mother were ushered into her room by a grim-faced Miss Jones who, from her expression, was mortified even to be associated with such a mad scheme as the one Mrs Hunter seemed to be embarked upon. The girl was as suitably dressed as the rest of their young ladies and walked with the same graceful and unhurried gait as her stately mother, showing none of the nervousness that Amy Jones expected in one of her class. Her dislike of the girl probably began then, if such a bland word could describe the feelings that grew in the flat bosom of the woman who liked to consider herself as Emily Hunter's friend. Miss Jones was not a teacher, but in a way she ran the school, for she attended to all the housekeeping, supervising the girls' food and general well-being. She engaged the servants, leaving Mrs Hunter to interview parents and pupils and teach how and when she pleased. And now it seemed it pleased her to take in this low-class person on what Amy Jones considered to be a whim and against all Amy's advice. They had argued, for the first time in their association, but Emily seemed set on the idea of bringing in a girl from some slum in the worst part of the city and turning her into a lady.

But that first interview amazed both her and Emily, for though the girl spoke with the most dreadful accent and mixed up her grammar in the most appalling way, she looked the picture of well-bred gentility. She answered Emily's questions intelligently, or at least those to do with the knowledge she seemed to have stored in her lovely head. She could quote books she had read and without recourse to pen or paper work out the simple sums Emily put to her. When asked to name some current event she asked politely whether Mrs Hunter meant in Liverpool or some other place in the world.

'Anywhere,' Mrs Hunter told her, delighted with the answer.

Gilly replied that she was aware of the terrible war in America between the northern and southern states and the distress the shortage of cotton was having in the cotton towns of Lancashire. She even quoted the fall in prices and the low stock of cotton in Liverpool at the beginning of the year. And she knew of the eventual capitulation of the Confederate Armies and surrender by General Robert E. Lee to General Grant at Appomattox in April. She knew that Paris was the capital of France and that the River Rhine ran through Germany. She could describe the visit of their Royal Highnesses the Prince and Princess of Wales to the town last month which she had read about in the newspaper. Did she read the newspapers regularly? Oh, yes, she was a frequent visitor to the William Brown Reading Room and borrowed books from the Free Lending Library.

What was she reading at the moment? Miss Jones asked her somewhat maliciously, believing she would mention some children's nursery story or comic book such as *Fun*, and was astounded and annoyed when she answered *Eugene Onegin* by Aleksandr Pushkin which Miss Jones herself had not mastered.

'Well,' she said when the woman and her daughter had left, convinced that despite the books she read and her knowledge of world events Emily was about to say it would not do. Not a girl of her class mixing with theirs.

'I shall take her,' Emily said calmly, pouring out the tea she had sent for.

'What?' Miss Jones said. She could hardly believe her ears and her frank incredulity rang in her voice.

'You sound astonished. Is it such a fantastic suggestion?'

'Fantastic? It's unthinkable.'

'Why?' Emily Hunter's tone was mild and questioning but there was a gleam of excitement in her eyes, which Amy Jones did not care for.

'You surely don't need me to tell you why, Emily. What will the other girls say and do? And then there are their parents.'

Emily Hunter shrugged her plump shoulders. 'This is my school, Amy, and I am prepared to deal with anything they might do.'

Amy tried another tack. 'But surely it would not be fair to the girl herself. She will never fit in. The girls will make fun of her.'

'Enough, Amy. I believe the girl is exceptional and that she is worth taking some trouble with. True, the way she speaks is appalling but elocution lessons and mixing with . . . well, with people like you and me and girls from good family she will improve. She has a mind that is quick and ready to be educated. She learned to read and write at Sunday school and from there it seems she is self-taught. I mean to improve that mind even more. God knows, for the most part I spend time on dolts and fools and it will be a pleasure to teach someone who is worth teaching. Oh, I know over the years we have had some exceedingly promising girls but the minute I mention to a father that his daughter has a good brain he tells me a good brain is worth nothing to the man she is destined to marry. He wants a girl who will make an excellent wife and mother, a good hostess who knows her manners and will be an asset to her husband. That is all they are destined for. As an appendage to some gentleman. This girl has no father. Her mother wants her to be better than she is herself and, who knows, perhaps the girl, when groomed, will make a decent teacher . . .'

'Here?' Amy's voice was faint.

'Why not?' Mrs Hunter had not the faintest conception what

plans Gillyflower Logan had for herself and would not have
been so confident had she known.

Mrs Hunter found to her dismay that there was really not a
lot she could teach the new girl since she admitted – to herself
only – that Gillyflower Logan had more learning than she had
herself. Gilly did not think it was wise to mention Jem or that
everything he himself had learned at the Mechanics Institution
he had passed on to her. Not draughtsmanship, of course, or
things to do with naval matters, but all the subjects that would
be useful to her. She it was who kept her mother's account
book, a simple exercise book that noted all Queenie's earnings,
her outgoings for their small household, their bank desposits
and even the small investments that Mr Field had suggested.

On that first day as she hung up her cloak on the peg
indicated, Gilly smiled inwardly as she reflected on the faces
of the neighbours when she had emerged from the cellar room
in Rose Alley dressed in her new gown and cloak. 'Keep 'old of
'em, our Gilly,' her mother had advised. 'An' mekk sure yer
petticoats are kept out o't puddles. Yer don't want ter arrive at
Mrs 'Unter's wi' yer skirts all a'draggle.' Their neighbours had
seen and become accustomed to Jem in his new finery, making
ribald comments regarding his sexuality, on the dandy in their
midst, his own father adding his voice to their crude remarks,
for Tommy Wilson harboured a deep grudge towards his son,
who refused to slip him a bob or two, and the women he lived
with. If he could do him, or them, harm, he would.

But the sight of Gilly Logan, bastard daughter of a woman
who could be described as nothing more than a female 'rag 'n'
bone' man, silenced them. She was like a fairy princess, though
if truth were told not one of them had seen such a thing. The
inhabitants of Rose Alley did not saunter along Bold Street as
those in society did and the outfit the Logan lass wore was
beyond their wildest imaginings. She held the skirt up out of the
stinking slime that was a hazard to all those who walked across

it, the shining black boots with their thick clumping soles the only incongruous note in her outfit, though they, naturally, did not use the word incongruous. Even her little bonnet amazed them as they had never seen her or her mam in anything but a shawl about their heads. They watched, voiceless, until Jem Wilson, Queenie and Gilly Logan had turned the corner. Tommy Wilson found he could not even speak so great was his resentment; instead, turning to Jess, he fetched her a clout that lifted her off her feet, then vanished into his own foetid room, leaving his dazed wife to pick herself up and, not daring to follow him, sit on the step with her youngest on her knee. Mind you, in her ragged pocket was the couple of bob their Jem had slipped her last night and thank God the coins hadn't jingled as she was knocked off the step.

Gilly had held Jem's hand tightly once they were out of sight of those in Rose Alley, the three of them walking quickly through the maze of alleyways and courtyards until they came out in Dale Street and then on to Whitechapel. She was dressed in the same pale blue dress that she had worn for her interview but over it she wore a plain woollen cloak of dark navy blue which Queenie had rescued from her handcart and put to one side for this very day. It was lined with beige wool and had a hood also lined with beige, which turned back to frame Gilly's face and show off her pretty bonnet. She had a great desire to cling to her mam, something she had not done for years, but she merely smiled and let both Mam and Jem go as she bravely climbed the steps to the unknown world beyond. This was the first day, the very first day of the life she had planned for herself and if she was to accomplish it she must get through *this*.

Mam and Jem had watched Gilly climb the steps and go through the double doors to the entrance hall, then, turning to sigh at one another, both wishing they could have gone with her on her first day, they parted, Queenie making her way back to Dale Street and the bank where she had a bit of business with

Mr Field, and Jem walking slowly on to Mount Street and the Mechanics Institution.

Gilly was first put in a class of ten-year-olds among whom Mrs Hunter thought she might hold her own and who might be kinder to her than girls of her own age. She was a head taller than the others and, despite her upbringing in the poorest part of Liverpool, strong, healthy and vigorous. When she sat down at the desk suitable for a ten-year-old she was as composed as if she had been a pupil at the school for years. She tucked her long legs into the small space beneath the desk and only then did she dare look around her.

Mrs Hunter, though she catered to the often spoiled offspring of what her father had called 'county' people, believed that they should be taught in an environment where luxury did not count. Though the rooms were warm the girls who took their lessons there had no more than a child in a small 'ragged' school might expect. Equipment was minimal, the only difference to the ragged school being that each girl had her own robust, slope-top desk joined by runners to a chair with a tilting seat. Inside the desk a girl was expected to keep her exercise books, pens and pencils, for Mrs Hunter, an enlightened teacher, had done away with the slates and chalk that might be found elsewhere. At ten years old a girl might be expected to write with a pen and ink. There was a sturdy blackboard at the front of the class on which was written in beautiful copperplate:

> *Train young minds*
> *Govern your temper*
> *Attend to education*

Then the alphabet came beneath in capitals in the same precise handwriting. The walls were whitewashed and decorated with pictures obviously drawn by the pupils. A large map of Britain hung on one wall, and on two others were informative charts of trees, birds and historical subjects such as Roman Walls,

Roads, and the Battle of Hastings. At waist level were shelves crammed with books. Gilly managed to read a few titles: *The Fat Cat, or 'do not ask for all you see', a cautionary tale*, was one, another *Struwwelpeter* which meant nothing to her, *Wonderful Stories for Children* by Hans Christian Andersen and a dozen others, many of which Gilly had already read.

She waited quietly for what was to happen next and was surprised when Mrs Hunter asked her to stand up and introduced her to the rest of the class as a new pupil. The girls turned to look at her but none spoke or smiled.

She resumed her seat, listening to Mrs Hunter as she told the girls to get their books out and not to make a clatter and would Amelia Turner please refrain from sniffing. Yes, she knew Amelia had a cold but she should use her handkerchief. Gilly listened intently in this confusing new world, not exactly afraid but somewhat dazed, speaking only when she was spoken to, and Emily Hunter could see she was an astute young woman who knew her own deficiencies and was not about to show them up on this her first day.

Mrs Hunter had decided that she herself would take the first class Gilly Logan attended. She wished to observe the girl, her reaction to the other pupils who stared at her in amazement, her quickness in answering questions, her attention span, indeed everything there was to know about the girl.

Gilly's first morning, though she did not show it, was a haze of confusion which, by the simple practice of picking out one girl and doing exactly what she did, she managed to get through. She realised that though all the other girls changed from their outdoor shoes or boots into some sort of light slippers, she would be forced to clump along the uncarpeted corridors her footsteps sounding loud and forceful to her ears, drawing attention to herself. First of all there were prayers and a hymn, both of which Gilly knew since she had learned them at Sunday school, and when Mrs Hunter beckoned to her she followed her to the classroom and, when told, folded herself into a desk among the little girls.

She thought she had lost her hearing at first, for Mrs Hunter's voice came to her from a long way away. It was a kind of buzz like that made by the bumble bees she and Jem had lazily watched when they ambled on a Sunday to the meadows beyond the outskirts of the town. The other girls, all beautifully dressed with their hair done in ringlets and tied with pretty ribbons, eyed her curiously and whispered behind their hands when Mrs Hunter's back was turned. They seemed to take little interest in what Mrs Hunter was saying. She had written something on the blackboard and with a stick was pointing to what she had written.

'Now then, Clarissa, surely you know what three times five is? We have been over this a dozen times and I did ask you to take your book home with you and learn by heart your multiplication tables up to three. Now then I will begin, one three is three, two threes are . . .' There was a pause while Clarissa struggled with how many numbers there were in two threes. Mrs Hunter sighed, for she knew as well as Clarissa that the child's head was filled with nothing but her own confusion.

'Very well, who does know what two times three is?' She looked round encouragingly. 'Come along, hands up who knows.'

'Six.' Gilly smiled at Mrs Hunter and Mrs Hunter felt her heart melt, for it really was the loveliest smile any girl had ever directed at her.

'Correct, Gilly.' The other girls turned as one and stared sullenly at the big girl whose voice had not been heard until now.

'Now the next, three times three?'

Gilly looked around her to see if anyone else wanted a go but as no one did, she answered, 'Nine.'

'Good, good. Now come along, girls, will someone else not try to tell me four times three.'

For the next thirty minutes Gilly and Mrs Hunter seemed to conduct a private lesson, since Gilly knew the answer to every question. Even when, to give the silent, obviously resentful girls, who did not care to have this outsider showing them up, a chance to shine, Mrs Hunter handed out plain paper and asked them to print their three times table, or perhaps if they were not quite sure of the three times, then the two times, some of them had barely put pencil to paper when Gilly's hand shot up and she handed Mrs Hunter a neatly written row of numbers.

Mrs Hunter knew then that she had made a mistake in believing that this young girl would do best in a class of ten-year-olds. She was thirteen, the girl's mother had told her, but she was ahead of those who were ten years old and even of those who were *fourteen*! But she must allow her to try and the first thing to be done was to take the girl to her own room and talk to her. What she meant was *warn* her because there was no doubt the child would have a bad time of it. Perhaps if she started her with . . . with elocution lessons, on her own with Miss Pedder for a day or two, she could then be put among girls of her own age. For a moment she thought uneasily that Amy had been right in her belief that the girl would have a bad time with these well-bred girls, not with her knowledge and learning, though even that might be resented, but in her manners – they had not yet seen her at table – and in her speech.

When they reached her room and were seated she paused for a moment, studying the face before her, noting the intelligence, the brightness in her eyes and, at the same time, the stubborn set to the pointed chin. She was the most beautiful young girl she had ever seen with a complexion like that of a creamy rose and a mouth as red as a hedge berry, her hair plaited and fastened in a huge and heavy chignon which tipped back her head. But even before she spoke, Gilly forestalled her.

'I know wha' yer gonner say, Miss 'Unter so I'll say it for yer. I don't talk right burr I will if yer'll learn me. *Teach* me. Lord, I do enough readin' ter know right way characters in me books speak burr it's pronunciation – is tharrit? – I need ter learn. Please don't chuck me out.'

'I have no intention of chucking you out, Gilly, and chucking is not a word we use here. I know you are a strong young woman and . . . well, you will need to be to get through this. I know you want to better yourself and I know your mother has worked hard to get you here so I mean to see you have every chance. I shall—'

'Don't stick up fer me, Mrs 'Unter. Not in't class. It'll only mekk things worse. If them girls see yer tekkin' my part they'll not like it. Put me in't class wi't big girls an' I promise I'll tekk care o' meself. I just want chance ter speak nice.'

'And so you shall. I mean to put you with Miss Pedder for a few days. Just the two of you. She teaches elocution and drama—'

'What's tha'?'

'You will learn what it is and you will also learn not to interrupt when an adult is speaking. You will learn manners, deportment, how to converse with a lady, how to arrange a dinner party, even if such a thing is not necessary. You will don the trappings of a lady – and I don't mean clothing – and all this, I suspect, is going to lead you somewhere, something you have in that clever head of yours. You *are* clever, Gilly, though I shan't tell you again, and determined, and the combination should achieve the goal you have set yourself. Now come with me and I'll introduce you to Miss Pedder.'

Miss Pedder had no need to order Gilly Logan not to slouch, for she had never seen a young girl with such regal deportment. The girl glided, that was the only word that came to mind, in a way Miss Pedder had a great deal of trouble teaching her other young ladies. She moved beautifully, turned beautifully, sat down and stood up in the graceful and proud way of a young queen and she only wished she had as much success with the voice exercises she set her. When told not to drop her 'aitches' as in Mrs Hunter, she mispronounced the aitch making it *haitch*. The alphabet, which she knew backwards and forwards, was spoken in such an appalling manner Miss Pedder despaired, and said so to Mrs Hunter, but gradually over the weeks she began to improve and Mrs Hunter decided that it was time she mixed properly with her fellow pupils. Girls of her own age who not only attempted arithmetic, spelling, English reading, drawing, needlework and vocal music, but who also gave small tea parties where the young ladies exhibited the pretty manners that Mrs Hunter did her best to inculcate in them.

'How do you like your tea, Mrs Hunter? With cream? Sugar?'

'Perhaps you prefer sherry, or Madeira?' this directed at a gentleman.

'Now ring the bell,' to whoever it was who was displaying their manners and the charade went on. It all seemed a lot of nonsense to Gilly but she knew she must attack it, for it would be vital to her one day.

There began a regime of daily lessons, which Gilly tackled with the strength of her mother and at the same time the humour of her father. It amused her immensely and she had her mother and Jem howling with laughter as she acted out Margaret Blackwood or Celia Morley struggling with the simplest sum which she herself had mastered at the age of eight, and they big girls of fourteen and fifteen.

These girls, and the rest of them, knowing she was not one of them, simply acted as though she were not there. Gilly and Queenie had bought a bolt of fine woollen material in a lovely tawny shade that matched her hair and, referring to patterns that were described in the women's magazine Queenie picked up cheap on a stall in the market, had made her a gown that was more suitable for winter wear than the blue silk. She had a pair of light slippers into which to change as they all did on entering the school and slowly but surely, letting no one alter her course, she began to speak as the others did. It did not come naturally to her so that at times she sounded stilted and, of course, when she was at home with Jem and her mam she let it slip, for she felt a fool speaking in what she called her 'false' voice. She began to realise, however, that Jem himself, though he had no lessons, was beginning to lose his Liverpool accent, for he mixed most of the time with gentlemen who were on a par with the girls at school. Unconsciously following each other, their way of speaking changed imperceptibly and the only one to notice was Queenie. Her girl, as winter became spring and then summer, was taking on the air of a lady, not putting on airs or anything like that but beginning naturally to speak as Miss Pedder had taught her. When she was alone she carried out the exercises she had been given and apart from now and again, when she was excited about something, when she dropped an aitch, or chopped off a word that ended in 'ing' Mrs Hunter prided herself that the girl could hold her own with any of the well-bred young ladies with whom she mixed.

Well, you could hardly call it 'mixing' since the young ladies avoided Gilly Logan as they might the kitchen-maid, making it plain that she was not one of them and though they accepted that Mrs Hunter might take as a pupil anyone she cared to, *they* wanted no part of it. Sometimes they even drew their skirts aside when she passed by, for they had heard that she came from a poor part of town though not even they could imagine how poor. They lifted their noses as though at a nasty smell and whispered behind their hands, but it seemed the 'new girl', as they still called her, was impervious to their scorn.

During the summer holidays when they all went home to their fathers' splendid estates, or grand villas on the edge of town, Gilly put on her old clothes and travelled with her mam to the cotton towns of Lancashire and over the Pennines into Yorkshire, standing behind the old stall as she had done in the past, and if the plain folk with whom she spoke marvelled at the strange way Queenie Logan's daughter had begun to address them they said nothing, for Queenie was known for her sharp tongue.

Gilly returned in the autumn to resume her education which Mrs Hunter thought might last for another three years. She was to learn a smattering of French this year which, though it might never be used, always gave a young lady what might be called polish.

8

Gilly had been sent by Miss Pedder to Mrs Hunter's study at Mrs Hunter's request as she had expressed a wish to hear her recite a piece of poetry of her own choosing and to hold what Mrs Hunter called a *conversazione*, which was a social gathering held by learned society. This was not, of course, a real one but Mrs Hunter liked to think that with a few of her cleverer pupils it approached such a level. She held these dialogues with them from time to time – most of the girls finding them a nail-biting experience – but a boring half-hour for Mrs Hunter. She felt it part of her duty to ascertain the progress of each day girl, particularly the older ones who went home at the end of the day and, one hoped, took part in dinner table conversation with their family. Perhaps there were even dinner guests which gave them a chance to learn how to behave in such circumstances. Boarders who did not have this opportunity dined each evening with her and her staff and were encouraged to practise for what, when they left school, would be rounds of afternoon calls, dinner parties, evening musical parties and such, where light conversation was necessary. These were examined each evening under her watchful eye.

And then there was Gilly Logan, who neither dined in splendour with her family, nor under the critical eye of Emily Hunter. Nevertheless Gilly had learned at lunchtime, when a simple meal was taken, which cutlery to use and when spoken to by the teacher at whose table she sat, answered intelligently.

Now, it seemed, Mrs Hunter wished to hear how her elocution lessons were proceeding.

As she stood before Mrs Hunter's desk, calm, her hands folded before her, her face serene, Emily, as she had done so many times before, wondered at the steadiness and dignity shown by this young woman in these unfamiliar surroundings, unfamiliar despite her time at the school. Compared to her own home this environment was surely still unique. Brought up in poverty, working manually from a young age, she had come on in leaps and bounds since the day her mother brought her here. She had made no friends, which was not surprising because girls who were pupils here did not mix with those they thought inferior to them. And Gilly Logan was one of the latter.

'Now, Gilly, which poem have you chosen to recite to me? I see you have brought a small book.'

She leaned back in her chair and steepled her hands beneath her chin. She smiled kindly, for she admired this girl who had overcome so much and who had achieved even more. What she was to do next year when she finished her education at seventeen, Mrs Hunter did not know, though she had her own hopes on that score.

'My poem is about the sea.' Gilly opened the book then paused for a moment. 'I love the sea, Mrs Hunter,' she said earnestly, 'and ships and if I had been a man I would have . . .' She sighed and shrugged her shoulders.

'Yes, Gilly?'

'Become a mariner. I want to see the world, visit the places we read about, climb the Himalayas, ride on a camel through the deserts of North Africa, trek through jungles, do what Mr Livingstone has done in Central Africa, sail from one continent to another on a sailing ship as a man would, as a sailor would but—' She stopped abruptly and the light that had gleamed in her eyes died away. 'As I am not I must—'

'What, Gilly?'

'I must do something more suitable to my sex,' Gilly said expressionlessly. She had no intention of telling Mrs Hunter what, being merely a woman and unable to travel as she longed to, she meant to do. She had told no one, not even Jem, but next year at the end of the summer term when she had absorbed everything this woman, all these women, and even Monsieur Suliot, the French teacher, could teach her, she would put her plan into action. Small at first. 'From little acorns grew . . .' as Miss Swindells was fond of saying.

'My poem is about the sea, Mrs Hunter,' she said in a resolute way. ' "A Burnt Ship" by John Donne. It's quite short.'

'Very well.'

Out of a fired ship, which by no way
But drowning could be rescued from the flame,
Some men leap'd forth, and ever as they came
Near the foes' ships, did by their shot decay;
So all were lost, which in the ship were found,
They in the sea being burnt, they in the burnt ship drown'd.

Six lines only and Gilly did not read them, as she knew them by heart. They were sad and even as she spoke the lines she wondered, as did Mrs Hunter, why they appealed to her. Mrs Hunter marvelled again at this astounding girl who stood before her. Most of her pupils when asked to read their favourite poem chose one by Marlowe or Wordsworth: 'Come live with me, and be my love . . .', 'I wandered lonely as a cloud . . .' Romantic as young girls are, but this one had chosen Donne. An unusual choice but then she was an unusual girl.

Emily Hunter shook herself out of her reverie, smiling, pleased, for it was a long time since she had taught a girl as intelligent as this one.

'Now then, *Parlez français, s'il vous plaît,* Gilly.'

'*Oui, madame.*'

'*Quelle heure est-il?*'

Gilly glanced at the clock on the mantelpiece. '*Il est une heure dix, madame.*'

'*Très bien.* Good, good, now . . . Sit down, Gilly and perhaps you would pour the tea.'

Gilly lowered herself gracefully into the chair beside the low table, smoothing the folds of her full skirt. A teapot, two cups and saucers, milk jug and sugar basin, all in matching bone china, were placed on the delicately patterned lace cloth, one worked by a former pupil and which Mrs Hunter liked to hold up as an example of what diligence could achieve. Gilly poured the tea as she had been taught, politely and correctly asking Mrs Hunter if she cared for milk and sugar, then handed her her cup and saucer. She sat upright, not touching the chair back. She answered Mrs Hunter's questions, smiling, nodding her bright, smooth head and when Mrs Hunter put down her cup and saucer, indicating that the session was over, she stood up, bobbed a small curtsey and left the room.

As she passed the doors of the large linen cupboard on the first landing, making her way to the sewing room, she became aware of the soft, muffled sounds of someone in distress. She hesitated, turning her head this way and that, listening, trying to locate the source of the sound. There was no one in the corridor. Windows lined it, looking out over the neat gardens which were just turning from the colours of summer, the roses dying, the herbaceous borders beginning to fade, the grass being cut by the gardener leading the donkey who pulled the mower. A lad was fighting a losing battle with the beech leaves which kept drifting from the trees on to the stretch of mown grass he had just swept clean. A flight of swallows flung themselves madly across the roof and with a great sighing of their wings vanished towards the river.

The sound was coming from the cupboard, soft, like that of a hurt child who does not want to draw attention to itself. Gilly hesitated, not wishing to intrude on what was obviously a private moment, then, squaring her shoulders, a gesture she was in the habit of making when disturbed or expecting a rebuff, which she did frequently, she opened the cupboard door a fraction and peeped in. As the light entered whoever hid there became completely silent and still so that Gilly could at first see nothing.

'Hello,' she whispered, wanting to say, 'Is anybody there?' but feeling somewhat foolish, for it was evident that someone was. Maybe one of the little girls just starting school, homesick, hiding herself away from prying or perhaps scornful eyes.

There was a movement from beneath the lower shelf and from a niche she had made for herself among the neatly ironed and folded sheets, a mournful face peeped out, a pale face from which enormous, tear-filled eyes gazed. Tracks down the cheeks attested to a storm of weeping. Then a girl crept out and stood up, her back to the cupboard. She looked hastily up and down the corridor then crouched, silently weeping, her head lowered as though expecting Gilly to reprimand her.

Gilly Logan had never, in the whole of her sixteen years, had anything to do with any female of her own age. During her time at Mrs Hunter's school she had become used to going about the business of obtaining the education she would need for her future life quietly. At first the other girls had covertly taunted her for the way she spoke but gradually they had become used to her. The novelty had worn off and now they simply ignored her. So she was not sure how to treat this little thing who stood abjectly before her. At first she had thought she was about eleven or twelve, maybe even younger, but on closer inspection she could see she had the breasts of an older girl. In fact, now that she had taken a closer look she remembered seeing her in Monsieur Suliot's class with girls of her own age. She recalled the girl's awful stammer, which had infuriated the French teacher because it made it all the more difficult to understand her halting French. Gilly had been sorry for her, knowing how she felt, since she herself had suffered the sniggers of other girls when she had first come to the school with her adenoidal Liverpool accent. She studied her carefully, knowing how cruel human beings were to each other, particularly to those who were smaller and weaker than themselves. She was tiny, neat, compact but in perfect proportion, no taller than Gilly's shoulder.

'Are you all right? No, I'm sorry, of course you aren't or you wouldn't be crying in a cupboard but . . . well, are you hurt or . . .'

'N . . . n . . . no . . . really . . .' the girl sniffed. 'I . . . I . . . I'm hi . . . hi . . . hiding . . . f . . . f . . . from . . . them because . . . sometimes . . . it . . . ju . . . ju . . . just . . . gets the be . . . better of me. I . . . sh . . . sh . . . should be used t . . . t . . . to it by now . . . b . . . but An . . . An . . . Angela Ryan . . . sh . . . she . . . frightens me . . . a . . . and . . . she won't . . . l . . . let me alone.'

Realising that here was a girl who was sympathetic, one who was not going to make fun of her, one who was patient and willing to listen, the girl's speech became more coherent. 'She won't leave me alone because . . . because she knows it m . . . makes the others laugh. Oh . . . d . . . d . . . dear . . . I'm so sorry . . .'

'Angela Ryan's a bitch, she really is and I'd like to smack her silly face.' Gilly was rewarded with a weak, somewhat shocked smile. 'She teases me too, you know.'

'Yes, I know.'

'So, you see, you and I are in the same boat. We should stick together.'

'Pardon?' The girl was clearly mystified. Her rather pretty face wore a puzzled expression and Gilly wondered for a moment whether she was 'pots for rags' as they said in the north, meaning she was not quite right in the head. But she seemed bright enough now she had overcome her first fear and realised that Gilly was not going to make fun of her. She glanced up shyly, her velvety grey eyes still drowning in her recent tears, but she had become more composed. She had short hair, fair and curly, and her dress was of the very best quality, Gilly could tell, for she had made a study of fabrics and design in the books that were on loan at the library. She apparently came from a wealthy family and Gilly tried to remember her name. It was part of Monsieur Suliot's teaching to make his pupils introduce themselves to one another but Gilly knew that this girl, made to stand up and speak before the class, had failed dismally, sinking back into her seat at the French teacher's impatient command.

She held out her hand which the girl looked at cautiously as though she suspected some trick, then, deciding that Gilly was to be trusted, put her own in it. Gilly thought it felt like that of an injured sparrow Jem had once found, soft, frail and thin, vulnerable as the girl was. She suddenly felt immensely strong and protective towards this little creature, wondering why, for the girl was nothing to her.

'My name is Gilly Logan. What's yours?' She still held the girl's hand, who left it there trustingly.

'Anne Barrie.'

Gilly felt a ripple of something move through her. She didn't know whether it was of apprehension or anticipation. The girl had the same name as the owner of the shipyard where Jem worked and for some reason it seemed to send a signal to her, a strange signal that she did not understand. Foreseeing, as though fate were at work this day but what the devil she meant by that she couldn't imagine.

'Is your father . . . does he own the shipyard over the water?'

'Yes . . . w . . . why?'

Gilly smiled and squeezed her hand. 'Nothing, except a very good friend of mine works for him. He's to become a draughtsman, an engineer, build ships and . . .' Her eyes shone with pride.

'My brother works at the same job. Perhaps your . . . your friend works with . . . with him.'

'I'll ask him tonight. What's your brother's name?'

'Lucas, and he's the . . . the b . . . best man in the world.'

'So is Jem.'

They both laughed, their hands still clasped and in that moment a friendship that was to endure a lifetime was formed.

Their friendship took its first step towards what was a rock-like foundation the very next day. Miss Pedder, as part of her elocution lesson, asked each pupil to read from a book of Miss Pedder's choice which at the moment was *Jane Eyre* by Charlotte Brontë. Jane had just arrived at Thornfield Hall and had alighted from the carriage, entering the square hall, when Miss Pedder told Gilly, who had been reading for five minutes, to sit down. Miss Pedder looked about her, smiling, then, with some hesitation, for it was well known to all the staff that Anne Barrie had a soul-destroying stammer, asked her to stand up. After all, she was the daughter of one of Birkenhead's most influential and wealthy gentlemen, sent here to gain an education and one could not simply ignore her, though all the teachers longed to, if only to save her the uphill struggle of coping with her impediment.

Anne stood and a noticeable snigger went round Miss Pedder's study where the older girls gathered to read. All the teachers had their own studies, a room where they might, at the end of the day, have privacy to mark papers, read, embroider, or whatever their choice of relaxation might be. Mrs Hunter knew that if she was to keep good teachers at her school she must pay them well and make them comfortable. There was a cosy fire in the grate, a cheerful if somewhat worn carpet on the floor and around the room half a dozen velvet-covered button-back chairs on which her pupils sat. They were girls in their last year at school, most of them sixteen or seventeen and deemed old and eligible enough to read in Miss Pedder's private study instead of the schoolroom. A delicate carriage clock with an oval face ticked pleasantly on the mantel in the centre of a line of Staffordshire ornaments, one of Florence Nightingale, two of members of the royal family, their connection to Her Majesty not quite recognisable, a sailor in a broad-brimmed hat and two lovers beneath an umbrella, all gaudily painted but quite appealing to the eye.

Miss Pedder sighed but she had no choice other than to ask Anne to start at the next line.

' " 'Will you walk this way, ma'am,' said the girl," ' she began encouragingly, indicating to Anne that she was to continue, which Anne tried to do. ' ". . . and I f . . . f . . . followed . . . h . . . h . . . er across . . . a . . . s . . . s . . . s . . ." '

'Is it a snake, I wonder?' Angela Ryan asked innocently, turning to greet the laughter that eddied about her.

'Thank you, Angela,' Miss Pedder said, 'that will do.' She nodded at the drooping figure of Anne Barrie. 'Go on, Anne: "across a square hall with . . ." '

' "W . . . w . . . with high . . . d . . . d . . . doors all r . . . ound: sh . . . she . . . ushered . . . m . . . me in . . . into . . ." '

Angela turned and whispered into the ear of the girl next to her and they both tittered behind their hands.

'Continue, Anne: "a room whose double illumination . . ." ' But Anne had lost her place and at once Gilly sprang up, her face pink with indignation.

'Please, Miss Pedder, won't you allow me to continue for Anne,' she began and for a moment, quite relieved, Miss Pedder was about to agree, but Angela Ryan interrupted, her face smirking with glee, for not only was she glad to make fun of Anne Barrie who was prettier and better dressed than she was and, of course, a good target for what Angela thought of as her own wit, but she despised and was intensely jealous of Gilly Logan who was one of Mrs Hunter's favourites.

'That's hardly fair, Miss Pedder, after all we must each of us learn to speak in public; by that I mean to people of our own class, on social occasions, you understand, and what better way to learn than reading aloud—'

'Now, Angela,' Miss Pedder began, but before she could utter some soothing words that would please everyone Gilly strode across the room and, with as much force as she could muster, slapped Angela across her rosy cheek. It knocked her head to one side and she was almost flung from her chair but in a moment she had recovered and with one leap was up on her feet and had grabbed at Gilly's plait which was as usual wound about her head. At once it came loose and a mass of russet tresses fell about her face and neck and flowed wildly down her back.

'Why, you . . .' and here Gilly let forth a string of foul expletives, commonplace in Rose Alley but which had never been heard in the prim confines of Mrs Hunter's school and were not even understood by anyone in the room.

They began to fling one another about the study, knocking over Miss Pedder's chairs and tables and her cheap ornaments which were, nevertheless, great favourites with her. Clarissa Wentworth began to scream shrilly and several of the others joined in, while Miss Pedder stood as though frozen to the spot. Anne wept silently by her chair but as suddenly as it had begun the fight was over.

'You stupid cow,' Gilly hissed contemptuously, shoving Angela back into her chair. 'You are supposed to be a lady or pretend that you are, whereas I, brought up in a back street where you soon learn to fight, have no such pretensions. I don't know who your father is but mine was an Irish drifter, a ne'er-do-well with nothing to his name but a sense of humour and a tendency to laugh, or so my mother told me. But my life has taught me one thing and that is how to defend those I care about. Anne is a person of value which you are not, but let me tell you that if you ever make fun of her again in my presence I'll knock your teeth down your throat.'

They all gasped in horror at the words, then, as she moved over to Anne and put her arms about her, stared in astonishment. She held her, then peered down into her face and asked her if she was all right. Anne nodded, blinking away her tears. She smiled tremulously and even the most insensitive realised that little Annie Barrie had found a champion; they also wondered what Angela Ryan would do to get her own back. Not a girl to be made a fool of, was Angela Ryan!

Miss Pedder let out her breath on a long sigh and they all waited to see what she would do. It seemed that the hullabaloo had not been heard by anyone else in the building. So would Miss Pedder report it to Mrs Hunter? Even Miss Pedder was unsure. The girls sat quietly now, turning to look first at Gilly Logan's face then Angela Ryan's but the two girls, who both knew that this was not the end of it, studiously avoided everyone's glance, and each other's.

'Very well, let us settle down,' murmured Miss Pedder, realising that she should say more or at least report this to Mrs Hunter, but she liked Gilly Logan and Anne Barrie. They all did, and she knew who would come off worst if this all came out. She took the line of least resistance, which proved to be a mistake!

It was dark as Gilly turned the corner from Vauxhall Road into the deserted Rose Alley. She had waited patiently for ten minutes for Jem outside the Mechanics Institution but it was a bitterly cold night and, besides, several men had glanced curiously at her as she shivered against the gate. She knew he would be cross and so would Mam if she walked home alone but it was not the first time and she had managed it safely before. Mind you, that had been in the summer when the nights were still light and there had been folk about.

But there were the cellar steps down to the basement area and her own door and a light shone from the small, barred window beside the door. Lifting the hem of her dress, she skirted the pools of filth, and was just about to reach out for the railing that surrounded the basement when a man's hand came from behind her and clamped itself over her mouth. An arm circled her waist and she felt herself being dragged backwards towards the horrendous heap of rotting brickwork which was the privy where all the inhabitants relieved themselves. The stench was appalling but it did not deter her attacker who was, presumably, used to it. The replaced door hung on its hinges and for a moment she managed to grab it as her attacker tried to shut it with his shoulder to trap the pair of them inside. His hand was already fumbling her breasts, tearing at the fine woollen fabric of her bodice and the hand he used, revealing his diminished thinking power, was the one he had held over her mouth. Taking advantage of his low intellect she turned her head and screamed shrilly into his ear, a scream that pierced him like a red-hot wire. At once he let go of her and, still screaming, she ran towards her cellar home where Queenie, a frying pan in her hand, stood outlined against the light. Tommy Wilson, who, mad with drink, had finally found the courage and the opportunity to grab what he had wanted for years, stood for a moment, a moment too long as it happened, with his hand to his ear and when Queenie threw the contents of the frying pan, sausages in red-hot fat, into his face, he screamed louder than Gilly. Queenie ran to him and hit him with the pan directly on his badly burned face then, as he fell, shrieking, she kicked him savagely before turning back to her daughter who sobbed against the railings. The occupants of the houses in the court had all tumbled out of their foetid homes to see who was screaming in agony, and they stood about, watching as Queenie Logan put her arms round her Gilly and guided her down the steps and into their home.

Tommy, his hands to his face, shouted hoarsely for Jess and when she came, helping him to his feet, he could be heard to mutter that if it was the last thing he did he would pay Queenie Logan back for this and as for that slut – meaning her daughter – she'd better watch herself, Jem or no Jem, who was known to be her protector, she'd be sorry she ever walked the earth when Tommy Wilson had done with her.

9

It was a repeat of the day several years ago when the *Rose Marie* was launched but this time Willy did not fall in the water and Jem, who had then been a mere labourer, was now allowed to mingle with the owners of the Barrie and Hughes Shipyard and their families, for it was he who had helped to design the steamship that was about to be launched. Of course, the shipyard had built and set forth on the Mersey many steam-ships of all sizes and for many purposes during the intervening years, but this was very special for Jem since on his arm was his young lady, Miss Gilly Logan.

Gilly had turned seventeen in February and wherever she went she excited comment, spinning men's heads in her direction; today it was the turn of Lucas Barrie who thought he had never in his twenty-five years seen a woman as en-chanting as the one who appeared to belong to Jem Wilson.

'Come with us, Mam,' Gilly had begged her mother. 'Put on the dress we made and that bonnet, you know, the one we bought from the villa in Everton with the feathered birds and ribbon. You'd look lovely and you'd be as smart as any of them.'

'Aye, until I opened me mouth, chuck. I'd only shame you an' Jem. God love us, the pair o' yer could pass as toffs now but not wi' me in tow. That there friend o' yours, Anne'd think nowt o' pound to yer soon as she 'eard me speak an'—'

'No, Mam, no. I'll not have you talk of Anne like that. She's dear to me and I know she likes me and she's kind and has a heart of gold. She wouldn't hurt a fly. She'd speak to you as she does to anyone, especially as she knows you're my mother. She'd welcome you into her family—'

'Mebbe, but wharrabout 'er mam? An' 'er pa? They'd not like ter think o' their lass mixin' wi' folk from Rose Alley an' though you an' our Jem'd gerraway wi' it, I couldn't. Lass, lass, I am wharr I am an' it's too late fer me ter change. I've nowt ter be ashamed of burr I'd spoil it for you an' Jem. Jem's doin' so well at that their job of 'is an' wi you beside 'im 'oo knows where 'e'll fetch up. Now, no more arguin'. Go an' get yerself dressed in yer lovely frock an' bonnet. Jem's brought yer some water an' it's on't fire ter warm so get yersel' a wash when Jem's finished and then when yer come back yer can tell us all about it.'

Gilly rose from where she had been crouched at her mother's knee, dropped a kiss on her brow, and turned to the red velvet curtain from behind which came the sound of Jem cursing as he did his best to tie his cravat before the mirror in his tiny quarters. It was getting very awkward now in the cellar home that the three of them had shared for so long. With Jem a fully grown man, tall, lean, but taking up a great deal of space especially with the wardrobe of clothing he had accumulated since he had gone up in the world, and Gilly a young woman who owned several gowns of her own making, plus bonnets to match, Queenie had quietly and without their knowledge, searched the suburbs around Liverpool for suitable lodgings where the three of them might settle and on Seymour Street opposite New Park had found exactly what she, Gilly and Jem needed: a small terraced house for rent in a respectable neighbourhood. Two bedrooms, of course, plus a parlour, kitchen and scullery and a secure back yard where she could keep her old cart. She and Gilly, as soon as the spring term ended at Mrs Hunter's establishment and the milder summer months allowed it, still donned their 'working' clothes and trudged Lancashire and into Yorkshire in their search for second-hand goods and to sell what Queenie had acquired in the winter months. They could still do the same from Seymour Street where the back yard led into a narrow alley.

With Jem's help, for he insisted on paying half their expenses in Rose Alley, and the pennies she carefully added week after week to her nest egg, plus the investments that Mr Field advised, Queenie had enough now to move them from the cess-pit in which they had survived for so many years to something better. Both Jem and Gilly knew of her hopes but not the exact whereabouts of what she secretly called the 'new place'. Gilly seemed inclined to persuade her to wait until she had finished her education, but she would change her mind when she saw the house in Seymour Street. Once her studies were done with and she had completed the elocution lessons, she told Queenie, the French lessons and the delicate sewing that was so important to what she herself was planning, though she didn't say so to her mother, a move would be vital, but not to some small house on the edge of the town as Mam envisaged.

Jem looked the picture of an up-and-coming young business-man. He wore a lounge suit, for dress and frock coats were now only worn in the evening. It was single-breasted with a narrow collar and fastened with only one button, the edges of the patch pockets bound with material of the same design as the jacket and it had a single back vent. Under it he wore a short waistcoat of the same material. His trousers were tight to reveal the shape of his calves and clung to his hips to show the small hollow in the curve of his buttocks. His legs were long and shapely and in perfect proportion to his tall frame. His deep blue eyes glowed with health, joyous vitality and with the content of a man well pleased with the world and his part in it, and his strong, uncompromising young mouth turned up at each corner in a most appealing manner even when he was not smiling. He was an attractive young man, not handsome by any means but completely and absolutely male and with an earthiness about him that came from his low beginnings. There was no softness in the smooth, taut skin of his face and neck and his golden blaze of hair curled crisply, cut short for the occasion, about his head. He carried a felt hat, not quite a bowler but of that general appearance and would put it on at the last moment for he hated wearing it and was still much happier in his cap.

Beside him, dressed with the tasteful simplicity that was to be her hallmark, Gilly wore a gown of dove-grey silk, the first time she had ever had a dress of such fine material, the colour so pale it was almost white. Her bonnet was the same dove grey, a charming frou-frou of nonsense wreathed in white lace and rosebuds, tied under her chin with broad silk ribbons and under it her hair, fastened back into a fat chignon, glowed a deep red, almost the colour of old burgundy. Her high-heeled slippers were grey kid and her gloves white lace. She carried a tiny parasol and the whole lot had cost her mother the profit from one whole season's trading even though most of it had been made by Gilly herself. Queenie didn't care about the cost, for her girl and the lad were going somewhere and she knew them well enough to know that wherever they went she would go with them. Not to affairs like this, of course, where she would be a total misfit, but in the home she had picked out for them and where she would look after them, and – her face softening at the delicious thought – any children they would have.

The dock from which the ship, to be called the *Emily Jane* after two of the daughters of Mr Barrie and Mr Hughes, was to be launched was crowded with those who had been invited and with the scores of men involved in her construction, from the moment when the keel was first laid until the last plate was put in place. The yard was almost as big and successful as Laird's further along the river. They built ships of every conceivable kind from packet ships to gunboats, ships intended for the Royal Mail company, great ships that were to cross to the other side of the world, steamers of every kind, several of these still fastened to the land in their cradles but seeming to be straining to be away as the *Emily Jane* was.

Working men stood about in groups of two or three, leaning upon massive pieces of machinery, which Jem explained to Gilly were cast-iron rollers just purchased from the Sandon Works which had gone bankrupt, and used for plate bending. There were barrels of pitch, a wrought-iron round shaft almost sixty feet long, wooden ladders, pulleys and planks and great stacks of logs which were being carried from one place to another, for, as Jem explained, the men were only allowed to stop work for the few minutes it would take the newly launched ship to go down the ways and settle in the water. Men who risked being hauled over the coals were standing idly to watch, a pipe between their teeth, the smoke wreathing about their heads in a thick blue mist. The weak spring sunshine was doing its best to get through the clouds which threatened rain but a curious silence fell as Mr Wilson, whom they all knew, walked by with his lady, a beautiful creature whose high-heeled slippers made a dainty clicking sound on the stone setts of the quayside. You could see he was made up with her and could you blame him, for wouldn't each and every one of them give their right arm to have such a beauty at their disposal. They might have been hewed from stone those rough, easy-going, hard-drinking, cheerfully swearing workmen, for they remembered young Mr Wilson when they had all called him Jem and it just showed what a bit of luck did for you. Their heads rotated from left to right as they watched the couple walk by towards the partitioned place where the high and mighty were stationed.

For a moment there was a lessening of the hubbub of polite conversation as Gilly and Jem approached, for not only were they unknown to the two wives of the shipbuilders but they were an exceedingly handsome young couple, especially the girl. Then, detaching herself from her parents' side Anne

Barrie hurried forward and took Gilly's hand in hers. There was a bit of a flurry as Gilly's parasol wavered but Jem allowed her to be taken from him, somewhat surprised when young Miss Barrie bent forward and kissed Gilly's cheek. She pulled Gilly forward to stand before her mama, her face rosy with delight, and so great was her joy that at last she was to introduce her dearest friend to her family, even her stammer seemed to abate.

'Mama, Papa, may I introduce you to my friend Gilly Logan. She and I are at Mrs Hunter's together. You remember I have spoken of her often and of how k . . . k . . . kind she has been to me. Gilly . . . this is m . . . my m . . . other and my father.'

Gilly bowed her head politely and held out her hand as she had been taught at Mrs Hunter's.

'How do you do, Mrs Barrie, Mr Barrie. It is a pleasure to meet you.'

'Miss Logan.' Mr Barrie was all smiles, for who could resist such a lovely and well-mannered young woman, but Mrs Barrie was somewhat more reserved because when you had a daughter, two daughters, you had to be careful with whom they mixed. Of course Mrs Hunter's school was well known for the high class of persons who sent their daughters there. She took Miss Logan's fingertips between her own, as was correct, and smiled coolly.

'And this is Mr Jeremiah Wilson, a friend of mine,' Gilly said, giving Jem his full name, turning to him and bringing him forward.

'Oh, we know Mr Wilson,' Mr Hughes, who stood to the side of Mr Barrie, said jovially. 'He works beside Mr Barrie's son in the design office. How are you, Jem. Looking forward to seeing yours and Lucas's ship set sail?'

'Indeed, sir. I have waited for this day a long time.'

'Good, good, oh, and here is Lucas now. Miss Logan, let me

introduce you to Lucas Barrie. He and Jem are the ones responsible for this day and let me tell you . . .'

What Mr Hughes wished to tell her drifted away into the depths of her mind, faint, disjointed, hidden where no sound could reach it, lost in the maze of confused colours, muffled noises, smells, feelings that drove all thought from her. The colour of silvery grey eyes surrounded by thick black lashes, the sound of a deep, soft and mellifluous voice as it greeted her, the faint aroma of cologne soap, the electric touch of a strong, bare hand, the fingers that grasped hers warmly and for just a moment too long. She was transported and completely speechless. She knew that Jem had taken her hand possessively, sensing something he did not like but it was too late. The eyes that looked directly into hers were clear, like deep pools of transparent rainwater in an almost colourless container, brilliant as if set in diamonds and yet nothing could really describe them, and nothing had prepared her for the thrill of quivering excitement that gripped her now, beginning in the middle of her chest where her heart lay, trailing delicately through the whole of her body right down to her knees which began to tremble strangely. She was aware that this was a moment of great importance, that she stood on the brink of a great revelation but could not yet understand the shape of it. They looked at each other with startled eyes, a look that spanned no more than five seconds and yet seemed to last an eternity before she lowered her eyes, hiding them with her long, chestnut-coloured eyelashes. She clung to Jem's hand as though to a lifeline that would prevent her being sucked under and down and down into the senseless sea of love. But it was too late. It had already happened. So this is how it feels, she remembered thinking. Not the sweet, wholesome, sustaining love that Jem offered her and which she had returned ever since she could remember, but this turbulence, this sweet longing, this longing for something she had never known before which this man promised her.

They stood, both of them, in the mass of shouting, cheering, laughing crowds as Lucas Barrie's mama aimed the bottle of champagne at the towering sides of the ship, her voice proclaiming her to be named *Emily Jane* lost in the thunderous roar, the whistles and hooters of other ships in the Mersey. There were people between them, Anne, Mrs Hughes, other members of the family including the naughty Willy who was still an imp, yet it was as though they were alone. Jem . . . oh, Jem . . . her heart wept and at the same it swelled with an emotion of such proportions she was overwhelmed. She could feel his gaze on her, *his gaze*, having no need to say his name, even in her head, and when she turned from the sight of the great ship sliding down the ways he was right behind her. Their eyes locked again and she sighed, sadly, gladly, for her future was fixed. All eyes were on the graceful glide of the ship so no one noticed when his firm mouth formed her name and then curled in the sweetest smile that was meant just for her.

Queenie was sifting through a heap of clothing on the table, holding up one garment for inspection and then another, placing them on different piles according to their saleability. Some were just rags and would be torn up to be made into dishcloths or dusters; others, after a bit of attention, would be sold to women at the stall in the market with only pence to spare but who would be glad of a little dress or a pair of breeches for a child. There were bonnets, most of which she discarded, for the women who were her customers wore shawls, but some she put to one side as their Gilly was a dab hand at turning some hideous thing into a sweet little bonnet, removing silk roses, bits of lace, ribbons that only needed a good wash and transforming them into a smart bit of nonsense that any woman of taste might wear.

The room was warm with a decent fire burning behind the bars of the grate and on either side of it were ovens, blackleaded to a polish in which you might see your own face reflected, gleaming like wet coal. Several pans stood on the top of one and an appetising smell wafted from beneath their lids, while on the bed of embers a kettle whispered steam. Who knew what Gilly and Jem might get to eat while they were at the grand launching, but just in case they were hungry when they came home she had made a big pan of scouse. She sighed contentedly, then, as a knock sounded on her door, a small frown creased between her eyebrows. Who the devil was this? the frown said. Probably one of her indigent neighbours wanting to borrow something. She would be glad when they got away from here, she thought as she moved towards the door. Left this hell-hole and into the little house she had got her eye on in Seymour Street, for it was in a decent neighbourhood where folk didn't go round begging a screw of tea, a spoonful of sugar, a cup of milk, or even, as Jess often did, a few pence to buy her kids something to put in their bellies.

As though the thought of Jess had brought him to her doorstep, Tommy Wilson stood in her doorway, his horny hands one on either side of the frame, his deeply scarred face twisted into what had once been an expression of resentment, a sullen bitterness at the way life had treated him and the rancorous feelings he held towards his son who had done so well and was unwilling to help out his old dad in his hour of need. A few bob here and there wouldn't hurt him, nor the woman who was now the lucky recipient of Jem's good luck. Now the look of malevolence that was added to his resentment and bitterness was quite terrifying because, of course, his worst grievance was the state of his face which this bloody woman had caused. The fat she had chucked at him had been hot and scalding, shrivelling his skin and puckering it up into lumps and pitted hollows, taking off his eyebrows and narrowly missing his eyes, one of which was now higher than the other. He had never been an attractive man, far from it, but his face had been ordinary and not one from which children ran screaming and men shuddered away. Even his old woman shut her eyes when he grabbed her and dragged her into the pit they called a bed. It had taken months to heal, treated by the old slut at the corner of the court whose remedies had made the bloody thing worse. He took it out on his wife, naturally, beating her black and blue sometimes, and the rest of his children who, in the last few months, those old enough, had hastily left home. Again a cause of acrimony, for had they stayed at home, bringing in a few pence, it might have made his life easier.

That had been almost six months ago and in that time he had brooded on how he might get his revenge, pay the bloody woman back for what she had done to him and had even enjoyed himself planning it. Once it was done he had felt he would have nothing left to live for but now, on this morning when his shit of a son and the girl he himself had been denied were out of the way he meant to make this woman sorry for her interference.

Queenie stared in astonishment at the scarred face of Tommy Wilson.

'Mornin', lass,' he said pleasantly. 'Can I come in,' he began but Queenie, who was not as yet scared, for the likes of Tommy Wilson didn't scare her, started to shut the door in his face.

'No, yer bloody well can't, yer daft sod. Why on earth yer should think after what yer did . . .' But it was then that she saw the two men at Tommy's back and she knew. *She knew!*

Her face lost every vestige of colour, turning to a shade like the grey ash in the pan beneath her fire. Her firm flesh fell in, deepening her eye sockets to black pits. She opened her mouth to scream but Tommy pushed her back, the men behind him quickly followed, and the door was banged to before any of the occupants of the court had time to notice that something funny was happening at Queenie Logan's basement home. The last man to slip inside was seen by an old man leaning on the wall, his pipe dangling from his toothless mouth, but he was beyond caring what happened in this terrible world of his.

Tommy gestured to one of the men who slipped behind her, clapping his hand across her mouth. She could smell him, smell Tommy and indeed all three of them, for they were ruffians of the worst sort who would do anything for the price of a pint of ale. Men who lived on the edge of violence, the dregs of the city, scraping a living at anything that came to hand, not concerned with the law and they were here at Tommy Wilson's request, probably not for any monetary reward, for where would Tommy Wilson acquire the brass to pay them, but for the simple pleasure of hurting someone, preferably a woman. And the woman was to be Queenie Logan who had defended her daughter from him and scarred his face in doing so. She didn't know why he had taken so long to get round to it, for after it happened she had expected some sort of retribution, taking great care to avoid the court at night or when it was empty. But she had grown careless and now she was to be punished for it. But she wouldn't let these buggers see her beg for mercy. Just let one of them give her the chance and she'd have the heavy poker that lay in the hearth in her hand and about someone's head as quick as a flash.

Tommy stood before her, his obscene face pushed into hers. 'See this,' gesturing towards the scars, 'yer gonner pay fer this, my lass. Me an' the lads're gonner punish yer fer what yer did ter me an' at same time we're gonner 'ave us a birra fun. Yer not the tasty tit-bit that lass o' yours would've bin but yer norra bad-lookin' woman fer yer age an' yer gorra cunny an' after all beggars can't be choosers, aye lads. Now, 'oo's first? I berrer warn yer Alf's a big lad an' e's a bit rough, and come ter think o' it, so's Mick. I'll watch fer a bit then it'll be my turn. Now then,

Alf, don't be so bloody 'asty . . .' for already Alf had his hand down the front of Queenie's bodice, tearing it and dragging out one of her heavy breasts, squeezing it until her face contorted in pain. She tried to kick backwards but he only laughed while the other two smirked obscenely.

'Best purra gag on 'er, Tommy,' Mick suggested, his own face twisted lecherously, gloating, dragging down his filthy breeches to reveal the enormity of his hot lust which stood out from his body like a flagpole.

'Right, Mick, good idea. Now let's see what we've gorr 'ere. Strip her and tie 'er ter't table.'

She did her best. She struggled so hard Tommy had to club her with his fist, hitting her so savagely he broke her jaw, then as she continued to fight twisted her arm behind her back until it snapped. She was unconscious when they had done with her, all three having what they called 'two goes' while the others watched and waited but Tommy was not content until he had taken a knife and slashed down both her cheeks, the point of the knife slicing through the bottom lid of her left eye.

'There, yer slut,' he crowed as the blood soaked into the wood of the table and he fastened his trousers up about his flaccid waist. 'See 'ow yer like it when folk turn away from yer like what they've done ter me. Right, come on, lads, let's bugger off before they come back, but first let's mekk a birrof a mess 'ere,' beginning to smash the pots and pans that were carefully stacked on shelves that his son had put up. He emptied the scouse on the floor and then, discovering his son's suits, slashed them to ribbons before starting on Gilly's gowns. Everything in the room was scattered and broken, only the table on which Queenie lay left untouched. It quite pleased Tommy to see her there in the middle of the devastation he had caused.

'Didn't yer say there were a young lass, Tom?' Alf enquired casually. 'Why don't we wait an' tekk a turn wi' 'er 'an all. This un's bin all right' – turning a contemptuous glance at the naked, bloody, badly bruised body of the woman whose head hung over the edge of the table and whose long dark hair touched the floor – 'burra birra young flesh'd be—'

'All in good time, Alf. She'll 'ave that prick wi' 'er which might complicate things a bit. No, there's always termorrer.'

They had been invited to stay to the celebration party held at the local hotel which was just a step from the shipyard, a rather smart hotel where the drink flowed and the buffet was magnificent. The guests were all influential gentlemen from both sides of the river, and their wives elegantly and expensively dressed, but neither Jem nor Gilly looked out of place. Lucas Barrie made no attempt to waylay the girl, the beautiful girl with whom he had fallen in love the moment he set eyes on her but his glance followed her about the room as he brooded on how he was to get to know her and not only that but detach her from Jem Wilson who was a friend of his and who was so obviously in love with her. Did she feel the same way about Jem? he wondered, but in his mind and in his heart, which had recognised her at once and what was in hers, he knew she didn't!

10

They sat one on either side of her bed both still in the clothes they had worn for the launching, both stained with her blood. It was daubed in their hair and smeared their cheeks and had dried in black crescents beneath their fingernails. Their faces wore identical expressions of deep shock, of horror, of total confusion and the agony one feels when a beloved member of a family is hurt. And not only had she been hurt she had been tortured! They did not speak, nor did they look at one another. It was as though they felt shame, guilt, that while they had been across the water enjoying themselves, leaving her alone, some monster had broken in and done this to her while they should have been at home to protect her. Later this would dwindle, this feeling of culpability, as they began to realise that Queenie Logan was a woman who had never needed defending, but at that moment they were in torment at being elsewhere, *at a party* when this had happened to her. She was forty-seven years old and had travelled about Lancashire and Yorkshire for the past thirty years, a tall, strong-boned woman whom many a man would not have dared insult and yet she had nearly lost her life in her own home, the door of which was always locked. It was clear that though hours had passed since they had found her they were both having trouble absorbing the horror of what had happened.

They had been laughing when they entered the cellar the three of them had shared for ten years, they could never remember at what, but as they opened the door they had both halted on the threshold, thinking for an unbelieving moment that they had come to the wrong house. That they had somehow stumbled into a charnel house that had nothing to do with them, that the nightmare sight before them was someone else's horror; then the thing on the table whimpered and the misted loveliness in which Gilly Logan had floated for the past few hours shredded away and she sank to her knees as the power to stand left her. She made no sound. The scream that was building inside her, looking for a way out, circled her body, hurting her, but her voice refused to function as her eyes took in the horrific scene.

'*Oh Jesus . . . Oh Jesus . . . Oh Jesus,*' Jem moaned, himself unable to move, for all capability of thought had left him. His eyes wandered about the room which bore no resemblance to the cosy kitchen he and Gilly had left earlier in the day and though he tried desperately not to look at the abused and battered body on the table some sense began to trickle back into his frozen, paralysed mind and, in an action born of instinct, he sprang forward and mindlessly threw the quilt on the bed over the woman who was Queenie Logan. By the very way she lay he could see, or his subconscious mind could see, that she had been violated in the most appalling way and that if she was to live it must be he who saved her. Gilly was still on her knees, gibbering, moaning, useless, for her mind had temporarily left her, nature cloaking her shock in mercy but it was no time to kneel or stand about bewailing what had happened. Queenie, whose face was a mask of blood, nevertheless thanked him with her one remaining eye, thanked him for covering her shame, the brutality she had suffered, and it was perhaps this that galvanised him into action.

He dragged a shaking Gilly to her feet, turned her to him, gripping her upper arms, and began to shout directly into her face.

'Gilly . . . Gilly, listen to me. There isn't time to weep. We must get your mam to the infirmary at once . . . *at once*, Gilly. Help me; help Queenie, she could die . . .'

'The infirmary . . .'

'Yes, and I can't do it without you. No doctor will come here and anyway I know of none near enough, so we must take her. Are you listening?' He shook her frantically and her head wobbled, shifting her pretty bonnet to the back of her head. Her hair was loosened and it tumbled about her face.

'You must run to the corner of Vauxhall Road, get a cab. D'you hear? Stand in the road and grab the first one that comes along.'

'A cab . . .'

'Gilly . . . Gilly, this is your mam's life we're talking about. If you don't help me she'll die.'

'No . . . no . . .'

'Oh yes.' He was savage with her now, flinging her about as though she were a rag doll and at last she began to come out of the stupor the sight of the woman – who could not possibly be her mother – on the table and the havoc of her home had thrown her into and her bone-white face showed a little understanding.

The cabbie had been most reluctant to enter the maze of courts and alleys that surrounded Rose Alley, for the worst, most brutal folk lived in the dense and foetid area but the lovely, shrieking young woman, who darted into the road right into the path of his bloody old nag which, despite its age and condition, managed to rear in fright, hung on to the horse's head until he brought his vehicle to a stop.

' 'Ere, what the 'ell d'yer think yer up to, yer daft bitch,' he shouted, but before he could say another word, or even tell the horse to 'gee up' she had climbed up beside him, gabbling some tale about her mother who was dreadfully injured and must be got to the infirmary.

'You'll be well rewarded,' she gasped, and he had time to

wonder why such a well-dressed lady was needing to get to Rose Alley which harboured the dregs of Liverpool and then to the infirmary.

Taking advantage of Gilly's absence, Jem approached the table, Queenie's one functioning eye following him. That eye had thanked him for covering her nakedness; now it fastened itself on his face, begging for something, he didn't know what. It seemed to him to be forgiveness, but why should Queenie who had given him affection, support, a home even, where he had been treated as her son, need his forgiveness? With infinite care, doing his best to reveal no part of her body, he wrapped her in the quilt, taking a torn shawl from the wreckage around him and winding it about her mutilated face. He found a pair of his socks that the marauders had missed and put them on her dangling feet and when Gilly swept back into the room, the cab driver behind her, he was ready, his precious burden held in his steady young arms.

The cab had been unable to turn into the narrow court but Jem carried her up the area steps and across the yard, conscious of the dozens of eyes that watched him, not one soul daring to come out and help him, for they all knew by now who had done this to Queenie. They were afraid of Tommy Wilson and his bully boys and what might be done to them if they 'squealed' so they stayed hidden, sorry, most of them, for Queenie was well liked. Jess Wilson cowered behind her door, weeping for the one woman who had been her friend but it was not enough to stand against the beast who only last night had beaten her with the buckle end of his belt.

The shawl slipped as Jem lifted her into the cab and the cabbie gasped when he saw her face and the blood-clotted hair. Gilly moaned and put her hands to her mam's mutilated cheeks then lifted the hem of her skirt in an attempt to stop the flow of blood. She wiped her hands on her lovely gown. Blood seeped all about them, coming from beneath the quilt and dribbling to the floor of the cab and even before they reached the infirmary on Brownlow Hill both of them were clotted with it. The cabbie watched them stagger up the steps and pass through the six Ionic columns that formed the front of the magnificent building. He was so distressed by the incident and by the anguish of the two young people he forgot to ask for his fare!

The vast entrance was busy, for the infirmary had space for over 1,500 in-patients and almost 1,300 out-patients. On the first floor there was a suite of twenty rooms for use by the various committees, the offices of the hospital and members of the household. In the left wing there was a room fitted up for the reception of patients requiring immediate attention which was where they headed. Wards filled with patients occupied the second and third floors and so enormous, new and modern was the building there was even steam power used to raise water. It was the very latest and best equipped hospital in the north, serving as a place for the ailing and injured, as it said on the sign at the door, and as a school for medicine and surgery. No other hospital could have been chosen to supply exactly what Queenie Logan needed.

The sister who was hurriedly summoned by the nurse at the reception desk immediately ordered a stretcher on wheels and Jem tenderly placed his burden on it. The sister, taking a peep under the quilt to ascertain the extent of the patient's injuries, recoiled slightly, then at once sent the nurse for the doctor. When he came Queenie was quietly wheeled away through doors that opened silently on to Gilly and Jem knew not what.

'I'll speak to you later,' the doctor said over his shoulder as he followed the stretcher through the swing doors. 'Wait here . . .' his voice drifted back and for at least five minutes both Gilly and Jem merely stood where they had been left, the focus of curious stares, for the pair of them were dabbled with drying blood. Other ailing or injured people wandered in and were seen by the nurse, directed to where they should go, until eventually she left her post and showed the stupefied couple to seats where they sat as though turned to stone, staring into the void, the black pit of hell from which they had brought Queenie.

It was several hours before the doctor returned. He looked about him and then beckoned them into a small office where he sat them down in front of his desk. He sighed deeply, contemplating them with compassion and Gilly looked back at him and knew he was going to tell her her mam was gone.

'She's dead?' Her voice was flat, expressionless. Jem took her hand but she shook it off.

'Oh no,' the doctor answered.

Gilly began to cry, to shake, to come to abrupt, merciless life, but even then she would not let Jem take her hand as he tried to do.

'She is . . . very badly injured.' The doctor, being a gentleman of good family, clever, but who had been raised to treat ladies as delicate, fragile creatures who must be protected from anything that might be an affront to their womanhood, was not sure how to continue.

'Raped?'

'Ah . . . yes, I'm afraid so,' surprised at the blunt question from what seemed a well-bred young lady who would not be expected to know about such things. His own sisters didn't!

'Please tell me . . .'

He turned to Jem as though he would rather speak to the man of the family but Gilly would not have it.

'She is my mother,' she told him harshly. 'I must know the extent of her injuries and . . . how . . . what . . . when will she recover?'

'Well . . .'

'Gilly, will you not go and sit in the—' Jem began but Gilly turned on him.

'Stop it, Jem. When I know what has happened I will do

whatever you and the doctor wish but I must know what has been done to her.' She turned back to the doctor and waited.

'She has been . . . sewn up,' he began.

'Sewn up?'

'She was badly damaged in her . . . well . . .'

'Yes, yes, I understand. And the rest?'

'She has a fractured jaw and arm, both of which I and my colleagues have set. Her face was . . . cut. We have repaired it but she has . . . I'm sorry, but she has lost her left eye.'

Gilly, although she was sitting, seemed to reel in her chair and both the doctor and Jem sprang to their feet. Jem was longing to hold her, to put his arms about her, to comfort her as he had done since she was a baby, but Gilly was not the same woman who had set out that day, or was it yesterday since they had lost track of time, and she resisted him.

'Can we see her, Doctor?' she asked, pulling herself to her feet by holding on to the edge of the table.

'She is still under the effect of the chloroform administered. Unconscious, you understand . . .'

'May I sit with her for just a moment? I will bother no one but I must hold her hand so that she will know I'm there. Please, Doctor . . . please.'

Doctor Jenkins, or to give him his correct title since he was a surgeon, Mr Jenkins, could no more refuse this tragic young woman than he could knowingly hurt a child or an animal. He was young, a brilliant surgeon and it was his genius, his gift for surgery, that had saved Queenie Logan's life, as she had lost a great deal of blood which could not be replaced. He nodded and, turning to the door, led them through it, across the great hall and up the staircase. In the corner of the ward closest to the door a screen was placed round a bed and there lay the bandaged figure of her mam. Unrecognisable, of course, since her face and head were totally covered except for three small slits, one for her nostrils, another for her undamaged eye which was closed and a third for her mouth.

And so they sat through the night, disturbed by no one but the nurse who slipped in periodically and bent over Queenie's prostrate form. She smiled at them and nodded, then went away to tell her fellow nurses that the young chap and the daughter of the patient had still not spoken to one another as far as she could tell but really, when Matron came round she was bound to send them home. It was only Mr Jenkins's kindness that had allowed them to stay so long, and them in such a mess with the blood still on them. She was not to know that neither of them wanted to go back to what had been their home but had been altered to such an extent by what had happened there, it was that no longer.

Lucas Barrie was supposed to be working on the design for the ocean-going liner the firm of Barrie and Hughes were to build for the American and Colonial Shipping Line. The ship was meant for the emigration trade but it was also to carry first-class passengers and therefore besides the commodious four-berth cabins available to those who were emigrating were fitted private state rooms, a ballroom, library, drawing room and every conceivable luxury passengers such as these might require.

Lucas was bent over his drawing board but his eyes were not on the board but were gazing into the distance across the Mersey to the furthest shore where *she* was. Though his eyes saw the busy shoreline, the rippling waters of the river and the scores of boats that sailed on it, her face was imprinted over it all and he was bowled over by his feelings as he had been bowled over by the sight of her yesterday. He was quite bewildered by the emotion he felt in the part of his body where he supposed his heart lay. He couldn't really describe what he felt for her because he didn't have any words. There probably weren't even any words for it. All he knew was that he felt wonderful, strange, different from anything he had ever expected to feel or would ever feel again. It was something that had just sprung up, not there one moment but there the next as if it had always been there, as if she had always been there or as if he'd spent his life waiting for her to be there. The words tumbled about in his head – sweet, fragrant, wonderful – filled with his feelings of . . . well, he supposed it must be love though he had never known it as yet. But then he had heard Jem talk about her, not taking a great deal of notice, he admitted, and he had understood that she was Jem's girl, the one he was to marry so what was he to do about that? He had known Jem was to bring her to the launching and had barely been interested, for he had his own lady friends. Not young women he would introduce to his mama, of course, but pleasing to him and ready to satisfy any need he might have. His mama was always introducing respectable young ladies to him, daughters of friends with whom she hoped he might form an alliance but he was not ready for marriage and had not planned to enter into it for years.

But this girl of Jem's was . . . was . . . Dear God, where was his mind leading him and anyway, where *was* Jem? It was after ten and he and Jem were usually at their desks by eight thirty. Both his father and Mr Hughes were sticklers for time and were at their own desks often before he was. They would not care for it if one or other entered the office where he and Jem and several draughtsmen pored over the plans for the next steamship and found Jem had not yet turned up for work.

He straightened up, concerned, for Jem was a conscientious chap, aware that he had been given a great chance by the partners and he would not do anything to jeopardise it. He was punctual and ever since he had been set to work in the designers' office had never missed a day's work.

'Seen anything of Jem Wilson, Soames?' he asked one of the men crouched over his own desk.

The man looked up and glanced about as though the missing designer might be lurking behind a cabinet. 'No, sir, sorry, sir.'

'Right . . . well . . .' Not wishing to draw even more attention to the missing designer, he stood for a moment then, nodding to the rest, walked to the door, opened it and left the room.

'Well,' said Soames, 'wonder where teacher's pet's got to,' for there was some jealousy among the office staff over the way a lad, an apprentice plate-layer, no less, had wormed his way into the owners' good graces and climbed far above any of them.

Lucas walked across the yard where men were busy at all the tasks that went into the building of ships. The labourers were employed with strong poles which they levered beneath great logs, putting their strength into moving them. The logs were rolled towards a sawmill which would cut them into planks to build the scaffolding of the ships, three of which were in different stages of construction. Workmen swarmed up and down the scaffolding like monkeys and a crane on a pulley lifted machinery into an enormous shed. Everywhere men sang or whistled or hummed tunelessly. A mongrel ran across the yard, narrowly avoiding a raised plank of wood which two men were lifting and one of them cursed colourfully. Lucas wended his way through them, looking out for Jem, though why he should think the man might be here, he couldn't imagine. Seeing no sign of him and reluctant to ask any of the men if they had seen him, again because he did not wish to draw attention to Jem's absence, he sauntered back towards the design office, nodding at one or two of the men who touched the peaks of their caps respectfully. For some reason he began to feel anxious, he couldn't say why, only that he thought it might be to do with the girl. *With Gilly . . . Gilly . . . Lord, what was the matter with him?* Why should Jem's absence – after all, he might be ill – have anything to do with this girl who was affecting himself so maddeningly, so amazingly, so *foolishly*?

He turned suddenly and moved towards the owners' office block where the books, ledgers, records, pay sheets and all the masses of papers concerning the business of the firm were kept. He entered noisily as though to tell himself he had every right to be here and even to put to the clerk who looked up at his entry his question, the answer to which lay here.

'Yes, sir?' the clerk asked respectfully, standing up behind his desk, as did his staff for after all this was the son of the owner.

'I want the address of . . . er . . .'

'Yes, sir?' The man waited expectantly.

'Jem Wilson.'

'Jem Wilson, sir?' It was obvious the clerk was wondering why Mr Lucas could not ask Jem Wilson the question himself.

'Yes, and I'd be obliged if you wouldn't take all day about it.'

'Of course, sir.' The clerk snapped his fingers at the man at another desk, not a little annoyed to be spoken to in such an arrogant way. Mr Lucas was usually so polite.

Within two minutes Lucas had Jem Wilson's address written on a scrap of paper.

'And I wish him luck of it,' the head clerk muttered, for he knew just where Rose Alley was!

'Where . . . what . . . where shall we go . . . where do you want to . . .?' Jem mumbled as they stood by the door that led out of the infirmary.

'I . . . don't know . . .' The words stuck in her throat, for the thought of returning to the shambles of what had been their home and with the violent picture of her mother, her beloved mam . . . stretched . . . stretched across . . . it would live with her for the rest of her life and she did not want to see it . . . never . . . never . . . *Mam, Mam . . . oh Jesus, Mam!*

'We could try for some . . . some lodgings until . . . until . . .'

'Who'd take us in?' She looked down at herself then studied her hands, which were caked with blood. She wondered dazedly what had happened to her white lace gloves.

'There's . . . dear sweet God, I can't think,' Jem groaned as though he were in actual physical pain and a passing nurse gave them both a concerned look.

Suddenly Gilly lifted her head and what might have been a snarl curled her top lip. She straightened up and lifted her head as though she were listening to something that only she could hear. Even her hair seemed to swirl in determination and she almost stamped her foot.

She took hold of Jem's hand and with a steady gaze looked up into his eyes.

'I don't know who did this to Mam, Jem. I don't know who hates her and us so much they would do this appalling thing but I'm damned if I'm going to let them drive us out. Rose Alley is, for the moment, our home and we've nowhere else to go so you and I are going back there and . . . and tidy up.' *Tidy up!* What pitiful words to describe what needed to be done to restore their home to them. Everything that could be smashed *had* been smashed except for the table where Queenie Logan's body had been so horribly violated. All they had left was what they stood up in, a pretty grey silk dress, a bonnet to match and the good suit worn by Jem. It would take a miracle to bring all three of them back to the contented life, the upward move they had been slowly making, the plans, the future, the goodness that was to be theirs through their own labour. When Mam was recovered, if she ever did, would she even want to return to the pit of hell from which they had pulled her? Could she face Rose Alley again? But whether she could or not, her daughter meant to try and when the time came she and Jem and Mam would move on to that secret dream she had been dreaming for years now.

For a moment, a man's face drifted across the dark wall of the hospital entrance. An engaging face with a warm smile that seemed to say something to her. Grey eyes like rainwater set in a strong, amber-skinned face over which tumbled an untidy sweep of dark, waving hair. She paused, putting her hand in Jem's as her heart turned over in her breast.

11

The horseman rode slowly along Hanover Street turning left into Church Street and on to Whitechapel. It was Sunday, a grey, misted day and the street was nearly deserted as swathes of fine rain drifted almost horizontally across his path. He wore a waterproof cape and a wideawake hat, the brim of which partly deflected the rain from his face but he had constantly to wipe his eyes to clear his vision. The forlorn figure of a police constable, also draped in a waterproof cape, stood on the corner opposite St John's Church where a row of carriages attested to the size of the congregation. The trees around the churchyard dripped dismally. The horseman reined in his animal, a fine coal-black hunter, a thoroughbred-Irish draught cross which looked decidedly out of place on a Liverpool street. Its coat was slippery with rain. It gave the impression that it longed to gallop freely, to jump, to race across flat fields as it had been bred to do, its confident, brave character very evident, and the constable took a hurried step back as the animal sidled nervously towards him.

'Good morning, Constable,' the horseman said politely, 'though the weather might be better.'

'Indeed, sir, proper parky an' all.' The constable touched the peak of his helmet.

'I'm looking for a certain street, Constable. I wonder if you could help me?'

'I'll try, sir. What was it yer wanted?'

'It's called Rose Alley and I believe it's—'

The constable's expression of geniality changed to one of horror and he even went as far as to move closer to the restless horse to make his point.

'Rose Alley! Nay, sir, 'ave yer got right address? That's a bad area an' . . . well, not really safe fer them as don't know it.' He shook his head at the very idea of a gentleman such as this one entering the maze of alleys, courts and streets that surrounded Rose Alley.

'That's the name I have been given. Rose Alley. I must say I'm surprised by what you say. It sounds so pretty.'

'Pretty!' The constable made a derisive sound. 'There's nowt pretty about Rose Alley an' if I was you I'd turn right round an' gerron me way. Pinch the boots off yer feet, they would, that's after they've beat yer ter pulp. Nay, I wouldn't go there meself, not fer a gold clock. An' you, dressed like that, sir. Yer wouldn't stand a chance. Burrif yer bound an' determined ter go I'd change inter summat . . . summat plain' – he eyed the horse-man's good boots, the cut of his breeches beneath the cape, his hat – 'an' if I was you I'd leave that fine animal at 'ome.'

While he had been back to his house to change and leave his hunter in the stable the streets of Liverpool seemed to have come to life. It being Sunday, those among the respectable working class who had the time and energy were off to see the sights, perhaps a saunter into the countryside that surrounded the city. Others were making for 'the sands' as they called it, beyond the Herculaneum Dock. At low tide it was possible to walk along Jericho shore and even bravely dip their bare feet in the icy water. They might take a picnic and eat their 'butties' watching the steady flow of sailing ships, the pageant of steamships which were becoming more and more familiar. Others were on their way to Princes Park to walk round the lake, peer over the fence at the Deer Park and eye the grand parade of real ladies and gentlemen in their finery.

As he moved quickly along Duke Street he was surprised by the large numbers of dawdlers making for Hill Street and the promenade along St James Walk from which, on a clear day, the far-off hills of Flintshire could be seen across the silvered waters of the estuary.

He made his way to Vauxhall Road looking out for Maguire Street as the constable had told him. In this, the poorer quarter of the town, young boys, barefoot, ragged and giving the impression they had not come into contact with water for a long time, if ever, were playing the popular Lancashire game of 'purring' where two contestants kicked one another until one was too badly beaten to continue. It was played in clogs which could do a great deal of damage but as these lads were barefoot they were laughing as they tumbled about, suffering no more than a graze or two as they fell. Along Vauxhall Street young girls, also barefoot, sat on doorsteps and voiced their opinion of him in the lilting tones of Ireland, for this was where many from that green but starving land lived. Even though he had returned to his house in Duke Street, left Ebony in the stable at the rear of the house and changed into his oldest clothing, he still felt conspicuous. The rain had stopped and sunshine filtered through the breaking clouds bringing out the denizens of the area, children screaming in play, their bare feet black, their hair lank, unwashed, stringy, their rags fluttering about them. Men leaned against the house walls eyeing him speculatively but he had had the foresight to bring a stout stick with him, warned by the constable, which he brandished threateningly. It was the smell that almost overwhelmed him, becoming worse the deeper he got into the squalid district. He could hardly bring himself to believe that Jem Wilson, who turned up for work every day as neat and well dressed as himself, lived in this squalid district, but there was the name on the side of a crumbling building in which he could not believe people lived. Rose Alley!

The court was empty save for a dog which was being tormented by three children. Evidently the women of the hovels were indulging in an afternoon siesta while the men took themselves off to a bull baiting which the constable had warned him was to take place at the back of the Crown and Anchor. There was activity only in one corner of the yard where two people, a man and a woman, were sorting out a jumble of what looked like broken furniture. They were both dressed in an assortment of garments, none of which matched, some of them roughly patched, the woman with her hair bound with a length of cloth pulled down to her eyebrows. The man he recognised, with astonishment, as Jem Wilson.

Slipping in some unmentionable mess which seemed to layer the court he hurried across to them, watched by the children who in their amazement left the dog alone. Even dressed as he was in his oldest clothing, a pair of worn riding breeches, a long coat that belonged to the stable lad at Duke Street, no hat but with decent riding boots, he attracted as much attention as if he had worn a crown and ermine cloak.

They saw him coming, Jem and Gilly, and for some reason immediately stopped what they were doing. Though she had borne up bravely for the past twenty-four hours, Gilly slumped against the slimy wall and tears oozed from beneath her closed eyelids. They dripped along the length of her incredible, fox-red lashes and fell on to the worn grey bodice she wore, and Lucas felt his heart turn over. He had not the slightest idea what had happened here but he knew it must be something horrendous, for not only was the beautiful girl with whom, in the tick of one second to another, he had fallen in love weeping silently, but Jem, who had not turned up for work yesterday, stood like a pale shadow of himself, looking so different to the cheerful young man Lucas worked with that he would hardly have recognised him. He seemed unable to meet his eye, biting his lip, slumped, like Gilly, his shoulders sagging under some great weight.

Lucas stopped at the head of the area steps, his hand on the rusted railing, longing to leap down and take the girl in his arms and tell her that whatever it was that made her weep he would put it right. She had only to tell him and he would move heaven and earth to stop her tears. And even in the midst of this – this whatever it was – he had time to wonder at the fact that though she wept she did not, as other young women did, sniff and choke, their noses reddening, their eyes swelling, but simply stood there while her crystal tears brimmed over and slipped silently across her pale cheeks.

He moved down the steps, avoiding the litter of rubbish that leaned drunkenly in his path, then stopped, uncertain how to go on, for not only was he stunned by this . . . this horror of a place where Jem . . . and Gilly seemed to live *together* – and what did that tell him, his agonised mind wanted to know – but what disaster had overtaken them that had them dressed like a couple of tramps and seemed to have changed them from the handsome young couple who had charmed his father's guests two days ago into this barely recognisable pair of . . . well, he didn't really know how to describe them. What in God's name had caused this change?

'Jem.' His voice was soft as though a harsh word might send the pair of them spinning off into further catastrophe. 'You were missing from the yard yesterday so I came to see if you were ill or had had an accident. I've never known you to miss a day's work.' His words implied that his concern was for Jem but he knew deep down that he cared only about this girl who was, in some way, connected to Jem. This silently weeping girl whose heart appeared to be breaking, so great was her distress.

They both stood still as though words were beyond them, their heads hanging and again he was bewildered by what seemed to be their shame, their guilt at something that had happened.

'Are you in trouble?' he asked, knowing what a foolish question that was, for it was so obvious they were. 'Perhaps if I were to come inside we could talk . . . you could tell me what troubles you. I might be able to help . . .' His voice trailed away.

Jem cleared his throat but seemed unable to speak. Though Lucas was not to know it the very thought of taking his employer's son into the savaged room, the room where savagery had taken place, appalled him. He liked Lucas. They had become not exactly friends, because there was too great a divide of class between them, but they had got on in their shared interest in ships and the seas beyond the estuary where they sailed. They had often told one another that they would go aboard a newly launched ship from the Barrie and Hughes Shipyard and take a look at some foreign land, and they had meant it. Perhaps they would one day but now . . . sweet Jesus . . . he had enough to think of, if only he could get his mind into some sort of order.

'Jem, you and I have been . . . can you not tell me?'

Jem found his voice. 'Gilly's mam . . . she's in the infirmary . . .'

'I'm sorry. Is she ill or . . .?'

Gilly came to life with an abruptness that took both men by surprise. 'No, she's not ill,' she screeched. 'She was attacked. Oh God, men broke in and . . . did what men do to defenceless women. While me and Jem were off enjoying ourselves, drinking champagne, all dressed up we were, as though we thought we were gentry – all thanks to her and her hard work . . . years and years she worked to help us to get where we are and what happened? She was nearly killed . . . blinded in one eye, and we should have been here . . .' Her voice sank to a whisper. 'We should have been here . . .'

Lucas did his best not to let his eyes run over the state of her, wondering bemusedly why she was dressed as she was, and Jem. He was not to know that, searching the cellar, they had found a pile of old rags, for that was all they could be called, which Queenie's attackers had missed. Stuff that Queenie had put to one side as unsaleable, and from which they had salvaged the odds and ends they wore. Overnight, by the light of a couple of candles, Gilly had roughly mended the rents and tears, sewing together a bodice and skirt for herself and a pair of breeches and shirt for Jem. They were not clean, since Queenie had meant them for what she called the rag-bag, but they were all that was available after Tommy and his henchmen had done with the place. Already Gilly could feel the itching begin and knew that there were probably lice creeping out of the seams of her outfit but somehow they had to clean up their home, mend a chair to sit on, the mattress on which she and Queenie slept and they could not do it in the bloodstained finery they had worn to the launching two days before and which was all that was left to them. As soon as they had tidied up the place, made it as much as possible a hole to hide in, she meant to take her dress and underwear and wash them somehow at the public washhouse on the Marine Parade where she and Queenie bathed. She would have a bath and wash her hair. Jem would clean up his suit as best he could and then they would both go to the infirmary.

Lucas put out a hand to her as he reached the bottom of the steps, ready to put his arms about her but she retreated, the lovely light in her eyes, the light that he knew to be yesterday's recognition of what was between them, gone completely. She seemed to hate him as though what had happened had somehow been his fault. The launching of the *Emily Jane* had taken her and Jem across the water. They had mixed with his family and friends, guests who had been charmed by her, accompanied by Anne who was her friend and thought to be one of them by everyone there. She had talked and laughed and she had responded in some way to his obvious admiration, shy, he had thought, delighted by it, her face rosy with her enjoyment of the day and then come home to this! Her guilt was a palpable thing and yet was so foolish, for none of it was her fault. He longed to tell her so, to force her to look up into his face and see the truth of it there but he knew it would do no good.

'I'm sorry . . . so sorry. Let me help, please . . . what can I do?' looking about helplessly at the pile of litter and the raggedly dressed man and woman who looked back at him in a daze. Jem had a chair back in his hands, broken, of course. Dragging his eyes away from Lucas he stared down at it as though he couldn't fathom out what he was to do with it.

'May I come inside?' Lucas said again. 'We seem to be attracting a lot of attention. Perhaps if you were to make a cup of tea, Gilly . . .' For it was well known that a cup of tea would pull you round, or so his mother said when some small thing came to try her.

'Tea? Make tea? What with?' Nevertheless she led the two men indoors then stood in the middle of the room which appeared to contain nothing other than what could only be called firewood. There was nothing whole in the room. Nothing. Every cup and saucer and plate was smashed. Even the pans had been bashed against the hearth so that they were dented and broken. And in the middle of the floor was some disgusting mess that might have been vomit but which was in fact the scouse Queenie had prepared, to which rats, attracted by the smell and the open door, were helping themselves.

Lucas was appalled. He simply stood for perhaps two minutes then, shuddering with horror, grabbed a broom from a corner, the handle broken, and, with a hoarse cry, swept the rodents across the room and out of the door, shutting it with a clatter behind them. He looked about him as though searching for something else on which to vent his anger but there was nothing in this destruction that could be mended.

Seeing the chaos in the minds of these two people who could barely withstand the shock of what had happened, he snapped into explosive life. Jem was a man, as old as he was, he thought, but Gilly, lovely, stunned Gilly, perhaps sixteen or seventeen and whose mother had suffered this nightmare, needed someone to take command and it seemed that just at the moment Jem could not cope. He knew very little about these two people, or the lives they had led. He was aware that Jem had climbed, with the help of his father and Mr Hughes, to the dizzy heights of a marine engineer over the past years but Gilly . . . Dear God, she went to school with his own sister and yet they lived in this . . . this hovel, this hell-hole so how could he possibly imagine what they had gone through. It seemed the mother, Gilly's mother, had been behind it all and, by God, if only for the sake of her daughter, he meant to put it right.

'Have you anything to fetch . . . er . . . worth fetching, I mean?' looking about him.

'Wha' . . . what . . .?' Jem put his hand to his forehead unable, it appeared, even to understand what the words meant, but Gilly did. She began to laugh, and through the laughter she wept hysterically, then ever so slowly sank to her knees and bowed her head. Both men leaped towards her but Lucas, with the clearer head, got to her first. He lifted her to her feet and put his arms about her and she sank against him. Jem watched wonderingly, since in the whole of their lives together Gilly had always turned to him for comfort, for protection, for his arm about her, for affection, or, as he thought, for love. He seemed unable to think at the moment but he knew something was happening that he could not quite grasp. Gilly must be taken care of. Her mam must be taken care of and though he had always been the one to see to it at this precise moment he couldn't even gather his thoughts together. Give him a day, an hour, and he would decide what to do; in the meanwhile here was Lucas to help and how could he begrudge Gilly whatever it was Lucas was about to offer.

'Leave this,' Lucas said roughly as Jem bent apathetically to pick up a saucepan, its handle missing. 'You must come home with me. No, no, not to my parents' home but to my house in Duke Street. I have three bedrooms, a bathroom, kitchen, all the things you need. You can't go to see your mother looking like that, Gilly,' he said, his arm still about her shoulders, looking down at her ragged dress, appealing to her in the way he knew would most get through to her.

'My gown . . .' she mumbled, meaning the lovely grey silk which lay across the table from which Jem had scrubbed her mother's blood.

'Leave it,' ordered Lucas, but she dragged away from him and bundled the dress up in her arms.

'Your suit, Jem . . .' And Jem did the same with the suit he had worn to the launching and which was the only decent clothing he now possessed.

'My . . . my mother. I must see her . . .'

'My housekeeper will find you something to wear, Gilly, and Jem can borrow clothes of mine.'

Jem came suddenly to life as though Lucas's determination to take over *his* role was not something he cared for. Ever since Gilly was born, the very *night* she was born, he had loved her and taken care of her, led her through her seventeen years, held her hand through so many mishaps and now this man who he worked with but scarcely knew was leading Gilly towards the door, his arm around her as though Jem was but a sympathetic bystander in all this.

'Just a minute, lad,' he stuttered, 'we can't just walk away from . . . from Queenie's home. That's what it is. Her home. When she's better she'll need somewhere to go, won't she, Gilly?' turning to her and reaching out for her arm. For a moment it gave the appearance of two dogs pulling at the same bone but Gilly stiffened and moved away from both of them.

'Mam can't come back here, Jem,' she said to him gently. 'Not after what happened to her on that . . . that very table. Don't you see? We'll find somewhere to take her when she's better. A new home away from Rose Alley but we have to stay somewhere until that day. Mam has money in the bank and I can get a job but we can't bring her back here. Mr Barrie has offered us . . . a place, and I think we should take it. We'll need so many new things, clothes for her, furniture . . . Please, Jem.' She stood in front of him and took both his hands in hers, looking up so lovingly into his face he relaxed.

Lucas watched and for a moment the bond between these two frightened him but for some reason he knew, for was he not a lover who knew the mind and heart of his beloved, that the love she bore this man was that of a sister for a brother. He too relaxed. He followed the pair of them to the door where they hesitated, ready to close it against intruders.

'Leave it,' he told them roughly, then, undoing the buttons of the stable lad's coat, he took it off and put it about Gilly's shoulders. Leading her by the hand and putting his arm through Jem's, he walked between them to the entrance of the court, conscious of the fascinated stares of the occupants of the tall, teetering houses that surrounded the stagnant court and who had all come out to see the fun.

It had soon got round that some toff was in Queenie Logan's place and they all knew what had happened to Queenie, poor sod. Now it seemed Gilly and Jem were to be rescued and the one who watched with most interest leaned in his doorway and snarled in his throat as his son was led away, the bitch with him. For a moment he stood with the rest then, without a word to Jess who hovered timidly at his back, he slipped along the wall and followed the trio as they moved back through the streets to Vauxhall Road. There was a cab passing and with that firm authority that the gentry have and which might have been called arrogance, he heard the toff hail it, put them both inside and climb in beside them.

'Duke Street, Cabbie,' he called out and the cabbie clucked to his horse. Tommy Wilson loped along behind.

12

'Your mother is a strong woman, Miss Logan,' the doctor told her, eyeing her poke bonnet and too short skirt with astonishment. 'There are not many who could withstand the punishment her body has taken, but even in such a short time she seems to have begun the process of healing and I don't just mean her body. She has spoken, whispered to the nurse that she must be getting home. She thinks you cannot manage without her and is worried about you.' He was enchanted as all men were by the wide-eyed beauty of Gilly Logan, despite her comical appearance. She hung on his every word, and he wanted her to go on looking at him as she was doing. He felt the need to take her hands in his but he resisted. Instead he smiled reassuringly. 'Though she is doing better than we expected she is, of course, still very ill and not yet ready to leave the hospital, but when she does she will need good nursing.'

'Which I shall give her, Doctor,' she told him breathlessly, longing to get into the ward and see her mam. 'We have somewhere clean and safe to take her as soon as you say she can be moved.'

Jem's face was expressionless as he listened to her and the doctor but there was a worm of fear in him. Although he wanted only the best for Queenie Logan, who had been like a mother to him, and knew that they had no alternative but to take up Lucas Barrie's offer of a temporary refuge for her, the disquiet he felt continued to grow. He felt deeply ashamed of himself, not only over what had happened to Queenie while he was not there to defend her but at his reluctance to take her – and Gilly – to Lucas's place where they would both be safe while he was at work. *And he must get back to work, for he did not want to lose his job!* He had seen the look on the face of his employer's son, the man who would inherit a part share of the shipyard, making him a wealthy man, the look that expressed the stunned admiration of every man who gazed at Gilly Logan. Even this doctor was enraptured and though he knew he had nothing to worry him here, for the doctor was no more to Gilly than the man who would restore her mam to health, the fear became ice in his veins as he considered the future with Lucas Barrie as a part of it.

Queenie was awake when they tiptoed into the ward and though they could not see her face so swathed in bandages was it, the one eye that was visible brightened and Gilly knew that beneath the bandages her mother was smiling. One work-roughened hand rested on the sheet, which crossed her breast and was tucked up to her chin, the other hidden beneath it in a splint to protect her smashed arm. She took her mam's hand, seeing the broken fingernails, feeling the cracked skin, knowing the damage to it, and the one beneath the sheet, had been done with love and a determination to give her, Gilly, what Queenie had never had. A decent life. Queenie could not speak but there was a questioning look in her eye.

Gilly sat down on the chair beside the bed and kissed the hand lovingly. 'I know we look a couple of cuts, especially me' – looking down ruefully at her outfit – 'but a kind friend has helped us, otherwise we . . . we couldn't really have . . . well, we would have come whatever we looked like because we wanted to be with you. The friend? He's the man Jem works with, isn't he, Jem? Mr Lucas Barrie.' She turned to smile up at Jem who stood on the other side of the bed and Queenie painfully turned her head to peer at him through the slit where her tawny brown eye could just be seen. She sensed at once that Jem was not happy about the arrangement. Nevertheless he put his hand on Queenie's shoulder and the three of them clung for a moment, silently reinforcing the bond that had existed for so long between them.

Jem actually didn't look at all bad, for he and Lucas were roughly the same build and height. He wore a tweed jacket and a pair of corduroy breeches, a high-necked woollen jumper of a quality he had never before known, all from Lucas's wardrobe, and his own boots.

It was Gilly who looked somewhat comical. As she smiled into her mother's face her mind went back to the moment when the cab had put them down in front of Mr Barrie's house. It was a tall, terraced house, identical to its neighbours. It stood in a crescent opposite another row and in between were railed gardens with paths, green, well-cut lawns surrounded by borders where the massed heads of daffodils, timid snowdrops, narcissi and tulips bloomed. It was a good neighbourhood, mostly families judging by the nursemaids in the gardens who were pushing perambulators, these contraptions made popular by Queen Victoria when her own children were small. They were large, high-backed, three-wheeled vehicles, pushed from behind and later, when she was more herself, Gilly would be quite fascinated by the sight of them since none from her world had ever owned, nor even seen one before.

The houses had long, highly polished windows with tiny, wrought-iron balconies on the first and second floors, steps that led up to well-painted front doors and steps that led down to area basements and a door to a kitchen. The window to the kitchen peeped over the steps to the pavement where only the legs and feet of passers-by would be seen.

Jem and Gilly huddled together on the pavement while Lucas paid the driver, then ran up the four steps to the front door, let himself in with a key and held the door open for them.

'Mrs Collins,' he called and from the back regions a short dumpling of a woman emerged, her face wreathed in a smile which did not waver at the sight of strangers. She was dressed all in black except for a snow-white apron tied about her capacious waist and the prettiest little white cap consisting of starched frills edged with lace framing her seamed face. Her hair was concealed beneath it but despite her efforts to be tidy, small endearing curls escaped about her ears.

'There you are, Master Lucas,' she pronounced. 'I were beginning to wonder where you were at.' Then she waited, asking no questions, showing no surprise as though Master Lucas turned up every day of the week with a pair of tramps.

'I've brought a couple of . . . friends who have . . . had some misfortune, Mrs Collins, but I'll tell you about that later. Miss Logan is in need of a bath and a change of clothing if you could find something for her. I can see to Mr Wilson.' He seemed to find nothing incongruous at the image of the tall, willowy figure of Gilly Logan fitting into any garment belonging to the dumpling who was Mrs Collins. Mrs Collins eyed Miss Logan with raised eyebrows though she made no comment.

'Right, my lad. Give me the young lady and you two go off with yourselves. There's plenty of hot water but before that I've got some pea soup on the hob, just as you like it. All three of you could do with a bowl and no arguments,' as both Jem and Gilly looked as though they were about to turn it down, for they were in a ferment to get to the infirmary.

'That would be grand, Mrs Collins but we must be quick. Miss Logan and Mr Wilson have to visit a sick relative and . . .'

'Right. Bath first, lass. Come with me and we'll see what's what.'

Mrs Collins turned towards a steep staircase that led up to a landing. There were several doors off the landing and further stairs leading to another floor. Mrs Collins indicated that Gilly was to follow her to a door at the back of the house which it seemed was hers. A comfortable bedroom, crammed with old-fashioned furniture, a brass bedstead, a dressing-table with a mirror, a tall set of drawers, a vast chair by a fireside where a small fire burned cheerfully and a huge wardrobe. Everything was spotless, from the white lace bedcover, the net curtains at the window to the embroidered headrest on the chair. There was a smell of lavender. A large black and white cat was curled in the chair, its tail about its nose, but it did not stir as the two women entered.

Mrs Collins opened the wardrobe door and began to rummage among its contents, bringing out a dress of black bombazine and, with a glance or two at Gilly who hovered at the doorway, placed it on the bed.

'What about underthings, lass, drawers and such? I've a chemise clean and you're welcome but I'm not sure—'

'Oh, please, Mrs Collins, you're very kind but don't bother about a dress. Just a shawl would do. Something to cover what I'm wearing.'

'Nay, lass, Master Lucas'd not like that. Now take off them . . . them things you've got on and let's get you into a bath first.'

Gilly did as she was told. She felt as though she had gone to sleep and wakened in a strange, dream-like world where she had never been before as she tried to assure Mrs Collins that she would manage until she got to the washhouse, but Mrs Collins was having none of that. Gilly didn't know the identity or the role of this woman whom Mr Barrie called Mrs Collins but she supposed, feeling suddenly calmer, that she would find out later and she certainly was very kind. Mrs Collins's unastonished and total acceptance of the situation lulled her into a state of even more composure and she allowed herself to be led to another room where she stood for several seconds, quite stunned by its splendour, in the doorway.

This was the bathroom! It had a white enamelled bath with brass taps at one end, a washbasin to match and what she did not recognise as a water closet, never having seen one before. The bath and washbasin were familiar in a certain respect for had she and Mam not used them at the public baths, but those were not as gleaming and luxurious as the ones in this bathroom. The whole room, walls and floor, was lined with sparkling white tiles, those on the floor set in small black diamond shapes. There were shelves crammed with a variety of fragrant soaps, shaving soaps, a brush and a cut-throat razor, bottles of all sizes on which she read strange words: lemon, cologne, musk, oil of cloves, cassia and verbena. It was the fashion among young men of class to take care of their appearance with pomades and lotions, brilliantine and macassar oil but all the bottles and jars were unopened as though Lucas Barrie did not bother with such things. Two tortoiseshell hairbrushes in a leather case stood on the shelf but Gilly had the distinct impression that Mr Barrie did not often use these either, for when she had seen him the other day, and today, his hair fell in dark, waving curls about his head. A toothbrush and a tin of cherry-flavoured toothpaste stood side by side on a lower shelf. A large potted plant flourished in one corner and there was even a fireplace. Over a rail to the side of the fireplace hung several thick, fluffy white towels.

Mrs Collins bustled across the white tiles, put a plug in the bath and turned on the brass taps from which water erupted, so hot from one that steam began to fill the room. Gilly was entranced: surely she had entered a magical, fairytale place.

'Use the water closet if you've a need,' Mrs Collins said casually, 'but don't forget to pull the chain.'

'The . . . the chain?'

'Aye. Now don't ask me how it works. That's a water tank,' nodding at a contraption supported by cast-iron brackets. 'Master Lucas talks about plungers and valves and ballcocks, all very new and modern and all you have to do is pull that chain,' nodding again at a pretty flowered chain-pull. She seemed to take it very much for granted but Gilly, invited to use it, not sure what to do, was relieved when Mrs Collins indicated delicately that she would leave the room.

'But where does the hot water come from for the bath?' Gilly gasped, the nightmare they had just gone through vanishing for a moment in her wonder.

'Nay, again I don't know, lass. We've a "gas-fired geyser" in the kitchen which is just below the bathroom and that heats the water but how it gets up here is a mystery to me. Master Lucas'd tell you was you to ask him. Now I'll leave you to it. Put them clean underthings on and then we'll tackle the dress.'

Had she the time Gilly could have spent hours in the lovely, sweet-scented room – Mrs Collins had poured something in the bath which smelled delicious – even using the water closet *twice* for the simple pleasure of watching the water flush away. But knowing Jem would be waiting she didn't linger and crept into the bedroom where Mrs Collins was ready with the dress, and while Jem was introduced to the marvels of the bathroom by Mr Barrie, Mrs Collins fitted her into the dress she had chosen for her.

It was enormous on her, sagging about the high neck and the bodice, the sleeves too short, and not until Mrs Collins found a broad band of black silk, which was actually a scarf, she told her, and tied it tightly about her waist did it come anyway near her. The bodice was slack and the skirt three inches short of her grey kid boots which were all she had and when Mrs Collins fastened an old-fashioned spoon bonnet on her head and posed her in front of the mirror she wanted to break into hysterical laughter. Only Mrs Collins's pleased smile stopped her.

'There you are, lass. Neat and decent as anyone could ask. Now, off you go. Mr Wilson's waiting for you. No, leave your lovely dress,' as Gilly moved to retrieve the grey silk gown, ready to take it, the moment she got back, to the washhouse. 'You won't know there's been any stains on it when I've done with it. I've got Mr Wilson's suit an' all.' Even what was obviously blood on the garments was not questioned.

Hospitals in the early parts of the century had been called 'gateways to death' with instruments employed on one person's wound used with a perfunctory wipe on the next patient. After an operation a patient was returned to the wards where they would be surrounded by others with open sores and fevers. Linseed poultices were used, which were a hotbed of infection, and blood poisoning was a common cause of death. The Crimean War and Florence Nightingale had helped to change that, for Miss Nightingale was a stickler for ventilation and cleanliness. A surgeon by the name of Joseph Lister began a movement which believed that bacteria entered wounds and caused suppuration, and Hugh Jenkins, who was treating Queenie, was an enthusiastic follower of Lister's methods. Only two years ago Lister had introduced a carbolic acid for dressing wounds and it was this method that had saved Queenie's life.

The ward where Queenie lay was spacious and well ventilated with a decent distance between each bed. The nurses were clean, competent women, trained in the care of the sick and injured. Besides Mr Jenkins, a surgeon, there were other medical men who had been employed when the old infirmary was knocked down and a new one erected, doctors who were chosen by men of their own profession and were qualified to administer the modern medicine the infirmary offered.

Sister Moore came bustling round the end of the bed and with an air of professionalism took Queenie's hand from Gilly's and held her wrist, feeling for her pulse. Gilly and Jem waited respectfully and when the sister told them that visiting time was almost over and her patient needed to rest, they stood up at once. Gilly bent and kissed her mother's cheek.

'We'll be here tomorrow, Mam, same time. Now you sleep and do as you're told and get better and when you are, me and

Jem have somewhere lovely to take you. You just wait until you
see the bathroom. It's a marvel, isn't it, Jem?'

Jem agreed with something less than Gilly's enthusiasm, and
Queenie noticed it and even in her battered state wondered
what sort of a man this Lucas Barrie was. Then, with many a
backward glance at Queenie, who turned her head to watch
them go, they left the ward and made their way to the front
entrance.

'Shall we go for a walk on the front, Lovedy,' Jem asked her,
apparently reluctant to return to Duke Street right away. 'Get a
breath of fresh air. And the Time Gun on Morpeth Pier at
Birkenhead is to be fired for the first time. It's to be fired every
day at one o'clock from now on, so they say. There'll be a good
crowd.'

'What, looking like this, Jem?' On a sudden whim Gilly
whipped off Mrs Collins's bonnet and loosened her hair which
blew about her face and head in a great swirl. Ladies did not
appear in public without a hat, and even working women
covering their head with a shawl or a man's cap. At once
everyone around them, men and women, stared at her, for not
only was she flouting convention, she was very lovely.

'Nay, put your hat on, lass. Everyone's looking,' Jem protested.

'Does it matter? No, I look hideous in it and the sooner we
get back to Mr Barrie's place the better. If I've nothing else to
wear at least I can alter this frock of Mrs Collins's, that's if she
doesn't mind, and do something with this bonnet. I mean to go
to the market and buy a length of material and make myself
something to wear as soon as possible and then if Mrs Collins
has cleaned up my grey silk . . .'

'Surely it doesn't matter what you wear as long as you're
decent, Gilly,' Jem began but Gilly stopped on the wide steps of
the infirmary and turned to him. There was a strange expression on his face and she peered at him as though doing her best

to decipher it. He looked somewhat sheepish, his eyes refusing to meet hers and she did not realise that he was, at one and the same time, ashamed, anxious and jealous. He didn't want Gilly to look elegantly lovely, for he had seen the look on Lucas Barrie's face and he was ashamed at himself for thinking such a thought. And he was anxious, for though he knew without a shadow of a doubt that Gilly loved him, Lucas was a handsome, wealthy gentleman and that was enough to turn any female's head. But then no matter what Gilly wore she was extraordinarily beautiful and he knew by the way men's heads turned as she went by that he was not the only one to think so. Some women are as lovely as a jewel with a jewel's hardness and brightness, others are pretty as a child is pretty, innocent and empty of face, but Gilly in the last year had become a woman, lovely, soft and eternally female with an honesty, a humour, a warmth, a young vitality that could not be hidden no matter what she wore. A woman, and yet still a girl for she was but seventeen. There was a brightness about her, a goodness, a kindness and Jem, who loved her with a passion beyond measure was terrified of losing her. He wanted her for his own before she began to realise that other men found her irresistible. And he knew Lucas Barrie was one of them! Her mouth, the softly curving short upper lip, the full lower lip, the square little jaw, the tilt of her golden-brown eyes and the vivid copper of her magnificent hair drew admiring glances to her like a bee to a beehive.

And into his mind's eye came the clear picture of Lucas Barrie. Tall, lean of waist and flat of belly, with strong muscled shoulders that filled the different jackets he wore in the office. His hair was thick and a rich, dark brown, ready to curl vigorously when unbrushed. His skin was a clear amber, clean shaven and his eyebrows dipped above eyes that were a compelling silvery grey, almost transparent, framed by long black lashes. His chin was firm, arrogant even, but there was a humour in him, a warm sense of fun which all those about him found they liked. Jem knew he did and the fear in him was that Gilly might, too. How could any woman resist him? Dear God, if he was a woman he knew he wouldn't and dear sweet God, why was he thinking in this way, like some . . . like . . . He was not a nancy but he could feel the attraction of Lucas Barrie just the same.

Was this why Gilly was so eager to get back to Duke Street?

Seeing the disappointment on Jem's face and completely misunderstanding it, Gilly slipped her hand in his. 'I know, let's walk back to Duke Street. We could go down Crown Street, along Upper Parliament Street right down to Queens Dock, along the docks to the Custom House and up to Duke Street. Come on, we could both do with some fresh air after this place.' For no matter how strict the medical staff were about cleanliness and the need for complete hygiene, a hospital had its own smell which consisted of sadness, illness, hopelessness and misery although it did its best to give hope to those who entered beneath the impressive portals.

They set off hand in hand, their heads close together as they discussed the future and the possibility of finding a place of their own when Queenie was returned to health. When they reached the corner of Duke Street neither of them noticed the man who loitered where it met Hanover Street, nor the constable who moved him on.

There was a carriage standing outside the door to number 7 Duke Street, from which a well-dressed young woman was just alighting, helped by a grand fellow in livery the same colour as the carriage, and a tall top hat. Another man, the coachman, sat erectly on the box, the reins in his hands. The carriage was a landau the colour of ox-blood drawn by two fine grey horses whose coats gleamed like silver. The hood of the landau was down and the interior could be seen to be lined in grey velvet.

Even in a respectable street such as this it was an unusual and breathtaking sight.

The girl turned her head as she prepared to go up the steps but when she saw Gilly coming towards her her face split into a delighted smile and she began to run, her arms wide.

'Gilly . . . oh Gilly, darling,' she cried, then, as though the thought had just occurred to her that in the circumstances she should be more decorous she stopped and waited.

It was Anne Barrie, the girl with whom she had been friends for six months. Her glance took in Gilly's comical appearance then she smiled tentatively and held out her hand, taking Gilly's.

'Lucas told me . . . oh dearest, I'm s . . . so sorry about your m . . . m . . . mother. I've come to see how she is and if there is anything I c . . . can do, please tell me. What a dreadful accident to have happened . . . oh and . . .' She turned to Jem. 'Mr Wilson, what a relief that G . . . Gilly had you to turn to.'

She knew nothing about the living accommodation that Gilly and Jem had shared. She was not aware of their special relationship since she had only been introduced to him at the launching, but it was clear in her mind that Jem had rushed from wherever he lived to be at Gilly's side in this emergency. She was the innocent, sheltered daughter of one of the most successful businessmen in Lancashire and it was evident that though Lucas had told her that Gilly's mother was in the infirmary after an *accident* she knew nothing of the details. How could anyone, especially her brother, tell her, for she probably barely knew how the act of love was performed, let alone the act of rape.

'How is she?' she added breathlessly. 'I came as soon as I knew to see if there was anything I could do. Lucas said your . . . your clothes were . . . well, he didn't seem sure what had happened to your dresses. He was very vague but I can see Mrs

C . . . C . . . ollins has helped out. Oh yes, I recognise that dress, Gilly. She used to be our nanny, you know. Oh, listen to me b . . . babbling on. I've come to take you to Bracken Hill to see if anything of mine will fit you. That is until your dress-maker can m . . . make you a new . . . See, here is Lucas come to open the door for us. Let's go inside and ask Mrs Collins for a c . . . cup of hot chocolate. Oh, Gilly, I can't tell you . . .' She took Gilly by the arm, turning to smile sweetly and encouragingly at Jem who followed behind, then led them both up the steps.

Lucas had eyes for no one but Gilly, for without the hideous bonnet loaned her by Mrs Collins, with her hair rippling down her back in a stream of copper, with her eyes smiling warmly into Anne's, how could any man with blood in his veins withstand her. As he held out his hand to her as though to help her up the last step his eyes met, for the fraction of a second, those of Jem Wilson's both revealing their feelings for this beautiful girl and it was as though a secret war had been declared. A battle, a challenge that would alter all their lives.

13

They sat in Lucas's drawing room and drank the delicious hot chocolate Mrs Collins brought them. She was inclined to fuss round Gilly, asking her kindly how her mother was doing and had she managed in the gown she had been lent and, though she hated to say it, did she think it advisable to remove her bonnet out of doors which a lady never did. She scolded Miss Anne for running about like a hoyden – oh yes, she'd seen her dash up the street to Miss Logan and what her dear mama would say if told she shuddered to think. Now then, Mr Lucas, she said to the tall figure of her master who lounged against the fireplace drinking his chocolate, what was he thinking about, couldn't he see that Miss Logan was worn out what with one thing and another, and really could do with a rest? She treated them all, even Jem, who hung about anxiously in the doorway, not sure whether to sit or stand, as though they were children. But she was kind with it and agreed with Miss Anne that Miss Logan should be driven to Bracken Hill, where she was sure Mrs Barrie would assent to Miss Logan being found something suitable to wear until her own wardrobe was replenished. Miss Anne and Miss Emily had more dresses than they knew what to do with and with a little lengthening, since Miss Logan was really quite tall, she was sure something could be arranged. Mrs Barrie would not like to see a friend of her daughter's in such dire straits, but what those dire straits were she did not question. She was aware that Miss Logan's mother had met with an accident but how Miss Logan and Mr Wilson came to be in such a terrible state of dress would be revealed in due course. In the meanwhile she did what she had always done for the Barrie children when they were small and had fallen down and scraped a knee. She provided them with comfort and a kind word and sent them on their way.

Rose Barrie was the daughter of a wealthy Liverpool merchant. She had been a spoiled, pretty girl when she married Herbert, declaring that she could not possibly live across the water in Birkenhead where the shipyard lay, for where would she do her shopping? She could not imagine life without the Misses Yeoland of Bold Street who had been her family's dressmakers for as long as she could remember. Mr Ireland of H.G. Ireland from whom her mother bought her furs, Mrs Dawson who supplied French corsets, Anne Hillyard who had a millinery and baby linen warehouse, also on Bold Street, Dismore's, the jeweller and silversmith, and Samuel Cutters, furnishers, were an integral part of her life, and surely Mr Barrie, her affianced, could more easily travel each day to his shipyard in Birkenhead than she could from Birkenhead to the splendid shopping area of Liverpool?

Herbert Barrie, who was in love with the pretty heiress and at the same time could not afford to lose the dowry she brought with her, gave in and looked around for a suitable family home for his bride. He found Bracken Hill.

The house was set at the end of a narrow lane that led from Princes Road surrounded by farmland. There was a high stone wall around the ten acres of garden and woodland and even a small lake and the wide, wrought-iron gates at the front led up a gravel drive in a curved sweep. The verges of the country road from Liverpool along which the smart carriage moved at a good pace were thick with the white of gypsy lace and big, white-faced daisies, and lush with the greenness of the coming summer's grass. In the hedges honeysuckle twisted round the growth of hawthorn and every few yards grew great hawthorn trees not yet laden with the white blossom of May. In the fields surrounding the house and land fat cows grazed and further on were flocks of sheep. There were wild daffodils and primrose shooting up in the soft spring warmth and overhead the sky stretched like blue silk above their heads.

'I don't think we need to accompany the girls to Bracken Hill, do you, Wilson?' Lucas had said casually as Gilly and Anne stood up to leave. 'I'm sure they can find a gown suitable for Miss Logan without our help.' His voice was cool. Lucas Barrie had known at once what Jem Wilson's feelings were towards Gilly Logan, since his were the same. He was a young man who had for most of his life been granted everything he wanted and he was not about to be thwarted by some working-class lad even though it was his own father, in agreement with John Hughes, who had put Jem where he was in the firm of Barrie and Hughes. He was not awfully sure in his mind what his next move was to be. He only knew he had fallen into love as quickly and as simply as once, as a boy, he had fallen into the small lake in his father's grounds. He was drowning in it, not thrashing about in cold waters as he had done then, but floating in a warm, delightful sea and until he had regained his equilibrium and decided what his next step would be he needed to keep this man who also loved Gilly Logan in his sights. It sounded churlish, which was not his style, but he sensed a real threat to his wooing in Jem Wilson. And anyway he liked the man. He had worked beside him for two years and they had got on well, but if Jem tried to stand in the way of his courtship – *courtship*, Jesus, was that the direction his thoughts were going? – of Gilly Logan, then there would be trouble. And not just for Jem!

'Shall we . . .?' Dear God, what could he suggest that he and Jem do to occupy themselves until his sister and Gilly returned? Their only shared interest was the ships they designed, but Jem forestalled him.

'While Gilly's with your sister I'm going to Rose Alley to see if there's anything worth rescuing,' he announced abruptly. 'She wasn't . . . wasn't herself earlier . . . afraid for her mam and we didn't really have the heart to do much, but without her I can have a good look round. There might be something. Something we can use when we get another place,' making it quite clear that he had no intention of staying with Lucas any longer than was absolutely necessary.

'I'll come with you.'

'There's no need.'

'I said I'd come. Two sets of fists are better than one and from what you tell me there are some rough characters around there.'

'My father for one.'

Lucas looked startled. 'Right . . . I see,' though it was plain he didn't. 'I'll call a cab.'

As the carriage turned into the drive its occupants were immediately shaded beneath the burgeoning branches of a small beech woodland, its beauty enhanced by a shimmering carpet of blue. Bluebells in a haze stretched from the drive and around the perimeter of the property, a sight so exquisite Gilly forgot for a moment the nightmare of the last days and even her beloved mam lying broken in her hospital bed.

'Oh, wouldn't Mam have loved to see this,' she whispered.

Anne, who had chattered all the way from Duke Street, took her hand and squeezed it. 'Then she shall. As soon as she is well enough Thomas shall t . . . take the carriage and f . . . fetch her to visit Mama.' She smiled lovingly, innocently into Gilly's rapt face.

At once Gilly wished she had never spoken. She was aware as Anne seemed not to be that the idea of Queenie Logan with her nasal Liverpool accent taking tea with the well-bred Mrs Barrie was a daft one, but then Anne was so naïve, so otherworldly could you wonder at it. Ever since the incident in the linen cupboard they had been friends, she and Anne, spending every moment in one another's company at school, ignoring Angela Ryan and her cronies. Angela had given up making fun of Anne, at least to her face and especially when Gilly was present. She knew that Gilly was not afraid of her and there was something about Gilly that made Angela hold her tongue, though she had not forgotten Gilly's attack on her and had vowed that there would come a day of reckoning.

They turned a curve in the drive and there was the house, a square-looking house of mellow red brick, flat windows, six on the first floor, four on the ground floor, two on either side of the front door, and at the side of the house two bays that looked out over a rolling lawn. There was a conservatory to the other side of the house, a very grand affair, painted white with a high roof in delicate fretwork, and beyond that a long, low building which was the stables and coach house.

The carriage drew up beneath a wide porch supported by four pillars and in front of a double door with long windows at each side. As soon as the carriage stopped the doors opened and a smiling maid stood there, neatly dressed in black with a pristine white apron and a white cap from which ribbons fluttered. She bobbed a curtsey, standing to one side as one of the coachmen jumped down and opened the carriage door.

Anne alighted from the carriage, smiling her sweet smile at the maid. 'I've brought my friend Miss Logan, Hetty. As you can see she is in need of something to wear and I thought . . . well, she has had . . . her mother has had an accident and . . . it's a long story but I'm sure Morna and I can find her something.'

'Oh, yes, Miss Anne.' Hetty peeped up at Gilly who was taller than her, her young curiosity getting the better of her, but it was not her place to question her young mistress's activities, nor the frightful attire the young lady visitor wore.

'Is Mama at home, Hetty?' Anne asked as she hurried Gilly through the front door. At the back of the wide hall another young maidservant peeped out of what appeared to be a kitchen door, then darted back when she saw she had been noticed. Gilly, knowing nothing of the workings of a house in the class of society in which Anne moved, also was not aware that Mrs Barrie was an indulgent, kindly woman whose children and servants were inclined to take advantage of her.

'No, miss, she and Miss Emily have gone to town. Miss Emily's having a fitting for her wedding gown and the brides-maids' headdresses are—'

'Oh glory!' Anne put her gloved hand to her mouth and grimaced. 'I had forgotten. I should have been here. Never mind. Come, Gilly.' And smiling at the maid who bobbed another curtsey she led Gilly towards the magnificent curving staircase that stood in the centre of the hall. Gilly would have liked to stand and stare at the splendour that surrounded her, merely catching a glimpse of an enormous fireplace in which applewood logs blazed, throwing out a sweet fragrance, a tall clock that ticked languorously and even as she hesitated for a moment struck the hour with a musical peal. The dial was painted with ships and flags celebrating, though Gilly was not aware of it, the Battle of Trafalgar, in which Herbert Barrie's ancestor fought. A deli-cately carved wooden hallstand set with a mirror was placed at the side of the front door and contained a dozen walking sticks, the handles of which were fashioned into horses' heads, owls and one had a beautiful porcelain bowl, gilded with gold and enamel. She wanted to loiter and gaze at the massed vases of fresh picked flowers, their scent vying with the applewood logs, a small round table on which a silver card salver stood, again an object she did not recognise, and a deep, red velvet chair. There were many open doors through which lovely things could be glimpsed but Anne was waiting for her at the top of the richly carpeted stairs and she had no choice but to hurry on.

Anne, who had known nothing but warmth, comfort, luxury, not only in her own home but in those of her family's
friends, could see nothing out of the ordinary in these objects at
which Gilly stared open-mouthed. She gestured to her to
follow her along a broad landing, leading her into what was
apparently her bedroom, going at once to a Chippendale
clothes press, or wardrobe as they were beginning to be called.
It was buff white with a chinoiserie landscape painted on it in a
pale apple green and there was a dressing-table to match with
an oval mirror placed on it. Gilly caught sight of herself in a
cheval glass, wondering for a moment who that positive fright
was! On the dressing-table lay beautiful objects in crystal and
silver, little ceramic pots, crystal scent bottles, a silver-backed
hairbrush and an elegant ivory case in which nestled sewing
needles, a pair of scissors and a thimble.

Turning round in a dazed circle, her mouth fell open at the
sight of the bed which had a sort of little tent over it, all in a
gauzy white muslin which was repeated in the curtains at the
window. On the bed was a quilted cover in shades of the palest
pink, cream, and blue-green, and the carpet across which Anne
flew, with no thought for what might be on her boots to dirty it,
was the palest cream. Gilly had thought Miss Hunter's room at
school was the pinnacle of luxury but this was overwhelming.
She was dazzled. She had not imagined that such loveliness
could exist and as Anne rummaged through her wardrobe,
pulling out this and discarding that, chattering all the time,
turning to consider Gilly, wondering what colour would suit
her best, Gilly suddenly came to her senses.

'Anne, love, stop a minute and let's think about this. I can't
wear anything as lovely as that silk affair. I have a silk dress, the
one I wore to the launching and which was stained when my
mam was . . . was hurt, and which Mrs Collins promised to
clean—'

'Yes,' Anne interrupted, holding a pale blue froth of silk, lace and ribbons in her arms. 'I was going to ask you how your . . . your mam . . . What sort of accident was she in? Was it—'

'She was attacked by some men,' Gilly said brutally, then was sorry as the blood drained from Anne's face. She swayed and at once Gilly was at her side, her arm about her, for this girl knew nothing of the brutal side of life and it had been cruel to blurt it out as she had. She took the dress from her, dropping it on the floor and led her to a low velvet chair, placing her tenderly in it, kneeling at her feet.

'I'm sorry, Anne. I should have told you more carefully. God, I'm sorry. You know nothing about – this sort of thing. Mam and me and Jem live in a . . . a very poor part of town and we left her alone, me and Jem, and these men . . . well, you must not worry about us, for we are all three strong and when she is better and out of hospital I shall find a place for her where she will be safe and where Jem and I will look after her. In the meanwhile your brother has offered us temporary accommodation. Oh, sweetheart, I'm so sorry to have upset you.'

'No, no . . .' Anne took her hands in hers. 'I'm sorry to be such a ninny. I want to help you, as you . . . h . . . h . . . have helped me in the . . . p . . . past. How can I forget . . . the way y . . . you d . . . defended me at school when A . . . Angela R . . . Ryan b . . . b . . . bullied me. We've been friends ever since, Gilly, and f. . . friends . . . h . . . help each other and I intend t . . . to help you.' In her distress her stutter became more pronounced. 'Tell me what I can do. Lucas has given you a home for now but in what way can I help?' She stood up, almost upsetting Gilly to the floor and ran to her wardrobe. 'See, take your pick. Anything at all if this blue silk doesn't s . . . s . . . suit. Mama won't mind, I'm sure, and then—'

'Anne, sweetheart, stop, stop.' Gilly rose to her feet. 'I should be glad of the . . . the loan of a dress but it must be something plain, something simple I can wear when I visit the hospital. And I need to go back to Rose Alley.'

'Rose Alley?'

'Where I live. Lived. There are things . . .'

Anne shook her head in denial and her pale face grew even paler. She grasped Gilly's hands frantically. 'Oh, no . . . n . . . no. You mustn't go there, Gilly, promise me. Those men who hurt your mama might be . . . oh, please, promise me.' She began to tremble, her slight frame pressed against the pretty wardrobe. She was a lovely young girl, small, dainty, her fair curls glinting in the firelight that lit the room, her slanting, silvery grey eyes so like those of her brother. She was dressed in virginal white with a buttercup-yellow sash about her tiny waist. She had thrown off her velvet cloak as they entered the room, dropping it carelessly on the carpet and Gilly was astonished at the attitude these people had to their possessions. She supposed they had so much and so many servants to pick up expensive garments from wherever they left them that they thought nothing of it.

'You must not worry about me, Anne, really you mustn't. Jem looks after me and would allow nothing to hurt me. Now, let's look through your wardrobe and see if you can find some plain gown, preferably grey or dark brown, or even black, that I can wear.'

Anne turned back dubiously to the wardrobe. 'I'm not sure I have anything in a dark colour. We mostly wear white, you see, or pastel colours . . .'

'Perhaps one of your maids has—'

'Oh, no, you could not wear a housemaid's dress, Gilly. It would not be proper.'

'Anne, for goodness' sake, lass, I'm sure your housemaids would be better dressed than . . .'

At that moment from the half-open window there came the sound of horses' hooves on the gravel drive and the scrunch of it beneath carriage wheels. A man's voice called, 'Whoa, Gypsy, whoa, Dancer,' and a woman murmured something.

A door opened and from downstairs the maid could be heard speaking to someone.

'. . . Upstairs, madam,' she was heard to say.

'It's Mama,' Anne cried and sped across the carpet to the door while Gilly stood rooted to the spot. The last time she had seen Mrs Barrie had been at the launching of the *Emily Jane* when all the ladies had been expensively gowned, smiling, nodding, believing her to be one of Anne's friends, from the same social group as the Barries. One of them, in fact.

Of course, Mrs Barrie was aware that Jem was an employee of her husband's, but not just any employee, for he was a qualified draughtsman, training to be a marine engineer, a designer of ships as her son was. He came from a lower social sphere than her son but he was a young man of distinction, John Hughes's protégé who would make his mark in the world of shipping. She would not, naturally, consider him good enough to marry one of *her* daughters but the young lady on his arm, a school acquaintance of Anne's, was very amiable and well mannered.

She was astounded to find that same young lady in her daughter's bedroom got up in some sort of mourning dress which was far too short and had obviously been made for another woman. She stopped in the doorway, her elder daughter Emily behind her, doing her best to move Anne out of the way.

'Anne, what is happening here?' she asked. Hetty said you had a friend with you but I did not expect Miss . . . er . . . Miss . . .'

'Miss Logan, Mama. Gilly Logan who is my friend from school—' Anne began but Mrs Barrie interrupted her with a lift of her imperious hand.

'Miss Logan, indeed, but might I ask—'

'Oh, Mama, Gilly is in a dreadful way of things. She has nothing to wear and I brought her here to—'

'Perhaps I might ask—'

'Her mam . . . her mama has met with an . . . an accident and—'

'I'm sorry to hear that but it does not explain why . . .'

Anne turned to Gilly in confusion for she too now wondered why the 'accident' to Mrs Logan should rob Gilly of her dresses so that she was forced to borrow from Mrs Collins. She had been told that men had hurt Mrs Logan but not that these men had also totally destroyed Gilly's home and ruined every stitch of clothing she possessed.

Mrs Barrie turned to Gilly enquiringly. She was a kind woman whose 'good works' were well known in the vicinity of Bracken Hill. She helped the poor and needy, moved graciously about the parish dispensing hot soup – not cooked by herself, naturally – old blankets, discarded baby clothes, and lectured women on the benefits of cleanliness. She was not clever or even very intelligent, but provided it was no trouble to herself would help anyone who asked. She drifted through her pleasant life, still pretty and plump and, though it filled her with no enthusiasm, was desired by her husband at least twice a week. She had given birth to seven children, four of whom had survived infancy, two of them sons, thank God. And it was through her children that she truly lived. Her placid nature allowed them many small indulgences: her two daughters attended school instead of being educated by a governess, for example, but let anyone threaten her children, sons or daughters and her easy-going nature turned to steel and she became a lioness defending her cubs.

Her mother's instinct told her that this extremely beautiful and unique young woman was such a threat. She didn't know how. Even this morning as she and Emily prepared to go into town to visit their dressmakers, the Misses Yeoland, they discovered that Anne was missing and they had been forced to go without her. And this girl was the cause!

'Perhaps Miss Logan could speak for herself, Anne,' she remarked sweetly.

'Of course, Mama, but you see—' Mrs Barrie held up her hand again and Anne subsided.

'Miss Logan?'

Gilly wet her lips and stepped forward. 'Please don't blame Anne, Mrs Barrie,' she began.

'I have no intention of blaming Anne, Miss Logan.'

'She has been so kind—'

'Gilly has nothing to wear, Mama,' Anne interrupted eagerly.

'Anne, must I ask you again to allow Miss Logan to speak for herself?'

Gilly lifted her head bravely. 'My mam . . . mother was attacked quite viciously, Mrs Barrie. Men broke into our . . . into our home and . . .'

An expression of horror froze Mrs Barrie's face. Dear Lord, she had two innocent daughters and surely this was not for their ears? This girl must be silenced and shown the door at once before . . . before . . . but Gilly could not be stopped.

' . . they did not stop at . . .'

'Please, Miss Logan,' Mrs Barrie all but shrieked.

'. . . hurting her, they wrecked our home and destroyed all my dresses, which is why I am here. Anne has promised me the loan of a suitable gown, something plain, until I can make myself a dress – I learned to sew at Mrs Hunter's – and then I shall leave at once. Your son is a friend of Jem Wilson who is also my friend and he—'

'*My son.* How is he involved?'

'He missed Jem at the shipyard yesterday – they work together – and called—'

'Where is he now?' For of all Rose Barrie's children her first-born was the most dear.

Gilly was surprised. 'Why, at his home, I believe. Anne and I left him there when—'

'You have been to my son's house?'

'Yes, Mr Barrie insisted we leave . . . my home, as it was so badly smashed up. My mother is in the infirmary. She has been blinded in one eye—'

'Stop, Miss Logan, I insist you stop at once. My daughters must not be subjected to this—'

'Mama, how could you? And if Emily is too frail to hear it then I am not.'

'Anne, I forbid you to—'

'No, Mama, I'm sorry, but Gilly is my friend and I will not desert her now. We must find her a gown she can wear, an everyday sort of gown, and a bonnet. In a dark colour, she says, and I seem to have none that . . . no, wait, I have it. Do you remember when Mrs Cass died Emily and I were made gowns of dark grey grosgrain with bonnets to match to attend her funeral? We had gloves and . . . now where did they go? Emily's should fit Gilly since she is so much taller.'

Both Emily and Mrs Barrie stood as though turned to stone as Anne darted about the room, opening drawers and pulling out white lacy garments, petticoats, chemises, under-drawers, gloves, stockings, then she suddenly clapped a hand to her forehead.

'I know, they will be in the trunk in the attic. You said—'

'Anne, will you stop this nonsense at once. Miss Logan—'

Anne turned to her mother in mid-stride, on her face an expression none of them had seen before. She had been brought up in a privileged class, bred from birth to have that quiet air of natural grace and authority that is unconscious in those without vanity. Though she was kind and sweet-natured she had been trained for what would be her position in life as the wife of a wealthy man whose household she would run. Finding a husband for her would not be difficult. With her spun silver and gold curls, the rich cream and rose of her skin, her soft, childish mouth and clear grey eyes, not to mention her father's fortune, she was a very eligible young woman. Her sister Emily, not as pretty or sweet-natured, had already captured the son of a local businessman – or had had him captured for her by her father – and it would be Anne's turn next.

But where Emily was compliant and dutiful, as her sister had been until now, Anne had an inner strength which at that precise moment made her defy her open-mouthed mother.

'I'm sorry, Mama, but I must help Gilly in her present trouble and at this moment the only thing I can do is to find her a dress to wear. That is not much to ask, is it? Now' – turning her sweet smile on Gilly – 'you wait here while I scoot up to the attic. Morna will help me. I won't be long.'

She pushed past her mother and sister and when she had gone, calling out to her maid Morna, Rose Barrie turned her grey eyes on Gilly. They were the colour of pewter and as flat and cold.

14

Mr Jenkins scarcely recognised her the following day as she and her gentleman friend entered the ward. In fact they were both the picture of well-dressed elegance, a lady and a gentleman of quality, or so they would be considered by all those about them. He was not to know that Miss Logan's gown and the casual lounge suit worn by her companion were the very garments in which they had brought in Miss Logan's mother on Friday. Then they had been bloodstained and dishevelled, the pair of them wild-eyed and desolate. Yesterday Miss Logan had worn a black dress of some sort, comical and ill-fitting and a huge black bonnet, obviously not hers, and he had wondered what had happened in this lovely young woman's life, apart from the attack on her mother, which he had advised her to report to the police, that caused her to wear what was evidently another woman's clothing. He could not have known that that other woman had somehow cleaned and sponged, brushed and pressed both the lovely satin dress and Mr Wilson's suit so that the garments looked as good as new. Mrs Collins's mother had been laundress to Lady Seddon of Seddon Hall and she had passed on her talents to her daughter, who might have taken up the same career but had chosen instead to become nursemaid, then nanny to the Barrie children.

Mr Jenkins spoke to them, assuring Miss Logan that her mother, considering her injuries, was doing as well as could be expected but her visitors were not to stay too long.

They crept quietly towards her bed. Queenie was still

swathed in bandages but her visible eye saw them approach and she held out her hand to her daughter. Every bed in the ward was occupied by women, all neatly tucked up beneath crisp, white counterpanes, their head resting on crisp, white pillows. A nurse, as immaculate as her patients and the beds they lay in, sat at a table in the centre of the room.

And on the table stood several vases of bright flowers. Spring flowers, mostly daffodils, that made a vivid pool of colour in the stark cleanliness that surrounded them. Gilly had brought anemones, or windflowers, as Sutton, the head gardener at Bracken Hill had called them. Glorious shades of scarlet, purple and blue, cut no more than an hour since and brought round to Duke Street by Anne. Anne had never defied her mother before and the measure had brought a flush to her cheeks and put a diamond sparkle in her grey eyes as she sent her very best wishes to Gilly's dear mama. Gilly was to tell her that Anne hoped to meet her soon. The flowers, in their own pretty water container, were placed on the locker beside Queenie's bed where, painfully turning her head, she could sigh over them.

There were visitors at almost every bed, working-class visitors whose loved ones, ill or injured, were fortunate enough to be nursed in the ward of this new, modern infirmary whose walls bore polished brass plaques naming its generous bene-factors. Of course, those of the privileged class preferred to be brought back to health, attended by their own physician, in the privacy and luxury of their own home.

'Mam, dear Mam, how are you feeling?' Gilly bent her head and kissed the back of Queenie's hand, holding on to it with both of hers. Jem leaned over and gently touched the top of Queenie's head where her dark hair had been cut away.

Queenie turned her head, rolling her one golden-brown eye from one to the other of these two who meant so much to her. She was in a great deal of pain despite the laudanum the doctor allowed her but she did not let it show.

'Smart . . .' she managed to say and at once they both smiled and leaned forward eagerly.

'We're staying with Mr Barrie, Mam. Mr Lucas Barrie, and his housekeeper cleaned our things. Everyone is very kind.'

Gilly resolutely shut out the hostile face of Lucas Barrie's mother who sensed a threat not only to her daughter but to her son who were both involved with this low-class girl. Herself, in fact. She had been driven back to Duke Street, as a great concession, in Mrs Barrie's carriage, simply, she knew, because Anne had made such a fuss and Mrs Barrie wanted no open rebellion until her husband came home to deal with it. She was not quite sure what to do with this daughter of hers who had always been good-natured and compliant and was now openly defying her. It was this young woman who was to blame, of course, and the sooner she was got rid of, the better.

'Anne, you remember Anne?' Gilly said now. 'She is Mr Barrie's sister. I know you've never met her, Mam, but you've heard me speak of her. Well, she gave me a dress. Plain it is, grey, but I'm to put a white collar and cuffs on it. It's even the right length and it's suitable for everyday wear, which this isn't,' looking down ruefully at the lovely silk gown which had been so miraculously restored by Mrs Collins. 'So you see, Mam, I can go about without drawing attention to myself.'

'Rose Alley . . .' her mother gasped.

'What about it, Mam?'

'Not go . . . you . . .'

'No, Mam, not me. Jem and Lucas.' Unintentionally she used Lucas Barrie's Christian name, not realising that she had done so, but Jem did, and so did Queenie. 'They went together and guess what, they managed to find quite a few things unbroken. Your pot dog that you loved, remember, and other things. They piled them in the cart . . . Lucas helped Jem to put the wheel back on and they dragged everything back to Duke Street and put it in the stable at the rear. That's where Lucas lives, isn't it, Jem? In Duke Street?' She had no conception of the expression on her face which both Queenie and Jem tried to decipher.

Gilly turned to Jem who up to now had not spoken.

'Yes,' he said quietly. No more.

'And hasn't he been kind? He and Anne. What would we have done without them?'

'I don't know, Lovedy.' His voice was tired, ragged even and had Gilly not been so busy being eternally grateful to the Barrie family who had smoothed out the thorny path she and Jem had walked since the moment they had found her mam so badly injured, she would have noticed. But something apart from her mam's state stood between her and her usual quick perception to Jem's mood.

'We stayed there last night and Mrs Collins made us a lovely meal, then she helped me to let out the bodice of the dress since Emily, she's Anne's sister, is smaller in the . . . in the chest than I am. I shall wear it tomorrow when I go to see Mr Field. Now, Mam, you've not to worry.' She brought her mother's hand to her cheek and smiled warmly into her bandages. 'I must see to our account. What is it?' as Queenie showed signs of distress.

'Jem . . . go . . .'

Jem understood at once though Gilly looked confused.

'Queenie, girl,' he murmured, using the affectionate term that Liverpool folk had made their own. He leaned closer to the face on the pillow. 'I would go if I could but I've got to get back to work. I must keep my job.' And Queenie was made to understand that with only one of them bringing in any money his job at the shipyard was essential. 'Besides, Gilly knows more about your bank account than I do. She can talk with Mr Field and see what can be done until you're back on your feet. You mustn't worry, lass. You rest and concentrate on getting better.'

Queenie freed her hand from Gilly's and clutched his arm. 'Soon . . . soon . . .'

He patted it tenderly then, as Gilly had done, brought it to his lips. It was true he must go across the water tomorrow with Lucas and put in a day's work, though he knew it would be hard to apply himself beside the man whose feelings for Gilly, *his* Gilly, were written plainly in his eyes, which last night had followed her about the room. There was something else he had to do as well, though he had said nothing to Gilly, and that was to find out who had brutally attacked Queenie and smashed up her room. He meant to make a few discreet enquiries – with the added incentive of a bob or two – among his old neighbours, for somebody in Rose Alley must be aware of who it was. He had no intention of going to the police as Dr Jenkins had advised because they would do nothing and besides, he was pretty certain it must be someone in Rose Alley or its vicinity who had been part of it. Men from another part of town might have attacked Queenie, as the brutal inhumanity that existed in the crowded courts and alleyways of the district and had been aimed at Queenie was well known. But they, whoever they were, would not have destroyed articles that could be sold. They would have taken everything that would sell for a few pence, clothing, pots, pans, bedding, even the handcart that was Queenie's livelihood. No, this had been done for another reason and he meant to find out why and *who*! It was someone who had a grudge against her, of that he was certain and a worm of suspicion wriggled in his brain though he kept it to himself.

The hospital was run on very strict lines, the patients' day arranged for the convenience of the staff, waking hours early and visiting hours restricted. One hour and then the bell was rung to indicate that visiting was over. They kissed her hand, both of them, for every part that was visible was bandaged, then left, promising to come tomorrow. Gilly glanced back frequently, wanting to weep but controlling it for she knew it would upset Mam, moving along with the stream of men and women, the men in caps, the women mostly swathed in shawls. The pair of them were eyed quite openly because it was not often 'toffs' were admitted to this hospital.

They were even more amazed when the couple were greeted at the bottom of the wide, shallow steps by another elegant young lady. Anne clasped Gilly's arm then leaned forward and placed a shy kiss on her cheek.

'I thought to take a cab and visit Lucas with you. Mama wouldn't allow me the carriage. Church, you understand,' she explained apologetically for her mama, not speaking of the frigid argument that had taken place in her mama's drawing room. Mama did not approve of Anne's friendship with Miss Logan who had turned out to be not their sort at all. She had accepted Papa's intention to bring on the young man at the shipyard, since it did not affect her family and she supposed that after all he had saved young Willy Hughes from drowning several years ago but that was no excuse for Anne to take up with this young woman despite their friendship at school. She was at a loss to understand how Mrs Hunter could have enrolled the girl at her exclusive school for young ladies. Anne was to remain at home where she belonged and discontinue this unsuitable friendship at once.

Anne had listened dutifully, her child's face pale and strained, for she disliked being out of favour with anyone, but the self-distrust that had served her all her life, that had created her stammer, left Anne Barrie at that moment, never to return. She forgot her shyness and the unease that filled her when confronted with opposition and her voice was steady, her stammer gone.

'I'm sorry, Mama, but I must disobey you.'

The silence that followed was as loud as a clap of thunder. Janet, a parlour-maid at Bracken Hill, who had just entered the drawing room carrying the tray on which was the hot chocolate always drunk at this time of the day, froze in the doorway.

Emily, rearranging a vase of tulips and daffodils on a table by the window, squeaked and turned so sharply that the vase toppled over and flowers and water slid to the floor.

'Anne, stop this nonsense at once.' Rose Barrie's voice was glacial. 'This girl has been helped by our family. We have done our Christian duty by her and that is all that is needed. Lucas has taken them in but I believe they are looking for suitable accommodation. I do not know what their . . . their relationship is to one another but whatever else and whoever else they are, that alone is enough to bar them from decent society.'

'I'm sorry, Mama,' she said again, 'but I cannot desert Gilly in her hour of need. I cannot turn my back on her.'

Rose Barrie's voice edged up a tone. 'She has her . . . her young man.'

Anne ignored this. 'I do not wish to upset you, or Papa' – who was ensconced in his study with his Sunday newspaper, happily unaware of the rebellion in his household – 'but I must go to her. I shall take a cab to Duke Street.'

'Anne, I forbid it.'

But Anne had turned away, brushed past the paralysed Janet, and ran into the hall. Opening the front door she called out to Dick, the gardener's lad, to run and fetch her a cab from the rank at the entrance to Princes Park.

They lunched with Anne and Lucas, Mrs Collins delighted to show off her culinary skills with dressed crab and a green salad followed by what she called The Hidden Mountain, a great favourite of Master Lucas's made up of eggs, slices of citron, sugar, cream and a layer of jam which, once mixed together, was fried in a buttered pan like a pancake. They drank a chilled white wine with the crab and followed the meal with coffee and macaroons made with sweet almonds.

Gilly was conscious of Lucas's eyes on her and whenever she caught them he smiled; each time her heart tripped in her chest and she found it hard to swallow. Anne seemed to have burst completely out of her shell, her artless chatter filling any silences that could have been constrained, turning again and again to Jem who could not help but be charmed by her childish loveliness. She asked him about his work, his schooling, his childhood just as though he came from the same background as herself and for a moment he was tempted to tell her how he and Gilly had lived, describe the squalor in which they had been brought up. In a way it was a credit to them both to have achieved so much but he knew he could not tell this sweet, innocent girl about the hideous state of the area where he and Gilly had lived all their lives. And the woman who had protected them, worked all hours God sends, hoarded every penny, doing without herself to give them their chance, was now lying in hospital in the pitiful state where some brutes, products themselves of this environment, had put her. Had it not been for her he himself would have still been a plater or some sort of labourer in the shipyard and Gilly, well, who knew what Gilly would have been? Perhaps his wife, living in rags on the pittance he would have earned; even as he thought these thoughts, watching something growing between Lucas and Gilly, with his heart in tatters, would he not have given it all up, been satisfied with the life they would have led had Gilly been beside him?

Lucas took them round to the stables at the rear of the house where his handsome horse wickered in welcome, pushing his nose against his shoulder and nuzzling at his pocket for a tit-bit. He watched with acid in his heart as Lucas showed Gilly how to offer the half apple on the palm of her hand to the animal, heard her delighted laugh as the horse took it, her shoulder leaning against that of Lucas Barrie. They were taken into the small coach house where stood the spanking, brand-new brougham he had recently purchased, he told them casually, since money was no object to the son of the wealthy shipbuilder Herbert Barrie.

'We could go for a drive if you like,' he said, including them all but looking at Gilly. Her face was bright. 'Oh yes, that would be lovely. Is there room for four?'

'Of course. Percy will hitch up the carriage horses and we'll have a run out.' He was the epitome of the young man about town, but at the same time Jem knew he was not one of the dandies who dashed about showing off their skill to the ladies. He was a serious young man, a clever, talented young man who would make his mark in his father's shipyard. His only fault in Jem's eyes was that he had fallen in love with Gilly!

They drove out of the city, heading north along country lanes past the Zoological Gardens where the roar of the caged lions could be heard. There was a great Sunday crowd at the entrance, people from all walks of life entering or leaving, for the Gardens were very popular, but Lucas guided the two carriage horses clear of the throng and on to empty country lanes bordered with wild primroses and violets, past orchards where the fruit trees were burdened with blossom, a beauty that squeezed the heart with rapture. Blackbirds sang recklessly in the hedges and swallows were flying high. The leaves shimmered and glistened and over the fields every imaginable tint of spring was burnished by the bright sunlight, and the grasses beneath the trees were starred with buttercups.

They clattered over a small wooden bridge that spanned a stream, the stream framed with willows and tall reeds. There were two children on the bridge, a boy and a girl, accompanied by a bright-eyed dog. The boy dangled a line over the water hoping for a fish, but his efforts brought no more than a brown speckled duck followed by a line of tiny ducklings.

Gilly sat beside Lucas where he had put her, his sister and Jem behind, and for the space of an hour or so the past few days were forgotten as she fell slowly but with an ever quickening beat into her love for Lucas Barrie. She had believed she could love no man but Jem and had indeed never done so. But she recognised at last that what she felt for Jem, the deep and abiding love she bore him, was that of a sister for a beloved brother. He had guided her, protected her, taught her, been her constant companion for the whole of her life, since even as a toddler he had been there to hold her hand, but as she turned to smile at him, to share with him this lovely day that had come so unexpectedly to them in the midst of so much horror, she caught the look on Anne's face as he pointed something out to her. She was half leaning against his shoulder as she looked to whatever it was, then he turned to her, smiling, and she smiled back and it was there for all to see, the shining devotion in Anne Barrie which was her nature.

Gilly felt the peace and *rightness* of it settle within her, then sighed deeply, her own shoulder touching Lucas's. He looked down into her face and on his was the identical expression to the one his sister displayed.

The clerk at the Royal Bank in Dale Street told her that Mr Field was with a customer but if she would like to take a seat he would see her as soon as he was free. The clerk smiled at her approvingly, for she was simply but properly dressed in a very suitable gown of dark grey. It fitted her perfectly, sculpting her high breasts and neat waist, falling gracefully in folds to her highly polished black boots. He was not to know that she and Mrs Collins had spent many hours altering the gown which had once belonged to Miss Emily Barrie, daughter of one of their wealthiest clients. She had added the touch of white at the neck and cuffs and lined the inside of the brim of her grey bonnet with ruched white muslin. Her gloves, borrowed from Mr Barrie's younger daughter, were also grey.

She had just come from the infirmary where she had spent an hour with her mother who, to her delight, had been allowed to sit up, propped up by several pillows. The doctor was pleased with her progress.

'She is eating well, only easily managed foods of course, since it is difficult with the bandages, but highly nutritious. I intend to remove the bandages from her face a little later. The wounds should have healed enough and it will do them good to be uncovered. Should you come tomorrow, you will' – he smiled at her, for she was irresistible to any man with blood in his veins – 'I thought you would . . .' Then he became serious. 'You must be prepared for a shock. Her face will be badly scarred and I cannot have you fainting.'

'I am not the fainting kind, Doctor. I love my mother and I shall not upset her by . . . by cringing from her.'

They had talked, she and Mam, she doing most of the talking, of course, but with Mam making suitable sounds which Gilly understood. Gilly held her hand lovingly, stroking it, looking beyond the bandages into her one eye which, now that she had come off the laudanum the doctor had administered, had brightened considerably.

'I'm looking for a house, Mam. What . . . what is it?'

'In . . . in . . . She . . . our Street.' Queenie struggled to make herself understood through the slit that had been cut in the bandages across her mouth.

'Where? What street, Mam?' Gilly asked urgently. 'Have you seen something?'

''Es . . . 'efore this . . .'

'Before this happened?'

''Es.'

'Say it again, Mam and I'll go and see it. Where?'

Queenie took a deep breath and swallowed the saliva that kept flooding her mouth. 'Shemour Street . . . off . . . Lonnun Road . . .'

'I don't think . . .' Gilly began doubtfully.

'Seymour Street off Lonnun Road.'

'Seymour Street off London Road?'

Queenie sagged against her pillows, nodding her head

emphatically, so emphatically her bandages wobbled and she winced in pain.

At once Gilly stopped her, taking her hand in hers. 'Mam, don't worry, I'll find it. Have you been before?'

Queenie, who was tiring rapidly, nodded faintly. 'Nishe . . . nice . . . Mishus Huggett.'

'Mrs Huggett. Now that's enough, Mam. I want you to lie back and rest. I'll go at once to the bank and then I'll call on Mrs Huggett to see Mr Field about our account. And I must visit Mrs Hunter and tell her I shall not be coming back to school. Anne said she would inform her that you had had an accident and I shall be needed at home for a while. Now, Mam, please, I must beg you not to worry. You won't get better if you worry and Jem and I want you home – perhaps to Seymour Street – as soon as possible. We'll manage.'

She was about to mention the handcart which, while she and Mrs Collins had been industriously sewing, Jem was giving the handcart a touch of paint with the help of Percy in the stable, but her plans regarding their old way of life must not be mentioned yet lest they distressed her mother. It would be a long time, if ever, before Queenie could take to the road again, but Gilly was young and healthy and there was nothing to stop her from doing something to bring in a few bob. She and Mam couldn't expect Jem to support them, though she knew he would be quite willing to do so.

She stood up as the clerk told her that Mr Field was free now and would she care to come with him to his office.

'It is a lovely day, is it not,' he said affably. 'I hope your mother is well. It's not often you come without her,' he went on, but she was not about to reveal to him why she was here to see Mr Field, and alone. Her plans were for Mr Field only.

15

She walked almost the length of Seymour Street, knocking on several doors before she came to number 17 to where she had been directed by a curiously fascinated woman who lived at number 11. She had knocked resolutely, watched by those on whom she had already called asking for Mrs Huggett and when the door opened to reveal a stern, even forbidding countenance she felt the need to take a step backwards.

Mrs Huggett saw a plainly dressed young woman, nervous, she was inclined to think, but she was prepared to admit that this was not a neighbourhood where young ladies such as this one often wandered so it was understandable that she should be nervous. Despite her imposing manner, at heart she was kind and fair and in the way of those who are homely was overcome with admiration for beauty in another. This young woman had a flawless face, a complexion of creamy rose with deep, velvety brown eyes in which flecks of gold floated and a soft, coral-pink mouth. A face to draw all eyes to it, even those of another woman, and a figure to match. She held her head gracefully, her back was straight and her breasts were high and pert above her narrow waist. From beneath her simple grey bonnet a shining tendril of hair drifted above her ear, hair streaked with the colours of autumn. Beech leaves came to Mrs Huggett's mind, for she and Huggett had been fond of a country walk, beech leaves mixed with cinnamon, gold and amber.

Nevertheless, despite her appreciation of her visitor's good looks, she raised her own head a fraction. 'Yes?' she said shortly, as it was not her way to be effusive even with this lovely young woman to whom, incredibly, she found she was drawn. Flo Huggett was not one to give way to her feelings, nor to let them be seen, but this one seemed so . . . so polite, so respectable, though as yet she had not spoken.

'Mrs Huggett?' she asked hesitantly.

''Oo wants ter know?' Flo Huggett asked severely, her Liverpool upbringing strong in her voice.

'My name is Gilly Logan. My mam gave me your name and address,' she faltered.

At once a picture of a tall, statuesque woman dressed poorly but cleanly, neatly, came to Flo's mind. In the face that woman was somewhat like the one on her white, recently donkey-stoned step but without the delicate loveliness this one pos-sessed. A working-class woman, a no-nonsense kind of a woman who had been looking for lodgings, decent lodgings, she had said, for herself and her daughter and a young man who boarded with them. That was a few weeks back now and Flo had given her up and was ready to let the place to someone else because she didn't like to see it empty. Huggett had called it her little nest egg, and standing empty was earning her nothing.

But still she would not let her guard down. She pursed her lips. 'So?'

'She said you had a house to let, Mrs Huggett, and I thought . . . well, I thought if it was all right with you I would like to see it with a view to renting it. That's if it's still available.'

Mrs Huggett liked her politeness but as was her nature did not show it. 'Did yer indeed? Well, yer'd best come in then and let me 'ave a look' – the word rhyming with Luke – 'at yer. I'm very perticler about 'oo I let to.' She opened the door wide and stood back to allow Gilly to enter. A pretty little grey cat twined herself about Gilly's skirts and at once Mrs Huggett swooped on the animal, clutching her in her arms, closing the door to with her hip.

'Follow me,' she told Gilly, leading the way up the narrow, achingly clean passage, a cold passage that led into a haven of warmth, cleanliness, brightness and comfort which was her kitchen. Everything in it gleamed and glowed with polish and elbow grease, from the set of graduated copper pans on a superb steel pan-stand to the blackleaded oven on either side of the bright fire where a kettle steamed. On a dresser there stood kitchen scales with a round brass tray and solid brass weights and on a shelf above the scales a variety of ceramic preserve jars, flat-lidded and salt-glazed in rosy shades of terracotta. The spotless tiled floor was in pleasing tints of fading red, beige and brown and the pine table in the centre of the kitchen was scrubbed almost to white. In front of the fire on either side were two pine rocking-chairs with low rush seats, both with a cushion for the back and between them a rag rug on which a low stool was positioned.

'Sit yer down then, lass,' Mrs Huggett ordered in a voice that was not to be disobeyed, sitting down herself, settling the cat on her knee and stroking her with a gentle hand. It was this gesture that gave away her true nature, usually hidden behind the inflexible façade she showed her neighbours.

'So, yer want ter rent my 'ouse, do yer?' she began.

But Gilly interrupted eagerly, her face turning a rosy red with some emotion. 'Oh yes, please, ma'am, that is' – she turned prim – 'if it is suitable.'

Mrs Huggett looked somewhat affronted then she gave a throaty laugh. 'Yer've no need ter "ma'am" me, lass. Mrs Huggett's the name. And where's yer mam terday? She 'ad a look t'other week an' seemed suited but then she never came back so I reckoned she'd lost interest. I were about ter let it to another woman, a decent widder woman wi' two bairns.'

'Oh, please, Mrs Huggett, don't do that.' Gilly leaned forward in her chair, nearly toppling out of it as it rocked. 'I'm sorry about the widow and her children but you see my mother has had an . . . an accident and has been unable to call back to you. She's in hospital and is unlikely to be out for . . . I don't know how long but in the meantime me and Jem—'

'Jem?' Mrs Huggett's eyes narrowed suspiciously.

'Yes. He lodges . . . lodged with us. We're staying with friends at the moment but we want to get our own place before Mam comes out of hospital. We can't go back to . . . where we were.' She screwed up her face, not knowing how to explain to this woman what had happened to Mam but she was to find that Mrs Huggett was not one to beat about the bush.

'What sorta accident an' why can't yer go back to where yer was?'

'Well, you see, when Jem and I . . . we'd been to . . . Jem works at Barrie and Hughes Shipyard and there was a launching. Jem's a draughtsman and he took me to—'

Mrs Huggett sighed. 'Look, lass, if you an' me's ter gerron there'd best be trust between us. 'Onesty an' truth an' if that's not possible we'd best part now.'

Mrs Huggett seemed as old and grey as granite, a tall and upright sentinel who appeared to be guarding her property against any intruder. Her kitchen spoke of a good housewife who bleached and scoured, scrubbed and beat her rugs each day in the back yard. Her snow-white linen could be seen hanging on the line outside the scullery window, which led off the kitchen, and the washing would no doubt give off a bracing smell of strong soap and lye. She was obviously a woman who spent her time keeping her place as clean as her rough hands and strong back could make it. And she expected it in others, especially if it was her property that was under consideration. Her strong, straight back was adapted by nature and the life she had led to carry burdens and she was demanding that Gilly tell her about hers.

'My mam was attacked . . . raped . . . in our home.'

Mrs Huggett put her hand to her mouth in an involuntary spasm of horror.

'The men . . . man who did it wrecked the place, and all our clothes were destroyed. I have had to borrow this dress from a friend and Mam needs somewhere safe and decent to live when she comes home.' It was baldly said and baldly received.

Florence Huggett was not generous with her affections, keeping them, as she reserved her physical stamina and the benefit of her sound advice, strictly for those she thought deserving of them. This girl was asking for no favours, no sympathy, just to be allowed to get on with her life in a decent place and that's what Flo had to give. A decent place, she said, which was the house next door to her own. Huggett had been in good work before he died, a harbourmaster down at the docks, or at least employed by one and he had done well. Flo had run a small stall at St John's Market, getting up early and driving out in a hired gig to the local farms to buy farm produce, eggs, butter, cheese and vegetables, which she sold at a small profit to working-class women. Between them she and Huggett had done well. No children, which had been a sadness to them both, but when Huggett was crushed to death by a broken spar he had had the misfortune to be standing under, she had some small savings and the house next door which he had bought her as a means of supporting herself. She was willing to do anything to earn herself a few bob and she managed very nicely.

'Right,' she said crisply and then, without another word, got up, poured hot water into a cheerfully rose-sprigged teapot and set it carefully on a mat on the table. She reached down two sturdy teacups and saucers, poured in milk and a teaspoon of sugar without enquiring whether Miss Logan took them, then poured them both a cup of hot, strong tea.

'Get that down yer an' then I'll show yer the 'ouse.'

'Is it far, Mrs Huggett?'

'Next door.'

Watched furtively by several of her neighbours from behind
their clean net curtains, for this was an orderly neighbourhood,
Mrs Huggett led Gilly out through the front door on to the
narrow pavement, the bit in front of her house evidently
scrubbed, produced a key and unlocked the door of the house
next to hers. The house was a replica of Mrs Huggett's only the
other way round. It was plainly furnished. A parlour with two
stuffed armchairs, a sofa, an empty cabinet, a small fireplace
set in pretty tiles and a rag rug similar to the one in Mrs
Huggett's kitchen. The kitchen held only the bare essentials, a
well-scoured pine table with two ladder-back chairs, another
rag rug and a dresser with nothing on the shelves. There was a
small scullery behind which contained a sink and led out into a
tiny back yard next to Mrs Huggett's. Gilly had time to
consider that the handcart might just fit in it. At the end
was a privy whose door was firmly shut but Gilly was prepared
to believe it would be as clean as everything else this woman
came into contact with.

At the top of the narrow uncarpeted staircase were two
bedrooms. In each was a double brass bed, the warm, golden
shine of the finials lighting up the rather dark rooms. On each
was a bare striped mattress and against the wall a set of
pinewood drawers. There was nothing else apart from the
plain cotton curtains at the window. Even the floors were bare
boards, well scrubbed, of course, and smelling of disinfectant.
Clean, neat and with only the basics. Gilly was vastly relieved,
for what was in the house would do very well. They would need
to buy bedding, pots and pans, crockery, cutlery, but the very
cheapest would suffice. Mam would be safe here and she had a
feeling that Mrs Huggett would make a very good neighbour.

'How much is the rent, Mrs Huggett?' she asked as they
came out into the quiet street and Mrs Huggett carefully locked
the door behind her.

'Well, seein' as 'ow it's furnished I charge six bob a week.

Now I wouldn't say this ter everyone but I took ter yer mam and you seem a likely sort of a lass . . .' She hesitated a moment. 'Will yer be workin'?' It seemed she was not about to let her property go to the unemployed who might get behind with the rent.

'Oh yes, I shall be self-employed and then Jem has a good wage.'

Mrs Huggett pursed her lips and stood for a moment on the doorstep. 'What d'yer mean, self-employed? P'raps yer'd berrer come in a minnit, lass, an' tell me what yer do. And this Jem yer mention. Where's 'e ter stay till yer mam comes 'ome? I run a decent place, Miss Logan, an' wi' yer mam in 'ospital . . . well, are you an' this Jem ter be 'ere alone, 'cause I'll tell yer now, I don't old wi' it.'

Gilly hesitated, looking confused, because the idea of Jem and herself staying alone at 19 Seymour Street and the implications it might arouse had not occurred to her.

'Well, you see . . .'

Mrs Huggett folded her strong arms beneath her bosom, a warrior defending her castle and her principles. Young men and women, even in her class which was, after all, as decent as any, did not share a roof until they were wed. It was not just the gentry who observed the proprieties.

'When d'yer want ter move in, my lass?'

'Right away, Mrs Huggett. Today, if possible. I shall need to buy bedding and—'

'Then you'll stay wi' me and this Jem can move in to number 19. I usually ask fer a month's rent in advance but seein' as 'ow . . . well, yer in a birr of a pickle an' I know yer mam from . . . so just give me a week's rent now and then your young man—'

'He's not my young man, Mrs Huggett,' Gilly declared hotly. 'He's me and Mam's friend and lodger. His own family is . . . well, being a respectable man who has got on and is wanting—'

'Rightio, lass. I understand.'

'He couldn't stay with them, you see. There were so many of them; nine at the last count and his pa . . . well, he wouldn't work and Jem wanted to prosper but I'm sure—'

'That's all very well but let me say this. I'm not lettin' my 'ouse to an unmarried couple, Miss Logan. This is a decent neighbourhood and the folk in this street are all law-abiding and respectable. So, 'tis up ter you. You can board wi' me at . . . five bob a week, all yer meals an' a clean comfortable bed while yer gerron wi' this self-employed work yer do an' this Jem can live next door on 'is own until yer mam comes out of 'ospital. Now, if that don't suit then yer'd best look elsewhere.'

She put the key in the lock and stepped inside her own front door, looking back enquiringly over her shoulder. 'Well?' she asked.

'Thank you, Mrs Huggett, that will do nicely. I shall be back later this afternoon. I have one or two things to bring, not much for they . . . they didn't leave us much but . . . well, thank you again.'

Mrs Huggett watched the tall, slim figure sway gracefully down Seymour Street, as did the occupants of the other houses that lined it, wondering how she managed that lovely way of walking. As Gilly turned into Bronte Street, which led directly to Brownlow Street, the infirmary and opposite it the Lunatic Hospital, none of them noticed the man who loitered at the London Road end of Seymour Street, a man with a badly scarred face. He did not attempt to follow Gilly, for it was late morning and broad daylight, the streets were crowded and there was a police constable at the far corner.

Pale spring sunshine lay in stripes across the road, filtering through the alleyways that divided it, which led to the backs of the buildings along the road. A broad band of sunlight spread out from Bronte Street, lighting up the piles of horse manure that steamed in the cool air and the barefoot scraps of lads who shovelled it up. When Gilly turned into Brownlow Street she was tempted to walk past the infirmary and sit in Pembroke Gardens next to it to think for a moment about what had happened this morning. There would be a riot of spring flowers, the beds crammed with early peonies, exotic with huge, bowl-shaped flowers that were already open. They had large, handsome leaves which set off to perfection the blooms of white, yellow and red; the smaller shape of polyanthus standing before them; delicate violas, white crocus, blue hyacinths, pink pearl and yellow narcissus with creamy petals and lemon trumpets, and tulips of every shade from white to scarlet. Wooden benches were arranged along the narrow pathway and as she approached the wide steps of the infirmary from one of them rose a tall, powerfully built young man, well dressed, attractive, the sunlight catching his dark hair and turning it almost to chestnut. He had obviously been watching for her. He did not seem to care to wear his hat, but held it in his hand.

She was mounting the steps, joining those who were taking advantage of the afternoon visiting when she heard her name called.

'Miss Logan . . . Gilly . . .' When she turned she was taken aback to see Lucas Barrie climbing the steps behind her. He was smiling, his teeth a white slash in his amber-tinted face and his eyes glinted like silver coins as the sunshine shone directly into them. When he reached her he stood on the step below hers, his hat held to his chest, his face on a level with hers. His smile closed like a fist about her heart and a leap of gladness nearly had her over. In fact he put up a hand to steady her just as though he knew how she felt, for he felt it too.

'Mr Barrie . . . Lucas . . .' she stammered, cursing herself for being so flustered. She was conscious of the hard lines of his body beneath his clothes and the hand he put on her arm was large, blunt-fingered but slender, and his smile was luminous, joyous, heart-stopping.

He turned grave when he saw how it was with her and his strong, handsome face became stern and uncompromising. He took her gloved hand in both of his and she left it there, accepting, trusting, with no attempt to hide what was in her heart and yielding to what she knew was in his. For a fleeting moment she wondered why he was not at the shipyard where Jem had gone early this morning but it did not last, for he was here and she was overjoyed to see him. They had breakfasted together before he and Jem had left for the ferry to take them across the river but it had been a silent meal, constrained, the three of them somewhat of a mismatch as Mrs Collins flitted in and out from the kitchen.

'I came to ask how your mother was, if I may?'

Visitors swarmed past them, tutting at the obstruction they caused, for Gilly seemed to be incapable of moving, speaking even, a small island around which the crowds were forced to part and divert round.

'Perhaps I might come in with you,' he ventured and it was then that she saw he had a small arrangement of lily of the valley in his hand tied up prettily with narrow white satin ribbon. Nothing as ostentatious as he might have brought, for the hothouses of Bracken Hill were crammed with out-of-season flowers and were his for the asking. She knew her mother would love the delicate, sweet-smelling flowers, their graceful stems clothed with pure white bell-shaped blooms, where she might have been overwhelmed by anything more showy.

He waited, still holding her hand, longing for her to speak. There was a sweetness and humour in his firm lips and warmth behind his alert gaze which told her he would only move at her pace, but what was in her mind and heart and soul was reflected in her face and he brought her hand to his lips, uncaring, indeed not noticing the stares of those moving up the steps.

Gilly felt the warmth of his lips on her knuckles and she shivered slightly, a shiver of delight. She wanted to put her other hand up to his cheek, to lift it to his hair, disarranged by the breeze, to smooth it back, but instead she heard herself whisper, 'What is it?' not even knowing what she meant, but he did.

'It's all right, Gilly, you must not be anxious, not about me or how you feel at this moment. You do feel something, don't you?' He leaned forward and smiled tenderly.

She nodded breathlessly, clinging to his hands for fear she might fall. She had begun to tremble but could not put into words what she felt. It was too soon. This was not the place. This had come upon her so quickly. She had felt the pull of his attraction the first time she had met him – was it only last week? – but then her mother had been assaulted and she had had no thought but for her plight. One thing had overlapped another, what she was to wear, the search for the house in Seymour Street, all piling up to cloud her mind, but through it all this man had been shining softly at the edge of her thoughts. She supposed that she had not really been aware of it, not consciously, but now she knew that he had been there, ready to help, unobtrusive, steadying her and Jem, taking care of the practical aspects of everyday living and leaving her free to see to her mam's future, her safety, her comfort, her nursing when she came home from the hospital. He had given them, her and Jem, a haven in which to replenish their strength and in such a self-effacing manner neither of them had given it much thought.

'May I come in with you,' his voice said, but in his eyes shone the words he had not yet spoken. "I want to be with you . . . Let me take the weight of your worries . . . You know my feelings, what I feel for you . . ."

'Of course,' she answered, her voice soft and inclined to falter and her own eyes shone with her emotion. "I feel the same

. . . Is this, can this be love?" unspoken words lying between them. "Oh yes . . . yes, this is love . . . I need you in my life . . ." Cross-currents of emotion but this was not the time nor the place so he put his hand under her elbow and they moved side by side up the steps towards what they knew was soon to happen.

Queenie was sitting up in bed. Knowing she had nothing to wear but the harsh hospital gown she had been put in after her surgery, Mrs Collins had insisted on loaning her a plain lawn nightdress she herself had made. It was edged around the neck and cuffs with fine crochetwork, and one arm had been pinned neatly to the shoulder. Under it her broken arm lay hidden. That morning Mr Jenkins had removed the bandages from round her head and the scars, neatly stitched where Tommy Wilson had slashed her, were revealed in all their obscenity. Her face was badly swollen, her eye which she had lost closed and glued together with some nasty matter. Her hair, lank and still clotted with blood, had been dragged back from her broad forehead, the jagged ends where the nurse had cut it standing up in spikes.

Her mother had not seen her. She was studying her hand which lay on the neatly tucked-in sheet and for a terrible moment Gilly was ready to turn back, for did she want her mother, her dearly loved mam to be seen for the first time like this by a stranger? It would be bound to upset her especially as she was not expecting him. Her appearance would be a shock for her own daughter and she would be dreading it, but she knew Gilly and Jem loved her and would accept it. But this man . . . this man who had her arm in an iron grip as though he knew exactly what was going through her mind and would support her with his own strength, *and Mam,* Gilly recognised that, was unknown to Queenie and might this not upset her hard-fought-for equilibrium?

Queenie turned then and saw them hovering in the doorway

of the ward. Her head began to shake when her one good eye saw the stranger with her daughter, but at once Lucas moved forward, taking Gilly with him. On his face was nothing but gentleness, compassion and another expression which told Queenie why this man was here. His goodness was apparent, as was the kindness in his heart. Yet he was a strong man, arrogant even, with the pride of his class and it was then she saw, as he turned to her daughter, why he was here.

He held Gilly's trembling hand as he led her to the bed and when she began to weep, unable at that moment to control her desolation, he said something in her ear and at once she stiffened her back and lifted her head, for her mam did not want this. Lucas did that for her. No pity, he had said and when she sat on the side of the bed, ignoring Sister Moore's frown of disapproval, she put her arms round her mother and then, with a loveliness that caught at Lucas Barrie's throat, kissed the scars on her face and then held her in her arms. He stood at the end of the bed, allowing mother and daughter to cling together. He himself had been appalled at the ruin of Queenie Logan's face but his love for her daughter kept him steady, as she must not see the horror in him.

They talked then, quietly, Queenie and Gilly, and when Queenie looked over her daughter's shoulder he smiled and held out the flowers to her.

'This is Lucas, Mam. Lucas Barrie,' Gilly said, turning to him, her smile lighting her face and Queenie saw how it was with them and her heart shrivelled in her breast.

16

The stallholders at St John's Market did not recognise her as the daughter of Queenie Logan who had on occasion rented a stall there. More often than not Queenie and Gilly had done business in Pedlars' Market in Deane Street, St Martin's Market in Scotland Road, the markets in Cleveland Square and Pownall Square, both in the open air and frequented by a poorer class of person than St John's, who could only afford Queenie's lower prices.

She left the handcart, which she had trundled through the back streets from Duke Street to St John's, at the side entrance to the market in Roe Street. Smiling beguilingly at a porter who stared at her open-mouthed, she asked him if it would be all right if she left it there for a few minutes.

'Wha'?' he quavered. She had left her bonnet in her bedroom at Duke Street and when Mrs Collins's back was turned as she 'knocked up' a few scones for Mr Lucas, since he was very partial to her baking, she had slipped the shawl from its peg on the back door, the one Mrs Collins used when she went shopping, draped it round her own shoulders, eased herself into the yard, opened the gate and pushed the cart into the back alley, praying the wheels would not squeak.

The porter was quite bowled over by her cream-rose loveliness. He couldn't make head nor tail of what she was meant to be, for she spoke in the accents of a lady but was neatly and plainly dressed and her head was covered by a shawl, the garment of a working-class woman.

'I won't be long,' she told him. 'I have one or two purchases to make.'

'Wha'?' he said again, removing his cap and scratching his bright red curly hair, but nevertheless he took up a stance near her cart. When she returned with her first purchase, staggering under three sets of sheets and pillowcases, six blankets, and three pillows, he was still there, stumbling over himself to help her stack them on the handcart.

'Is tharrit?' he asked her, hoping to engage her in conversation, for she was an extremely pretty girl.

'Well, no,' she apologised. 'I have some more . . .'

' 'Ere, Perce,' he called to another porter. 'Watch this lot while I give an' 'and ter this young lady.'

Perce looked somewhat taken aback and indeed quite a group of willing young men had gathered. Before long Gilly had her handcart piled up with bedding, crockery, pots and pans, cutlery, and even a clock and a couple of pretty pictures to hang on the wall for her mam. All at knock-down prices, for her saviour, whose name, he told her hopefully, was Ginger on account of his vivid red hair, was well known in the market and with a wink and a nod at the stallholders, the men as captivated as he was, she did well.

'There's just one more thing, Ginger, if I may call you that?' she told him prettily, smiling inwardly at how easy it was to get the male of the species to do one's bidding.

'Eeeh, girl,' was all he managed to stutter as if really she had no need to ask. He would lie down on the market floor and let her wipe her dainty feet on him, she had only to ask.

'I want some cheap materials, good quality, mind, but cheap.'

'Yer'll need Mrs Fletcher then. She's at back in't corner on account o'she deals wi't those who can't afford flash prices. Bu' she's fair an' 'onest. She goes round ware'ouses an' buys end o' rolls an' such.'

'Thank you, Ginger. I don't know what I would have done without you. You must let me pay you . . .'

He was deeply offended. 'Aay aar, girl, there's no need fer tha'. Glad to 'elp, I were. Now, let's get yer over ter Mrs Fletcher an' then, when yer finished I'll 'elp yer get yer stuff back 'ome.'

No matter how she protested he would not allow her to carry the small rolls of fabric she purchased from Mrs Fletcher's stall. The stall itself looked as though a whirlwind had whisked through the market and played havoc with Mrs Fletcher's materials, but ask her for some particular fabric and with a bit of a rummage and some good-natured muttering she produced whatever Gilly asked for. Nothing fancy, as Gilly knew exactly what she wanted. Dimity, which was a stout cotton, some plain, some printed. Drill, a strong twilled linen. Jaconet, another thin cotton between a muslin and cambric. Foulard, which was a soft, light twilled silk. Gingham and panne, which was a soft silk between a velvet and a satin. A mixture of practical everyday wear and that special Sunday best for women of the middle class who could not afford the smarter more expensive ranges of the Misses Yeoland and their like but who, nevertheless, wished to be elegant. And all in lovely shades from pale dove grey, tawny brown, buttercup yellow, cornflower blue, apple green through to crimson for those of a more adventurous nature. Colours she had seen on fashionable ladies in Bold Street.

'Right, where to, chuck?' Ginger asked cheerfully when the whole lot, bedding, pots and pans, fabrics were all piled up in a tottering tower on the handcart. He gripped the handles firmly and with a wink at his admiring colleagues, turned to Gilly expectantly.

She was mortified! 'No, Ginger, I can't let you push this lot all the way to . . . to my home,' she told him fiercely. 'Not unless you will allow me to pay you for your time. You have

been more than kind but I can manage this from here.' She tried
to take over from him but he merely grinned and began to
trundle the rickety handcart along Roe Street towards Great
Charlotte Street, going in the right direction, as it happened,
and Gilly had no choice but to keep up with him.

'Wheels on this 'ere cart need a birra oil on 'em, chuck,' he
told her, his face, covered with the freckles that seemed to be
the mark of those with hair his colour, split in a wide grin that
told her the minute they got to her place he would have it all
sorted out.

The inhabitants of Seymour Street were highly entertained
when the young woman who'd visited Mrs Huggett's that
morning and looked to be moving in to number 19 came
stepping lightly up the street with a young man pushing a
handcart. She produced a key and opened the door, saying
something to the young man who vanished up the covered
ginnel that ran from the street to the back alley, taking the
handcart with him. What went on at the back of the house they
could not see but the young man, a workman in some sort of
uniform and a cap with a badge on it, came out of the front
door, tipped his cap to the young woman and went whistling up
the street.

Gilly surveyed the pile of her purchases which Ginger had
carried in for her and placed on the kitchen table. She wrapped
herself in a large sacking apron, which she had bought that
morning, and from the small brick lean-to at the side of the
privy where Mrs Huggett had told her she could help herself to
kindling, wood and coal, she brought in the makings of a fire
and soon had one burning brightly in the fireplace. She filled
the kettle from the tap over the shallow sink in the scullery and
placed it in the heart of the fire. While she had been at the
market she had bought tea, milk, sugar, bacon, potatoes, a loaf
of bread and a pound of best butter, food for the meal she
meant to cook for her and Jem when he got back from the

shipyard. She would make up Jem's bed but would store the rest of the bedding ready for when Mam came home.

She was actually humming when someone hammered on the door. She was so startled she almost dropped the kettle from which she was just pouring boiling water into the teapot in readiness for a cup of tea. Perhaps it was Mrs Huggett, but surely her landlady would not make such a commotion that it seemed the door would come off its hinges.

She opened it slowly, peeping out at her visitor and was astonished when Lucas burst through the doorway with a face on him that was thunderous. She fell back before him, astonished.

'What the hell d'you think you're playing at?' he roared. 'I couldn't believe my ears when Jem said you were moving. He had received a note from you with this address. Are you mad to be wandering alone about the city with those madmen who attacked your mother still on the loose? It's beyond me why you felt the need to leave the safety of my house at Duke Street but I'm afraid I must insist you come back at once.'

All the time he was shouting directly into her face he was forcing her backwards into the kitchen where, on seeing the pleasing fire, the kettle still boiling in its hearth where she had replaced it, the pile of goods on the table, the feeling of *permanence*, he stopped abruptly. Gilly could feel her own fury bubbling up inside her but as yet she could not seem to find the strength to fight back. How dare he feel he had the right to question her actions. How dare he shout at her, order her about as though she were his to direct. How dare he come bursting into *her* house, just as though he had a perfect right to do so.

She did her best to hold in the resentment she felt. To be dignified, as a lady of his class would be, but it was very hard and her expression was icy. He had been very kind, in fact what they would have done, her and Jem, without his help she

couldn't imagine, but that did not mean . . . that did not mean
he could take her over as he seemed to be doing, and when she
had regained her equilibrium she would tell him so.

'So,' he said dangerously, moving further into the room, his
face working with the strength of his emotions which had, for
the moment, got the better of him. After what he had seen done
to her mother he could not bear to think of her where she was
not under his protection. 'Are you to give up this nonsense and
come—'

'Nonsense! Nonsense! What are you talking about? And
who the bloody hell d'you think you are?' she hissed, losing that
layer of breeding Mrs Hunter had given her. 'Laying down the
law and telling me what I should or should not do. I am a grown
woman' – which at her age and in the circumstances under
which she had lived she considered herself to be – 'and I am
quite capable of running my own life without—'

'I won't have it, Gilly.' He could barely speak, so great were
his rage and fear for her. 'There is room in my house and you
will be safe there. I don't know what you intend doing to earn a
living but whatever it is it can be done in Duke Street. Jem can
live here if he wants to but—'

'I go where Jem goes,' she told him flatly.

His face whitened, the rush of furious blood under his skin
ebbing away at the implication of her statement. He seemed to
tower over her, for though she was tall for a woman he was even
taller. His hands clenched at his sides and he looked as though
he would like to hit her into submission.

'And then there is my mother,' she went on. 'She must have
somewhere to live when she is recovered and ready to leave the
hospital. Are you to offer *her* a room at your house? Are you to
fill it with waifs and strays? Your mother would not be best
pleased if you did, I can tell you. Especially the likes of me! She
made it quite plain that—'

'What's my mother got to do with it, I'd like to know?'

'Ask her,' she spat out.

Her chin rose and her lips quivered but before she could prepare herself for the next onslaught he would surely aim at her, his arms rose and dragged her to him, pinioning her own arms to her side. His mouth fell savagely on hers, crushing her lips so fiercely their teeth touched and she could taste blood in her mouth. She felt the strength of him against her body, breast to breast, thigh to thigh and inside her something rose and shouted for the joy of it. Her heart was pounding in her breast and she could feel his beating against hers to the same rapid rhythm. She sagged against him, not with distaste or fury but with delight, with something she had never felt before, which she knew was the female in her responding to the male in him. His lips moved on hers, the fierceness changing to softness, to the velvet touch of intoxication, then moved down to her jawline and along it until they reached her ear where they nibbled and sucked the lobe before returning to her mouth. She responded eagerly, pressing against him, lifting her mouth, which had rested for a second against his throat, back to receive his soft and savage kisses. She made a sound in the back of her throat and he threw back his head in exultation for a moment.

'You feel the same,' he triumphed. 'You love me, say you love me, say it, say it.' His arms loosened their grip, his hands grasped her forearms and began to shake her.

She was dazed, her eyes unfocused with that loveliness that comes when a woman is deep in the pleasures of the flesh and her head wobbled, her glorious hair falling about her in a vivid curtain of copper and gold. He cupped her face and began to kiss it, placing the tender love he felt on her eyelids, her cheeks, her jawline, and finally on her mouth. Her hands rose to grasp his wrists as though to ensure he did not leave go of her and she swayed closer to him.

'My love, my love,' he murmured. 'You really are mine. I

knew it. From the moment we first met I knew it. Dear sweet God, I love you.'

He was a man, a virile and very masculine male who was accustomed to the women in his arms allowing him whatever he asked of them. Paid women, of course, and very occasionally the bored wives of his father's business acquaintances who were eager for a little excitement. A man well used to the lusty pleasures that were always available to him. He had not, until this moment, held a woman in his arms who was not only young but innocent. Untouched. Pure. A woman who had never known the hands of a man on her. He was certain that Jem Wilson, a decent man who also loved this girl, had not dishonoured her. She loved Jem as a sister loves a brother and this was her first encounter with the intimacy and power of love between man and woman, of desire that melted the bones, inflamed the flesh and caused all coherent thought to flee.

He held her unresisting body close, his lips smoothing her jaw, moving beneath it, down to the hollows of her shoulders, pushing aside the neat white collar on her gown. The buttons gave way as though by magic and she began to sigh. He looked about him for somewhere to lay her, for he was beyond thought himself, his whole body concentrated on the next step of this wonder that had come about. The logical conclusion to his love and her response to it. Her pliant young body strained against his, her arms wrapped about his neck and head, their mouths fastened hungrily on one another, hers moist and warm and full. She was a young girl with a serene beauty that delighted him, but suddenly some small voice deep inside him began to gnaw at him and though he did his best not to listen, the voice grew louder and louder. His male body demanded to go on, to satisfy itself as it had always done, to explore and experiment, but she was not that kind of woman and her innocence and trust held him back. *And he loved her!* He was not awfully sure where this was to lead but he did know that until he was absolutely certain that what was in his mind was *right* he must not dishonour her.

He pulled back, his breath ragged, but she clung to him and he had forcibly to remove her arms, dragging them down from his neck.

'Darling, don't . . . don't. I mustn't let you. I love you . . . love you and this, wonderful as it is, must not happen yet. We must wait until . . .'

'What?' Her breath was sweet and warm against his mouth as she tried to cling to him, her senses, her *sense* completely overruled by this magic that had sprung up between them. She had had no idea that it could be so . . . so . . . *beautiful*, this between a man and a woman but now, as he held her away from him she began to realise that he was right. She wanted nothing more than to stay in his arms, to be kissed and . . . and . . . well, whatever else he had in mind but it must not be. Not yet, wondering what she meant by those last two words. She must be by herself for a while, be given space and peace to mull over this wonder, to think what it meant and where . . . where it was to go. She was aware that Lucas was an honourable man and she was also aware that had he not stopped when he did she would have gone on and on, swept away by her vulnerable woman's body and the feelings he had aroused in it. She loved him, oh yes, she loved him, she had known that even before today, but she was also sensible enough to realise that women from her class and gentlemen from his did not marry. She wanted to lie down with him, anywhere, here on the well-scrubbed floor of Mrs Huggett's rented kitchen but her practical mind, trained by Queenie, knew there was more to a relationship than the submitting of two bodies one to the other. She must have time. Lucas must have time, for though he said he loved her, she hardly knew him. *She hardly knew him* and besides that there were the plans she had made which were already being put into practice. Wait, her balanced young mind told her.

He smiled at her, then leaned forward to place a gentle kiss on her parted lips. His hand rose and caressed her cheek. 'Don't look so serious, my sweet love. We love each other, let us be content with that for now; in the meanwhile, run upstairs and get your things while I call a cab. Leave a note for Jem to tell him where you are or . . .'

He stepped back hastily, for the expression on her face told him that though he thought he had won her round to his way of thinking and that she was willing to come and live under the protection of his roof until he had . . . well, sorted out what they were to do, it was not so. Her face had changed from sweet acceptance to one of furious indignation and he was convinced she might strike him in her anger.

'You can just go to the devil, Lucas Barrie, and take your offer of a room at your place with you. Just because you kissed me and . . . and . . . don't think you own me. This is my house and I'd be obliged if you'd leave it at once and don't come back until you're invited. You're so bloody high-handed, you men, ordering women about as though we were—'

'Stop it, Gilly, stop it at once.' His face was as maddened as hers. 'God in heaven, you'd think I was asking you to . . . to . . .' He couldn't think of anything bad enough to say. 'I love you.' His voice was stiff. 'I want to protect you against what happened—'

'Give over. I've lived among the most degraded and evil men on this planet and I—'

'That's what I mean. You need looking after and—'

'Jem will look after me.'

'Like he did your mother, you mean.' Though he had not meant to say it, his voice was contemptuous and he knew he had made a horrendous mistake. She might not love Jem as she did him, but he was very dear to her and it had not been Jem's fault that her mother had been so abused.

She drew herself up and the blaze of golden copper in her

eyes became a flat, muddy brown. She lifted her head, then, with a stiff movement that was not at all like her usual graceful stride, she pulled her dress about her, moved to the street door and opened it.

'Get out, get out of my house and until you're invited back don't come again.'

He strode angrily past her into the street, beyond coherent thought as she was, his face the colour of lead and his eyes the same. Without a word he almost broke into a run as he made for the corner. They did not speak again. She banged the door to behind him, almost having it off its hinges, then, sinking down behind it to her haunches, she put her arms about her knees, rested her head on her arms and began to weep broken-heartedly.

She was cutting out the first of the gowns she was going to make when Jem knocked on the door. There were no signs of the anguished tears she had shed and Jem was surprised and pleased with the warmth of her greeting.

'Oh, come in, come in, Jem and see our new home. I've made your bed up and after we've had something to eat we'll go and see Mam and tell her all about it. I've put a couple of pictures on the wall. You know how Mam loves pictures and Mrs Huggett says she will help with the nursing. She's given me a spare key for you but she says I must sleep at her house until Mam comes home. She's very respectable, Jem, and wouldn't hear of us being alone and even . . . Oh, Jem, isn't it wonderful? So far away from Rose Alley and look, I've started making one of the gowns I've planned for . . . for . . .'

Her face was flushed with something, excitement, Jem supposed and her eyes were as bright and glowing as an amber gemstone. For some reason he felt a frisson of anxiety, he didn't know why, then it receded. Of course she was excited. This was the first proper home she had ever had. A decent home in a respectable neighbourhood and she was like a child playing at doll's house, making up beds and hanging pictures. She had set out crockery on the dresser, plain white dinner plates, side plates, soup bowls, cups and saucers on the lower two shelves and on the top one an assortment of pans. There was even a vase with a bunch of daffodils arranged in it on the window bottom. The fire burned brightly, reflecting on the white walls and vivid red cushions on the two chairs were a splash of colour, vying with the rag rug which it seemed Mrs Huggett had bestowed on them as a moving-in present. It seemed Mrs Huggett had taken a liking to Gilly, as she had taken a liking to Gilly's mam and, apart from the fact that their landlady insisted Gilly slept in her house until Queenie came home, he was prepared to accept her friendship for his womenfolk. That is how Jem Wilson saw Queenie and Gilly. His womenfolk. His! Queenie had been his surrogate mother ever since he was seven years old and Gilly was his love and the one he would marry.

It seemed Jem's world was complete! He had a wonderful job which would one day bestow on him the title of Marine Engineer. He was learning his trade and when he had passed his examination and had the necessary qualifications he would be his own man. Set up in the business of designing and building boats on his own and be ready to marry his Gilly. His plans were firm in his mind and it did not occur to him that Gilly, who had loved him since she was a nipper, might have plans of her own. When she told him of them over their simple meal, and showed him the patterns, the materials, the scissors, the tape measure folded neatly away in a piece of spotless muslin, he was speechless; speechless and horrified.

'But you can't do that,' he floundered. 'You need . . . well, finance and . . .'

'I have it, Jem. Mr Field is to lend me the money, all on a sound financial footing, of course, paying interest on the loan and—'

'But . . .'

'I know it's a bit of a shock but I've had it in mind for a long time, Jem. While I was at Mrs Hunter's and learning the ways of a lady I was already planning—'

'But what about me?'

She looked surprised, leaning her elbows on the table over which she had thrown a snowy white cloth. She peered into his stormy face, bemused and disappointed, for she had expected some show of enthusiasm, or at least *interest* in what for her was to be the start of a brand-new life. He had his career that promised him so much and which would lead to a wonderful future, so why should she not put her own talents to the same, but different future for herself? Mam would never have to work again, indeed it was doubtful Mam *could* ever work again, for Gilly was well aware that folk would not want to look into the ruin of Queenie Logan's face. Half blind, perhaps forced to wear a black patch like some pirate, Mam needed a place where she could be useful and safe and not have to see the avid looks on people's faces. She would look after her and Jem and be as happy as a skylark in this, her new place.

'Jem?' she questioned softly, reaching out to take his hand but he snatched it away.

'We'd best get our things on if we're to reach the hospital before visiting time's over,' he said shortly.

She sighed, her heart, which had already taken a terrible beating that day, aching in her breast.

17

In Remington Place, a narrow street just off Bold Street, in an airy workroom at the top of the building, Gilly sat down slowly in the straight-backed chair before the work table. She placed her hands palm down on its scrubbed pine top and looked about her. There were two other tables like the one at which she sat, both bare, waiting for the industry that was soon to start, and two more chairs. Lining the room from the sloping ceiling to the floor, except for one wall that consisted of a large window, were shelves on which every kind of fabric, in every imaginable shade of the rainbow, was neatly folded. Above her were more windows let into the sloping roof and above that nothing but the arch of the sky. If she stood on a chair she might see chimneys, thousands of chimneys, house chimneys and ones that poured forth smoke from the hundreds of factories. The sky was a hard blue, but the pall from the chimneys turned it to a yellow grey through which the sun could only faintly glimmer. Standing sentinel about the perimeter of the room were tailor's dummies, patiently passing the hours until the day and their futures would start in this new endeavour like dutiful employees waiting on the command of her who employed them.

The light, even so diffused by the smoky pall that hung over the city on six days a week, fell across the table and on to the face of the girl who sat so quietly, lighting her skin to pale honey and illuminating her tawny eyes with the luminous quality of an amber gem. Her abundant copper-gold hair was brushed smoothly back from her forehead and gathered into a pretty grey chenille net at the crown of her head, the grey perfectly matching the fine wool of her gown. The gown was very plain as befitted her employment, with a high, round neck and long, tight sleeves. The bodice fitted her young breasts and neat waist like a second skin, and the skirt flared out into fullness, under the hem of which was a glimpse of the lace on her white petticoat. She smelled fragrantly of lavender.

It was a bitter day and she was two months shy of her eighteenth birthday. Her thoughts, as she waited for Anne to arrive, carried her back over the past few months.

Mr Field had been taken aback by her first request for a loan, looking beyond her for the strong woman who was her mother and with whom, over the past years, he could not remember how many, he had done business. And now here she was again. The girl! Not in a big way, of course, for where gentlemen of the standing of Herbert Barrie or John Hughes and other success-ful men of business dealt in thousands, guineas that is, Mrs Logan conducted her small affairs in shillings and pence. Nevertheless she had a nice little account at his bank which, though small, earned her a respectable interest.

'A loan, Miss Logan? What had you in mind? Your mother has monies in an account here and if you needed . . .'

Miss Logan wasted no time in telling him. Her mother was to leave hospital within a few weeks and as soon as she was able would come to see him and instruct him to release what was in her account to her daughter but it was not enough. Miss Logan intended to open her own business and with the loan, which she confidently expected Mr Field to advance her, and which she would pay back in instalments, and what her mother was to extend to her, she had put a small down payment on premises in Remington Place where she meant to set up as a dressmaker. A seamstress. Not to cater to the social élite of Liverpool, though that would come in the future, but to ladies of the middle classes who wished to be as smart and elegant as those of a social status above them but could not afford the prices of the Misses Yeoland and others of their standing. She knew fashion and was able to assess what colours, what styles suited the ladies she studied and whom she had encountered in the smarter streets of Liverpool. She said so to the bank manager and Mr Field was inclined to agree she knew what she was talking about as he surveyed her over his desk. She was dressed in a grey gown, a simple gown that became her perfectly and so exquisitely fitted it might have just come from some Paris couturière, and not from Anne Barrie. It had a crinoline, which he knew from his wife and her irritation with its width, was the height of fashion, and it did away with the dozens of petticoats necessary to hold out one's skirts. Miss Logan's was wide but not so wide that it could not squeeze through his office door and she managed it gracefully. The huge cage did away with the need of corsets, too, since the skirt made even the biggest waist look small! Though trimmings were the thing, or so his wife told him. Miss Logan wore none.

She smiled at him. 'You are looking at my skirt, Mr Field,' she said, causing him some embarrassment. 'But let me say that the crinoline has had its day and by the end of the year it will be bustles at the back and . . . Oh dear, I'm so sorry. I get carried away, but already in Paris and London, according to the magazines I receive, these fashions have taken hold and I mean to introduce the ladies of Liverpool . . . there I go again boring you with the frivolities of ladies' fashions.' She leaned forward eagerly. 'So, Mr Field, will you help me with this business I mean to set up?'

She sat back again in her chair as though embarrassed at her own outburst and her bonnet, which Mr Field thought must be of the very latest design, dipped intriguingly over her forehead. It was of straw, lying flat on her head so that her chignon was revealed beneath the brim at the back and was tied beneath her chin into a bow with wide ribbons of tawny satin. Around the brim was a ribbon to match. She wore no jewellery and her boots were of a serviceable and sturdy black leather. Apart from these last she might have passed for a lady of fashion, even of great wealth, for such would have worn boots dyed to match the colour of her gown.

'If we are to do business, Miss Logan, which I hope we will, I must speak to your mother. You are no more than a girl and as such to put money, quite a good deal of money into your hands would be taking a great risk. I know Mrs Logan and I admire her for what she has done over the past years. If she is to share in your venture then I will consider it. Bring her to see me when she is recovered.' He too sat back, considering the matter concluded.

Gilly lifted her head imperiously. 'I cannot wait for that, Mr Field. It will be many weeks before my mother will be able to get about. Her face was . . . was badly injured and it will take time to heal. The landlord of the premises I wish to rent is demanding three months in advance and I have not got such a substantial sum. If you will not let me have it now I must go elsewhere. Probably to a money lender which I am loath to do.'

Mr Field looked horror-stricken for a brief moment, then cleared his throat and fiddled with his cravat. She was an exceedingly lovely young woman and her defiance had brought a soft flush to her silken cheek and a flash to her eyes which was very appealing. By God, he thought, this young woman will go a long way. She has only to lift her head and fix a man with those magnificent eyes and what chance has he? And she was her mother's daughter. He had found Queenie Logan to be honest, scrupulous and clear-headed and though her account would hardly be missed should she withdraw it, he found he did not wish her to do so which she might well do if he refused her daughter.

He studied Gilly Logan for several moments, his eyes steady on hers, then he smiled.

'Very well, Miss Logan. I will advance the first quarter's rent but anything else you may need in the way of fitting out this shop of yours must come from your mother's account. Do you understand? This will give you three months to find your first customers and begin to show a profit. Bring Mrs Logan to see me as soon as she is recovered enough and we will discuss it further.'

He stood up and so did she. They shook hands in the manner of gentlemen concluding business. She smiled brilliantly and again he marvelled at her beauty. She bowed her head in thanks, turned and moved gracefully to the door. As she opened it and made to go through with her wide skirts, she turned to smile again as though to tell him that next time she would be in a more up-to-date gown. He began to laugh.

Her next visit an hour later was to Mrs Hunter's School for Girls in Williamson Square. The hallway was as usual bustling with girls from five-year-olds to those who were ready to leave at the age of eighteen. Miss Jones, who happened to be on her way to Mrs Hunter's office, stopped dead in astonishment and those behind her, two little girls on their way to ballet class, walked into the back of her, almost knocking her over, much to her annoyance. But she was too busy glaring at Gilly as though it were her fault, to turn and berate them.

'Yes?' she enquired shortly, as though Gilly were a total stranger, shooing the girls past her impatiently.

'Might I see Mrs Hunter, if you please?'

'Mrs Hunter is far too busy—'

'I would like a word with her, Miss Jones, and if you would tell her I won't keep her long.'

'I happen to know . . .' Miss Jones began angrily, but Gilly drew herself up and without another word turned down the corridor in the direction of Mrs Hunter's office with a squawking Miss Jones behind her. Gilly knocked on the door and without waiting for an answer walked straight into Mrs Hunter's office where the lady was sitting before her fire drinking a cup of chocolate. She turned and to Miss Jones's chagrin, smiled with delight when she saw Gilly in the doorway. Hastily she put down her cup and stood up, lifting her hands to take Gilly's.

'Gilly, my dear Gilly, how lovely to see you, come in, come in and sit down.' Turning to Miss Jones who hovered, thunderstruck, in the doorway, she told her shortly to bring another cup for Gilly, dismissing her as though she were a scullery-maid.

The cup and saucer were brought by a kitchen-maid, for Miss Jones apparently considered it beneath her dignity to wait on the girl who was a student at the school, especially one with Gilly Logan's background. Miss Jones had not forgotten the mother, the imperious but terribly common woman who had called herself *Mrs* Logan though there had never been a sign of a Mr Logan. Mrs Hunter had favoured the girl, in Miss Jones's opinion, and now here she was about to sip hot chocolate in Mrs Hunter's study as though she were the daughter of a good family. She would have loved to linger at the door to hear what the little strumpet was saying but reluctantly she moved away to her own small office on the first floor.

'Now, my dear, first tell me how your mother is,' Mrs Hunter began solicitously. 'Anne Barrie conveyed to me the news of her . . . accident. No details, since she seemed to be somewhat vague about what happened but I have wondered . . .' Mrs Hunter looked suitably sympathetic, waiting for Gilly to supply those details, but Gilly had not come here to discuss her mother but to explain why she must give up her schooling so suddenly and earn a living and Mrs Hunter might be of help to her there. She was the headmistress of a highly thought-of school for young ladies and if she was to mention, casually of course, to their parents that one of her former pupils was to open a smart but not expensive outfitters where the very latest Paris and London designs might be purchased it would give her a good start. She meant to advertise in the *Liverpool Mercury* and, since Remington Place was a good address off Bold Street, she had high hopes.

'My mother is recovering well, Mrs Hunter and should be home very soon. We have moved from . . . from Rose Alley to Seymour Street where I shall have a sewing room to do local work. I intend to cater not just to the middle classes or even higher, but to the woman who has a husband in decent work and can afford to pay a small amount to look well. But that is not really why I came. I wanted to thank you for what you have done for me. Many ladies would have turned my mother away when she came seeking an education for me but you recognised something in her and helped her to realise her dream. I am not a lady and never will be but you have shown me that even a woman of my class can make something of herself given a helping hand. You have given me that helping hand and at the same time added something to my mother's life that has brought her a great deal of satisfaction. I'll bring her to see you when she is fully recovered.'

'I should enjoy meeting Mrs Logan again, Gilly, and of course, you must still visit me from time to time. I might mention to the mothers of my young girls who grow so quickly that one of my former pupils can accommodate them at reasonable prices. They are not all fabulously wealthy and some of them have four or five daughters to dress,' saying exactly what Gilly had hoped to hear.

'Thank you, Mrs Hunter. If it had not been for you I—'

'No, no,' protested the headmistress. 'It was not me who set you on the path you have travelled and will continue to travel, but your mother. A remarkable lady.'

Gilly rose to her feet, her eyes misting with the tears that Mrs

Hunter's words had induced. She looked round the pleasant room. The fire snapped and sent fiery sparks up the chimney and a rosy glow about the room. There was a vase of peonies on a small table, pale pinks and a deeper red mixed with greenery. On the walls hung small prints of rustic scenes and the curtains at the windows moved gracefully in a small breeze which blew through the fractionally opened window, for despite the warmth Mrs Hunter was a fiend for fresh air. Everywhere winked and glowed and twinkled, shining on brasses and gilt, the silver chocolate pot and the rich pattern of the carpet.

One day I'll have a room like this for my mam to sit in, she thought as she took Mrs Hunter's hand then, impulsively, leaned forward and kissed her cheek, which was soft and wrinkled, crumpled like that of a fading rose.

'Thank you, Mrs Hunter,' she said.

'Good luck, my dear, and please don't forget to come and bring your mother. She was a brave woman to confront me in this school of mine but what a wonderful result her bravery had.'

And so she looked about her at the big room at the top of the building which waited expectantly for its life to begin, for those who would create the lovely garments she meant to design. She would be the only seamstress to start with, since she could not afford to employ the girls she would eventually need but Anne would be here soon, for Lucas's sister intended to be part of this new endeavour. She couldn't sew, at least only a bit of embroidery, she said, which Gilly knew to be exquisite and might be worked somehow into the garments that were to be brought to life in this very room. Perhaps underwear, night-gowns, even baby clothes if she could expand to it because there were other rooms, empty rooms for now, in the tall building that might be incorporated into the business. There were hundreds of dressmakers in Liverpool, all catering to different classes of women. A first-rate house drew its clientele from the top echelon of the gentry, even the nobility, for many of them attended court up in London. A second-rate house such as the Misses Yeoland attracted those who were wealthy but not in the same class as the first. Both these types of house did not make up the skirts of their dresses on the premises but put them out to be made up by freelance needlewomen. Third- and fourth-rate houses made up the whole garment in their own workrooms, dressing the wives of tradesmen and me- chanics, and it was these that Gilly was aiming for. *To start with*. She had acquired on hire purchase a second-hand sewing machine, made nearly ten years ago by a man called Singer on which she could run up a cheap dress in a quarter of the time it took to hand-sew. Her ability lay in the design and the cut and the gowns she had already created were a testament to her cleverness. She had also fashioned several hats and bonnets in the latest style, buying the cheapest chip and straw from the market and trimming them with her own simple designs.

The premises were entered by climbing wrought-iron steps to a wide arcade along which other shops were situated. There was a hatter, a shoemaker, a corset maker, a furrier, a photo- graphic portrait establishment, all high class and frequented by the quality of Liverpool, which was why the rent was so high on Gilly's premises. Her shop front was small with a bow window and a newly painted door that led into the shop which was not large, since her mother's money and what Mr Field had loaned her did not allow for luxuries. She and Jem had painted the walls a tranquil and delicate shade of duck-egg blue, even in the workshop because she wanted her seamstresses, when she had them, to have a calm place in which to work. The tables were high enough to avoid the ache in the spine that was a sewing girl's lot, with chairs and footstools. There was an ironing room ready for the pressing and goffering that were part of the trade.

Downstairs, where her customers first entered her shop,

were small velvet chairs in a darker shade of blue, tables on which the latest fashion magazines would lie to tempt what she hoped would be her clientele and at the back of the shop behind a rich blue velvet curtain was a tiny kitchen where hot chocolate, coffee or tea might be made to tempt those who wanted to sit and chat, perhaps with each other or even with Miss Logan herself, or to peruse the magazines. Even if they bought nothing they had seen what was on offer and would surely return.

Her bow window held two lovely gowns against a background of cream velvet. One was in a rich satin in a colour between peach and the palest grey depending on which way the light fell on it. Round the low neck and edging the short sleeves were sewn hundreds of tiny crystals, falling in a narrow cascade to the hem. There was a tiny reticule and satin slippers to match, a perfect combination for an evening. The second gown was of the finest wool, the colour that of the poppies that grew during the summer in the fields about the town. Again it was simple, but with the added style of the bustle, the fabric drawn up at the back into a pleasing fall. On a small placard in an elegant copperplate written by Anne were the prices of the gowns, which astounded those who ventured to look in the window, for fashion houses did not advertise their prices. This practice, in Gilly's opinion, frightened off the woman who had not a great deal to spend and did not dare to cross the threshold. The evening gown, made to measure, was four and a half guineas, the day dress twenty-nine shillings and six pence! The shoes and reticule were extra, of course, and the discreet sign in the corner of the window informed the customer that there were even cheaper garments to be had tailormade. She meant to change the window display every day in the hope that the ladies of Liverpool, high and low, would take a walk along the arcade to see what *Gillyflower's* had on show.

She thought of her mam now, despite her poor sight which

meant she could no longer conduct her business with her handcart, as happy as a mother cat in a new basket placed in front of a fire, ready to purr at the slightest provocation. They had brought her home from the hospital with strict instructions from Mr Jenkins that she must be brought back every four weeks so that he could check up not only on her healing wounds but on her state of mind, for if any woman was justified in losing her reason after what had happened to her it was Queenie Logan. Her face was horribly scarred, left puckered and ridged despite the doctor's careful stitching, each cheek split from eye to chin, the left eye no more than a hollow where Mr Jenkins had been forced to remove the eyeball. Her arm was still in a splint and she walked painfully but she was longing to get 'home' meaning the little house in Seymour Street which Gilly had described to her. She had, of course, seen it but not as it was now that Gilly and Jem had made it into a proper home. Mrs Huggett, who took a great deal of interest in the young couple, had helped, diffidently passing things on to them that she said she no longer had a need for. Several rather good blankets, a rag rug she had made from old cut-up bits of clothing to go before a fire and since she only had one fire this might as well go before theirs. There was an old tin bath, a rather hideous ornament of a dog and a cat entwined and other objects that were dear to her but which she knew would have a good home with Gilly and Jem. She had called them by their Christian names from the start, since to her they were no more than bairns and besides, she had taken a great fancy to Gilly and was sorry to see her leave when her mam came home.

What a day that had been. The cab they had ordered stopped at number 19 and, with a solicitous arm about her, Jem had almost lifted Queenie from it. The whole street seemed to be out to welcome her on that warm end of summer day, for it had got about that their new neighbour had been in a terrible accident and they wanted a scen at her. They weren't exactly sure what had happened and Flo Huggett, who would know, wasn't saying, but she was whisked over the doorstep before any of them caught more than a glimpse of a woman in a shawl who seemed to be wearing an eye-patch. Flo was there, and Mrs Logan, whose name they had learned, had her lovely daughter by her side and that was all they saw of her that first day!

But Queenie was not one to lurk indoors and hide her ruined face and though the neighbours had gasped in dismay when they first caught sight of her after several weeks when she came out to donkey-stone her doorstep, as they all did, she had smiled and shouted, ''Ow do,' to Mrs O'Reilly across the road who was doing the same, and they all got used to her and her eye-patch. In fact they barely noticed it in time, for she was a kindly soul who, though she wasn't forever traipsing in and out of their houses, would do anyone a good turn.

She and Flo Huggett got on like a house on fire, as they were strangely alike in their outlook on life: clean to the point of obsession, honest as the day is long, stubborn as mules when they believed in something that was important to them. Neither of them was generous with their affections except for the two people, three if you counted Jem, who had made their world. One was Gilly Logan, the other had been Huggett who had died young. They had no patience with lazy layabouts and both had a sharp, faintly bitter sense of humour. Sensing kindred spirits, they had taken to one another at once.

Now Gilly walked towards the window overlooking the roofs that soared about them. It had rained in the night and then frozen and the tiles gleamed like ebony in the bit of sunshine that touched them. She sighed deeply with satisfaction, because she knew somehow that what she was about to do, starting today, would be a success. How could it not be when her determination, the stubborn streak and strong will she had inherited from her mother, surged through her, making her fingers tingle as they itched to start the future.

There was a rustle of starched petticoats at the door and she turned to smile at Anne who was dressed, not by the Misses Yeoland as she had been in the past, but by the new dressmaker and milliner at Gillyflower's in a rich pink trimmed with silver grey, her fair curls doing their best to escape from beneath her cream straw hat.

She smiled, her silvery grey eyes narrowing. It was Lucas's smile and Gilly felt her heart break a little, for it was many months since that day when he had left her at Seymour Street and not once had he been near her.

'Are you ready to unlock the door?' were the first words Anne spoke.

'Are you?'

'Yes.'

They took a deep breath and, turning, began to descend the stairs, one behind the other.

18

The tinkle of the doorbell lifted both their heads and they turned to look at each other in what appeared to be wonderment. Anne had jumped as the bell sounded, pricking her finger, which she put in her mouth at once, for to get blood on the petticoat she was embroidering would be a disaster. Gilly snapped the pencil she had been sketching with, working on designs she meant to make up and place temptingly in her window against the draped cream velvet background. They both turned to stare at the door leading to the stairs.

'Oh Lord,' Anne whispered and Gilly knew she did not mean the possible mark on her sewing but the distant noise of the doorbell which had sounded for the very first time.

'Oh Lord,' she said again and stood up in agitation, turning in a circle as though her whirling mind could not decide where she should go.

'It's all right, Anne,' Gilly said soothingly, though she felt far from all right herself. She must run down the stairs and enter her *salon* as Anne grandly called it and attend to whoever had entered her shop. Please, dear Lord, let it be a customer, someone who wants to buy one of my gowns, for if something didn't sell soon she would have a shop full of outfits, all crammed together on padded hangers and no materials to make more, although there seemed little point in sewing any more.

Anne followed her downstairs, so closely she was in danger of treading on the hem of Gilly's frilled train which fell from her bustle, but by the time they reached the door that led into the salon they had both regained control of themselves, moving slowly into the smart, pleasant little shop, smiling in readiness for whoever had entered, noting automatically that everything was in order, dusted that morning by Gilly herself, her pattern books and fashion magazines spread neatly on the tables, the blue velvet chairs arranged so that customers might take their ease as they consulted her, or Anne, on the cut of a gown, the colour of it, the design, the occasion for which it was to be made up and anything else they might have to say. Her shop window sparkled – cleaned by herself with vinegar – in the first of the spring sunshine and standing between the two lovely dresses in the window was a delicate arrangement of lily of the valley. Bonnets were perched on plaster heads, set on shelves that Jem had put up and painted, shawls were draped across chairs, there were displays of fans, embroidered gloves made by Anne's clever fingers, lace caps and collars, again designed and made by Anne and easily seen by anyone passing the pretty bow window. Parasols and beaded reticules, all so lovely and *clever*, and yet not one garment, not one bonnet or parasol had been sold.

There was a young girl standing in the shop, hesitant, shy, inclined to back away as though her own presumption in entering this wonderland alarmed her. A working-class girl with a shawl about her head and a much patched skirt, black boots, but clean, neat, and somehow, though Gilly was not sure how, familiar. She stood by the door and as Gilly and Anne entered she put her fingers on the handle ready, it seemed, for a quick getaway. Her shawl slipped, revealing her hair and as soon as Gilly saw it she knew who she was. It was a bright, carroty red.

'Please, do come in,' she said, as though the girl were a valued customer while Anne stared in surprise, for it appeared to her that this girl was not, as they had hoped, about to order one of their gowns.

The girl let go of the door handle but did not come any closer. 'Our Ginger sent me,' she said in her nasal Liverpool accent. 'I can sew,' she added simply. 'Yer remember our Ginger?' she asked hopefully.

Oh yes, Gilly remembered their Ginger, for had it not been for his help and guidance she would not have achieved what she had. Lacking Jem, at work each day in the shipyard across the water, she would have been hard pressed to find Mrs Fletcher who had provided all the materials with which she made up her gowns. Mrs Fletcher had taken a great interest in Gilly's endeavour, going out of her way to search out factories and warehouses who let her have their ends of rolls, fabrics that had not sold as they had hoped since most had a slight flaw, perhaps not obvious to the uninitiated but reducing their value and selling power. Rich gisele velvet, barathea, faille, Ottoman satin, a rich shaded satin embroidered with white flowers, algerine, a twilled shot silk, satin veloute, rich as velvet and as supple as muslin, sultana, a mixture of silk and mohair, poult de soie, satin merv, shantung and the more durable patterned cotton, tweed, gingham linsey-woolsey and marcella, as these would make up into outfits for the woman who longed for smartness and style but at a price she could afford. Colours of the rainbow such as garnet, poppy, wheat, rose, apple blossom, gold, plum, heather, greengage and honey all shimmered about the walls of the workroom. Although Gilly had read that Frederick Worth, who came from Lincolnshire and became a Parisian dressmaker, was a rude little man who would dress no one unless they had been presented to him by some important personage, she had seen his designs and dreamed of watching his success in the fashion world. And Ginger had been her tireless helper in all this. It was Ginger who had introduced her to Mrs Fletcher – who now allowed Gilly to accompany her to her source of fabrics – and it was Ginger who delivered the heavy rolls to the shop in Remington Place.

'Yes, I know Ginger but what—'

'Me name's Nell Goodwin, ma'am. I allus wanted ter sew, ter mekk lovely things, burr I never got no further than Sampsons sweat shop at back o' Chapel Street. Bent over a sewing machine fer twelve hours a day in bloody awful conditions . . . eeh, I'm sorry, me mam don't like me ter swear burrit were enough ter mekk a saint say summat bad. Anyroad I've bin lookin' round fer somewhere ter go but all of 'em want a premium o' thirty pounds at least an' I've not gorrit an' neither 'as me mam. I'd work fer nowt, Miss Logan, if yer'd learn me. Me mam's willin' ter feed me an' I could live at 'ome. I'm sixteen an' a good girl an' our Ginger – 'e's me brother, see – said 'e'd 'elp out wi' a few bob an' then if—'

'You're Ginger's sister?'

'Yes, Miss Logan,' the girl said eagerly, 'an' if yer'd give me a chance, p'raps let me tekk summat, a scrap o' material what's not valuable to yer, I'd mekk it up at 'ome an' fetch it in't mornin' ter show yer wharr I could do. I'd not let yer down, 'onest.'

Gilly looked helplessly at Anne who looked helplessly back. Anne knew that though she was very willing she was of absolutely no help to Gilly apart from the exquisite embroidery she did. And then there was her mother. Rose Barrie was incensed every time she sent for her younger daughter to be told nervously by the maidservant that Miss Anne had gone out and though she knew perfectly well where she had gone, against all her vigorous and Herbert's half-hearted wishes, there seemed to be nothing she could do about it, short of locking the girl in her bedroom. There was one consolation to be had and that was her son's loss of interest in the Logan girl, which was indeed a blessing. For a few months when the mother had been injured Lucas had been involved with the awful family and Rose had been mortified, afraid that he might try to involve the girl in family occasions. It had been bad enough with that young man who had saved the life of Willy Hughes, the fellow John Hughes had taken a fancy to and had educated above his station, but thank goodness Herbert had decided that his son should work beside him in the office. Lucas would be, after all, the senior partner when Herbert and John retired, so it was logical that Lucas should move on to a position of management. The whole thing had thankfully been forgotten. But there was still the worry of Anne's determination to be active in the girl's shop. A shopkeeper! A dressmaker! And when the circle in which Rose Barrie moved became aware of it, how was she to find a suitable husband for her younger daughter? At least Emily was safely married!

It was strange, almost as though some power beyond their ordering had entered the shop with Nell Goodwin, for as they stood there, the three of them, dithering, Gilly could describe it in no other way, over what should be done next, the doorbell tinkled for the second time that morning and a young woman entered the shop, a well-dressed young woman accompanied by a maid who carried a small dog under her arm.

As though something in Nell's mind, and Gilly was forever to marvel at it, told her exactly what her place was, she vanished behind the curtain that led to the tiny kitchen. Anne, with a great show of interest, and following Nell's lead, removed a hat from one of the plaster heads and tried it on, just as though she herself was a customer who had never seen it before, even though she had sewn on the pale gold ribbon that tied beneath her chin. She studied herself in the mirror, then turned to Gilly and casually asked its price.

'But please, do attend to this lady while I browse through your stock, if I may,' she added artlessly.

Gilly moved forward and smiled at the newcomer who, somewhat coolly, returned it.

'I am interested in that cream silk gown you have in the window,' she announced with a drawl, the drawl of the privileged classes which usually meant *money*. 'And that cream straw hat is a wonderful match. Perhaps I might try it on.'

'Of course, but which—' Gilly began.

But the young woman, imperious and almost rude, interrupted her. 'Both, of course, since they match so superbly.'

A customer of her class did not buy tailor-made gowns and just as Gilly was about to tell her that an outfit could be made exclusively for her and by the very next morning, she cut in as though she hadn't a moment to spare. 'I hate all the fuss of fittings and so on, er . . . er . . . I'm afraid I don't know your name . . .'

'Miss Logan.'

'. . . Miss Logan, which my mama deplores but since I have my own money I can please myself. If that gown fits me I shall buy it and then, once you have my measurements in your records I can order from you with no need to waste time at Mama's dressmakers. I like to dress well, you see, but I have neither the time nor the inclination to spend hours in a place like this. My name is Helen Moore and I am involved with the new women's movement led by Mrs Millicent Garrett Fawcett of whom you will have heard. No! How strange,' as both Gilly and Anne looked totally bewildered. 'Well, I don't suppose you are concerned with my pastimes, if you can call them that. Now, you sit down, Marie, and make sure Clover does not—' She stopped speaking abruptly and peered intently at Gilly. 'Do I know you?' she asked. 'I'm sure I've seen you somewhere but I just can't place . . .' She whirled then to Anne, the skirt of her rather chic dress with its wide crinoline dipping like a bell. 'And your face is familiar, too. Do you go to the suffragist meetings, is that it?'

Anne, a pretty little bonnet of dove-grey grosgrain with tiny pearls sewn under the brim on her head, put her hand to her lips in horror, her vivid grey eyes widening to great pools of amazement as she recognised what Miss Moore was talking about.

'Dear God, no,' she gasped. 'My mama would sooner I threw myself into the river than . . .'

Miss Moore sighed. 'Yes, I know, mine is the same but as I am twenty-one and have money from my grandmother, who would throw me in the river herself rather than see me interested in . . . well, never mind, but I seem to know your faces. Both of you.'

From behind the curtain the small, shy figure of Nell appeared. She had discarded her shawl and was wearing a perfectly decent white blouse, beautifully pin-tucked down the front and a snowy white apron which had hung on a hook behind the curtain and covered her patched grey skirt to the hem. She carried a tray bearing a gleaming pot of hot chocolate, a white cup and saucer in bone china so fine it was almost transparent, a sugar bowl and cream jug to match, all set on a white cloth.

'P'raps madam'd like a cuppa chocolate,' she said, placing the tray on a table beside the maid. She poured a cup for Miss Moore. Though she had not been told, she did not bring the maid a drink! Miss Moore reached for the cup and sipped absentmindedly without a word of thanks. One did not notice a serving maid in her society.

Anne came to life after recovering from the shock of realising that this forthright young woman was one of those who thought they, and the rest of the female population, should have the vote. 'Perhaps we all went to school together,' she said. 'Mrs Hunter's School for Young Ladies. I was a pupil there and so was Miss Logan.'

'Really? So was I,' Miss Moore said, losing interest. 'Now, if I may I'll try on that dress and the hat and have a look through some of your stock. Many of my companions in the movement will be glad to hear that they can buy decent gowns at a decent price without going to all the fuss of spending hours in a dressmaker's salon, so I'll pass your name on to them. There is to be a meeting in Manchester with the intention of forming a Manchester society, the women's movement I spoke of, one in Edinburgh, another in Birmingham, so I will need something suitable for those occasions. Something sensible and yet feminine as we must all look our best. We are not trying to ape the men in politics but universal enfranchisement is of the utmost importance.'

The two girls stood in silence, since neither of them had the slightest idea what she was talking about. Gilly read the newspapers and remembered vaguely something that had been written in *The Times* but had taken no interest because it all seemed to be part of another world where women who had nothing better to do interfered in what was essentially a gentleman's concern. They were overwhelmed by this handsome, forthright young woman who spoke casually of travelling to Manchester, perhaps to Birmingham, to attend meetings, to move about the country with only that wisp of a maid to accompany her on business they could neither of them comprehend. They were both women of their times, even if from different levels of society and their destiny in life was to marry, make a home and have children. The only difference between them was that Anne had a father to support her and Gilly had to support herself until she too married and had children, for that was what she, as a woman, was intended for. In the meanwhile she would make her little business successful and then, one day, would probably marry Jem, who was already hinting that they were both old enough for the next step. He was climbing the ladder at the shipyard and his designs for the next ship, a cargo ship that would sail to Australia, had already been approved by Mr Barrie and Mr Hughes.

For a misted moment a strong and uncompromising face swam across her vision. That was how it had been the last time she saw him when she had refused to take refuge at his house in Duke Street. He believed that a woman must allow herself to be sheltered, protected by masculine strength, and as a wife be subordinate to her husband. He would love her, certainly, for she already knew he had loved her as she loved him, but he was a man who would expect his woman to be as the women of his class were. Oh, yes, she realised that he would eventually have married her because his love, his need, his care for her were very evident. She would have lived a life of great luxury, been loved with passion and consideration and even respect, her slightest desire satisfied, except for independence and a will of her own. She would be his, his to adore, to keep safe in the home, his to command. He would provide for her and the children they would have but she would be as his mother was: a respectable married woman with no thoughts in her head but those put there by her husband. Her heart broke with the loss of him, a loss she must keep hidden from Mam and Jem, a pain that pierced her in the night when she lay sleepless next to her mother in the big, comfortable bed in Seymour Street. She was astounded to feel such grief, for she barely knew him. She only knew that her heart recognised his and what was in it, and though it could have been hers she had turned him away from her with a few harsh words and he had gone. He was a proud, complex, clever man and she had lost him because she would not be what he wanted her to be: totally dependent on his masculinity.

Miss Moore's voice brought her back from her pain-filled memories, the drifting memories that plagued her when she was alone. She shook her head and moved to fiddle with a fan, which it seemed was not quite in its correct place.

'. . . And I have to have something for the Hunt Ball, and my cousin, who is to be married next month, will expect me to turn up in something decent.'

Miss Moore, whose carriage stood at the corner of Remington Place and Bold Street, causing chaos to the passage of traffic, the footman and coachman totally unconcerned by the exhortations of the local constable to move off, drank her chocolate and with the decisiveness of a sergeant major directing his troops chose six dresses, four hats, two bonnets, a shawl, a fan and a parasol to match the cream dress, since she was going to the Grand National at Aintree, she told them, and had it on good authority that the day would be sunny. It took her no more than three-quarters of an hour. She summoned the footman, parcels and hatboxes were packed into the carriage, and Miss Moore, with her silent maid in tow, swept from the shop with a reminder that she would be back and she would send her friends, for they were all of the same mind as herself, too busy with the important work of gaining female representation in politics to waste valuable time on light-minded trifles. Miss Logan was to send her a bill for what she had bought and she would be in to see her about the dress for her cousin's wedding. And she was badly in need of a new riding outfit, in a shade of pewter, she thought, would Miss Logan agree? Good, good!

They danced round the shop with Nell watching in open-mouthed astonishment, performing a polka that threatened to knock all the hats off their perches and the tables spread with magazines spinning against the chairs. Their wide skirts were a danger to everything and their hysterical laughter rang up the stairs to the workroom where Gilly said she must go at once, for if all Miss Moore's friends were to be fitted out she must make haste with new designs. At last they quietened.

'Can you believe it, Anne?' Gilly asked, sinking down into one of the pretty velvet chairs and accepting the cup of chocolate Nell thrust into her hand. It seemed Nell Goodwin's future was already decided! 'Six dresses in one day, hats, a fan . . . Dear Lord, it will pay the rent for six months and if she does as she says we will be inundated with orders. Do you think she means it?'

Anne sipped the chocolate handed to her by Nell, her face

thoughtful. 'I shall ask Mama who she is. Mama knows of all the quality folk in and around Liverpool and if she doesn't she'll soon find out. I hope . . . I hope . . .' A frown creased her smooth young brow and she bit her lip.

'What, what is it, dearest?' for that was what Anne had become to Gilly, her dearest friend.

'Well, she's just waltzed out of here with six dresses, hats, bonnets and all the rest, without paying us a penny.'

Gilly stared in alarm at her friend's face. 'You don't think she's . . .?'

'Lord . . . oh, Gilly, have we been . . .'

'I'll gerr our Ginger on to it,' Nell said stoutly, to their astonishment as she took the empty cups from their hands and put them on the tray, ready to whisk it behind the curtain. ''E knows everyone in Liverpool an' if 'e don't 'e's friends 'oo do. Moore, she said, wi' a carriage an' footmen an' all. Shouldn't be 'ard ter find. You leave it ter me. Now, do I work 'ere or not?'

Nell proved as good as her word, taking away a length of gingham, a pretty piece decorated with buttercups, and returning the next morning at goodness only knows what time, for she was on the doorstep when Gilly arrived, with a beautifully made bodice wrapped in tissue. She must have worked all night for it was hand-sewn, *beautifully* sewn with tiny pearl buttons down the back, the neck high with a frill about it, long sleeves, again frilled and ready to put with a skirt in the window. She also had news about Miss Moore whose family, it seemed, was well known in Liverpool; her father was what was known as a merchant prince dealing in every kind of goods, importing and exporting, a self-made millionaire, while her mother was the daughter of an earl who was entitled to call herself 'Lady' Harriet Moore, though she did not use the privilege.

'So yer see, Miss Logan, Miss Moore comes from a good family. Walton House they live in, at Walton-on-the-Hill, a big 'ouse, our Ginger ses, wi' dozens o' servants. 'E's a mate o' the under-gardener, our Ginger, I mean, 'oo's mam lives in't next street, Alfie's mam, I mean, an' 'e ses they're a great family. Miss Moore's the only one an' when the old man goes she'll get the lot.'

Gilly and Anne exchanged glances of triumph, both remembering the reception they had met with when they got home last evening. Anne's had been frosty, for Mrs Barrie had, for the umpteenth time, begged her husband to forbid their daughter to go down to that *place* again, saying the word as though it were Liverpool's lowest brothel. Her father, so astute and forthright in business, was quite the opposite in his own home, and left all that sort of thing to Rose. He had frowned and sighed and mumbled before escaping to the privacy of his study. He himself could see no harm in his younger daughter indulging herself in a little hobby, which was how he saw it, and she would soon tire of it, as she had tired of all the other pastimes she had taken up. Her stammer had held her back but now that it had gone, thanks, she told him, to Miss Logan, she was happy and occupied in what was, after all, a lady's world of fashion and could come to no harm in a dress shop. Only Lucas showed the slightest interest in the wonder of selling six dresses, bonnets, a fan and a parasol, his face fixed in the strangest expression as he listened to Anne argue with her mother over the dinner table while the maids, who missed nothing, wondered if there was a chance they might visit this *fashion house* as Miss Anne described it, for it seemed Miss Logan was not to cater just to the very rich but was willing to sew for any class.

They were transfixed when Mr Lucas stood up abruptly during Miss Anne's argument with madam, his chair crashing to the floor. He threw his napkin to the table and strode out of the room, ignoring his mother's plaintive query as to what was the matter, then she followed him, the easy tears that they knew so well flowing down her cheeks, leaving Miss Anne alone and deflated at the table.

The news was received in a completely different manner at number 19 Seymour Street. Gilly was hugged and kissed, first by Queenie, then by Jem who longed to put his kisses on her lips but restricted himself to her cheek, then by Flo who was called in to share the joyful exultation of Gilly's triumph.

'Now don't let's get too carried away, Mam. This is one customer we're talking about and though she spent nearly fifty guineas and promises to come back, we haven't actually got the money yet.'

There was silence as Queenie and Flo, who owed not a penny to a living soul and had never, as so many of the poor did, bought stuff on 'tick', absorbed this piece of news. Jem's young face became serious, for more than the others he knew the ways of the wealthy. Not that he had ever had wealth but he knew for a fact that the bill for the suit of clothes Mr Barrie had presented him with to wear at the office and the Mechanics Institution nearly six years ago had taken more than six months to be paid, though it had been presented to Mr Barrie a week after the suit was purchased. This is what happened between tradesman and customer in their circles. Would this magical woman who had floated into Gilly's shop and bought so much be the same? Was Gilly beginning to crow too soon? Would this lady, for she was that, a lady, never be seen again, along with the purchases she had made and would she ever settle the bill which Gilly was to send to Walton House in a day or two? In one way, a selfish way, he knew, he hoped it would all end in disaster, for then, when her little shop failed, she would turn again to him, as she had not done for a while, claiming pressure of work as an excuse for missing their Sunday walks. He loved her and would marry her one day but something in her, which had come about recently, held him back from pressing her. There was plenty of time. After all, she was only eighteen.

19

Gilly was dressed in an outfit the colour of forget-me-nots, a tightly fitted jacket with a pleated peplum which sat sublimely over the frilled flounces of the bustle at the back of her skirt. The skirt was flat at the front across her stomach and when she walked the pale grey kid of her new high-heeled boots peeped out. The straw bonnet on the back of her head was cream, decorated with forget-me-not blue satin ribbons and white lily of the valley, tied beneath her chin, and from the high brim at the front her copper-gold hair escaped in curling tendrils above her brow. Her enjoyment of the moment had flushed her skin to rose and her eyes were great drowning brown pools shot with liquid gold. She looked quite, quite glorious and it seemed everyone in the park thought so, for heads turned to watch her admiringly and to smile at her companion's antics. Two young working girls, both dressed neatly and soberly but with pretty bonnets on their heads, stopped to watch her go by, convinced she was some lady of quality, little knowing that she had made the whole outfit herself with the help of her indispensable young apprentice.

The man whose hand she held, almost as though she were a child walking with her father, could not take his eyes from her and had she not laughingly guided him would have walked into other couples, families, children with hoops and balls and dogs on leads.

'Stop it, Jem. People will think we're mad, especially if you walk backwards, you idiot.'

'I can see you better if I walk like this.' Jem was elated, for his Gilly was returning to the girl he had loved devotedly for the past eighteen years, becoming what she had been for most of her life, probably due to the success of her young business. She was lively, enthusiastic, ready to laugh with him, take walks with him on a fine Sunday such as today, the forlorn, quiet, withdrawn young woman who had agonised over her mother and what had happened to her, thankfully fading away. He told himself that that was what had been wrong with her for months, that and her preoccupation with the daunting task of starting the dressmaking and millinery business that she had wanted to call Rose Alley. They had talked her out of it, he and Queenie, for how could they refer to *Rose Alley* without remembering the real Rose Alley which was part of their past life and all its horror. He had persuaded her, with Queenie's help, to have the sign painted out and another put in its place: *Gillyflower's*. Round the name, copied from a book that Anne brought from the library at Bracken Hill, were images of gillyflowers, a delicate pale pink against the apple-green wood of the sign. Gillyflowers were clove-scented, the book said, but as Jem told them practically it was not possible to paint a smell. Gilly had even had hat boxes made adorned with the name and flower.

It seemed that since she had changed the shop's name and had Miss Helen Moore's custom bestowed upon her she could do no wrong, and in the last three months not only had Miss Moore paid her bill promptly and ordered gowns for every occasion and time of the day or night, including night attire since Miss Logan's embroidery was so exquisite, plus a riding habit and a gown for the grand ball at the Town Hall, she had also introduced half a dozen of her fellow 'suffragists', as they liked to call themselves, to Gillyflower's. Gilly and Anne barely saw her, for now that Miss Logan had her measurements, Miss Moore relied on her to send over to Walton House whatever apparel Miss Logan thought suitable for Miss Moore's perusal. It was very seldom that a garment was returned.

The ball was in honour of the visit of Prince Arthur, Her Majesty's third son, and Prince and Princess Christian, who were guests of the Earl of Derby of Knowsley, and other distinguished individuals. Nearly 3,000 of the elite of the town and neighbourhood attended, ladies and gentlemen of good society, among them Mr and Mrs Jonathan Moore and their daughter Helen, Mr and Mrs Herbert Barrie, their son Lucas, their married daughter and her husband, Mr and Mrs Ernest Davidson, and their younger daughter Anne. Mr and Mrs John Hughes were included but their children were not, being too young. It was a huge affair, the recently erected New Exchange Room, connected by a gallery from the Town Hall, having been elegantly fitted out for the dancers at the enormous cost of £3,800!

Anne's ball-gown was designed and made entirely by Gilly and her young apprentice, whose skill and ingenuity had repaid Gilly a thousandfold since she had taken her in. The gown was of silver gauze over white satin, the bodice cut very low off the shoulders, so low in fact Mrs Barrie told her husband she did not know how he could allow his daughter to enter the ballroom, but the sudden rush of young men who clustered around her pretty daughter helped to stem her anxiety, particularly as one was a young relative of the Earl of Derby! She was undoubtedly the most beautifully gowned young woman in the ballroom with her flat stomach, her pert breasts half revealed, her gauzy train and neat bustle, decorated with a cascade of tiny stars. Gilly had attached a satin ribbon to the train so that when Anne danced, as she did from the moment they arrived until the National Anthem was played, she looped the ribbon round her wrist so as not to impede her dainty silver slippers. The young men almost fought with one another to take her into supper and Mrs Barrie spent the evening in a delirium of joy.

It was her laughter rising on the warm air above the hubbub of the crowds that he recognised. He stopped dead where he stood on the flower-bordered pathway in Princes Park and the young lady on his arm almost tripped over the hem of her expensive, beautifully made gown, gripping his arm violently in order to avoid falling. Jem, still foolishly walking backwards, also nearly came to grief, because Gilly stopped and for a confused moment the two couples, Gilly Logan and Jem Wilson, Lucas Barrie and Angela Ryan, almost crashed into one another. Passers-by also got caught up in the muddle, gentlemen muttering as they guided their female companions round the silent group who blocked the pathway.

For several seconds no one spoke. Jem, who no longer worked with Lucas, ran his eyes over him and the lovely, supercilious girl at his side and had time to think that she was exactly the sort of woman Lucas's family would approve of and, though he did not know why, his hand tightened on Gilly's and he drew her protectively to him. Lucas had steadied the girl on his arm, who was beginning to smile. Not a pleasant smile. A malicious smile as though she knew something that none of the others knew. Her periwinkle-blue eyes had stars in them and she clung to Lucas's arm like a limpet. He's mine, Gilly Logan, her expression seemed to say, and Gilly wondered why, since no one, as far as she knew, was aware of the feelings she and Lucas had once shared. But she remembered the encounters she had had at school with Angela Ryan when she had defended Anne and instinctively, with that feminine intuition that recognises what is in another woman's mind, she knew that Angela wanted Lucas and was telling Gilly, who was a possible threat, to keep off.

Lucas's eyes were colder than an icy winter sky and there was a thin, white line about his mouth. Still they stood, the four of them, and a gentleman at Lucas's back asked them politely if he and his wife might pass. The grass had a dew on it, he said, and his wife was reluctant . . . His voice was lost in the dense silence that had fallen over them though Angela continued to smile jubilantly.

'Wilson,' Lucas said, nodding at Jem. He did not acknowledge the presence of Gilly, his cold eyes sweeping over her shoulder and looking into the distance. The sight of her holding the hand of a man, and laughing as though she had not a care in the world, was crucifying him, since he had told himself, and believed it, that she was nothing to him. That the strange incident in her new home had been no more than that. An incident with a pretty girl who had caught his eye at the time. One whose mother had been in trouble and whom he had helped over a tricky period and yet here he was rigid with shock, nausea attacking the good breakfast Mrs Collins had cooked for him that morning. He wanted to shake off Angela's clinging hand, stride across to Jem Wilson, punch him in the mouth and fling him away from the lovely, silent girl whose rosy face was now ashen. How dare he put his hand on what was . . . what should be Lucas Barrie's . . . Dear sweet Christ, what was wrong with him? How could he let a woman affect him as this one did? She was not for him, coming from the class she did and yet last year he had held her in his arms and felt the glory in her and the answering glory in him, but she had denied him, sent him away and all he had been doing was trying to protect her. He had thought of her since, of course he had, he could not deny it, in his head at night, in his dreams, in his arms, his mind full of her and yet she was handfast with this . . . this man who also loved her. He knew that, for a man will recognise it in another. And could you blame him? There was something about Gilly Logan, a beauty not just of her face but in her heart and soul. It shone from her and when men looked at her they recognised it. She was completely unaware of it, of her loveliness, the glow that shone from her and that was what was so special about her.

But she is not for you, something inside him snarled, so just walk away. Take the simpering creature on your arm and walk away, for these two, especially *her*, are nothing to you.

Gilly looked at him, looked deep into those cold grey eyes, which had once smiled and glinted like silver, which had once narrowed and meshed his incredibly long eyelashes in that smile, and she saw fear. She saw the wildness that he was just about holding on to, the anger and the love, the deep tearing love in him for her and it gentled her, for she felt the same.

'Good morning, Lucas, Angela,' she said softly, doing her best to defuse the situation, as she could feel the terrible tension in Jem whose own love for her sensed her anguish and, what was worse, its mirror in Lucas Barrie.

But what could he do? What could any of them do, for even Angela realised, as women will, the danger that lay in the woman opposite her. The woman who had been the only girl to defy Angela at school. She had made Angela look small and petty in the eyes of her cronies and Angela had not liked it. She had sworn revenge but somehow the chance of it had not come, not at school, but now, surely it was in her power, through this man to whose arm she clung, to hurt the beautifully dressed girl who was looking at Lucas, her eyes filled with agony. Why? There was nothing between them that she knew of, but her nerve endings told her there was something strange, odd in their reaction to one another. Lucas's arm was tensed like iron beneath her gloved hand and he seemed to tremble somehow although he did not move. His face, which had been smiling at some remark she had made, was clamped tight and the expression in his eyes was quite frightening. It was as if he loathed Gilly Logan and though she didn't understand it, not yet, she would. Oh, yes, she would question the naïve girl who was Lucas's sister, for Anne was so innocent she would see nothing wrong in confiding in the girl who had tormented her at school but was now so nice to her. Angela, who had meant to have Lucas Barrie from the first time she set eyes on him at the dinner table of a mutual family friend, had been sweetness and light to Anne Barrie ever since, and the stupid girl actually thought Angela had changed and wanted to be her friend. Angela had heard of Gilly Logan's dressmaking business, as who had not in her group, and of Anne's interest in it and if she played up to the little fool, expressing her admiration, she could worm out of her all that there was to know.

'Your mother is well, Miss Logan?' Lucas managed to say through stiff lips.

'Thank you, yes.' Their eyes met and clung and spoke and it was as though those about them, not just Jem and Angela but the irritated man whose wife was reluctant to walk on the damp grass, the children doing their best to roll their hoops, the dogs on leads, the families, nursemaids with perambulators, ladies and gentlemen taking a sedate walk in the park in the summer sunshine, faded away to a hazy place on the periphery of their vision. Angela was ready to stamp her foot in temper, for she had always claimed everyone's attention whether it be her doting mama and papa, the servants in the mansion where she lived, her friends who were still afraid of her and her quick temper, and now this man who was staring at Gilly Logan with that peculiar expression and she was prepared to fight for him.

Jem began to fidget and his fists clenched, his eyes turning to the frozen blue of the Norwegian fjords from where, though he was not aware of it, his ancestors came. He did not care for the intensity of Lucas Barrie's gaze nor Gilly's answering one.

"You knew I loved you and yet you sent me away . . ." Lucas's expression silently told her.

"Yes, I don't know why now . . ."

"You know this woman means nothing to me and your love for Jem is for a brother . . ."

"Yes . . ."

"Walk away, come with me. If I hold out my hand will you take it . . .?"

"How can I . . .?"

"Easily . . ."

"I cannot . . . please, let me go . . ."

No word had been spoken and yet they both knew exactly what was in the other's mind and when hers told his she could not, would not come with him, his face closed, tight as a clam, grim and ugly with his hatred, not just of Jem Wilson who he believed stood between them, but of her. The gentleness that had momentarily warmed his eyes to grey velvet dissolved and his breath seemed to gasp from between his thinned lips.

'Good morning to you both,' he said icily and, putting a hand to Angela's in the crook of his arm, he brushed past them and walked along the path to the gate.

'Wheer's our Jem?' Queenie asked as Gilly stumbled into the kitchen. She was patiently stitching on a hem, for she and Flo often helped out with the plain sewing that would not show on the garments Gilly and Nell turned out. She was wearing the wire-rimmed spectacles Mr Jenkins had ordered for her to help her sight, which had once been as sharp as a razor, and she peered over the top at her daughter. 'An' what's up wi' you? Yer look as though yer'd seen a ghost, dun't she, Flo?' turning to her companion for confirmation.

She and Flo sat with their knees up to the cosy fire which, though it was summer, was always kept in because a good deal of the cooking was done on the fire. A kettle was always simmering in the coals and next to it stood a big pan of scouse ready for their mid-day meal. Beside the fire on each side was an oven in which Queenie baked bread, cakes, scones, meat pies, and the fragrant smell in the well-scoured kitchen told a visitor that fresh bread had been baked this morning. The room was spotless, the reflection from the fire glowing in the rich polish of the oak dresser that stood against the wall, in the whitewashed walls touched to gold, in a copper bowl filled with the massed heads of yellow-centred daisies. Overlying the mouth-watering smell of the bubbling scouse and the fresh bread was the fragrant scent of Queenie's pot-pourri, the flowers for which Gilly had gathered with Jem last Sunday when they walked across the country fields on the outskirts of the city.

'Well?' Queenie added, her needle poised ready to take the next stitch. She and Flo had just been conjecturing on the lovely possibility of a wedding sometime in the near future, for what could be more appropriate than her Gilly and Jem married and sharing the double bed Gilly now shared with her mam. In fact they had decided happily between themselves that Queenie might move in with Flo and let the newly-weds have this house to themselves. She and Flo got on so well it was as though they had been friends since they were little lasses and the thought that they might share grandchildren – though naturally they would be Queenie's by blood – was a great joy to them. They went about together, to the markets and for walks down to the Pier Head now that Queenie had recovered, Queenie holding on to Flo's arm, and had even ventured across the water on the ferry. There was money to spare now that Gilly was doing so well, and so was the lad who had had a rise at the beginning of the year.

'Wheer's t' lad?' she repeated, feeling a sudden flicker of apprehension whip at her chest just where she supposed her heart was. Gilly was flushed, her eyes over-bright and for a brief moment Queenie toyed with the lovely thought that she and Jem had been . . . well, canoodling in some quiet corner of Princes Park where they had gone for a walk.

'I left him . . .'

'Left 'im!' Queenie's mouth dropped open and Flo hissed in the way she did when she was surprised.

'Yes, he wanted to . . . to . . .'

'What, fer God's sake? 'E wouldn't leave yer ter walk 'ome on yer own.'

'Well, he did. He wanted to . . . to get a look at the new bridge,' she lied. 'Runcorn Bridge. They say it will shorten the distance to London by nine miles and you know how . . . how interested Jem is in such things.'

They both stared at her in astonishment for they had *not* known of Jem's interest in bridges. Jem had only one interest: well, two if you counted the stammering girl who stood in the doorway, and that was ships. Ships, ships and more ships. She was lying! Their Gilly was lying and the apprehension that prodded at Queenie's heart increased.

Gilly removed her lovely bonnet in the casual manner of someone without a care in the world and placed it on the kitchen table. She smiled brightly. 'Is there any tea in the pot?' she asked and sat down on the pouffe by her mother's chair, the one Queenie had used to rest her tired legs when she first came out of hospital. Gilly's head was bowed as though in great sadness and Queenie and Flo exchanged glances. What the devil had happened in the few hours their girl and Jem had been out? Something surely had.

She took the cup of tea Queenie put in her hand and sipped it silently, seemingly unaware of the presence of the two women, gazing with blank eyes into the fire and when Flo's cat, which followed Flo everywhere, rubbed against her she picked her up and put her in her lap where she curled upon herself. How could she reveal to these two the magnitude of the pain she had suffered at the sight of Lucas Barrie with a woman on his arm? For it had nearly felled her. She didn't know why really, for had she expected that during the last year he had calmly gone across the river every day to the shipyard and at night come back to Duke Street and sat before his fire reading his paper? Had she imagined that his social life had ended on the day she had sent him away from this house and told him not to return? That he would have nothing more to do with women? He loved her, somehow she knew that with a belief that never faltered, for it had been apparent, at least to her, in his every movement today, in his every glance, and in his *refusal* to glance at her, in his voice and the contemptuous tilt of his head.

And how could she tell them of the words that had passed between her and Jem as they left Princes Park.

'He's taken a fancy to you,' Jem said, baldly voicing the fears he had felt stirring last year when Lucas Barrie had made such a fuss about Gilly and Queenie. He and Lucas had worked together at the shipyard but that was all. They had not been friends and yet Lucas had gone out of his way to help them when Queenie had been attacked. He had insisted on them staying at his house, had provided clothes for them when theirs had been in such a state, he had visited Queenie in hospital and generally been of great support to them when they had both been in the deepest of shock. All right, it might be his nature to be a Good Samaritan, to go out of his way to help those in distress, but somehow Jem hadn't thought so and his suspicions, his male instinct where Gilly was concerned had been aroused. He had watched closely, not realising that he was doing so, for signs of . . . of something; what he didn't know, but something that might perhaps reveal Lucas's real purpose, his real motives and he had begun to think there was a bond of some sort between Gilly and Lucas. Then, to his great relief, Lucas had lost interest, which seemed typical of his sort, and they had seen him no more. He and Lucas had stopped working together, Gilly had been absorbed with her mam's recovery and settling her into Seymour Street, then her business, and no more had been heard nor seen of Lucas Barrie.

But today every bone in his body, every pulse, every surge of blood in his veins had warned him that there was some unspoken link between Gilly and Lucas Barrie. The tension had been unmistakable, a crackle of energy, an excitation, an agitation for which he could find no explanation. Barrie had been tight, rigid, as though he were furious about something, every line of his tall body stiff with an emotion Jem could only describe as outrage and he had been provoked beyond the state where he knew what he was saying.

'Jem, what a silly thing to say. As if there could be anything between me and—' Gilly had begun.

'I didn't say there was anything between you. Is there? Is there, Gilly? I said he had taken a fancy to you. He was incensed about something and that bloody girl on his arm knew it.'

'You are being quite ridiculous, Jem Wilson, and I'll not have any more of this talk. Lucas and I—'

'I see, you are defending him.'

'No, I am not.' They no longer held hands. They strode out along Princes Road and what they both suffered was a palpable thing between them. Folk strolling towards the gateway to Princes Park stepped hastily to one side as they saw them approach, for there seemed to be madness in the faces of the couple coming towards them. The words, or perhaps not the words, for he had spoken little, but the attitude of Lucas, which he had aimed deliberately and accurately at her heart, had quenched her dashing spirit and now Jem was attacking her and all she wanted was to get home and hide somewhere to grieve for the love that was lost to her, the love that Lucas had done his best to kill. He had not succeeded, of course, for nothing could and that was what Jem sensed and that was why he was striding jerkily along beside her, his face tight, his hands clenched into the fists that he would dearly like to aim at Lucas Barrie. Or perhaps her, for she had been his all her life. As a toddling child, a growing girl, a young woman, he had thought of her as his, his to love and support and one day marry. They were both of an age for it to happen and now this man had come into their lives and all because, years ago, Jem had saved the life of a drowning lad. He should have left him in the bloody water!

'Have you been seeing him . . . meeting him?' He swallowed painfully and the sinews in his neck stood out. The colour beneath his skin flared and then receded and he clamped his jaws together, his merry blue eyes now flat and lifeless.

She stopped abruptly, again disturbing the flow of passers-by while he continued to walk on.

'What?' She was clearly so astonished Jem should have seen it but he was stalking on and had his back to her. She ran to catch up with him and those about them stared in amazement. She caught his arm but he snatched it away, moving so swiftly he was almost running in his devastation, for he knew in his heart that he had lost her. He knew he was not imagining their connection. He had seen it for an instant in her eyes and in Lucas Barrie's and he could not stand it.

'Jem . . . wait . . . please, Jem . . .'

Jem had reached Rodney Street, heading for Brownlow Hill which he would cross to reach Seymour Street when suddenly he stopped and stared, then with an oath began to run, really run, and Gilly lost sight of him in the crowds.

She slowed down and with the jerky movements of a marionette walked the length of Russell Street until she reached the corner of Seymour Street.

20

It is doubtful whether Jem Wilson, had he been in his right mind, would have given chase to the man he had seen lurking in the entrance to a ginnel in Seymour Street.

For the past year, on and off, Jem had been making enquiries in the vicinity of Rose Alley about the attack on Queenie Logan. He had knocked on every door about the court, even the one that sheltered his own mother – when his father was absent – going about it in what he thought was a discreet manner, but the denizens of Rose Alley, who all had their suspicions, and some more than suspicions, also went in terror of the perpetrators of the crime and knew that if they were to speak to Jem about it they would in their turn be the ones who would suffer. Tommy Wilson had a fiendish temper. In fact it could hardly be described as a temper, he just lost control of his already overheated mind and his malevolence was something nobody in Rose Alley wished to encounter. Ask his poor wife. She and Tommy and their umpteen children lived and screamed and fought and somehow survived in the festering filth Jess Wilson was too dispirited to overcome. Not that she fought much with Tommy unless she wanted a black eye, a split lip or a vicious 'seeing to' as Tommy called it, which left her unable to walk for a week.

When her son had turned up on her doorstep months ago asking questions about Tommy and his mates she had been torn between delight at seeing him and terror for his safety because if Tommy should find him here he would tear him to pieces. Tommy loathed and detested their Jem with a snarling hatred that came, she knew, from an envy of his son's rise in life and his contemptuous refusal to share his good fortune with his father. And he coveted Gilly Logan, who had once been a neighbour, with a menacing lust that had made him dangerous, wanting what he was convinced his son had. He had taken the mother instead, when she had defended their Gilly with a pan of hot fat, maiming her for life, blinding her in one eye, Jess had heard, putting her in hospital, Queenie Logan who had been friend more than once to Jess, but it was more than Jess's life was worth to say anything. *To anyone.* Jem had been round a few times when Tommy was at what was laughingly called work but which was no more than an hour here and there to earn a few bob for a pint in the four ale bar at the Crown and Anchor. Or when he had taken every penny she had put aside in an effort to feed her often starving children, pushing her and her remonstrations aside as though she were no more than the scrawny cat that lurked about the courtyard.

Jem had come more than once over the months, trying to discover the names of the men who had shared with Tommy what they had found that night in Queenie Logan's cellar but nobody would speak out. Jem had wanted to go to the police, he said, but unless he had some proof to take with him he was beating his head against a brick wall. Tommy used Jess's body frequently, brutally, noisily, as all the neighbours heard and the only man to speak up, not in defence of Jess, for who cared how a man abused his wife, but because Tommy had, in a drunken stupor, pissed down his cellar steps, had been beaten to a pulp by Tommy and his cohorts and never worked again. His wife and children were even now in the poor house.

Jem had seen the man in Seymour Street with his face turned away several times over the last months, but had attached no importance to it, and certainly had not linked it to the Logan family. For all he knew the man might live in Seymour Street, though it was a bit strange as this was a decent neighbourhood where the men had proper jobs, where they went to work in the morning and came home in the evening and put their wages in their wives' hands. Not prosperous by any stretch of the imagination, but living within their income and perhaps saving a penny or two for a rainy day. They didn't hang about in the middle of the day, loitering in ginnels, turning aside when anyone passed down the street.

It was as though the horror of the morning, the realisation that his dream, not just his dream but his life, was nothing but smoke and shadows, that his Gilly, *his Gilly*, was loved by another man and that in all probability she loved that other man, had clouded and yet at the same time *cleared* his mind and the moment he saw the figure lurking at the corner of Seymour Street and Rodney Street he recognised him. It was his father! Tommy Wilson! And what else could he be doing in this vicinity but getting up to no good? Jem realised now that Tommy had been hanging about ever since they had moved here, watching and waiting for an opportunity to do some harm, to him, his son, to Queenie who had recovered from the horror he had inflicted on her, if you could call being blinded in one eye recovered and, more than anyone, to Gilly. It was Gilly who had been defended by Queenie on that night she had thrown the contents of her frying pan in Tommy's face, disfiguring him for life. Not that he had been much to look at before but now he was scarred, his face puckered and twisted and raw and because of it, and because he had been denied what he had wanted of Gilly, he was here again. He must have followed one of them, obsessed with his need, not only for the sweet flesh of Queenie's daughter but for more revenge against Queenie. He had not got his ruffians with him this time, the sodden toss-pots who had aided him, shared with him in abusing the woman Jem loved as a mother, but he was still after Gilly and, he supposed, himself, for he had steadfastly refused to hand out any of his earnings to his father who would immediately make his way to the Crown and Anchor and pour the lot down his throat. He often gave his mam a bob or two, knowing it would be spent on food for his brothers and sisters, however many there were now. He had lost count long ago. But he'd be buggered if he'd let the old stoat menace his family, as he thought of Queenie and Gilly.

His normally placid nature, his easy-going sweetness of humour, the insouciance with which he meandered through life, had shredded away at the sight of Gilly and Lucas Barrie eyeing one another with something in their glance he recognised. He had felt the hot blood of jealousy pump violently in his veins, the pain of it unbearable. He hated Lucas Barrie with every fierce and furious beat of his heart and he had wanted to take him by the throat and choke the life out of him, slowly, of course, so that he would suffer, anything to remove the expression that was etched on his face. Perhaps beat him with his fists, sinking them into the man's face, see the blood spurt and hear the satisfying crunch of bone breaking. He was almost mindless in his painful rage, and had no thought of danger as he sped swiftly along Seymour Street, for what he could not do to Lucas Barrie he could do to Tommy Wilson. Beat out of him the confession that it was he and others who had raped Queenie Logan, then drag him to the nearest police station and have him locked up.

Though his father must have been in his forties and for many years had done nothing more strenuous than lifting a tankard of ale to his lips, he was surprisingly fast. Not that it mattered much how far ahead he got, for Jem knew where he was going. Along London Road and Shawsbrow, turning into Byrom Street and on to Scotland Road the two men flew, passersby getting hastily out of the way, staring in open-mouthed astonishment. Perhaps the first man, who looked a low fellow, had stolen something from the second, who was well dressed, and one or two men made a half-hearted attempt to catch the low fellow and were viciously pushed to one side for their troubles, one falling so hard he cracked his head on a lamppost where he lay still. A small crowd gathered about him, impeding Jem's progress but he elbowed his way through and was just in time to see his father turn into Rose Alley.

There was no sign of him as Jem followed him into the court and for a second he hesitated. Should he march boldly up to his mam's cellar door and demand that his pa come out and . . . what? Fight? He did not want to fight, at least he did but not the sort of fight where two fellows squared up to one another with their fists. He wanted to *beat* Tommy Wilson, beat him to a bloody pulp for what he had done to Queenie and what he hoped to do to Gilly, Gilly who had been Jem's one love for eighteen years and now was . . . Christ Jesus, it wasn't Tommy he wanted to smash to the ground but that other sod, the one who had laid covetous eyes on Gilly. This last thought melted the final vestige of good sense in him and he strode towards his mother's cellar steps, moving round the foul privy in the centre of the court. When the door sprang open he was taken completely by surprise, turning his head, and making a perfect target for the iron bar that smashed across his forehead. It felled him with one blow into the evil-smelling filth that overflowed and surrounded the small wooden shack and there he lay, blood spreading from the appalling wound his gloating father had inflicted.

'Theer, yer bastard, that'll learn yer ter interfere wi' yer pa,' he jeered, just as though Tommy Wilson was the one who had been the victim in this chain of events. ''Appen yer'll keep yer bloody nose outer my business in future. Now get back ter yer fine job an' yer fine new life and leave me an' mine alone.' For good measure he aimed a vicious kick into his son's ribs, breaking two with the iron-tipped cap of his boot. He was just about to land another, for he had gained the greatest satisfaction from downing the son who had refused to help his poor old pa out on many an occasion, when a screaming virago flew across the court and jumped on his back.

'Leave 'im alone, yer daft sod. D'yer want ter kill 'im? Gerroff 'im or I'll call the scuffers meself an' tell 'em it were you what interfered wi' Queenie. Leave 'im alone . . .'

It was like having a limpet on his back, since Jess Wilson had her arms in a stranglehold about his neck and her scrawny legs wrapped tightly about his waist. He was confused, his triumph muddling his brain and he could not seem to function properly. Though he reached for her over his shoulder as she sank her teeth, what she had left, into his neck and, when the blood spurted, seemed to relish the taste of it. Round and round they went in a grotesque dance and it might have gone on for ever had not Patty Wilson, thirteen years old and who had suffered the attentions of her father for the past three, screamed for their Rosie, a year younger, to run for the police, as when their father finally dislodged their mother he would undoubtedly kill her as it seemed he had just killed their Jem. Their pa had done nothing for his family except abuse them all, her and Rosie getting the worst of it. Sadie had gone long ago, saying she'd had enough of the old bugger with his hand up her skirts. It seemed to Patty, as this crisis exploded round them, that though her pa might do untold damage should he be cornered, to her, to Mam, to the neighbours, what had they got to lose? It was Mam who did her best to defend them, who fed them when she could, who kept the old bugger from the girls when she could and though the police would be reluctant to enter this court unless they were in numbers, the removal of the old bugger, as they called him, could not fail to improve their lives. And if their Jem was dead, Pa would swing for it and good riddance to him.

The inhabitants of the court talked about the events of that day with avid relish for weeks. Poor old Jess had been badly injured before the police finally overcame Tommy, for he had put up a ferocious fight, but a lucky blow from a truncheon had felled him and when he collapsed in the muck in which his son lay, the women had rushed to pick up Jess who was crumpled on top of her husband. The 'bobbies', wearing their smart, full-skirted, knee-length tunics with gilt buttons down the front, and holding on to their top hats, all except one who lost his in the scuffle, had hauled away the stupefied figure of Tommy Wilson, bundled him into a horse-drawn van and driven off.

'Wharrabout the lad an' 'is mam?' Peg O'Dowd ventured, since the pair of them looked to be on the verge of expiring, that is if Jem had not already done so.

The sergeant in charge scratched his head. They were used to these commotions in the back streets and courts of the city and it had been known for the police van to carry the injured to the nearest hospital, but he could hardly put an unconscious man and woman in the back of the van that carried the dangerously truculent instigator of this dreadful incident.

'P'raps a cab?' he suggested hesitantly.

'Wheer's likes of us ter get money fer a cab?' Peg demanded to know and those who had gathered to watch nodded their heads.

'P'raps Jem's gorra bob or two on 'im,' one suggested.

' 'Oo's Jem?' the bobby asked.

' 'Im,' pointing to the still figure lying in the filthy matter about the privy.

'Well,' the sergeant murmured, strangely reluctant to go through the pockets of an injured man.

' 'E looks badly, an' so do poor Jess.'

'Aye, poor lass. Tommy's done fer 'er at last.'

Jem proved to have the cash in his pockets needed to hire a cab and the presence of the policeman persuaded a cabby to stop at the entrance to the court. With the policeman's guidance mother and son were lifted gently into the cab and driven off towards the infirmary with a rather proud Peg O'Dowd in charge.

'Yer'd best run an' tell Queenie,' she shouted to Rosie Wilson, leaning out of the cab for a moment to whisper Queenie Logan's address, for even now, with Tommy Wilson in handcuffs, his reputation for violence was feared.

They were sitting down to their scouse, asking one another anxiously where their Jem could have got to, when the knock came to their door.

Gilly rose to answer it. It could not be Jem, for he had a key and when she saw the ragged girl on the doorstep she could not at first remember her.

'Yes?' she asked politely. 'Can I help you?'

'It's me, Gilly.'

'Oh . . . I . . .'

'Rosie Wilson. Jem's sister.' The girl's face was ashen and her eyes, the same shade of brilliant blue as Jem's, were shadowed with what looked like fear. She kept looking over her shoulder into the quiet street, for though her pa was safely locked up what about those ugly brutes he knocked about with and of whom she was terrified? Of whom they were *all* terrified, not just her and Patty but every female in Rose Alley.

'Who is it, chuck?' Queenie's voice asked her as she came from the kitchen into the narrow passage. She stood behind Gilly, peering over her shoulder with her one eye and for a moment Rosie, who had not seen Queenie Logan since before her pa had broken into her cellar, gasped with shock and took a step backwards. Queenie's good looks had been ruined by the encounter and the black patch over her eye gave her the air of an outlaw or one of the low creatures who hung about the back streets surrounding Rose Alley.

'It's me, Mrs Logan. Jess's lass,' Rosie said bravely. 'Me mam's in a right mess an' they've tekken 'er ter't infirmary. She were that brave. I couldn't o' done it, I can tell yer, leapin' on 'is back like that, but then 'e's 'er son so 'appen she thought . . . but me pa were in such a temper, mad 'e were, outer 'is mind wi' it an' if bobbies 'adn't o' bin fetched 'e'd o' done fer 'em both. Peg sent me, Mrs Logan. Fetch Queenie, fer that lad looks in a bad way, she sed, so I run 'ere . . .'

Queenie elbowed aside the bewildered figure of her daughter who stood gape-mouthed in the doorway and dragged Rosie inside and through to the kitchen where Flo was loitering anxiously by the doorway. Rosie had a cup of tea thrust into her hand and was pushed into a chair. The colour returned to her face as she sipped the tea and she began to enjoy herself in an odd sort of way.

'Start from't beginnin', chuck,' Queenie told her, while Gilly hung over her and Flo poured herself a cup of tea, as she had a feeling she was going to need it.

Rosie told her tale, the tea pulling her together, sorry to be the bearer of bad news, for she had had no idea of the damage her pa had done to Mrs Logan's face. She could not stop staring at it, then from Queenie to the beautiful creature who was, it seemed, Gilly Logan. Dressed like a bloody queen she was, with her hair all shining and piled up on top of her head in a sort of crown and her eyes like great golden pools in her face from which every vestige of colour had fled.

Queenie pulled Rosie to her feet, spilling what remained of Rosie's tea which she had been enjoying, since it was not often she had a hot, strong cup with sugar and milk.

'Do us another favour, Rosie. Run ter't corner an' fetch a cab, will yer? Us'll need ter get ter't infirmary. Yer can come wi' us since yer ma's involved an' if what yer say . . . well, come on, lass,' turning to Gilly. 'Stir yersel'. Yer'd best put on yer old cape if we're ter go ter't . . . Look after everything, will yer, Flo?' She gazed somewhat wildly about her, not knowing exactly what she meant and neither did Gilly as, stunned to speechlessness by this second nightmare in their lives, she followed her mam to the door where a breathless Rosie had a cab waiting. The cabby had been somewhat reluctant to stop for the ragged young woman who had hailed him but the respectable figure of Queenie reassured him and at once, at Queenie's request to go like the wind, he set off at a gallop in the direction of the infirmary.

Mr Jenkins could not believe his eyes when the woman whose face he had mended and her lovely daughter accosted him in the waiting room of the infirmary. There were casualties in every corner, for this was where those who could not afford to pay for medical service came in their dozens every day. There were women dragged down with whining children, men with gashes to their heads, mangled hands, since the machinery in the factories hereabout was lethal with the careless, children wheezing as though they had a saw in their frail, narrow chests and needed a bottle, and those who, like the men, had been caught in the whirling machines in the cotton factories. Mr Jenkins and the other doctors were run off their feet, for though it was Sunday the Lord did not grant them a holiday. There was blood on the doctor's white coat and Gilly stared at it in horror, still in the shock Rosie's gabbled words had spun her into, for it might be Jem's blood and how could she bear it if it was. She knew very well what had sent Jem into the madness that had directed him to Rose Alley because the meeting with Lucas and Angela in the park had paralysed her, stopped her heart and then raced it to a violent, agonising beat and it must have shown in her face. How could she have hidden what she felt for Lucas Barrie in that moment before she got a grip on herself? Not only Lucas and Angela but Jem had seen it. Lucas's eyes had sent their message and hers had answered and *Jem had seen it*, though what had sent him racing off to Rose Alley was a mystery.

'Ladies,' Mr Jenkins exclaimed and could not help himself from studying Queenie's face with a professional eye, congratulating himself on a job well done, even though she was no longer a handsome woman.

'Mrs . . . and . . .'? He could not quite remember their names.

'Logan, Doctor.'

'Of course, and . . .'

'This is my lass, Gilly.' Hugh Jenkins looked at Gilly with a man's approval for he remembered her as quite the most beautiful creature he had ever seen.

'Oh yes, and what can I do?'

'We've come about our Jem.' Queenie dragged Mr Jenkins quite roughly from his contemplation of their Gilly.

'Jem?' he said, turning back reluctantly to Queenie.

''E were brought in about . . .' She turned to the third member of the party who stood anxiously at her side. ''Ow long, Rosie?'

Rosie, who had never owned a watch, shrugged. 'An 'our?'

'And what was wrong with, with . . .?'

'Jem.' Queenie began to be irritated. ''E were 'it in't face wi' an iron bar. That's right, innit, Rosie?'

Rosie nodded speechlessly.

'An' Rosie's mam . . . Jem's mam, fer Jem's Rosie's brother.'

Mr Jenkins, doing his best to keep his admiring gaze from Gilly who had not spoken one word but seemed, of the three women, to be the worst afflicted, turned back to Queenie. His face took on a grave expression and Gilly put out her hand to him, which he took gently.

'Not . . . not dead. Doctor, please, not dead . . .'

'No, not . . .' He had been about to say, 'not yet' but changed it hastily to 'not dead'.

'An' me mam?' the girl with them, a scrawny, ragged little thing, interrupted.

'Your . . . mam?'

'She came in wi' our Jem. She's 'is mam an' all.'

Mr Jenkins studied them, wondering how to tell these three females that Jem Wilson, who had been stripped and searched for a clue as to his identity, and the woman who had come in with him, apparently his mother, whom the police constable had told them had tried to defend her son against his maddened father, were both hovering on the brink of death. He and his colleagues had worked on the pair of them, lying side by side in the operating room, and they were still there. The woman had been stitched and bandaged but the man, though his dreadful wound had been cleaned and pulled together, could be said to be in the hands of the Lord, for there was nothing else *they* could do for him. They had seen his brains, he and his fellow doctors, through the gaping hole in his forehead, something that very few of them had viewed before and when they had the sufferer had never recovered.

'Come into my office, Mrs Logan and . . .'

Gilly began to weep, not the heaving, sniffling weeping the doctor had encountered in his medical profession but great fat tears slowly sliding down her cheeks and dripping on to the sensible grey wool of her old cape. They were silent, heart-wrenching, and Mr Jenkins wanted to take this lovely, devastated woman into his arms and comfort her as though she were his to comfort, which she was not. She had suffered so much, now he recalled, only last year flying in here with the man who lay close to death on the operating table but the victim then had been her mother. Her mother had been abused, tortured and from what Queenie and the girl, Rosie, were babbling it seemed the man who had been the perpetrator then was the man who had inflicted that great gaping wound on poor Jem.

'He mustn't die, Doctor, he mustn't die. This is my fault. I must be given the chance to make it up to him. What happened today was nothing and I must tell him so. Don't let him die, please, Doctor.'

'Miss Logan, please, come into my office,' for people were turning to gawp at Gilly Logan who was becoming hysterical. A child watching began to weep and a nurse hurried across as the doctor must not be harassed by patients, or their relatives.

He led her into his office, her mother and Rosie following and those who had come into the infirmary for treatment wondered what you had to do to get preferential treatment from the doctor! His office indeed!

Tommy Wilson was brought before the court two weeks later, struggling and cursing in the grip of two powerful warders, for he was known to be violent. He had attacked a fellow prisoner in the cells and declared that he was bloody innocent of all the charges brought against him, which did not go in his favour with the judge. To save them further distress the court had allowed the victims of his crimes, the woman he and his mates had raped and beaten up, and his own son who was still in hospital after Tommy Wilson had attacked him, to make written statements. These were written by Mr Barrie, the reputable son of the well-known Liverpool family, since Queenie was unable to read or write and Jem had been blinded, and he read them out to the court.

It did not take long. Only the two policemen who had arrested the culprit were called, for it was felt that Mr Lucas Barrie's word was sufficient to complete the case. Tommy was sentenced to ten years' hard labour!

21

She brought him home six weeks later, leading him lovingly from the hospital under the guidance of Mr Jenkins and Sister Moore who had taken a great liking to the brave lad who still believed that soon, one day, perhaps next week or even next month, he would regain his sight. They had not liked to disillusion him or the girl who held his hand as they put him in the cab.

'God, I'd forgotten how noisy the streets are,' he said cheerfully, for as long as his hand was in Gilly's he was happy. The other ladies who came to see him were as kind as any man could wish, bringing him little tit-bits the one called Flo had made for him, tasty meat pasties they told him he had liked, macaroons, coconut biscuits and home-baked scones spread with the jam she said she had made. The one they called Queenie fussed over him, begging him to tell her if he was in pain, asking if she could plump up his pillow for him, pour him a drink of the special lemonade Flo had brought, agonising that she could not read to him as she had never learned, but as soon as Gilly came in the evening she would read him the news from the *Liverpool Mercury*. She told him things he didn't really understand about his mother who had been in the same hospital but who had been discharged and who had promised Queenie she would come to visit him but she never did, and for some strange reason he didn't seem to care. You'd think he would, wouldn't you, her being his mother, but Queenie told him he had not lived with his own family for a long time. It appeared that Queenie had adopted him in some way when he was a bairn and though he'd never called her Mam, she said, she was in all respects but one his mother. He and his real mother had been in the same accident together, the details of which were curiously vague and he found it hurt his head if he tried too hard to remember the past.

He couldn't even bring back the image of Gilly's face, he only knew deep within him that she was very beautiful and he had loved her. Her hair was the colour of a fox's pelt but with streaks of gold and amber and cinnamon and her eyes were a golden brown as Sister Moore had told him when he had begged her. Her hair was long, curling down below her waist and she had let him put his hands in it, feeling the silkiness of it and the sheer vitality that made it crackle when she brushed it. He longed for the day when his sight would return and he would see her again. He didn't worry about his memory too much because Gilly and Queenie had told him all he wanted to know. He had been there on the day Gilly had been born, Queenie said and had looked after Gilly through the years as though she were his little sister. He loved her and he wanted her but he didn't tell Queenie that. She might have been his little sister in the past but as soon as he had recovered his sight and his memory he would return to . . . to . . .

It was here that he felt the sharp edge of anxiety, for they had told him he was a designer of ships, that he had qualifications that had secured him a good job at some shipyard – Barrie and Hughes – across the water, meaning the River Mersey as they were in Liverpool, but for the life of him he couldn't imagine how one went about designing a ship, even when he got his sight back. He supposed he could read and write, they told him he could, and if he applied himself perhaps he could . . . well . . . it was here that his musings ran out when he lay quietly in his bed between visiting hours.

A chap had come to see him who said he was called Lucas

Barrie, the son of the shipyard owner and had spoken pleasantly to him, telling him that his job would be kept open for him
until he was himself again, taking his hand to shake it in the way
men do, lifting it from across his chest where it lay helplessly,
saying he would keep in touch and Jem had thanked him
politely. He had gone away and had not come back, though
fruit and flowers had arrived from Barrie and Hughes, or so
sister told him. He had not eaten the fruit but had told sister to
give it to some other patient, he didn't know why, and the
flowers were put in a vase on sister's table in the middle of the
ward.

He could tell when she came into the ward, for he could smell
the special perfume she wore. Over the antiseptic aromas and
sometimes others not so pleasant he caught that special fragrance she brought with her. The smell of her workroom in the
shop she owned, of fine materials, of straw she used to make
hats and the unmistakable freshness of meadowsweet. He did
not remember that he and Gilly had gathered the creamy,
fragrant wild flower that grew beneath hedges lining the fields
they had wandered or that it was related to the rose. From it
Gilly had made a perfume that was peculiarly her own.

And he knew the sound of her. The way her skirt rustled
when she walked, the measure of her footsteps, even the sound
of her breathing as she approached his bed. He would turn to
her, looking at her with his sightless eyes and hold out his hand
for her to take. She would bend to kiss his cheek and he longed
to turn his face so that her lips would touch his but he never did,
not yet. He wasn't quite sure what they had been to one another
. . . before . . . so he let her take the lead, desperately hoping it
would take him to where he longed to be.

That last day he was dressed ready in the clothes she had
brought in the day before. A fine chocolate-coloured corduroy
jacket and beneath it a beige casual jersey knitted by Flo which
she thought would, until he felt totally recovered, be more

comfortable, and woollen breeches with well-polished boots. Flo had another jersey on her needles in a soft blue, which would match his eyes, she privately told Queenie.

'I'll be far too warm in this get-up,' he had protested laughingly as they wrapped a scarf, this time knitted by Queenie, about his neck, but he found that after being confined to his bed and the ward for six weeks he felt a bit strange, chilly and vulnerable, a bit shaky. It was frightening not only to lose the life you had led up to six weeks ago but your sight as well, even if it was only temporary, so was it any wonder he felt a bit queer. He sat in the chair by his bed and waited for her.

She stood in the doorway and studied him for a few minutes, gathering her strength, getting in the way of several nurses who were going in and out of the ward. They were ready to be irritable with her until they saw who it was, then they curbed their impatience for could you help feeling sorry for her? She had a hard row to hoe what with the terrible tragedy of her mother and now this, her young man apparently set upon by the same devil who had injured her mother.

He always seemed to sense when she entered the ward but this time, for some reason, perhaps the passage of the nurses in the doorway as they changed shifts, he was unaware that she was there. His face was calm and as attractive as it always had been except for the appalling weal across his forehead. It had been split open by the force of the iron bar his father had struck him with and though Mr Jenkins and his colleagues had done their best, it seemed as though the inside of his head where the core of Jem Wilson dwelled was ready to spill out and they had been unable to avoid the disfiguring scar. It had taken many hours to sew him up, to attempt carefully to put back its contents without damaging him further, as very little was known about the brain and they had been on uncharted territory. Mam had told her so, for the doctor had spoken to Mam. Mam was strong and practical and though she herself was willing to do anything, or be told anything that would restore Jem to the endearing young man he had been it was to Queenie Logan and, standing behind her, her friend Flo Huggett, whom the doctor confided his fears. Besides, Gilly had to attend to her infant business every day, for without Jem's wage they all depended on her to support them. She and Nell, with Anne's help, were designing and making up the outfits her customers ordered. 'Keeping up' was how Gilly described it because it was agony to be forced to open up the shop each day with Jem so ill, to sew and stitch, smile at customers, chat to them, attend to the demands of Helen Moore and her friends and several other ladies who, on hearing that Lady Harriet Moore's daughter frequented the new dressmaker and milliner on Remington Place, had decided to give it a try.

Anne, still fighting her mother, was an enormous help for, being a lady herself, she greeted the customers as though they were guests in her mother's home, smiling, talking of mutual friends, sipping endless cups of chocolate that Rosie made and brought out on a silver tray from behind the discreet curtain to serve to the ladies who had begun to treat the establishment as though it were Anne's! Rosie was still inclined to break into hysterical tears in her new neat black uniform, white frilled pinny and cap, and at the marvel of having this job that Miss Logan had given her.

'What you did for Jem and your mother saved their lives, you know,' which wasn't strictly true. 'Running here to tell us, fetching the cab, and then looking after your mam when she went home. And you must tell her that when she's better she can come and clean for me, that's if she wants to,' she added hastily. And as soon as her broken arm was out of its plaster Jess was to do so. In the meanwhile Rosie learned to make tea, coffee, hot chocolate, to bob a curtsey, to hand out dainty little biscuits and smile at the ladies, to hide her terror and to obey whatever commands were directed at her even if she didn't understand half of them. Upstairs on the top floor Nell worked like a Trojan, her sewing machine whirring away as she turned out the 'tailor-made' outfits which were so much cheaper than those made to measure. The materials were just as attractive and colourful and the styles elegant and fashionable and, when put on the 'mannequins' Gilly had purchased through the good agency of Mrs Fletcher from St John's Market, scarcely looked any different from the ones in the salon on the ground floor where the ladies were fitted. She was helped by Gilly, who was thinking she must take on another young apprentice if trade continued to expand as it was doing, since the ladies in the salon liked to be attended to by the proprietor and she was often called away from her workbench on the top floor to chat to Helen Moore, to Mrs Margaret Clarke, to Mrs Lucinda Braithwaite, friends of Miss Moore's mother who thought they were entitled to the owner's full attention, or any other of the ladies who were beginning to have their gowns made up at Gillyflower's.

There had been a dilemma when it came to serving ladies who were not strictly speaking ladies of the quality of Miss Moore and her friends but who wanted a well-made gown at a reasonable price and were in awe of the likes of Miss Moore. They were reluctant to enter Miss Logan's premises when, through the bow window, they could see ladies of quality perched on Miss Logan's velvet chairs drinking hot chocolate and chatting as though they were in their own drawing rooms. Not that any of them would do anything to threaten the women of the lower orders but Gilly knew the two classes would not mix. The gentry did not shop with working women and certainly they would not look through her designs shoulder to shoulder with a woman whose husband might be a clerk in the office of their wealthy husbands.

She and Anne and Nell had put their heads together and had

come up with the idea of turning the first floor into a reception room for the 'ready made' customer. A discreet sign was put in the window which informed that 'ready made' outfits were on show on the first floor and that customers should go directly up the stairs where costumes for every occasion might be seen.

This proved a success, and when Nell's mam who worked hard in her job as overseer in a pickle factory and could afford to spend a bob or two, especially now that Miss Logan was paying their Nell a decent wage, ventured inside and up the stairs, she was relieved that she would not be made to mix with the 'nobs' from Walton-on-the-Hill and the exclusive suburbs of Liverpool. She bought a lovely frock for her niece's wedding which her own daughter had helped to design. She didn't seem to mind that she did not mix with the likes of Lady Harriet Moore, and as for Lady Harriet and her friends, it is doubtful they even knew about the upstairs room, let alone noticed the respectable women who climbed the stairs to it.

It was four weeks after what they called Jem's accident. It was eight o'clock and dusk was beginning to fall when Gilly heard the doorbell ping downstairs. The workroom tables were bare as she and Nell liked everything cleared away ready for the next day. The workroom floor had been swept clean of pins and tacking thread, every frill and feather and flounce packed into their compartments and she was alone. Nell had promised she would bring Sadie, a friend of hers who was keen to leave her present employment in a shirt-making factory at the back of Exchange Street and follow in Nell's footsteps. Start at the bottom, of course, Nell had hastened to add, even though she was an experienced machinist, but she could vouch for Sadie's honesty and her penchant for hard work. She didn't use such words, of course, for Nell could barely read or write but if Miss Logan would give Sadie a chance Nell herself would make sure Sadie gave satisfaction. She was to bring her next Monday.

When the bell rang she went to the top of the stairs, which

were in shadow and her heart missed a beat. Although she knew
Tommy Wilson was in the Borough Gaol and could no longer
menace her and her family there were still those louts with
whom he used to drink and who had been involved in her
mother's ordeal. She wished she'd gone down with Nell and
locked the door behind her but she had been putting the
finishing strokes to the design she had drawn for a wedding
dress for the young daughter of one of Miss Moore's acquaintances.

'She's a bit hard up, Miss Logan,' Miss Moore had confided,
'for her husband's a skinflint and wants to do everything on the
cheap. Her eldest daughter and he won't allow her to spend as
she should. Now I told her about you and she's coming to see
you. I promised her she wouldn't be disappointed. You won't
let me down, will you?'

No, she wouldn't let Miss Moore down because had it not
been for her Gilly would never have done as well as she had.
She had escaped the trap of poverty into which she had been
born and from which she was slowly, by the skin of her teeth
perhaps, but surely lifting herself. If she lost on this order she
could afford it, and she owed it to Miss Moore.

She stood at the top of the stairs and watched him climb
them slowly and the shock of it struck her a blow that made her
gasp. Her heart began to gallop wildly and she felt the blood
drain from her brain, which had been filled with fabrics, with
crystal and diamanté, with velvet and satin ribbons, and she felt
faint. She stood rigid and paralysed and her mouth dried up so
that she could not have spoken if her life depended on it.

He reached the top of the stairs and stood before her and
they looked at one another across the days that had gone by
since they had come face to face in the park. He was dressed in
black. Nothing about him of contrast other than the snowy
waterfall of his cravat. His dark hair was smoothly brushed, he
was freshly shaved. He smelled of lemon soap and cologne and

he looked immaculate. He was frowning, deep forbidding lines from his nose to his mouth and for a moment she was struck by how much older he looked than the last time she had seen him. Perhaps it was the shadowy passage, for there was little light now coming through the windows in the roof where the last of the sunshine had faded.

'What are you doing here?' she threw at him harshly.

His face closed up even more but there was a strange look of vulnerability about him which he was doing his best to hide.

'I don't know. I don't like you being here alone when the others have gone. Anyone could break in. They don't need to break in when you leave the bloody door unlocked. Don't you see . . . the danger . . . I've been watching each day since . . . keeping you safe from . . . I love you, you see, think of you all the time. I can't work, sleep, my mind is full of you and you are so deep in my heart it hurts me. I'm blind. I can see no one but you . . .'

He bent his head and groaned in despair and without a thought for the consequences, her own heart in agony for his pain, she went to him and put her arms about him, drawing his head to her shoulder.

At once his arms lifted to hold her against him, clinging to her in what seemed desperate need, trembling as though, should she let him go, he would fall. She was, for the moment, the strong one, the support, her female instincts flooding to comfort, to relieve his pain.

He was hurting her, crushing her, the bones in her back, her ribs, his own body a taut, shuddering length of bone and muscle. He lifted his head and looked down into her face and his eyes, which could be as flinty as the rocks up on the moorland of the Pennine range beyond Liverpool, were like the soft grey wings of a dove, like the velvet with which she worked. His love for her, which he had tamped down deep inside him where no one could see at their last meeting in Princes Park, shone and glowed and a tentative smile played about his strong mouth.

'I love you, Gilly.'

'I love you, Lucas.'

Her eyes were warm, filled with that velvet-textured softness that betrayed the depth of her love for him and he sighed with satisfaction, with thankfulness. She did not try to hide it.

Her eyes were steady, a glowing, golden steadiness as they looked into his and when his mouth came down on hers, hers leaped to meet it. She could feel the warmth at the pit of her belly, tendrils that worked their way up and up until they reached her breasts and her nipples rose and hardened. She could feel a responding hardness in him as he pressed her to him and his manhood jutted arrogantly, for she was a woman, his woman and it demanded he take her. It demanded he lay her down, here in her workroom which surely would have a place, soft and warm and fit for his love. His penis flared inside the tight breeches he wore as he lifted her up, his mouth still on hers as he looked round him for some place, a heap of material, the workbench or even the floor, but she began to struggle, pushing at him with her clenched fists, dragging her mouth from his and at once he put her down, lifting his head and standing back from her, his hands upraised.

'I beg your pardon. I did not mean to offend . . .'

'No . . . no, Lucas, please don't . . .'

'Please don't what? You say you love me and your manner seemed to imply . . . that you were not unwilling . . .'

'Unwilling! Dear God, I was ready to lie down and let you take me like . . . like a . . .'

He moved towards her but she stepped away, for she yearned with every fibre, every pulse, every bone and muscle in her body to allow him to – *allow* . . . Dear God, she would glory in it – strip her and himself and make love to her here on the bare floor which Nell had brushed so scrupulously only an hour since. The thought strengthened her resolve, for Nell was part of her life, part of this endeavour that she was slowly carving out for herself and not only for herself but for Mam and for *Jem*. Jem who was blind and though no one had said so she sensed that he always would be. He didn't know himself yet and when he did he would be in torment. To know that he would be dependent on herself and Queenie would surely drive him to want to take his own life, for Jem Wilson had achieved so much in the past ten years and to have it taken from him would be a blow he might not be able to bear.

'Don't . . . please don't touch me,' she whispered and again he took a step back, seriously offended.

'I beg your pardon again.' Then suddenly he reached for her, crushing her to him, frantically raining kisses on her hair which had become a tangle of warm, flowing copper, on her pale face and eager lips, for though her mind told her this just would not do, her female body told her mind to go to the devil because this was what it wanted.

'My darling, my lovely darling, don't you know that you belong to me. That I belong to you. We will be married . . . oh yes, that is what is to happen. I want to look after you. I want you for my wife who will be in my care and protection and these men, this man who has almost destroyed your life can no longer harm you. As my wife you will be safe and loved.'

For a lovely moment, the image of what he was saying flooded through her and she wanted nothing more than to sink against him and let him look after her for the rest of her life. Put her in some lovely house, and it would be lovely knowing Lucas, be pampered as she had never been pampered, her mam allowed to live the rest of her days in peace and security. No need to struggle and worry, rushing frantically between St John's Market, Seymour Street and this place. To be one of the ladies on whom she now waited, to sit with Helen Moore and drink hot chocolate while she flipped through fashion magazines. To be safe, loved, cared for, protected as she would be Mrs Lucas Barrie . . .

And what of Jem?

She dragged herself forcibly from his arms, panting, her eyes glaring and dangerous as though she hated him, her hair streaming wild, for it was only thus that she could withstand him and what he offered.

'Stop it, *stop it*. You know I cannot . . .'

'I know nothing of the sort.' He was seriously insulted, for what man who has just offered the respectable estate of marriage should be asked to put up with this? It was as though he had asked her to be his mistress. To hide her away in some isolated house where, when he felt like it, he could visit. To keep her separate from his life in a box like a toy that he could take out and play with now and again.

'And what about Jem?' she hissed.

He looked genuinely surprised. 'What about Jem? You love me. I love you and have asked you to marry me. What is wrong with that?'

'Sweet Jesus, he is *blind, blind*. Blind and helpless and who is to look after him?'

'You are not responsible.' His face was stony and in his eyes there was hatred, for her or for Jem she could not tell. Probably both of them because they were depriving him of what he wanted more than anything in the world.

'I am. I am. He has no one . . .'

'He has your mother.'

'She is getting older and cannot manage.'

'I will pay for a private nurse to look after his needs.'

'Go, for God's sake go. I can stand no more.'

'Gilly, my love, don't do this. I love you so . . .' His eyes gleamed with what looked like tears but she turned away, her face to the shelves of cloth that glowed like jewels in the fast fading light.

'Go, Lucas, I cannot . . . cannot stand much more.'

He turned his back on her and quietly moved down the stairs.

She had not seen him again though Anne was full of what she was sure was to be an engagement between him and Angela Ryan. No, nothing had been announced but they were always together, she told the silently sewing figure of Gilly Logan whose heart, broken on the rocks of loss, hurt her so much she bent over, pretending she was searching for a pin on the floor.

She moved across the ward and when he turned, knowing she was there, though he smiled with delight, her face was blank, pale, her eyes unfocused. He held out his hand and she took it, bending to kiss his cheek, beginning to smile, for the nurses were looking at her curiously.

'Are you ready then?' she asked him. 'Flo's cooked all your favourite dishes, there's a cab waiting at the front of the hospital and if you behave yourself and eat up your dinner I promise to take you for a walk along the Marine Parade this afternoon.'

'Yes, Nurse.' He grinned and he was Jem again, the Jem she had known and loved ever since the day she was born. He put his hand through her arm and, nodding and smiling at nothing and nobody in particular, allowed her to lead him from the ward.

22

She was in the fitting room with Mrs Septimus Raines and her daughter Kathryn, putting the last pin in the hem of the exquisite wedding gown she had designed and made for Kathryn, when the bell tinkled, heralding the arrival of a client. Kathryn, who was to marry Magnus Wills, son of the cotton merchant Angus Wills of Wills and Hodson, next month, was utterly thrilled with her gown, she told Gilly ecstatically, for she had believed that her father, enormously wealthy but known as the biggest skinflint in Liverpool, would deny her what was every young lady's right, and that was a perfect wedding day dressed in the gown of her dreams. Thanks to Miss Logan, who dressed Miss Helen Moore, and many other ladies from leading families, some of whom were at that moment seated in Miss Logan's salon, she was to have it, and at a price to which her father had agreed.

Gilly rose from her knees and stepped back to survey her handiwork in the mirror where the reflection of Miss Kathryn Raines stood sighing in her pure white virginal innocence. The gown was suitable for a winter wedding, made from panne velvet embellished with swansdown, simple as befitted a bride of seventeen, with a high neck and long sleeves. She carried a muff on which white rosebuds were to be pinned, and was to wear a simple coronet of the same delicate flowers from the hothouses of the Raines' mansion to be rushed to Gillyflower's on the day of the wedding and fashioned by Miss Logan herself. Her face veil, which was now the fashion, reached her chin. Her mother studied her with satisfaction, for though Septimus had allowed her the smallest amount of cash possible Miss Logan had made it stretch so that it looked as though a great deal had been spent on his eldest daughter. She herself was to look splendid in purple silk which Miss Logan had privately told her would not be expensive though she guaranteed that Mrs Raines would not be outshone by any of her guests. Mrs Raines mixed in illustrious circles, the quality of Lancashire, and had standards to keep up, not to mention the future which contained no sons to be married but only daughters. God only knew how she would manage the four coming up behind Kathryn, girls ranging from nine years old to fifteen, but she would think of that when the time came. Thank God for Miss Logan!

Beyond the fitting room was the polite hubbub of ladies who had wandered into Gillyflower's not to buy anything in particular but to see what the clever Miss Logan had on show. She was known for her imaginative designs, her competitive prices, her ability to produce a gown or a mantle at a moment's notice, telling one another that it was difficult to believe she had been in business for a mere eleven months. Her beaded reticules were quite breathtaking and her Spanish parasols a dream, and lately she had put on discreet show facial preparations of which their husbands would probably not approve. Made by some woman – unaware that the woman was Flo Huggett in the back kitchen of her terraced house in Seymour Street – from lemons and cucumber to freshen the skin to herbal washes to lighten or darken the hair, all in fancy bottles, floral perfumes, pots of rouge and powder, all for sale and husbands none the wiser. One never knew what one was to find at Gillyflower's and that was why it was such a delight to enter the salon, drink tea or coffee or chocolate, eat the delicious ratafia biscuits, baked by Flo Huggett though naturally they were not aware of it, served by the polite wisp of a girl in the fetching maid's outfit devised, they supposed, by Miss Logan herself. Miss Logan was always dressed in dove-grey silk, plain, beautifully fitted, with a tiny arrangements of violets pinned to the bodice.

'Well, I think that will do, Mrs Raines. I shall need one more fitting when this hem has been adjusted. Nell here will help Miss Raines and take the gown upstairs to see to the hem. Come in when it suits you for the final fitting and I will personally check that everything is perfect. What is the date of the wedding? . . . The twelfth of December, only three weeks to go, and I shall need the bridesmaids to have a final fitting.'

'Miss Logan, will you run up half a dozen petticoats in the next week?' Mrs Raines asked her worriedly. 'I'm not sure whether Kathryn has enough, and perhaps a morning gown,' her expression cunning as she brooded on the expense, on the possibility of hoodwinking Septimus into believing that the wedding gown was just a trifle more than they had thought.

'Of course, Mrs Raines.' Not by a twitch of her lips or the flicker of an eyelash did Gilly Logan allow the woman to realise that she was run off her feet and with only two needlewomen, Nell and Sadie, and with the ladies already beginning to think of their Christmas outfits for the dozens of parties and balls they would attend, she would need to work far into the night to fill all the orders. Not that she was complaining, not even in the dark recesses of her heart where pain constantly lurked, for Lucas and for Jem, because this was what she wanted, this was what she needed to keep her mind off the desolation that hit her the moment she laid her head on her pillow at night. This frantic need to keep up. To bustle here and there in her cool dove grey, smiling and murmuring soft words to her customers, issuing crisp commands to her staff, not a copper hair out of place, not a nerve anywhere in her body out of control. Even Jess Wilson, who now cleaned the shop every morning, coming in before it was light, despite the incongruity of Jess *cleaning* when one remembered the muck and muddle she had lived in in Rose Alley, added to the success of Gillyflower's.

'So if you'll excuse me, Mrs Raines,' she said with a smile, 'I'll leave you in Nell's capable hands.'

The salon was crowded, ladies sitting gossiping, or flicking through the pages of the *Ladies' Journal*, debating on lace edgings and pearl beads, a social occasion one might think, but Gilly was aware that many of these ladies who had come in merely to look would almost certainly buy something, even if it was only a lace fan. Anne was sitting beside a very pretty, expensively dressed young lady whom Gilly at once recognised, listening to what she was saying but at the same time constantly turning her gaze from the young lady's face towards the door from which Gilly would emerge, and when she did she jumped up, pale and seeming to be distraught, then sat down again abruptly.

Gilly was disorientated for a moment and through the polite buzz of conversation and the movement of nodding heads the figure of the man lounging beside the door had no significance, but at the sight of Gilly, as though she had been waiting for this moment, the woman talking to Anne jumped up and with a malicious, triumphant smile crossed the room and put her arm through that of the man.

'Good morning, Gilly,' she said, raising her voice so that she might be heard, though there was no need, for every lady in the room, sensing some tension here, fell silent. 'I believe you know my fiancé, Mr Lucas Barrie. I am here to see what you might have to offer in the way of a trousseau and Lucas, since he is a gentleman who likes his lady to be well dressed, insisted on coming with me, didn't you, darling?' She turned an enchanting smile into the blank face of the man by the door.

He did not return her smile. In fact he looked grim, harsh even as though this were really nothing to do with him and Gilly knew he had come for one reason only and that was to confront her. To let her see that he was willing to go to any lengths to get her to see reason. He had wanted her, asked her to marry him and she had refused. A man such as he would not countenance a refusal. Indeed she believed he had never known one, for he was rich, handsome, a powerful man in the city, or would be when his father stepped down. There was talk that Herbert Barrie was ready to retire in favour of his son who had proved to be not only a clever designer of ships, but also a businessman who had begun to take an interest in other commercial schemes, such as the railways, mining, and investing in various businesses in and around Liverpool.

It was nearly six months since she had seen him when he had asked her to marry him. The shock of seeing him in her salon struck her a blow that made her gasp quite audibly and almost bent her double. She felt the blood drain from her face and something strike her in the middle of her chest where her heart thudded painfully, galloping wildly to a beat that threatened to have her off her feet. But she must not faint. She must show no concern and certainly not distress, for the salon was filled with ladies on whom her business depended. She must smile, smile, smile and pretend that this was nothing to her. *They* did not know, nobody did, what was between her and Lucas Barrie and she must keep it hidden even though every bone in her body ached as did even her teeth as she clamped her jaw tight then relaxed it to *smile, smile, smile*!

Angela Ryan clung possessively to Lucas's arm, turning to smile and nod at the ladies who were friends of her mother's and who had been guests a week ago at the dinner party when the engagement had been announced. She felt the jubilation flood through her, for she had seen the anguish that had rippled momentarily across Gilly Logan's face and knew that her instincts had not let her down. She had sensed it when they had met in Princes Park, that spark of something between Lucas Barrie and Gilly Logan and though she was absolutely certain

that the Barrie family would not countenance a connection
between their son and a dressmaker she had gone out of her way,
with the help of her mother and father, who had business ties
with Barrie and Hughes, to trap Lucas Barrie. She had got
nowhere. He had been polite, smiling, ready to dance with her at
balls, sit next to her at dinner parties, engage her in conversation
but showed her no more attention than he would any other
young lady until several months ago when he had suddenly
begun to squire her about, to her and his family's delight. His
proposal of marriage had not been quite the romantic one she
had hoped for, in fact she had been slightly disturbed when he
had spoken quite coldly then pushed her gown down from her
shoulders, partly revealing her white, full breasts, kissing them
with a passion she did not think proper. But she had allowed it,
not knowing its full cause nor the despair that had occasioned it.
He had done it several times when they were alone but she had
made it clear that that sort of thing was not to be indulged in until
after the wedding ceremony. She would have been wise to allow
it, for Lucas Barrie was an honourable man who would have felt
compelled to marry her rather than take advantage of her in a
physical sense and then let her down.

Lucas and Gilly looked at one another over the heads of the
seated ladies and once more, as though their minds were linked
by some invisible thread, their eyes and hearts gently spoke to
one another.

"I would give her up in a minute if you would only say
yes . . ."

"You know I cannot . . ."

"Why? You don't love him as I don't love this foolish child
on my arm . . ."

"It's not possible . . ."

Lucas Barrie was so strange, so rigid and still, rooted to the
square of blue carpet in Miss Logan's salon, that the ladies who
watched this interchange with deepening curiosity fell silent,

for there seemed, even to their minds in which nothing more stupendous than the fit of a gown or the latest fashion in hats moved, to be something unusual going on here. Miss Logan was smiling, as she usually was, wearing her normal courteous expression, ready to move forward and chat to whoever wished it, but her gaze remained on Lucas Barrie, not shifting at all to the lovely girl by his side who was, after all, the bride-to-be and the one who was to be fitted for her trousseau.

Lucas was aware of nobody but her. She looked stricken. She was his dearest love. He had thought that with the passing of the months and his engagement to Angela he could put her out of his mind and yet he had come here, surprising Angela, to give his opinion on what she should purchase to become his wife. As if he cared what she wore! And in that moment as he looked deep into the eyes of his true love, he was appalled at what he had done, to her, to Angela even, for he knew he would not marry her. He had been prepared to do anything, not caring how it affected them, to get her. To get *her* meaning Gilly Logan. He was a man who was accustomed to having his own way in most things and just recently, since he had more or less taken over from his father, he had become even more sure that his way was the right, the *only* way of doing things.

A slight wash of colour flowed beneath his smoothly shaved cheek and his grey eyes narrowed, a prick of light turning them to silver, a look that his mother would have known spelled trouble. Not that he had ever been a hot-tempered child or young man, not one to get in a tantrum over what he was told he couldn't have, but somehow, none of them knew how, his nanny, and then his teachers at school had found he had achieved what it was he had set out after. He had always been a favourite with the ladies, tall, lean, with strong, muscled shoulders, for as a lad he had worked manually in his father's shipyard. His thick dark hair curled vigorously, his dark-complexioned face was slashed with dark eyebrows, his chin thrustingly arrogant and his mouth firm, yet a lift at the corners spoke of humour. His teeth were a brilliant white, not quite perfect for one was slightly crooked.

Not that he was smiling now, for what had he to smile at as he regarded Gilly Logan with a look that had the ladies wondering what the dickens was going on. Here was Herbert Barrie's boy, apparently betrothed to Joseph Ryan's girl, Joseph Ryan of Rosemount Lodge and one of the wealthiest and influential merchants in the city. Dealt in timber, he did and had a warehouse on the river and if his daughter cried for the moon he would get it for her. She'd wanted Lucas Barrie, hadn't she, everyone in their elite circle knew that and she'd got him, due no doubt to some deal between their respective fathers, though they had to admit Lucas would not have agreed to it had he not wanted it.

It was apparent to them all that he did not feel humorous now, despite the wry lift to the corners of his mouth, and they deliberated in whispers among themselves as to what he was up to. They were not to know that the casual stance of his long body was a pose he had affected to show Gilly Logan he no longer cared about her, that she could go to the devil and he wouldn't give a damn, marry that half man she lived with, but his eyes denied it.

He wore the finest of dove-grey trousers and an exquisitely pleated and tucked shirt with a snowy fall of a linen cravat. His coat was plum-coloured and his boots a polished black. He carried a hat that was the exact colour of his trousers. A beautiful young man, beautifully dressed with a girl on his arm whom most men would have been proud to escort but, making them all jump and Kathryn Raines, who had just come from the fitting room, squeak, he extracted his arm from Angela's, turned abruptly, opened the door so violently it set the bell ringing and ringing, then crashed it to behind him. The ladies, including Angela, stared in open-mouthed wonder, then the ladies turned to her, for she was not a girl to accept submissively what was surely an insult to her. Her *fiancé* as she had called him, leaving her stranded, ridiculed, for that was how she would see it, shown up in front of the high society of Liverpool, abandoned without a word and what they wanted to know was *why*. Could it be something to do with the immobile figure of the proprietor of this establishment whose golden tawny eyes had clouded into an unfocused stare as she studied the door through which Lucas Barrie had just blundered?

Anne Barrie stood up suddenly and they all turned to look at her, ladies with cups of delicious hot chocolate halfway to their lips as Lucas Barrie left. Now what? their avid eyes asked, but Anne merely smiled at them all, including Angela Ryan and moved gracefully across the deep textured carpet to Gilly. She took her arm and turned her towards the stairs.

'Come, Gilly, we must get Miss Raines's patterns for her . . . her . . .' for a moment she couldn't think what it was that Miss Raines, or rather Mrs Raines had ordered. Her wedding dress was all but finished so what . . . 'That morning gown you promised her,' she finished, leading her up the stairs and putting her into the surprised arms of Nell with hissed instructions to look after her. Then she ran downstairs again and, with a graciousness and politeness of a hostess in her own home, ordered fresh biscuits, chocolate, chattered to this lady and that on any subject that came into her head and led Miss Ryan to a chair, for she seemed temporarily stunned. Not that it would last. Angela Ryan's temper was well known and when she recovered her wits the first person in her line of vision would get the full blast of it. Anne did not mean it to be her. Angela Ryan had made Anne's life a misery at school until Gilly came but she was strong now, thanks to Gilly and the purpose in life her friend had given her. She still had stupendous arguments with her mother over her determination to *do something useful* rather than accompany her on calls, receive callers, sit at home and embroider, go for carriage drives and spend hours in places like this poring over fashion journals. She was Gilly's right-hand man, Gilly told her a dozen times a day, for it was Anne who knew the right thing to say to these ladies, how to treat them. She could not sew a straight seam though her embroidery was quite beautiful and Gilly did not know what she would do without her.

They had all gone, Angela cowering in her mother's carriage which had been sent for, the other ladies making their way to their next appointments, most in their own carriages, but all still whispering about the strange events in Miss Logan's smart salon, the story of which would be all over Liverpool's upper classes by nightfall. They wouldn't like to be in the shoes of whoever had caused the affront to Miss Angela Ryan, not awfully sure who it was, for neither Lucas Barrie nor Miss Logan had spoken a word. Still, *something* had taken place and Angela Ryan and, more to the point, Joseph Ryan would want to know what it was.

'Why didn't you tell me he was engaged to her? You must have known and yet you said nothing. I can't believe you didn't warn me so that I would be ready for the—'

'Darling, I didn't know it would mean anything to you. You and Lucas have never . . . you have never spoken of him and he certainly has not said anything to me about his feelings for . . . for you. I know you have met a time or two . . . at the launching of the ship but even then you showed no sign. I thought you and Jem were . . . Dear Lord, Gilly, forgive me but I didn't know you . . . you and he were . . .'

'We're not.' Gilly's voice was savage and her face contorted with the intensity of her denial. 'He is nothing to me and I am—'

'Then why are you so upset? What happened downstairs was quite appalling and all of Liverpool will be gossiping. You don't think Angela Ryan will forgive him, do you?'

'Do you honestly think I give a damn about Angela Ryan?'

'No, I don't suppose you do but she will do her best to get her revenge, not only on Lucas, for there is nothing more sure than that he will not marry her now, but on you. You know she has always been jealous of you, of your beauty—'

'For goodness' sake, Anne.'

'She hated you at school when you protected me. Do you remember my stammer? That was her fault and yet you cured me with your affection, your kindness and your goodness in allowing me to work here with you. My mama doesn't like it and I keep expecting Papa to say . . . but that's neither here nor there. What is there between you and Lucas because it will—'

'Nothing, for God's sake. Nothing! We are nothing to each other and I told him so when—'

'So you have seen him. Oh darling, what is it? Tell me. Let me help you, for you are dearer to me than a sister.'

'He came here.'

'Here? To the shop?'

'Yes. You had gone, I was alone and he . . . he asked me to marry him.'

Anne's face lit up and she leaped to her feet ready to embrace this girl, for she could think of no one whom she would rather have as a sister-in-law, but Gilly bowed her head, leaning forward in her chair as though she were in great pain. She was in great pain and yet in the core of her, in her heart, was a feeling of joy. Was it joy? She could think of no other way to describe it because what Anne had said about Lucas had lit a tiny candle in her. A candle of . . . of what? He would not come again and if he did she would not accept him, but Anne was adamant that he would not marry Angela. And what was that to her? To Gilly Logan? Even with Angela out of the picture it did not mean he would not marry someone else. But he wanted *her*. It had been in his eyes and in the tension of him as he stood, at ease he would have her believe, in her shop doorway. He had challenged her in some strange way, had humiliated Angela who had been bursting with malicious pride in her capture of him.

As though catching the drift of Gilly's thought Anne's voice was quiet, sad even, as she spoke.

'You know she will not forget this. She may not be clever but she's not stupid and she will have recognised that you were the reason for Lucas's behaviour. She came to your shop to parade him before you and her friends, though you were the main target. You, or Lucas, have in the past given her reason to believe that there could be something between you. That is why she came to the salon. To show you that she has caught him and that you are, for some reason, to dress her for her marriage to him. But Lucas bolted, showing *her* up in the most appalling way. And she will not forget it. Nor forgive it. She, or rather her father, has a great deal of influence in Liverpool and there are those who would listen to him, and obey him, if he says that their wives and daughters are not to put business your way. Through her father she could hurt you badly.'

Gilly bowed her head even further and began to rock gently, her arms about herself as women do who are badly hurt, not physically but emotionally. She had fallen deep in love with Lucas Barrie. And he felt the same about her, she knew that in her woman's heart which beat steadily and irrevocably to the same beat as his. She had done nothing to encourage him. Just the opposite and he had gone away. He had chosen another woman and it had been announced to all Liverpool society that he was to marry Angela and yet with just one meeting, one wordless exchange that had dazzled them both, he might have ruined her. It was not to be borne. *It was not to be borne* and yet it must be. He had left his fiancée in the full glare of the ladies with whom she and her family socialised, exposed her to their unkind curiosity and, when she had recovered her senses, for nothing like this had ever happened to the pampered daughter of Joseph Ryan, she would raise her proud, vengeful head and strike back.

'What shall I do?' Gilly moaned. 'Dear God, Anne, you paint a pretty picture of what is to happen. I know Angela is a . . . a . . .'

'A vindictive bitch,' Anne spat out, her usual sweet face contorted in fury.

Gilly laughed weakly, lifting her head. Her eyes were bleak, their golden lights quenched. She did not weep though she felt like it, for she was a fighter and had not worked her fingers to the bone for most of her life, and especially this last year, for nothing. She was the sole breadwinner in her family as Jem no longer brought in any wages. How could he, the state he was in. Jem, poor Jem . . . Dear God!

She stood up jerkily, smoothing down her skirt. She reached out and put her arms round Anne, then kissed her cheek.

'Well, we must just do our best to hold on to the customers we have, Anne, love, and hope they are not all led by Angela Ryan.'

23

Jem reached for his stick, which was hanging on a knob on the hallstand, flung his cap on his head and opened the front door on to Seymour Street.

'I won't be long. Just to the end of the street and back,' he shouted to someone in the far reaches of the scullery, but he hadn't even shut the door before Queenie came screeching through the kitchen and into the passage, her face a picture of disapproval and at the same time anxiety.

'Lad, lad, wait fer me an' I'll come wi' yer. I need a few bits an' pieces from't grocers an' a walk'd do me good. I've a fancy ter mekk some scones fer us tea an'—'

'Give over, Queenie.' Jem sighed irritably. 'When will you realise that I've got to learn to get out and about on my own. I'll never do it if you or Flo or Gilly keep treating me like a child out for the first time without its mam. I've got my stick and like Mr Jenkins said I've ears on me head. When you can't see other senses take over and, God's honour, I could hear a pin drop a hundred yards away. Let me go, Queenie, please.'

'Listen, our Jem, I've stuff ter get at market so why don't me an' you walk over there an'—'

'Leave me alone, Queenie, for God's sake leave me alone. When will you accept that I've to get on with my life and I've to do it in my own way. I want to get about the city without—'

'Eeh, no, lad, not yet,' Queenie agonised, wanting to get hold of this beloved man who was like a son to her and drag him back to the safety of 19 Seymour Street where she could watch over him. It was six months since Tommy Wilson, now languishing in the Borough Gaol, thank the good Lord, had damaged his son so badly he would never see again. But not only had he blinded the lad, he had taken away his spirit, his joy of living, his pride, his manliness, the very essence of the bright, engaging young man he had once been.

Jem had nothing to live for now. The clever brain that had forged his will to clamber to the heights he had reached was slowly withering away with nothing to occupy it, nothing to think about but his pain, for though he told no one he had headaches that nearly crippled him. His memory had returned in small flashes and that was partly to blame for his melancholy because he remembered what he had lost. They all loved him and would have given anything, Queenie her life, to restore him to who he had been. Aye, they all loved him, he knew that, and would take care of him until the end of his days but he was still a bloody man, and what he wanted from Gilly was not the pitying love she felt for him. He was a proper man, wasn't he, and what man wanted to be a burden to the women in his life, no matter how they loved him. They were all three patient and cheerful, unnaturally so, he was inclined to think. He had lost the knack of making them laugh, the merry and auda-ciously comical man he had once been burned out of him as he realised, week by week, that he was never going to see again. What was he to do with the rest of his life? He asked himself this question day after desperate day and the truth was, he hadn't the faintest idea. Squat at the corner of Bold Street with his cap on the pavement before him begging for charity from passers-by? If he could just think of something to give him a reason for living, some occupation, preferably one that would bring him in a wage, he might hang on, but what in God's name could that be?

He had asked the question of Mr Jenkins on one of the check-ups the doctor insisted upon though there was really nothing more that Hugh Jenkins could do for the tragic young man who was ebbing away before his very eyes.

'Why don't you go to the Free Library on William Brown Street and teach yourself Braille?' he asked him one day. 'I believe they have a few copies there. The man who invented it was himself blind. You read by touch, using embossed dots. Louis Braille died years ago and at first his method was not accepted but it is becoming widely used. I believe they even have a newspaper, one a week, which might be useful. You could at least read independently without having Gilly read to you.'

But so far, deep in his depressive state, Jem had not taken up the doctor's suggestion. All he wanted to do at the moment was get away from Seymour Street, from the suffocating ministrations of Queenie and Flo and away from his deep and hopeless love for Gilly Logan which was slowly killing him.

'No, Queenie, no, no no. Let me go by myself, lass, please. I promise I won't go far. Bloody hell, I know this city like the back of my hand.' He laughed bitterly. 'I used to say I could find my way round blindfold, well, now I intend to do it.'

'Well, at least purra scarf on, lad,' Queenie begged, longing to follow him to make sure he was all right crossing that busy road at the bottom of Seymour Street, since not for a minute did she believe that he would turn back obediently at the corner. London Road was one of the busiest in Liverpool, crowded at this time of day with wagons, brewer's drays, carriages, enormous shire horses with dangerous hooves, gentlemen riding their thoroughbreds and though he swore he could manage, his hearing acute, he could be run down by any one of them.

'Let me come wi' yer,' she pleaded one last time but he was off down the street, tapping at the wall of the houses, waving to her with his free hand. Oh aye, he was confident enough, but then he had walked along Seymour Street on his own a dozen times and what's more the residents knew him and of his disability and when they saw him coming they got out of his way. They shouted a cheery greeting to him but none stopped to speak, for to tell the truth they didn't know what to say to him, poor lad.

He reached the corner of London Road without mishap. Listening carefully, he decided there was a break in the traffic and crossed from one corner of Seymour Street to the other, holding his stick up as a signal to anyone who might be approaching on a horse that he was blind and to give way to him. He knew he could reach his destination through side streets but there were too many corners, too many alleys and ginnels to manoeuvre so he had decided on the main roads as they would be more direct. He knew that the hesitant manner in which he walked and his stick which wavered out before him would warn pedestrians, and with the good humour and hearts of the Liverpool man or woman they would move over for him. It was the roads and their heavy traffic that would be the challenge. But, Jesus, he had to start somewhere because if he was to achieve any sort of independence he must do it now before he became a total invalid.

He reached Lime Street, tapping his way, waving his stick and repeating to all those who, it seemed to him, got out of his way, 'Thanks . . . thanks . . .'

'Need any 'elp, lad?' one sympathetic male voice asked and one woman actually touched his arm and asked if she could take him to his destination. His attractive face lit up with the smile that had been so active once, and his good teeth gleamed in his flushed face, for the unaccustomed exercise was pumping his blood round his body. His cap was set at a jaunty angle and his thick curly hair sprang out from beneath it, the winter sun touching it with gold. He wore the good jacket and breeches, the warm knitted jersey made for him by Flo, a vivid blue that matched his eyes and the hearts of many of the women who watched him go by could have cried for him, since it was a sin that a lad, a good-looking lad like him should be so cruelly afflicted.

He progressed slowly along Lime Street. The sound of the trains from the railway station, the whistle of engines, the shouts of porters and the stamping of the hooves of the horses that pulled the many cabs drawn up at the bottom of the entrance steps confused him and he was tempted to ask someone to guide him, but he gritted his teeth and blundered on, apologising profusely when he walked into the back of a gentleman who turned to swear at him.

The man glared at him, then seeing his condition became apologetic as though he should not have been standing innocently at the bottom of the wide steps.

'I say, I'm sorry, old chap,' he stammered, and Jem felt his heart weaken, not physically, for he knew he was as sound as a horse, Mr Jenkins had said so, but at this test of his resolve, which seemed to tell him that everyone was sorry for him but damn glad it was not them. Their compassion, their pity, unmanned him and for a dreadful moment he wanted to shout to anyone who would listen that he would be grateful if they would put him in a cab and send him back to Queenie. To Queenie's arms and Queenie's loving understanding, but, good Christ, he could not give up. He *would not* give up! He had crossed no streets yet except Seymour Street, for at each corner he had turned left, but now he was beyond the station he had to navigate several narrow streets. He was opposite the Town Hall; he did not know how he knew but some sense of direction, which he was glad he had not lost, told him, but then came the difficult part: Ranelagh Place which had *five* roads leading into it.

He had felt the lift to his spirits as he had shuffled along but now stood helplessly on the kerb, listening to the concerto of the traffic, the sound of heavy wheels on the cobbles, the clash of hooves, whips cracking, men shouting at others who got in their way, the hubbub of voices and his heart sank.

'Where did you want to go?' a quiet voice said at his elbow and he turned his blind gaze to the man who had spoken.

'Just get me across this junction and I know my way from there.' It galled him to ask for help, since he had been determined to get to Remington Place on his own. Not to go in, of course, since that would not be appropriate. Her shop would be filled with ladies and for the life of him he couldn't understand why he should need to get there. It wasn't as if he could see it, watch the customers come and go, but something in him wanted to get there, to stand on the other side of the road and know that she was there, making a success of her life, fulfilled by it, part of the world as he was not. He shouldn't have come, he realised that. A wander – which was what it would be – down London Road, William Brown Street, Dale Street and Water Street, a direct route to the docks would have been more sensible for his first outing and from there he could have sauntered along the Marine Parade, seeing nothing, but smelling the freshness of the sea, the sharpness of tar from the rigging of a sailing vessel, coffee beans, Indian tea, citrus fruits, nutmeg and the clean smell of timber. All the aromas with which he was so familiar and which he missed so desperately. To hear the shouting of labourers, the cry of the seabirds, the hooting of ships' sirens, the whistling and banging . . . Dear God, he thought he would run mad with longing, but there was this man at his elbow who seemed inclined to drag him across Ranelagh Place by force.

He pulled his arm away so rudely he felt sorry, but then his rage took over, not at the helpful man but at life itself which had made him so bloody helpless he couldn't even find his own way home. Turning away he began to flounder back in the direction from which he had come and though Lucas Barrie, whose voice he had not recognised, knew that this was the man who stood in the way of his determination to win Gilly Logan, he could not help but be sorry for the poor sod.

It took him a long time to get home, for on the way he happened to pass The Ship Inn, a public house on the corner of Pudsey Street, and the sound of laughter drew him towards it. He hadn't had a good laugh for a long time, he brooded, and it sounded as though those inside the four ale bar – he couldn't remember the name – were having a good time. He went inside, bringing the laughter and the boisterous uproar to silence for a minute as he stumbled to the bar, brandishing his stick before him. Men, mostly sailors, drew aside to let him pass and when he ordered a rum, downing it in one gulp, they looked at one another suggestively, for here was what looked like a toff, and a *blind* toff into the bargain, who might be persuaded to buy a round or two.

To give them their due they led him to Seymour Street, or half carried him, when his money ran out, and left him to tap his way to his own door where Queenie frowned in great disapproval when she opened it, for she knew a drunken man when she saw him. He had done his best to get his key in the lock and the sound of it had alerted her, but his drunken laughter, his mumbled protests that he was perfectly all right frightened her to death. She knocked on the wall between her house and Flo's, a prearranged signal between them, and when Flo came running, her hand at her mouth at the sight of him sprawled in Queenie's chair, they looked at each other aghast.

'Dear Lord, wha' next?' moaned Queenie. 'I didn't want 'im ter go on 'is own but would 'e listen? Norra birrof it an' now look at 'im. Drunk as a fiddler's bitch an' 'ow the 'ell did 'e gerrome, I'd like ter know.'

Jem must have caught the drift of what she was saying, for he assured them slurringly that his 'friends' had fetched him to the end of the street and he thought he might go to meet them again as they were a good laugh and there was not much of that in this bloody world. All spoken in broken snatches which the two women found difficult to understand.

Jem had been sleeping at Flo's for the last couple of months. Well, it seemed daft, Flo said, when she had two bedrooms and Queenie and Gilly were forced to share so Jem, who didn't care where he slept, he said in that indifferent manner he had assumed ever since his beating, had been moved into Flo's spare bedroom. They had made it 'nice' for him though they might as well not have bothered since he couldn't see the pictures of ships on the wall, the pretty curtains at the window with a counterpane to match, the rugs they had made for his feet, nor the best English stoneware jug and basin decorated with birds which they thought he might like and which stood on the washstand under the window. He ate his breakfast at Flo's, for she said it was a blessing to have someone to cook for again, but he spent the rest of the day with Queenie and, when she got home from the shop, with Gilly.

Grumbling loudly, protesting that he was comfortable in the chair, they got him to his feet, half carried him round to Flo's and somehow propelled him up the stairs. With little exercise he had put on some weight since his father had injured him and he was heavy, but they managed to undress him, mumbling that he was not a little lad nor a baby to be treated thus, and got him into his bed where he fell at once into a deep sleep. He was still there when Gilly came home.

It was two weeks since Angela Ryan and Lucas Barrie had entered her shop and in those two weeks three of her customers had cancelled their orders for Christmas gowns. The engagement between Lucas and Angela was broken, so Anne told her, and the conflict at Bracken Hill was indescribable. Papa had threatened to disown Lucas, for he and Joseph Ryan did a lot of business together and this rift caused by Lucas's shameful conduct and affront to the Ryan family would surely create dissension not only between the two families but would ruin their business association. She had slipped out unseen by the kitchen door, to the amazement of the servants, since her mother had expressly forbidden her not only to go out but to cross the threshold of that hussy ever again.

'But why do you call her a hussy? Gilly is not to blame for what happened,' Anne had alleged vigorously, her face pale and rigid, an expression reflected in that of her mother. 'It is nothing to do with her. Lucas and Angela came into her shop and after a few minutes Lucas simply turned and walked out again. He never said a word to anyone so it is he who caused all the fuss. I was there, Mama, and saw it.'

'Yes, and that is why you are not to go again. Your papa and I have been very lenient with you but you are not a shop girl, nor a dressmaker. Yes, yes, I know you consider Miss Logan a friend and that she was kind to you at school but she is not our sort, Anne, and the association must end. You are to stay at home and do what a "daughter at home" would do. What your friends do which is to—'

'I have no friends other than Gilly. She relies on me to help her in the salon.'

Mrs Barrie tutted impatiently. 'Salon indeed. I never heard the like . . .'

'Many of our friends go there, Mama, and are delighted with what she—'

'So I believe but I don't think Miss Logan can count on their custom for much longer. I blame her entirely for what has happened. They say Angela is distraught. To be treated as she was in front of people with whom her family dine and then to be tossed aside by my own son . . . Oh yes, he has informed her that he no longer wishes to marry her and it all stems from that visit to that woman's shop. Hilda Ryan told me that she thought Joseph would attack Lucas he was so outraged by his high-handed behaviour. To become engaged one week and to cancel it the next is not the way of a gentleman and your father is beside himself. He and Joseph Ryan do a lot of business together, timber and such . . .' Her voice was vague, for she had no idea nor any wish to know what her husband did at the shipyard. 'If Mr Ryan takes it into his head to cut off the supply of timber your father would . . . well, he would not be pleased.'

'But what has that to do with Gilly, Mama?' Anne had begged to know plaintively.

'It was in her shop that the . . . the incident occurred and surely that tells you that—'

'What, Mama, what?'

But Rose Barrie would say no more except to reiterate that Anne was to go nowhere near Remington Place again.

'Perhaps it would be better if you were to . . .' Rose lifted her head imperiously. 'Your father and I forbid you to associate with Miss Logan from now on.'

'I must disobey you, I'm afraid, Mama. Gilly is my friend and I cannot desert her.'

The tension from the drawing room spread, like a gentle wave on the flat mud at the edge of the River Mersey, through the house and into the kitchen where the servants fell dumb. Miss Anne was so pleasant and kind, so *mouse-like*, she never argued with either of her parents but would you listen to her now. Mrs Barrie would not be best pleased and they were right.

Rose Barrie put her hand to her breast where her heart was beating out of control and she thought she would swoon. When had the mouse turned into a lion, she wondered frantically, but she would not be beaten. Not by a chit of a girl who had up to meeting that hussy been the perfect daughter.

'Then perhaps it would be advisable for you to visit your Aunt Isobel in Scarborough. A few weeks away might allow you to recognise who you are and the importance of your father's position in this city. It will not do, Anne so if you will ring the bell and ask Hetty to pack . . .'

'No, Mama, I'm sorry, but that would be impossible.'

Rose Barrie's mouth fell open and she goggled at her daughter in utter amazement. Never in her eighteen years had her sweet-natured, pliable young daughter defied her. She watched as Anne stood up and left the room, her safe and respectable world crumbling about her. First Lucas and now Anne had thumbed their noses at the society in which they moved and she hadn't the faintest idea what to do.

She rang the bell for her maid, falling back into the depths of the sofa until she came with the smelling salts.

Now Anne took Gilly's hand and peered lovingly into her forlorn face. She did not tell her about the scene with her mama for it was obvious Gilly was brooding about something. The cancelling of the three outfits was a blow indeed since all three were ladies of quality who might influence others. Joseph Ryan was enormously influential in commerce and a word to those he did business with, the word passed on to their wives would do enormous damage to Gilly Logan. But it seemed to Anne that this was not the only thing that troubled Gilly. It occurred to her as she studied her friend's face that Gilly had lost weight, her face had hollows that had not been there before and her eyes were dulled. She had lost somewhat that look of rosy good health; even her hair, when it was let loose, was curiously lifeless.

'What is it, dearest?' she murmured. 'Something else is troubling you, isn't it? I know we have suffered a blow in the last fortnight but there are other ladies who will be glad to give us their custom. The "upstairs" ladies are growing in number,' meaning the wives of the hardworking and respectable working men who were spreading the word among their friends that Gillyflower's could supply all their needs and at a reasonable price. They would still give her their custom, for

Joseph Ryan had no leverage over them since he simply did not
know they existed in his important world, or of that side of
Gilly's business. They were beneath his notice, the small
businesses that proliferated and thrived in many of the back
streets of Liverpool. Ironmongers, scale beam-makers, rope-
makers, men associated with ships and the sea, those who
supplied ships' provender, ships' chandlers, sail-makers, small
men, but successful, who owed Joseph Ryan nothing. Their
wives did not mix in any way with the upper-class ladies and as
Gilly drooped in her empty salon, upstairs Nell was at this
moment fitting Mrs Atkinson, wife of a ship's chandler, with a
gown for her niece's wedding in West Derby. Sadie was going
ten to the dozen on her sewing machine and Rosie was helping
her. She had made Mrs Atkinson a pot of tea since the lady was
not partial to chocolate or coffee, she said, being used to
neither, and she was well satisfied with the attention she
received and the lovely gown designed for her by Miss Logan.
She meant to bring her great friend Mrs Lawley whose husband had a corner grocer's shop on Clayton Street at the back
of the library, for Mrs Lawley had a daughter who was about to
be engaged to an up-and-coming bank clerk.

'Tell me what's troubling you, Gilly, please. We are
friends . . .'

'Yes.' She longed to pour out her hopelessly aching heart to
this dear girl who, despite her family's disapproval, continued
to be her friend, and tell her how deeply she loved her brother.
Tell her that her heart was breaking into a million shards, all of
them piercing her so badly until she thought she might slowly
die of it. Anne knew of his proposal and Gilly's refusal and had
not mentioned it since, waiting, she supposed, for something to
occur that could change Gilly's mind but it was hopeless,
hopeless.

'It's Jem,' she blurted out suddenly. 'He's . . .'

Anne's good heart ached not only for this girl but for Jem

who was so cruelly afflicted, wondering why it was that so much trouble could come to one small family.

'Yes?' she asked softly, thinking that she knew what was troubling Gilly, for it was obvious, had been obvious ever since they had become friends that Jem loved Gilly. It had shone from the brilliant blue of his eyes which were now opaque and staring and though she knew that had he not had this trouble he would have married Gilly, had she been willing, what man will attach himself to a girl who he could not see. Nor support and protect.

'Is he . . .?' She paused delicately, for Gilly Logan was not the only one whose feelings were involved here.

'He's beginning to drink,' Gilly said bluntly. 'Once upon a time he was reluctant to accept the few bob we gave him, for a man must have a few coins to jingle in his pocket but now he . . . he asks either me, or Mam or Flo for . . . He has taken to going out alone. We followed him and he goes straight to the four ale bar on Pudsey Street where they greet him like a long-lost friend. I spoke to Mr Jenkins who tells me has tried to interest Jem in learning to read Braille—'

'Braille?'

'It's a way for the blind to read. At the library on William Brown Street but he . . .' Her head drooped in despair because Gilly Logan knew there was only one way to get Jem back into a world in which he could survive. But she loved Lucas Barrie and her body shrank at the thought of giving it to any other.

She did not see the light of something glimmer in Anne's eyes nor the lift of her head as she stared over Gilly's bent head.

24

She saw him tapping his way along London Road, not giving a damn for those who got in his way, it seemed to her, grunting when folk apologised profusely when he bumped into them. When he approached Pudsey Street and the Ship Inn, just as he was about to enter she stepped out in front of him, colliding so heavily with him he instinctively put out his hand to steady her and she clung to it though she had no intention of falling.

'Oh thank you, thank you so much,' she murmured, a frail woman who needed the strong hand of a man to guide her. 'I might have fallen but for you.' She appeared not to notice the stick or the unfocused stare of the man to whose arm she clung.

'I'm sorry,' Jem mumbled, strangely pleased, for it was not often, in fact never during the past six months that anyone had needed his support.

'I was looking for the museum but I seem to have missed it. And I wanted to look something up in the reference library . . .' Anne hesitated, still holding on to Jem's strong, manly arm, as there were several rough men about, sailors and such who were intent on entering the Ship Inn. She was not exactly a pretty girl but her fresh, neat appearance in the rich blue winter outfit made for her by her good friend Gilly Logan, her charming bonnet to match with its ruched muslin beneath the brim from which several golden curls had escaped, her dainty fur muff and her lovely bright smile were attracting some attention. Jem was dressed in his usual corduroy jacket, his well-pressed breeches and the knitted jersey and scarf Flo had made. He was never allowed to leave the house in the state of disarray in which he entered it, for the minute he undressed either Flo or Queenie had the flat iron out. He had shaved that morning at Queenie's insistence, mainly to shut her up, and brushed his tumble of fair curls. His boots were polished to a high shine and he looked very presentable.

'Aren't you Jem Wilson?' Anne said hesitantly, clinging still to his arm, as at her words he tried to pull away. For a moment he had been a young male who had attracted the interest of a young female, both of them unknown to each other, but when she seemed to recognise him he was at once conscious of his blindness.

'Yes,' he said roughly, doing his best to dislodge her hand. 'So what?'

'I'm Anne Barrie, Gilly's friend. You seemed familiar but I could not quite place . . .'

'Well, I suppose the stick would give me away.' His voice was rude, ironic, and his sightless eyes bent to hers as though he were doing his best to pierce the darkness about him. The sound of the hated name, the name that belonged to the man who had laid covetous eyes on Gilly, stiffened his arm and Anne felt it but she still would not let go of him.

'I had forgotten,' she said simply, 'but I would be most grateful if you could guide me to the library. I know it is in William Brown Street which was once Shawsbrow and when I asked a gentleman he seemed unsure of where I meant. In fact he seemed more interested in smiling and looking me over as if he thought I had designs on *him*.'

'Well, he would, and really you shouldn't be on your own at this end of London Road at all. There are a great many public houses where sailors and . . . disreputable fellows hang about.' He sighed deeply but at the very centre of him a small glow warmed him. Here was a young woman who had lost herself, silly little fool, a woman from the quality folk of Liverpool who had no idea of the danger she could be in, but who seemed to need something he could give her. He knew where he was and he knew where the library was but getting across the busy roads that lay between was impossible. On his own.

'All right, Miss Barrie . . .'

'Anne, please. We have met before, you know.'

'I don't remember, I'm afraid.'

No, your eyes were filled with Gilly Logan as were my brother's.

'Well, never mind,' she said out loud. 'If you could take me there, seeing that you seem to disapprove of my being in this part of town, I should be so grateful.'

He laughed bitterly. 'Miss Barrie, you seem to have over-looked the fact that I cannot see. You say you are a friend of Gilly's so you will know of my accident.'

'Of course, but what has that to do with taking me to the library? I will be your eyes as we cross the road and you will be my . . . my guide and protector.' She held his arm tightly and was relieved to feel him relax.

'Sweet Jesus, you're a persistent little bu—er . . . lass. Very well, I'll take you to the steps of the library but how am I to get back to where *I'm* going?'

'And where is that, Jem?' she asked innocently.

'Into the Ship.'

'The Ship?'

'Aye, the pub.'

'Really. Could I not come into the pub with you?'

He laughed out loud again and several passers-by looked round curiously. His 'pals', those he had taken to drinking with at the Ship and who were entering at that moment, hung about in the doorway, wondering what the hell old Jem was doing talking to the attractive young lady who, it seemed, knew him and was holding his arm. They were even more surprised when the couple began to walk in the direction of St George's Hall.

'Aye up, Jem lad, are yer not comin' in?' one shouted after him. 'We've a rum set up for yer on't bar,' which was not true, for Jem was the one who usually ordered and paid for the drinks, at least until his money ran out when they lost interest in him. He could find his own way home now.

'No, I've somewhere to go but I'll see you later,' he shouted over his shoulder.

No, you won't, Anne said to herself, leading him to the kerb. If I've anything to do with it you won't go in that place again. No wonder you've gone off the rails, coming home drunk and in dire danger of losing your way and I don't just mean between here and the Ship. Left with two elderly ladies as your only company, two elderly ladies who have nothing else to do but fuss about you, not meaning to do you any harm but nevertheless doing it. Gilly is away all day and sometimes into the evening, struggling with her business which, because of a vindictive, spoiled girl and a man who is unsure how to proceed with his life, is beginning to flounder. She, Anne, was not really needed in the salon any more, as the ladies who still brought their business to Gillyflower's did not need to be flattered and fawned over. They were the wives of artisans, successful tradesmen, professional men, who were themselves outspoken northern women who stood *beside* their menfolk and were not kept in the place gentlewomen were, bowing to their husband's commands. Joseph Ryan had spoken to his business associates and they, in their turn, had spoken to their wives and the custom they had taken to Gillyflower's had been withdrawn. The only lady of the privileged class who still had her outfits designed and made by Gilly was Miss Helen Moore who was twenty-two and unmarried and what's more she was a suffragist. Her mother had long given up trying to keep her at home and since she had her own money she was one of those rare birds in this day and age, a woman who could do as she pleased. With Nell and Sadie and Rosie, who was now allowed to hem a garment under supervision, Gilly was able to manage the work she had, which was why Anne was here, holding Jem's arm.

They made a handsome couple really, for they were both well dressed and though the man seemed disinclined to smile, she did, chatting amiably, looking up into his face, her own quite animated, doing her best to keep up with his long stride. She was small, her head barely reaching his shoulder but with an occasional skip she kept in step.

Anne Barrie had been attracted to the young engineer from the very first when he began to work in her father's design office. She had been drawn to his merry, endearing grin, his vivid, smiling blue eyes, to his infectious good humour and to his seeming disregard of the division between them, for he was a working lad and she was the daughter of a wealthy ship-builder. She had not been in his company often, as it was no part of her life to go to her father's shipyard but as he progressed and had been included in the company at several launchings she had been drawn in some strange way to his kindness, his inclination to talk to the youngsters, to share a joke with them, treating them as equals instead of naughty children, almost becoming one of them. It was as though he could be comfortable in whatever company he found himself. He had no 'side' to him as though he were not really aware that he was, in many ways, beneath the Hughes and Barrie families. He had chatted to her, unaware, it appeared, of her stammer which still had a tendency to appear when she was with strangers and she found that when she was with him, as when she was with Gilly, it disappeared. She was at ease with him, relaxed and she sometimes wished that he and Gilly were not so attached to one another. She knew, of course, that her family would never agree to any sort of relationship between herself and a man from the lower classes but then it didn't seem to be of importance since he loved Gilly and it seemed to be accepted that one day they would marry. But Gilly loved Lucas and

Lucas loved Gilly so what was to become of poor Jem? He was blind, useless, bitter and angry at his fate and Anne knew that should Gilly have wished it, which she didn't, Jem would never accept her pitying love.

Something had flourished unseen in the heart of Anne Barrie, small as a bud about to open on the branch of a tree, a bud that would grow and become a leaf in the spring and Anne cherished it. Whenever she was in his company, which happened now and again when Gilly took her to Seymour Street for a meal, she could look at him, study his young face, which was sadly ageing in his resentment, his frustration, the bitter cup he held to his lips, and she began to understand, to recognise what it was she felt for Jem Wilson. Had he had his sight, had Gilly loved him and not her brother, that bud, that leaf that was blooming would have been firmly squashed, pruned from the branch and Anne Barrie would have found a life for herself in some way, some occupation that her good heart would have found rewarding. But none of these things signified and her compassion for Jem, this feeling that grew in her must be allowed full rein. For his sake and for hers. She sometimes smiled to herself in the dark of her bed, seeing herself with a mission, foolish girl, but was it not something that was worth trying? A challenge! But no, that was not it, for in the very core of her where no one could see she accepted that she was more than just attracted to him.

'Rightio,' she said gaily, 'step out now with me. There's a break in the traffic.' She began to laugh, clinging like a limpet to his arm and he found his own mouth twitching. 'Quick, run for it . . . no, don't hesitate, Jem. Trust me.' And he found he did, quickening his step to run with her to the other side of the road.

'Perhaps when I've finished my business at the reference library we might take a walk along the river. I've always wanted to go as far as . . . well, I don't know, how far can you go along the Parade? I've never been since my father believes it's not ladylike to be interested in such things.'

'What tommy-rot! Why shouldn't you look at the ships as you walk the Parade? I suppose he thinks women should be kept in their place and their place is not where lads like me go. It's grand along there and I only wish . . . You can go as far as the Fort.' His voice was gruff but there was something in it that told her he was pleased. Not pleased that he was not to see it but that he should be the one to show it to her.

'Would you like to take me?' knowing in some way that to suggest to him that without him she could not even attempt it would surely soothe that hurt, that male pride, that feeling that he was worthless.

'I suppose I could.' It was all the same to him, his manner seemed to say, but with that instinct that comes to a woman interested in a man, she had done the right thing.

'What is it you want to know at the reference library?' He was not really interested but he was doing his best to be polite as she steered him, without seeming to, through the press of people who crowded the pavements along William Brown Street.

'Oh, it's something for a friend who is interested in . . . well, never mind. If I nip in to the library you could wait for me, if you don't mind, and then we could take a stroll along the Parade. But I tell you what.'

'What?'

'I'm really hungry. Shall we take lunch at the Adelphi before we . . .?'

She knew she had made a mistake before she finished the sentence. It had been said without thinking, but how was a blind man to eat a meal in public and, what's more, at the Adelphi which was the smartest hotel in Liverpool. It was unthinkable and his reaction told her so. He pulled his arm from her clutching hand and turned, crashing into a gentleman who was coming up behind him, hitting him so fiercely the man's hat fell over his face and he dropped the newspaper he was carrying.

'Dear God, man, can you not watch what you're doing?' he snarled, setting his hat back on his head and bending down to pick up his newspaper and at once Jem fell over the man's back and landed in a heap in the path of another chap who almost went over *him*.

Jem steadied himself and when she went to help him he threw off her hand and turned about, disorientated and absolutely livid with himself, with the man who had just noticed his stick and was apologising profusely and with the man, his own father, who had thrown him into this appalling state. From being a strong, cheerful young man with a fine future ahead of him he had become a cripple, a man dependent on others and he could not put up with it much longer. The dread canker of hopelessness was sapping his will and he knew he was slipping into the pit his own fertile mind had dug for him. What was he to do with the rest of his life? he asked himself. Why the hell had his father's blow not killed him, for surely he could not be expected to stumble through life holding on to some kind hand.

'Why the bloody hell don't you look where you're going,' he snarled at the contrite gentleman who, seeking to atone for what was his fault, or so he would have Jem believe, was ineffectually brushing him down. 'Give over, you fool.' He struck out at the poor fellow with his stick and when Anne sought to hold him back he turned on her.

'I don't know what your bloody game is, miss, but whatever you have in mind, forget it. I was minding my own business, going in the Ship for a drink with my mates and you have to come along with your daft notion of *me* helping you to find the library. You could have asked anyone in the street but no, you decide to pick on the poor blind chap who knows no better. Leave me alone, damn you. All of you leave me alone. Don't I have enough of them at home what with Flo and Queenie forever fussing round me and Gilly, when she's there which isn't bloody often, doing her best to make me believe nothing has changed. Now, if you would be so good as to get me to the corner of London Road and Lime Street I'll be on my way. No, let go of me, you daft bitch . . .' for Anne was desperately trying to take his arm. There was quite a crowd round them now, all sorry for the man who was out of his mind, it seemed, his blindness making him crazy, and also for the young woman who was doing her best to calm him.

'Jem, Jem . . .' she was crying, as she struggled to get him up the steps and through the pillared entrance to the library, but he kept stumbling and tripping at each one and his fury was further kindled by his inability to get up them by himself.

'I swear I'll knock you down if you don't leave me alone.'

'Very well, then, knock me down but I have no intention of taking you back to the public house and letting you drink with those rough men.'

'Those rough men,' he mimicked, his face twisted into a cruel parody of a smile. 'Those rough men are my friends.'

'No, they are not. You have money in your pocket and so they have latched on to you and your . . . your . . . condition.'

'My blindness, you mean,' he sneered in her direction. She had him by the arm and was steering him more successfully up the steps and into the entrance of the library.

'Yes, I do, and if you weren't so damn sorry for yourself you would realise—'

'Oh, for God's sake, leave me alone. I'll find my own way back.' He twisted away from her and began to blunder back towards the entrance and the lethal steps but she stepped in front of him, barring his way. The place was busy as the library, the museum, the reading room and the reference library were very popular. The William Brown Library and Museum had been open since 1860, a gift made by William Brown to the town of Liverpool. The foundation stone had been laid in April 1857 and the library had been built at William Brown's own expense and presented to his fellow townsmen as a means to promote their social improvement. And that was what it was doing, the crowds that swarmed in and out testifying to its success.

'Will you stop making such a fool of yourself,' Anne said quietly, surprising herself with her forcefulness. 'You've a face on you like a yard of gravy, as my nanny used to say, so sit here . . .' directing him to a seat against the wall, 'and wait for me. Yes, I insist you do as you're told or I shall be as cross as my nanny was when we misbehaved. The trouble with you is that for the past six months or so you have been spoiled by those ladies who have you in their care. They long to protect you, to make sure you come to no harm in your . . . your changed state. Gilly's mama and her friend have been so eager to please you, to do and say whatever you want them to do or say that you have become a tyrant. No, don't struggle with me or I shall call the attendant. Now sit down and wait here for me and then when I return you shall take me down Dale Street to the Pier Head and we shall either walk along the Parade or take the ferry across the water. I shall allow you to choose. Please, don't argue, for I have made my mind up.'

He began to laugh and Anne knew she had won this first round. He was laughing at her impudence, at the very idea of a woman who was like a kitten challenging a bulldog, ordering him about like a child. It was a bit of a novelty in his long and tedious days and so he was prepared to allow it. He knew his temper had become very short over the past months, ever since he had realised that his sight had gone for ever and with it his chances of having Gilly for his own. He wanted her just as desperately as he had always done but his pride, his masculine need to be the leader, the stronger, the breadwinner, the protector would not permit him even to consider what he had hoped for for years. He wanted to marry her, he always had, but not now, now that he was no more than a stumbling, blundering caricature of what he once had been. He was in the hands of two kind, elderly women who wanted nothing more than to look after him, for they didn't know what else to do. Their pity was a tangible thing, wrapping round him like a soft, smothering blanket, and to be truthful he had rather enjoyed being told off by this scrap of a lass. He had a picture in his mind of how she had been the last time he had seen her, for he *did* remember her whatever he said, small, fair, dainty with grey eyes like velvet. It was very vague, but then did it matter if she was as ugly as Punch's hump? He couldn't see her, could he?

Anne looked back over her shoulder as she walked away from him. He was doing what he was told, sitting impatiently on the seat, both hands on his stick which he had stood between his legs. His head constantly turned and she knew he was listening, doing his best to pick up sounds he might identify, his face still and wary, for he was as defenceless as a child. Her heart surged with some emotion that had nothing to do with pity, although she knew she did pity him but at the same time she knew quite positively that the three women who had him in their care were no good for him. Not even Gilly who genuinely loved him. She was frantically doing her best to keep her business together, leaving him each morning in the clutches – which was not a good word but correct – of her own mother and her mother's neighbour. He was being beaten down not only by his affliction but by sheer boredom. He did nothing. He had nothing worthwhile to do. She knew Lucas would willingly help him at the yard but what could a blind man be employed at, especially one who had trained to be a designer, a draughts-man, one who put his ideas on paper? Something must be done for him, and for Gilly and Lucas!

The clerk in the reference library was very helpful. Yes, he had heard of the Braille system of reading and writing, and if she wished to know more about the subject she should go to the School for the Blind in London Road where so many estimable – that was the word he used – persons had been educated. He

believed books might be had and not only that but the person
who wished to use them, since the dot system needed special
training, looking carefully at Anne's fine eyes, would be taught
how to do so. There were classes in spinning, hamper- and
basket-making, weaving, and many other occupations in which
a blind person might eventually make a living.

'Have you no books or newspapers in the reading rooms
where, once a blind person has mastered the dot system, he
may come and read them?'

'We have, miss, but I would advise you to take the person to
the school first.' He smiled admiringly, for she was an attractive
little thing and he had enjoyed showing off his knowledge to
such a lady.

'Thank you, you have been most kind,' Anne said, smiling in
return, then went slowly back to the entrance hall where she
could see Jem fidgeting impatiently on the seat.

'Here I am.'

'And about bloody time too,' he declared. 'I was beginning
to think you'd abandoned me here and to tell the truth I
wouldn't have blamed you.' He stood up and at once began
to make for what he thought was the way to the wide steps at
the front of the building but in fact was the opposite
direction. He waved his stick threateningly in front of
him, causing great alarm to a party of visitors who scattered
as he approached.

Anne took his arm and turned him about. She began to lead
him towards the steps, warning him as they came to them.

'Now, one at a time, if you please. I have no desire to be
dragged down into the road and under the hooves of a passing
horse. Just go with me, Jem, and stop trying to manage by
yourself.'

'You're a bossy little bugger, aren't you,' he told her pleasantly.

'Not really but you're enough to turn anyone into a despot.'

They reached the foot of the steps and she turned right and he had no choice but to go with her.

'And did you get what you wanted in the library? I hope so after making me wait for hours.'

'It was ten minutes, no more, and yes, I did,' wondering how she was to force the truculent, moody, fierce-tempered man whose arm she held to learn not only how to read and write in the Braille system, but one of the trades open to him as a blind man.

25

The daffodils were trumpeting the golden arrival of spring in the new grass of Princes Park, Sefton Park, the Zoological Gardens, St James' Cemetery and about the old gravestones of St Luke's Church. In fact wherever there was a bit of grass they pushed up towards the warmth of the sun. In the churchyard, grouped in no particular pattern where the grass had not been mown, were wildflowers, oxslips, early purple vetch, daisies and the deep blue of violets and lady's smock, silver and white. Along the verges beneath the church wall grew the more regimented harbingers of spring, anemones, primroses and crocus, neatly planted by the church gardener, all picked out by the bright April sunshine, and against the outer wall a wild cherry tree was in delicate bloom.

It was Sunday, the morning service had just ended and the minister stood at the porch to greet his flock as they came out of the church, the gentlemen frock coated and top-hatted, the ladies in their flowered hats and expensively designed spring gowns. Not all were stylish, despite having cost a lot of money, and not all were new, for many of the matrons were of the opinion that a gown, well made, could easily last more than one season. They bowed and dipped and smiled the smiles of the respectable and respected gentlefolk they considered themselves to be, ignoring the more inferior worshippers in their sombre Sunday best, which had to last a lifetime, who slipped past the minister and began to make their way home to their Sunday dinner.

Gilly sat with the sun on her face and watched them idly, thinking it was time she moved, for though she had lost so many customers there were still many jobs to be done and she needed to catch up on a Sunday. She had regretfully let Sadie go. Her wage had been hard to find, besides which there was really only work for two. Rosie still made the tea and swept up at the end of the day and hoped that Miss Logan would keep her on, even if it was only for these mundane tasks, and her mam, Jess Wilson, was glad of the couple of bob Gilly gave her to clean the place. Gilly was hard pressed to find their meagre wages but with Tommy in prison and with rent to find Jess needed every penny she could earn. She was not a very *careful* cleaner since she had not had much practice and one of the jobs that awaited Gilly at the salon was what Queenie would have called *bottoming*.

Gilly sat up slowly as a group of the better class of persons came out of the church and barred the way to all those behind them as they commandeered the minister as was their right. A stocky, middle-aged, expensively dressed gentleman in a well-tailored frock coat which hid his paunch and on his arm a woman several years younger, stylishly dressed in a gown of burgundy silk. It had a bustle and a small train, and perched on her severely coiffed hair was the latest fashion in hats, a spoon bonnet with a frill over the back of her neck and vastly decorated about the brim with a wealth of artificial flowers. Around the couple were their grown-up children and the husband of one of their daughters, all properly dressed for church-going and all somewhat subdued as was proper on such an occasion. Among them was their younger daughter, the only one with any pretension to fashion, her full-skirted gown in a lovely shade of apple-green silk and a simple silk bonnet to match with a ruched frill of white muslin beneath its brim. Pinned to her breast was a small posy of lily of the valley. Next to her, looking decidedly out of sorts, was her brother, immaculate in a black frock coat, grey striped narrow trousers, and carrying a black top hat. Anne and Lucas Barrie!

She stood up, ready to run, then regretted it at once as her movement caught their eye and for the first time since before Christmas she and Lucas looked at one another. The shock of it struck her a blow that made her gasp. Though she was caught by the silvery depths of his startled grey eyes she saw Anne smile and begin to move towards her. Rose Barrie, having shaken the minister's hand, turned bemusedly to watch her daughter as she made her way towards the woman on the bench, wondering who she was. When she recognised Gilly her expression, which had been self-satisfied, even smug, for had she not got her handsome, well-brought-up family about her, became icy with disapproval. She had been weak in the past and had allowed her daughter to associate with the woman on the bench, but recently, after a good talking-to, she had come to believe that Anne was at last willing to listen to reason. She had taken to visiting the library and the museum, the art gallery and had even taken up sketching and was no longer to be seen at this woman's shop. Not that many of her friends still employed Miss Logan to dress them, for Angela Ryan's bitter enmity towards the woman did not relent and her father was too powerful to defy. Anne visited her sister Emily who was to have a child later in the year and was pleased to have her company, Emily told her mother, since she felt she should not be seen out, except to church, naturally, and on several occasions called at the homes of the friends she had made at school whose families were known to Rose Barrie. All in all, the outcome had been very satisfactory. Curiously, she did not question the identity of these friends, seeming to have forgotten that the only friend Anne had had at school was the very girl with whom she had been forbidden to associate.

Rose had been gratified when it was conveyed to her by her elder daughter that Angela had been seen to dance with Lucas at a grand ball at the Town Hall on St George's Day. This was before Emily had discovered she was with child, of course. Rose had not dared to ask her son how it had come about and Emily could not tell her, only that they had danced the waltz and had smiled at one another in a most pleasing way. So was there hope that her good-looking son had come to his senses and might, one day, pay his addresses once more to Joseph Ryan's lovely, well-brought-up and very wealthy daughter. Dear sweet Lord, she did hope so, but the sight of Anne almost running to reach *that woman* made her heart leap in a most uncomfortable way and she thought she might choke. She clutched at Lucas's coat sleeve as though to prevent him from making a fool of himself, and them, as Anne was doing, but it seemed it was not necessary for he looked away across the gravestones and appeared to be totally indifferent to the hussy.

'Oh, Gilly dear, how lovely to see you. Are you waiting for someone?' Anne enquired smilingly, continuing before Gilly could answer. 'Mama is watching so I must be circumspect since she has refused to let me out of the house unless I promise not to come to the salon but I mean to disobey her when she is convinced . . . Oh dear, I suppose I should have ignored you but I miss you, Gilly and, really, this is ridiculous. See, Papa is coming over . . . I must go, but I will manage somehow . . .'

Without giving Gilly a chance to speak she turned away quickly and moved in the direction of her papa who looked awkward and embarrassed, for he had never been able to understand his wife's aversion to Gilly Logan. Such an exquisite creature and kind to Anne and what's more he admired anyone who had spunk which is what the girl had in abundance. To start a business from virtually nothing was to be admired and, besides, what harm could his girl come to mixing only with females and those of the same class as themselves. The poor girl, meaning Miss Logan, had known nothing but the most trying of circumstances. First her mother and the ordeal she had suffered and then the blinding of poor Jem Wilson who, it was rumoured, she was to marry. Two people to support and because of the vindictiveness of a silly girl as a result of the shilly-shallying of his own son who had discarded her, the poor young woman was struggling to survive. His own girl, of whom he was fond, had tried to help her but Rose was adamant.

'You had best come to your mother, Anne,' he said quietly, taking her arm. 'Good morning, Miss Logan.' He bowed and smiled at Gilly, to his wife's annoyance, and even as they returned to her side, father and daughter, Gilly could hear her begin to warn Anne that if she didn't listen to . . . The sharp voice became fainter as the family moved off down the path towards the gate where their carriage waited. She saw Lucas take his mama's hand, bending to kiss her cheek, then he strode away along Berry Street towards Duke Street.

She straightened her back and lifted her head, unaware that she had been holding herself stiffly, her shoulders slightly hunched as though to defend something vulnerable inside her. Taking a deep breath, she placed one foot in front of the other, taking great care as though the church path were full of potholes, moving through the press of people who were still coming out of the church. Carefully she put out her hand to the gate and stood for a moment, then, scarcely looking, for she was held in the grip of anguish so great it was ready to have her over, she crossed Berry Street and into Bold Street, almost senseless until she reached Remington Place. She moved heavily up the wrought-iron staircase to the first floor of the arcade and he was there at the door to the shop, his face so stern, so formidable she was ready to step back from him. He took her reticule, searching in it until he found the key. Unlocking the door, he pulled her inside, closed it behind her, then dragged her into his arms, her back to the door. His lips found hers, savage, so savage she felt her teeth break the skin and tasted blood in her mouth but she clung to him, her arms about his neck, one leg wrapped about his as though to hold him even closer, his name moaning in her throat. Their bodies fitted together, breast to breast, thigh to thigh, their mouths fused, moving, caressing, enfolding, their tongues touching. He put his hand to the back of her head, wrenching off her bonnet, entwining his fingers in her hair until it fell about her, a tangled mane of living copper. She lifted her chin and his lips slid beneath it and along her jaw. He was gasping her name as he took the lobe of her ear between his lips and with a groan they both sank to their knees as though the strength had gone from them. She held his head, wrapping her arms about it as his mouth slid to her breast, then his hands went to the buttons and tore open the front of her bodice releasing the fullness of them, the hardness of her rosy nipples in his mouth. She cried out and he answered her, his voice harsh and gasping.

'I love you, Gilly,' and she was made to realise that there was no going back, no escaping what was to happen and at last she accepted. He swung her up into his arms and began to climb the stairs to the top floor. He laid her down in a pile of silks and velvets, a lovely bed of rich colours, soft and ready for them and she watched as he stripped himself of the packaging of civilisation to reveal his beautiful male body, brown and hard and eager and she had but a moment to admire it before he had done the same for her. He pulled her naked body against his, his arms tight about her, her full breasts against his chest, his flaunting manhood questing between her open thighs for she was as eager as he. There was no gentleness in him, nor in her and when she wrapped her legs about him he entered her at once, hurting her which she gloried in. He was the first man she had known and he knew it too and his triumphant shout echoed about the rafters, telling her she was his now. He had put his masculine mark on her and she was his until eternity. He knew it and she knew it and the white-hot, ice-cold joy raced through her body and her voice joined his.

The whole encounter had taken no more than ten minutes.

They lay fast together, not speaking, her face buried in his neck and shoulder, his against her tangled hair, then he sighed, replete for the moment.

'My dearest, dearest love,' he murmured at last, then raised himself to look down into her dazed face, kissed it tenderly, and lifted a hand to brush back a shining strand of copper hair that had wrapped about them both.

She sighed and stretched, lifting her arms above her head, deliberately displaying her proud breasts for his hand to cup and it began again, this time slowly, lingeringly, exploring one another's body, kissing, licking, sucking, smiling until he knelt over her, male triumphant, plunging into her again and again until she wept with the rapture and glory of what he did to her and he groaned as though he were in agony. He devoured her and she knew that nothing would ever be the same again. She belonged to this man and no other.

Afterwards he leaned against the workbench, stretching out his legs and she rested between them, her back against his chest, his hands cupping her breasts, the thrust of him gently probing between her buttocks. The last of the April sunshine had gone and the light in the room was dusky but they were reluctant to leave this moment, this time, this marvel they had discovered together. Lucas Barrie had made love to many women but he had loved none of them. He knew the difference now and the ecstasy he had just experienced was a marvel to him, for he had thought he knew it all. But he had not, not until now.

'You are mine now, you know that, don't you, Gilly.' His voice was very serious. 'You know what is to happen?' It was not a question but an order.

'Yes, my love.'

'Good girl, so there will be no arguments.'

'No, Lucas.'

'I must be allowed to look after you. I need a lover, a friend as my wife, laughter, love, what we have shared this day with no looking back. Your family will be cared for. I cannot let you go this time. I appreciate that . . . that certain people, on both sides, will not be happy but I will not let you go. Tomorrow I shall go and see the parson and have the banns called and then we must make arrangements for this place. I suppose it will be easy enough to end the lease and . . .'

Slowly she sat up, turning to look into his face, a face that was at last ready to smile with satisfaction, for it seemed to him she was willing to allow him to do something for her. She had struggled for so long, setting up her salon, working far into the night, supporting her mother, nursing her when she was injured, caring for her as she recovered, and now she had another one dependent on her and he, Lucas Barrie, was quite willing to support him too. The whole boiling lot of them, for he was a wealthy man. She would live in luxury; he would shower her with all the things she deserved, all the things he thought she should have, all the expensive things he wanted her to have. They would buy a house, a big house where she would be mistress, waiting for him at the end of the day, where she would have his children and, if she needed it, he would even bring her mother to live, not with them, of course, but in some comfortable corner where she would be safe.

But he did not care for the growing expression on her face. He could not as yet describe what he meant but he only knew he did not like it. He smiled and lifted his arms to pull her back into his embrace but she edged away from him, and with a muffled oath, stood up and began to rummage for her clothes.

'Darling . . . Gilly . . .?'

She had pulled on her petticoat and for a moment he was distracted by the picture of her naked from the waist up, her breasts moving and lifting as she searched for the rest of her clothing which had been flung willy-nilly about the room. Her gown was next, tugged over her head and the buttons, some of which were torn away, done up anyhow. Her face was crimson with some emotion and, feeling at a disadvantage in his nakedness and his own anger rising, he stood up and reached for his clothes which were scattered in the oddest places.

'What the hell is up now?' he demanded to know, his voice harsh with his disappointment. He had expected delight, not what looked strangely like offence. Just as he had thought everything was going to be all right, that she was to agree on what he had hoped for, planned for, despite the disapproval of his mother and probably *her* mother and certainly Jem Wilson, she had turned truculent and for the life of him he couldn't see why.

'I . . . I don't know exactly but . . .'

'What, for God's sake? Tell me and I'll put it right. My love, my dearest love, I would do anything to take that tired look from your face, that droop from your shoulders. I want to take care of you, look after you . . . and your family.' His own face worked with emotion, for he was not a man who liked to plead. All his adult life he had done and been just what he wanted to do and be. He had never been denied, as his parents doted on their clever, handsome son and he had proved himself again and again in the world of commerce. His father was willing to allow him to take over his place in the firm of Barrie and Hughes, even John Hughes trusting him implicitly until his own young son could take his place beside him. Lucas would be senior partner, given his head, and his head, his heart and his loins told him this woman was the right wife for him. She too was clever, and would soon learn the ways of the privileged class of which he was a member and he could see absolutely no reason why she should not marry him at the first opportunity. There was nothing to stop her, nothing; nothing except Jem Wilson who loved her as he, Lucas, did. Not as much, of

course, not as ferociously and besides, what could he give her, a
blind man sitting at home, depending on *her*.

He reached for her and pulled her into his arms, resting his
cheek on her tumble of hair.

'Gilly . . .' He could not hide his eagerness. 'Could we not
try, start afresh, give ourselves another chance. We have loved
one another . . . oh yes . . . for two years now and no matter
what you say' – she had said nothing yet! – 'we are meant to be
together so why—'

'I'm to give up the shop then?' Her voice was muffled against
his chest and he bent his head to hear her more clearly. 'You are
taking it for granted that I must give up what I have built and
come and live with you in some fine house, is that it?' Her voice
was expressionless, flat and empty.

'And what is wrong with that? You will be my wife and will
have no need of—'

'Am I to have no say in the matter?'

He looked amazed. 'What is there to say?'

'I am not to consider my mother and . . . and . . . Jem?'

She almost fell as his arms dropped away from her and his
face registered his outrage. 'I knew it was him. I bloody knew it
was him. Tell me, what the devil has he got to do with you and
me? You don't love him.'

'I do.'

'Not as you love me. I know you have been friends, sister and
brother if you like, but are you to let that hold you back from
your true destiny which is to be my wife? He cannot support
you. In fact the opposite since he depends on you and your
mother. Dear Lord, I'm sorry for the poor chap. I cannot
imagine what he has suffered . . . to lose one's sight . . . but it
has nothing to do with you and me. I'll make sure he and your
mother want for nothing, believe me. If I could find some
suitable work for him at the yard, I would, but without his sight
there is nothing.'

'I know, don't you think I don't know. But . . . but to tell him, you and I . . . it will crucify him. But it's not just that.'

'Tell me.'

'It's your high-handed belief that I will give up my business. That I will sit at home, your home and do nothing.'

'Nothing! You will be my wife and as such—'

'Cannot I be your wife and keep my shop and—'

'And what about the children we will have? Are they to be left in the charge of servants while you flaunt yourself . . .'

She tore herself from his arms and reached up to bundle her hair into a mass of tumbled curls on the top of her head. She searched round wildly for her bonnet and when she found it jammed it on her head. He watched her, his anger fierce and knife-edged, hating her, loving her, wanting her all over again. His face softened for a moment, since he adored the very ground she walked on but when he put out a hand to restrain her she shook him off.

'You'd best go,' she spat at him. 'It seems we cannot agree.'

'Damn it, you . . . you . . . don't do this. Don't send me away again for I won't come back. Believe me, I'm not a man to beg and if—'

'Don't threaten me, Lucas. I will not be—'

'Bugger it then. I'll find someone more amenable to a perfectly proper offer of marriage. Someone who—'

'Like Angela Ryan, you mean?' she said raggedly.

'Why not?' His voice was mocking and his eyes gleamed sardonically though he was still white-lipped with anger. He reached into his pocket and withdrew his cigar case, extracted a cigar and stuck it jauntily between his lips. He lit it, eyeing her over the flame of the match, then reached for his hat, tipped it in her direction and ran down the stairs, banging the door to behind him.

She sank to her knees and put her trembling hands to her face.

★   ★   ★

It was dark when she reached home and as she entered the hallway and shut the door behind her, a shadow loomed towards her.

'Where in hell have you been?' Jem snarled, catching her wrist with a cruel, savage hand, one that meant to hurt.

'Jem, you frightened the life out of me, hiding and jumping out like that. What were you doing?'

'Never mind that.' His dead eyes glared into hers. 'Where have you been all day? You left here this morning to catch up on some work and here it is almost nine and—'

'Lord, is it that late—'

But he chopped off her words, wrenching at her arm in his anguish. 'Where have you been and who with? No, don't tell me since I know already. Don't lie to me, Gilly, please don't lie. Jesus God, I can smell cigar smoke. Oh yes, it's true that when you lose your sight your other senses become more acute and I won't have it, Gilly. All my life I have loved you and wanted you but I waited, I was patient with you. You loved me, I know you did until that sod came on the scene but now . . . now it's too late. I always believed that if you acted decently and hurt no one it would all be . . . but I was bloody wrong, wasn't I? I might have had a chance if my own bloody father hadn't . . . I can't bear myself, Lovedy. Self-pity is the worst but . . .'

'Jem, please listen.' She put a warm, steadying hand on his where it still clutched hers painfully. His face was haunted and he twitched away from her, putting his hand to the wall as though to get his bearings, turning from her, not at all prepared to listen to her, for he was deadly afraid of what she might say.

'Listen to what?' His voice was savage with pain and a vicious anger which, curiously, she thought was not directed at her. But she had to tell him something. She knew he wanted her but since he had been attacked and blinded his bitterness had grown and even if she was to agree to . . . to be with him, his pride would not allow it. So what was there to do, to say?

She and Lucas had quarrelled violently so would she see him again and if not what was the use of telling Jem of their love?

He was frozen with his hand on the wall, suspended in the ice of his pain, twisting about as though to escape it.

'Are you to marry him?' His voice was hoarse.

'No. I don't know . . . he has gone . . .'

'Gone where, for Christ's sake?'

'I don't know.' Pushing past him, her own pain something she could not deal with, she ran upstairs and into the bedroom that had once been his, closing the door silently behind her.

26

The couple were arm in arm as they sauntered along the drowsy peace of the lane. Bees were busy from flower to flower, their humming competing in the summer air with the noise made by linnets and warblers, whinchats and titlarks and, high in the sky, so high as to be almost invisible, the sweet song of the skylark. Butterflies danced deliriously over moon daisies and the pink and white of clover, the lovely creatures dark green, white, peacock and tortoiseshell as though the very air, sweet with the smell of summer, had driven them wild.

They had taken a cab from the end of Seymour Street to Breck Road from where they had begun their leisurely stroll, passing fields on one side that were a yellow carpet of buttercups starred with the scarlet of poppies and on the other side meadows that waved with grasses and rue where a herd of cows was grazing. The cows raised their heads and stared curiously at the two humans, their eyes a liquid brown in their placid faces, their udders limp and empty since they had just come from the milking shed. On the banks that lined the lane dusky cranesbill grew against dry-stone walls that were gradually being submerged by sweet Cicely. The plant was almost waist high, its full green foliage and luxuriant white blossoms making the senses reel with its fragrance. There was hedge parsley, dock and nettle and, standing tall and dignified, foxgloves, their rich colour vivid against the greys and browns and blacks of the stones in the wall. One of the loveliest effects were the stems and leaves of the shining cranesbill, seen against the light and assuming the translucent beauty of scarlet and crimson.

'I think I'd like to paint this wall, Jem,' the girl said. 'The colours are perfect. Can we stop a while? We could have a picnic here, if you like, while I set up my easel. What d'you think? On the other side of the wall where no one can see us. Look, there's a stile.'

'It's no good telling me to look, sweet Annie,' was the surly response, but Jem allowed Anne to lead him to the stile which he climbed over without her help despite it being anxiously offered. He kept his hand on her shoulder though as they waded through grasses that reached their waists and when she advised it, he sank down, his back against the wall.

'Will this do?' Anne asked him.

'Well, you're the painter so you decide. It's no good asking my advice.' He struggled to remove his jacket and she longed to help him but resisted the temptation, for Jem Wilson's temper was tricky these days. He pulled at his collar and loosened his tie which he then slipped from his neck. His warm brown throat was revealed, brown from the summer sunshine in which, for the past weeks, he had strolled and sat and even slept as his companion painted. He leaned his head back against the wall, raising his face to the sun, and Anne Barrie felt her heart soften with love and with something else that she was too innocent to recognise as desire.

They had been what she liked to call friends ever since that day when she had accosted him outside the Ship Inn and coerced him into taking her, or rather she had taken him, to the William Brown Free Library on William Brown Street over six months ago. She had managed to get him interested in the idea of learning Braille and several times a week he had attended the School for the Blind in London Road. He would not even contemplate making baskets, spinning or shoe-making, which were taught at the school, and had told her to mind her own bloody business when she had tried to persuade him, but he had made good progress with reading the books available there. Braille books, the first of which had been devised by John Alston at the Asylum for the Blind in Glasgow. There was a printed Bible which he had been allowed to take home with him and though he held the religious principles within its covers in great contempt, for where had God or Jesus Christ been when They allowed his father to blind him, it gave him a good grounding in the language and he had enjoyed some of the fairy stories, which was all they were to him. Not that he would admit it to Anne, the woman who had opened up his world for him, guided him solicitously about the city, broken him free of the prison Queenie and Flo would have caged him in, a loving prison but with bars on it nevertheless.

'Shall we have our picnic first?' Anne smiled questioningly in Jem's direction but he shrugged indifferently, his eyes closed, his hands behind his head, his long legs stretched out before him, his ankles crossed. Anne sighed, thinking how lovely he looked, the sun striking golden shafts from his curly hair which fell over his forehead to his eyebrows. He hated having it cut, or rather hated going to the barber who, along with everyone in the shop, stared at him with various degrees of curiosity and pity. He couldn't see it, of course, but he sensed it and almost one of the first things he had asked Anne was whether she thought she could have a go at it.

'But I wouldn't know where to start,' she gasped, appalled.

'Oh, for Christ's sake, what is there to do but pick up the bloody scissors and cut it off as short as you can. Queenie and Flo won't attempt it.'

'What about Gilly, surely she . . .'

But Jem's face had closed up and his mouth tightened, for there was nothing in this world he could think of that would crucify him more than to be touched by Gilly. She whored with that sod Lucas Barrie, and why the pair of them didn't marry he couldn't imagine. It would be done with then and she could get out of his life for ever. Go and live in the house the bastard would undoubtedly put her in. Not that he saw a lot of her these days, for he had breakfast with Flo and the evening meal that they all shared at number 19 was a silent one except for the forced chatter of Queenie and Flo. The moment it was finished he made his way back to his room at number 17 and read his books by Flo's fireside. Let Gilly cut his hair? He would rather die and Anne was made to understand that Gilly Logan was a subject not to be discussed.

They sat with their backs to the wall and ate the picnic Queenie had packed for them in a small lidded basket. Anne could not, of course, ask Mrs Dobbs in the kitchen at Bracken Hill, as it would get straight back to her mother and the question of why she needed a picnic when she was visiting her sister would be an awkward one. There were little meat pies, baked by Flo, two chicken legs, fresh white bread and a pat of best butter, and fairy cakes with a cherry on top. A jug of milk, fresh that morning from the chap who brought the milk cart round, and two glasses, for Queenie and Flo could not get out of the habit of 'feeding up' whoever they held in their affections. Miss Anne had become one of them, since had it not been for her, their Jem would not have learned the magic art of 'reading'. They were distraught over the way Gilly and Jem had fallen out over something, neither of them knew what but with Miss Anne prepared to take Jem out on little jaunts at least he got out of the house and he certainly looked better for it. The sun had darkened his face most attractively and though he was blind his eyes were still that vivid blue they had always been. His long eyelashes, though his hair was so fair, were dark and thick and altogether wasted on a man, they told one another! His temper worsened though, and the joyful, engaging young man they had once known was hidden beneath the increasingly morose and bitter chap he had become.

Anne sighed as she packed away the remains of the picnic, then leaned back again and as she did so her shoulder touched Jem's. She was astonished when, with a small sound that she could not identify, he turned towards her and pulled her clumsily into his arms. They closed about her and with some initial fumbling his mouth came down on hers, hard and almost cruel. She did not struggle, for it was as if she had known from the first that this was what she wanted but at the same time she did not respond as she did not know how. Both she and Jem were virgins with no experience of the opposite sex and for a moment they floundered together in a sea of doubt. His lips became more gentle and it was then she began to kiss him back and when she did his became fierce again.

He crushed her to him, capturing her arms, pushing her back among the long, sweet-smelling grasses, one of his legs crossing her body as though to hold her down. She was not reluctant, for she had wanted him in some way for a long time but she did not know how to deal with his vigorous male clamour. He groaned, which frightened her somewhat but she was totally captured by his strength. His hand went to her face and chin, his kisses moving along her jawline and up to her ear and she felt something move in the pit of her stomach, a lovely feeling that made her want to sigh. His hand moved to the swell of her small breast, cupping it, fingering the peak of her nipple then to the buttons on her bodice, and when he began to undo them she did not stop him. One by one they came apart and with a fierce pull he dragged her bodice down over her shoulders, followed by the pretty lace chemise she wore beneath it until her breasts were naked in his hands. He fondled them, murmuring something, which she was not to know were the names of her brother and Gilly Logan, then slid his mouth down to her nipples, taking them one at a time into his mouth, nipping them, making her wince, but she did not stop him, nor resist when his hand went to the hem of her skirt and pulled it up to her waist. He caressed her thighs, parting her legs, dragged at her drawers then rolled on top of her and with a great shout, which attracted the attention of a labourer on the far side of the field, entered her fiercely. She herself cried out, for the pain was excruciating but when, after some bewildering noises which sounded as if he were in agony, he fell on top of her she cradled his head lovingly to her breast and smiled, for his actions had told her he loved her.

'I love you, Jem,' she said, her breath ragged in her throat. She had not enjoyed the experience, only the kissing of her breasts, and the rough sweetness of his mouth on hers, but from whispered words she had overheard between her mother and sister, women were not supposed to. He had made love to her, roughly, for he was inexperienced in such matters, but she was not to know that as so was she. But he loved her, she firmly believed it, and she loved him and they would be married as soon as she had told her parents. Her heart quailed at the thought but it had to be done.

Jem smiled into the curve of her naked breast, amazed at her naïvety and yet, at the same time, the deeply hidden Jem who had burrowed down into the one who now existed was sorry for her, and ashamed of himself. He had taken her because she was there and willing but at the same time he was triumphant. Lucas Barrie had taken the woman Jem loved and now he, Jem Wilson, had . . . well, here in his coarser side he used a word that men use when they enjoy a woman . . . Lucas Barrie's sister. He had used her to get his own back. It was as simple as that. He didn't love her as she seemed to love him and the sooner she knew it the better.

'That was nice,' he said airily, as though complimenting her on the picnic, as he sat up and adjusted his breeches which were round his ankles, pulling them up and fastening them, but she continued to lie there, her vulnerable woman's body exposed to the prurient eye of any passer-by, though of course there was none. The dark bush at the junction of her legs was damp with his semen and her bare breasts bore marks where he had nipped them. But he could not see what he had done to her, nor that she was making no attempt to cover herself up.

Anne Barrie slipped into a pit of despair, for his words, his indifference were not the actions of a lover. He was putting himself together with the casual air of a man well used to such occurrences and her heart broke a little, because she had just given him, or had taken from her, the most precious gift a woman can give a man: her virginity. But not just that, she had given it to him with her love.

'Jem . . .' Her voice had a quiver in it.

'What?' He turned his sightless eyes to her, hearing the sounds of her struggling to button her bodice, the rustle of her petticoats and the distress in her voice.

'I love you, Jem. I wouldn't have done this . . . had I not loved you.'

'I realise that, sweet Annie,' he said carelessly.

'Do you love me, Jem? Please say you do.'

'Very well, I love you. Are you satisfied now? But . . .'

'Yes?' Her voice was eager with longing for him to say something to reassure her, to let her know that this meant as much to him as it did to her.

'We'd best keep this to ourselves. A secret, for the time being.'

It seemed to tell her that soon, one day, they would announce their feelings for one another to the world and at once her heart lifted.

'Oh yes, until we're . . . well . . .' She didn't know how to go on really. She knew that he was not of her class and that it would be difficult but with a young girl's romantic heart she rather liked the idea that for the time being she and Jem would share this lovely thing. She had hoped for declarations of undying love such as those she read in *Jane Eyre* and *Sense and Sensibility* but Jem was not a man for words, apparently, so she was content. He was here with her. She loved him and would look after him for the rest of their days and . . .

'Is there anything left to eat?' he asked carelessly, shattering her thoughts. 'I seem to have worked up a good appetite. I wonder why?' And deep in the heart, the soul, the goodness of Jem Wilson who had lived in Rose Alley, he wept for this lovely, innocent girl.

She was just putting her key in the lock as Jem and Anne were climbing the stile from the field to the lane. That afternoon she had fitted Mrs Atkinson's new dress, a lovely creation of cream silk with which Mrs Atkinson had declared herself delighted.

'My sister-in-law, Mrs Ward, is looking for a dressmaker to design my niece's wedding trousseau, the wedding gown, of course, the bridesmaids' dresses, a going away outfit, several gowns for morning and evening wear, and petticoats, night-gowns, all the usual things a new bride feels entitled to, and after seeing your work I'm inclined to recommend you to her, Miss Logan. Would you be able to manage it, d'you think? The wedding is in September, a bit of a rush. Not that there is any need to rush, you understand,' she added hastily, 'but the gentleman she is to marry is to travel to New York on business, for he is a coming man, Miss Logan, and . . . well, careful with his . . . anyway, it has been decided that Nora will go with him. A wedding journey of sorts.' Mrs Atkinson preened, for she was not yet quite used to the new riches her husband had garnered and the position it gave her.

Gilly put the last pin in the trailing hem of Mrs Atkinson's train which was attached to the bustle of her gown, then stood up gracefully, smiling in the courteous way she had developed for her customers. Mrs Atkinson was not a lady, but her husband was in a fair way of business near the docks. He had a growing ship's chandlery and was considering an extension to the premises since business was so brisk. Both his sons worked with him and Mrs Atkinson had an extensive allowance to spend as she pleased. All her family, including her brother whose daughter was to marry in September, were connected to the shipping that bustled up and down the river and Henry, her own husband, was moving into commerce, not only to do with the ships in the port but the railways. They were an extensive family with brothers, sisters, nieces, cousins, all with new money and their business meant a great deal to Gilly. Now that she had lost so many of her *county* clients, thanks to Angela Ryan's influence, excluding Miss Moore and several of her suffragist friends who had stayed loyal, she was relieved that those lower in the class chain, still wealthy, some of them, but not *quality*, had taken her up. She was being recommended by them to their acquaintances and business was beginning to pick up.

She needed to be busy. Ever since the day when Lucas had asked her to marry him for the second time and she had refused, she needed her days to be filled with a hectic work schedule. She had even asked Sadie Knowles to give notice at the shirt factory where she had gone when Gillyflower's seemed in danger of collapsing and come back to her. At this moment Nell was busy on her sewing machine making up an evening gown for a Mrs Lawley whose husband was in the grocery business and Rosie Wilson, hastily taken away from her tea-making duties, was hand-sewing a hem on a petticoat for Mrs Girvan several shops along the Arcade with whom Gilly did business in Parisian flowers, French flowers, headdresses, bouquets and wreaths. Miss Hawkins, who made and sold stays and corsets on the Upper Arcade, was also a client, for it was very handy to pop along to Miss Logan's place and be fitted, almost overnight, for a gown or a bonnet.

As she shut the front door behind her and made her way along the narrow passage to the kitchen, the conversation that was taking place there stopped abruptly.

She removed her hat and threw it on the kitchen table, smiling brightly at her mam and Flo who were drinking tea, their feet up to the fire as though it were a cold day. They had their skirts hitched up to allow the warmth to reach their shins and both turned guiltily as she entered.

'Someone talking about me?' she asked, seating herself at the table and reaching for a cup and saucer and the teapot which nestled under its cosy on the plush tablecloth.

'Wha' mekks yer say tha', our Gilly?' Queenie exclaimed. 'Why should we be talkin' about yer?'

'Well, if not about me, then who? Is it Jem?'

'Eeh, lass . . .' But Flo looked what Queenie would have called flummoxed and Gilly shook her head.

'I know he goes to the library and I know who takes him. I'm not daft, Mam. He's never here and when he is he doesn't talk to me.' She remembered his accusation on the night she had returned late from the shop, the time when . . . when she and Lucas had . . . Oh God, Lucas, my love . . . my love . . . and the pain struck her again as her heart broke again as it had done every single day since. She had rarely seen him in the company of others, such as the launching of the *Emily Jane*, but she could remember it so vividly. Every word he had spoken in the group of spectators, every time he had made eye contact, or laughed, or frowned she had felt she could watch him for ever, the way his dark hair covered the back of his neck and touched the collar of his jacket, his hands which were long-fingered and yet strong as they had cupped her breast that last time . . . Lucas . . . ah Lucas . . .

She was jerked back to the present by her mother's voice. 'An' why is that, chuck?' Queenie asked quietly. 'That's wha' me an' Flo was talkin' about. You an' 'im were that close onceover an' now it's as though you can't abide one another. All he does is go out wi' that lass. Not tharr I mind,' she added hastily, 'since it did 'im no good 'angin' about 'ere wi' me an'

Flo but I can't bear ter see you an' 'im . . . I keep thinkin' when 'e gets more used ter bein' as 'e is 'appen 'e'll . . .'

'What?'

'I dunno, chuck.' Queenie sighed. Just when everything was looking up for her and Jem and Gilly, when they had this cosy house and both Gilly and Jem in decent work, it had all fallen apart thanks to that sod from Rose Alley. Everything bad seemed to come from Rose Alley. They had escaped the poverty and the squalor but they had left their happiness behind in the cellar that had been their home. She was content, for they had no money worries now and she had a good friend in Flo but the misery she suffered over the estrangement between Gilly and Jem was hard to bear. They had been so close for years, but Jem was an embittered man and even the friendship between him and Anne Barrie did not seem to give him any joy. And as for Gilly, she carried a haunted expression about with her, the cause of which was a mystery to them. That was what they had been discussing when they heard Gilly's key in the lock.

'I don't know what 'er mam would 'ave ter say if she knew 'er lass were out an' about wi' our Jem. Where she thinks she is I don't know, but she seems ter be allus on our doorstep. She tekks 'im ter't library an' tha' an' . . . well, they've gone on a picnic this afternoon. I medd 'em up a basket o' food an' God alone knows where . . .'

'Now, now, Queenie, don't gerr upset, love. She's a nice lass.'

'But norr our sort, Flo. I don't want 'im ter gerr 'urt. Not more than 'e already is. Classes don't mix, Flo, yer know that.'

She turned suddenly as her daughter rose jerkily to her feet, picked up her hat, leaving the cup of tea she had just poured on the table, and almost ran from the room and clattered up the lino-covered stairs.

'Now wharr 'ave I said?' she blurted out. 'God's love, yer

can't open yer damn mouth these days wi'out upsetting one or t'other.'

She looked up into his sunbrowned face, her hand in the crook of his arm as she guided him along Breck Road, her love for him aglow in her face and eyes. She was his now and though he had not said anything she was perfectly certain in her innocence that they would be married soon. Her thoughts took her no further than that. To the altar where, as a bride in white – even though she was no longer a virgin, blushing at the thought – she would put her hand in his and be his wife. Where they were to live, how he was to support her, what they would do for the rest of their days did not even enter her mind. They loved one another and for the present that was enough.

'Shall I come home with you, Jem?' she asked shyly.

'If you like.' His answer was indifferent, and yet Jem Wilson could not help but think about the last couple of hours when he had, for the first time in his life, known a woman. He had always believed that when he lost his virginity – no, that sounded as though he were a milksop – when he became a true man, which was not much better, he would have gone through that lovely process with Gilly. He loved Gilly, even now when he knew she had probably taken Lucas Barrie as a lover and in a madness, an antidote to the agony she had caused him he had, cruelly, taken Lucas Barrie's sister. Thrown her skirt up about her waist and taken her maidenhood with no more thought than his own bloody father when he had raped Queenie Logan. No, that was not true. He had not forced her. Anne had been willing. She loved him, she said and she meant it, for she was a good, kind, sweet-natured young woman who had believed that he felt as she did. She would want marriage and why not? Dear sweet Christ . . .

They hailed a cab at the corner of Breck Road which

dropped them at the end of Seymour Street. Anne paid the fare, bustling to get out and help Jem down.

'There's no need to act as though I was six years old and you were my nanny,' he said ungraciously, and perhaps it was as well that he could not see the expression on her face.

'I'll walk home with you,' she began but he brushed her hand away and strode off in the direction of number 19, his stick tapping the pavement before him. She watched him go, her eyes heavy with unshed tears because although she had no experience of men outside her immediate family, she was sadly aware that he did not love her as she loved him. But it didn't matter, she told herself stoutly as she climbed back into the cab and gave him her sister's address. She had enough for both of them.

27

There was to be a fair, a bazaar and games of cricket to celebrate the grand opening of Sefton Park, rumoured to be the most magnificent park in the country, or so said those who were born and bred in Liverpool and had already visited it. The official opening in May had been a splendid affair, conducted by Her Majesty's third son, Prince Arthur. There had been parades led by a detachment of the 5th Dragoon Guards and their route had been lined by many thousands of cheering spectators, for Liverpool folk did love a good procession!

The park was undulating with a valley down the centre and cascades of sparkling water which ran down to a lake where rowing boats might be hired from a boathouse to the side. There were many activities to be enjoyed, tennis courts, a cricket pitch, a football pitch, bowling greens, not to mention the beautiful ribbon gardens along each path, which had been designed in curves and ellipses to create circular spaces where the sports were held. The paths were dotted at regular intervals by park benches. There were pavilions where those wishing to partake of refreshments might sit at dainty tables to eat cream puffs, chocolate éclairs, fresh scones and drink tea, bandstands where Liverpool-based bands played stirring tunes and with striped deckchairs around to relax in. Best of all the whole park was free to anyone who wished to enjoy it. There was even a new omnibus tramway from the Town Hall to carry those who could not walk so far, since the park was in Dingle which was a fair way out. And to top it all there was to be a flower show and

August was the best month for summer flowers, everyone knew that. You had only to look at the rainbow colours of snap-dragons and petunias, the heavenly blue of delphiniums, the cream, crimson and butter yellow of lupins and the majestic salmon pink and warm red of gladioli.

'Eeh, I'd love ter see it,' Flo sighed wistfully one sunny Sunday morning as the four of them sat round Queenie's breakfast table dutifully eating the fried eggs, bacon, tomatoes and mushrooms to be followed by toast and best butter, the sort of meal Queenie thought necessary to start the day.

'Well, why don't we walk down ter't Town 'All an' 'op on that there new tram ter Dingle? We could 'ave us a walk on Jericho Shore an' then stroll up ter't park. It's a lovely day.'

'No, I'm sorry, I have far too much to do at the salon. Nora Ward's gown needs—' Gilly began, casting a furtive glance at Jem with whom, when the two elderly ladies were there, she did her best to chat, though he was just as stiff and formal. It seemed he would never recover from the belief that she and Lucas were lovers and knowing there was nothing he could do about it, he withdrew from any confrontation. And the irony of it was that she had never seen Lucas since the day they had loved one another on a bed of rich velvet and silk in her workroom. Three months, and every day Jem went, they were told, to the library or the School for the Blind where he was learning to accept that he would never see again and must start a new way of life. Find something to fill his days and his life. He had become friendly with Anne who it seemed was eager to take him out into the country where they picnicked and she painted her little pictures of flowers and grazing cows. Gilly rarely saw her now, the excuse being that her parents had forbidden her to work at Gillyflower's, saying that no daughter of theirs was to be associated with trade and it seemed she was now willing to obey them! Now and again they met in Seymour Street where Anne came to pick up Jem, and Gilly felt a stirring of suspicion that it was not just Anne's public-spirited benevolence that prompted her attachment to Jem.

'And I'm off to the library,' Jem interrupted.

'Fer God's sake,' Queenie said in exasperation. 'Library'll be closed on a Sunday an' me an' Flo fancy a day out. An' it wouldn't 'urt you none neither. Pair o' yer 'aven't 'ad a day out since Adam were a lad. Yer always off somewhere or other. Now I'm not tekkin no fer an answer so go an' put yer 'ats on an' we'll be off. I'll just side the table an' wash up,' for nothing would persuade Queenie to leave her place in a mess.

'I'll 'elp yer, lass,' Flo volunteered, but Queenie shooed them all out and within half an hour they were making their way down London Road, past the library, along Dale Street to the Town Hall. Flo, being more sprightly than Queenie, held Jem's arm and Queenie and Gilly walked behind.

It was a glorious day, hot and sunny, and the weather had brought the crowds out and they had to queue for the horse-drawn omnibus, for it seemed everyone was going in the same direction. Despite the park having been open for three months still they flocked there, Liverpool folk determined on having a good time and, though her heart was heavy, as it had been for weeks now, Gilly could not help but feel it lift a little as they crammed on to the tram, Queenie and Flo guiding a stony-faced Jem who, she thought, would have turned round and gone home had the two women not kept a good hold on him. He looked very attractive in his corduroy jacket and open-necked shirt, a cravat tied round his neck. His trousers were a mixture of beige and brown and his boots were well polished. Queenie waited on him hand and foot, cleaning his boots, pressing his trousers, making sure he had a clean shirt or jersey every day and in Gilly's opinion was slowly ruining him, for his high-handed presumption that this was his due was burying the lovely chap he had once been. She had seen Anne do the same, guiding him along Seymour Street as though he were an invalid.

She herself wore a new gown of corn-coloured silk with wide ribbons of saxe blue about her waist. Her straw hat tipped over her forehead had the same coloured ribbons about the brim, tied at the back and falling down to her shoulder blades. Her cream boots were of kid, an extravagance she allowed herself since in the past three months trade at the salon had picked up and her clientele was growing. Even one or two of her quality customers had trickled back.

They walked with the rest of the multitude along Aigburth Road to the entrance of the park, the wild roses in the hedges blooming profusely and even blackberry bushes beginning to show signs of the fruit that would come later. The park was set on the outskirts of the city, in what could still be called the countryside and even as they drew near they could hear the 'oom-pah-pah' of the Liverpool City Brass Band playing with great enthusiasm and in contest with others of the same ilk.

The fairground was just inside the park entrance to the right of the lake in what would later be a deer park and the noise and colour and movement struck them forcibly as they crossed Aigburth Vale, a series of lawns and flowerbeds, and a lined path that led to the cacophony! The fairground was a kaleido-scope of whirring, whizzing colours, of dizzying wheels and flying swingboats and rocking roundabouts. There were screams of mock terror from those who were already being swung and whirled and lifted to great heights then dashed down at great speeds. There were the cracks of rifles from the rifle range where young men were bent on showing their prowess to groups of giggling young girls as they did their best to win a prize, the shrieks of excited children, the clamour of an organ grinder who was prodding a monkey into perform-ing tricks and the cries of vendors extolling the virtues of their wares. Queenie and Flo hung back with Jem between them. It appeared it was all too much for the three of them and even

Gilly, who once would have delighted in the sheer excitement, the colour, the noise, was overwhelmed.

She took her mother's arm and began to lead the three of them towards the lake where a path led to a great glass structure where an arrow stated that the flower show was open.

'Right, Mam, let's go in here and then when you've seen what you want we'll go and have a cup of tea. The pavilion is at the top of the lake and then we can have a look at the tennis courts and the cricket. They say there's croquet and—'

'I'm sitting out here,' Jem interrupted abruptly. 'What do I want with bloody flowers when I can't see them.'

'You could smell them, Jem,' Gilly said patiently. 'The roses will be in bloom and—'

'You go then. Put me on a seat and leave me.'

'But—'

'For God's sake, Gilly, leave me alone. I don't know what the hell I'm doing here in the first place.' His voice had started to rise and several people stared curiously at the two elderly women who looked quite distressed and the lovely girl who seemed to be trying to persuade the young man to do something he didn't want to do. Surely . . . surely he wasn't *blind* and him so young, they whispered to one another, noticing the stick he held and the curious unfocused stare of his eyes. 'And you three can go and get a cup of tea, if you want. I'm not sitting at a table slopping my tea and . . . and . . .'

Queenie pushed her wire-rimmed spectacles up her nose and tutted impatiently. It was not often she lost patience with Jem whom she loved dearly but sometimes he tried her too far and now was one of those times. She herself looked at the world with severely restricted sight and while she knew that was more than Jem had he had her, Flo, Gilly and now the sweetness of Anne's love to sustain him. It was terrible to be blinded at his young age but the sooner he accepted it the better.

She told him so. 'Now you listen 'ere, lad, me an' Flo get

right fed up wi' you forever whinin'. I don't see that well
neither.'

'Give over,' Jem sneered. 'You can't compare what was done
to you with what my bloody pa—'

'So we're gonner 'ave a competition now, are we, ter see 'oo's
worse off?'

'Mam, stop it. Everyone's looking.' Gilly tried to take
Queenie's arm and Flo grabbed at Jem. A small crowd had
gathered and it was this that gave Gilly the strength to draw her
mother away towards the flower show and, realising that she
had let her temper get the better of her, and sorry for what she
had said to her Jem, Queenie allowed herself to be led away. It
was true that with her one good eye and the spectacles the
doctor had prescribed for her she could see a lot more than Jem.

'Jem . . .' she murmured but he turned away and she had no
option but to let him go in the direction Flo was urging him.

'Please, Jem, come with us. I'll hold your arm and—'

'Lead me about like a child who can't be trusted out on its
own. Jesus, if I could go by myself I'd go home and bugger the
lot of you. The only one who—'

He stopped speaking suddenly, for he had been about to say
the only one with whom he felt comfortable was Annie, sweet
Annie, who had learned not to fuss him and for the last three
months, during the long hot summer and their wanderings in
the fields and woods about Liverpool, had given him some sort
of peace and comfort with the sweetness of her body. She had
allowed him to undress her and helped him with his own
garments and they had lain together in the drowsing peace
of the empty glades of woodland with the sun shining in golden
shafts on their naked bodies, and though he could not see her
loveliness he had felt it and his gratitude to her had been
immense. She talked of marriage but so far he had put her off,
since he knew very well that the moment the Barrie family knew
of their relationship they would pack her off to some distant

relative and he would lose her. He didn't love her. His love had been given to Gilly Logan on the day she was born and would always remain with her. He had begun the enticement of Anne Barrie in revenge, a nasty way of getting back at Lucas, though how it would work he didn't know, nor care really. He had lost Gilly to Lucas Barrie and he had taken, in the most cold-blooded way, Lucas Barrie's little sister. God, he must be out of his mind, and he supposed he was, for the man he had once been was gone and the mind and heart of that man had gone with him.

'Promise you won't move, Jem,' Gilly begged him. 'I'll take Flo and Mam into the pavilion and then come back for you. Perhaps we can walk over to the cricket, sit in the sun for half an hour while Mam and Flo have a cup of tea. Please, Jem . . .'

'Oh, all right,' he conceded ungraciously. 'I don't have much choice, do I?'

They sat together in a small, select group, the upper crust of Liverpool, nodding and smiling and clapping at the appropriate time as their team of gentlemen played the workforce of Barrie and Hughes Shipyard. There was Herbert Barrie and John Hughes and their wives, the ladies shaded under their pretty parasols, sipping the lemonades Ernest Davidson, husband of Emily who had once been a Barrie, had brought them from the clubhouse. The ladies were dressed in light, summery dresses in pale colours, their bonnets dipping with the weight of the artificial flowers that adorned them. Angus, the Barries' second son, was there with his fiancée, Miss Dorothy Coop, and Miss Coop's parents, her father being in cotton. Anne sat quietly between her mother and father and wished she didn't feel so nauseous, telling herself she would never eat prawns again, for they did not seem to agree with her. The Hughes family sat on the tier above them, naughty Willy, who had started the whole devastating catastrophe when he fell in the

River Mersey years ago, still getting up to mischief, untying his sister Jane's hair ribbons. And smiling triumphantly on the tier below the Hughes family was Miss Angela Ryan and her parents who had been invited to watch what the Hughes and Barrie families hoped would be a victory for the gentlemen, among them the Barries' son, Lucas. Angela looked unbelievably pretty in a white muslin dress with a broad apple-green sash, her parasol tipped over her glossy ringlets on which a wisp of an apple-green bonnet was perched.

The cricketing gentlemen were clothed in traditional white and even the working lads had managed a pair of white duck trousers, the latter determined to beat the hell out of their superiors, for there was a special trophy and a cash prize donated by Herbert Barrie. Over it all, the polite clapping and the occasional 'well played' or 'good shot, lad', the bands continued to vie with one another in playing stirring martial music. It was a scene that took place on every village green and cricket pitch the length and breadth of the country and as Gilly, holding Jem by the arm, led him to a bench under the wide, spreading branches of a venerable oak tree, every spectator's attention was on the gentleman who had just swung his cricket bat, hitting the ball so high and so far every eye lost sight of it. It had gone into the branches of one of the oak trees which had been there before the park had been built. When the architect, a Frenchman, had planned the gardens he had cleverly incorporated many of the fine trees that had stood there for generations and there was still a small woodland towards Ullett Road. The ball fell through the thick foliage and hit the ground, landing in the undergrowth at the foot of the trees. Wood anemones, violets, miniature wild orchids were all trampled underfoot as the fielders searched frantically for the ball while the man who had hit it stood grinning at the stumps, his even white teeth adazzle in his brown face as he grinned in acknowledgement of the crowd's applause.

The ball was found and for the next five minutes Gilly sat and watched Lucas Barrie knock the ball all over the field and when, finally, he was bowled out she still sat there, uncaring that he had apparently scored over a hundred runs with which the crowd, the *gentleman's* crowd, was delighted. Angela Ryan was standing up with the rest, clapping and turning about as though it were all down to her and as Lucas left the field, lifting his bat to acknowledge the applause, Gilly felt something start to thump and shake inside her, as if her heart had come loose. Jem was fidgeting beside her, longing to be off, unaware of the company across the cricket field and of the identity of the cricketer who was making such an impression on the spectators.

'Can't we go, now Gilly?' he complained. 'This is no fun just sitting here listening to some other men enjoying themselves. Let's go and find Queenie and Flo, if we can in this crowd. To be honest I don't know why I let you talk me into coming . . .' His voice faded from her hearing. He had not stopped talking but she had stopped hearing him as Lucas's team came out of the pavilion and began to spread themselves about the field. As she sat there in her dream-like state Lucas walked towards the tree where she and Jem were seated. He stopped short of the tree and stood with his back to them watching as two men from the other side took their place at the wickets. He stood with one hand on his hip, his tall, gracefully proportioned body indolently at ease, the fine white cambric of his shirt stretched across his back which was damp with sweat.

The lad who was batting hit a spectacularly high ball into the air and Lucas watched it as it flew over his head and with a crack hit one of the branches of the oak tree and landed with a thud in the uncut grass at Gilly's feet. Lucas had been running backwards, ready to catch the ball, but when it vanished in the foliage he turned in a spin and dodged beneath the leaves.

'What the bloody hell was that?' Jem exclaimed, then with his sharp hearing picked up the brush of Lucas's footsteps in the grass. 'What's happened? Who's there?' But neither Gilly nor Lucas answered him, for they were captured in the net of delight that had them fast at this unexpected meeting. They had parted in bitterness but that feeling had been a false one, their wondering eyes told one another, for their love had overcome it, would overcome the rocks and pitfalls that life had strewn before them. It had been battered but it had not faltered. And as Gilly stood up, moving from beneath the umbrella of the oak and into the sunshine it was as though the crowd, which had come to watch the gentlemen get thrashed by the working lads, or the other way round depending on your station in life, held their breath in amazement. Lucas reached out and took both her hands in his.

'My love,' his lips mouthed silently, lifting at the corners in his joy, and her eyes were a brilliantly deep golden brown, clear and sharp in answer. Their love was a tangible thing, as though it might be visible to the eye and she allowed her hands to remain in his. What he was showing her in his velvety grey eyes told her of his feelings. When he was at odds with the world, or with her, his eyes were a silvery, sometimes a slatey grey, but his love turned them to velvet, a pale, dove-grey velvet. In a daze she watched his face close on hers and there, before the crowd of silent spectators, Lucas Barrie kissed her, a declaration that none of them could ignore, especially those in the spectator stand. His lips were warm and she trembled with delight, a strange delight but sweet as the incident had been sweet.

There was a long moment of absolute silence in which even the birds rustling in the oak seemed to hold their breath, then, 'How lovely you are.' His voice was no more than a soft whisper so that even Jem, bristling on the bench behind them, could not hear. Then he turned and sauntered back to his post on the field. Suddenly he realised he had forgotten the cricket ball and with a grin in her direction strode back to get it and from the stands where the working-class folk sat there came a resounding cheer.

They did not cheer at the other end, where the better sort were congregated. Angela Ryan's pretty face turned the ugly colour of a beetroot then paled as every vestige of blood drained away. She clutched at her father's arm who himself looked violently displeased since he had high hopes for this lovely lass of his and Herbert Barrie's lad. She was clinging to her father's arm and he patted her hand, but the expression on his face had Lucas seen it might have alarmed him. Joseph Ryan was in the habit of getting his way in all things and the best of everything for his daughter who was more precious to him than anything he had ever owned. His little girl who had sat on his knee from the minute she could climb up on it, prettily asking for this or that, whatever might have taken her fancy, and it had been his joy to get it for her. Now she wanted Barrie's lad and though the sod had let her down once she was still determined to have him and that was good enough for her father.

Behind Gilly Jem spluttered angrily, demanding to know what the devil was happening, then stood up, brandishing his stick and at once Gilly came from the loveliness of the last few minutes. If Jem could have seen her face he would have understood at once who had put that dreaming smile there.

'It's only one of the cricketers retrieving his ball,' she said, putting his arm through hers and leading him away from the cricket pitch towards the pavilion where she could see Queenie and Flo sitting in the sunshine. The crowds had grown and the noise was overwhelming as the brass bands, the organ grinder and the hurdy-gurdy all vied with one another for the crowd's attention. The Punch and Judy show was in full swing and the children's screams added to the cacophony.

''Ave yer seen enough, our kid?' Queenie asked hopefully, for though she and Flo had had a cup of tea in the pavilion it was nothing like the drink they were used to. 'Maiden's water', she had christened it contemptuously and Flo had agreed. They liked it hot, sweet and almost black!

'Well, I certainly have,' Jem remarked petulantly and Gilly felt sorry, for really what fun could it be to a man without sight, the roars of the crowd, the high-pitched squeak of the Punch and Judy, the bright array of flowers in their summer beauty, all the things that she and others in the park took for granted. He couldn't even hear the lovely song of the water falling in cascades down to the lake because of the hubbub of noise that surrounded them.

Jem released Gilly's arm and took hold of Queenie's, allowing her to guide him along the pathway. He could smell the roses which were a feature of the gardens around the pavilion and brooded on the fate that had deprived him of his sight. He was startled when for a fraction of a second something seemed to glide across the inside of his eyelids, or the blankness of whatever it was he looked at – as he thought of it – every waking hour. He could still 'see' in his mind's eye all the things he had known since he was a baby, or he supposed he should say he remembered from his earliest memories. Some of the scenes and sights he remembered were not pleasant but the one memory that had never faded was that of a laughing baby with a mop of red, curly hair, well, not exactly red but copper and gold and amber blended together into a ripple of blazing light. Arched baby eyebrows a soft brown and the most amazing golden-brown eyes surrounded by long brown lashes, the eyes glinting in the light. And now, as he walked beside Queenie Logan he had the strange feeling that he was looking at something, or *for* something that had just crossed his vision. A colour, or was it a shape, a blur, a shade, and then it was gone and he was staring at nothing as he had done for over a year now.

'You all righ', chuck?' Queenie asked as they waited for Gilly and Flo to catch up at the tram stop where the omnibus tram would take them back to the Town Hall.

He sighed deeply and Queenie put her hand on his, her compassion for this dear lad flowing through that hand and into his.

'Eeh, Queenie . . .' he sighed. No more but she understood.

'She's got to be stopped, Papa. I want her to be so discouraged she and her low family will move away from Liverpool and settle somewhere else. She must have spent all her ready money on that shop and the . . . well, the fittings and the fabrics and all the things she sells there. She nearly went under last time when our friends stopped buying her gowns but somehow she managed to keep going. You know I want him, don't you, Papa?'

'Yes, sweetheart, and so do I, for Barrie and I can do business together.'

'I'm sorry, Papa, but I don't care about that.' His daughter's voice was vicious, strident with it and her young and pretty face was distorted with hatred. 'I had him here . . .' She put out her white hand, which had never lifted a thing in its life if it could be lifted by a servant, and she had plenty of those, and pointed at the palm. 'We were engaged and then he . . .' She lifted her fingers to her hair and seemed ready to tear it out by the roots. 'Dear God, why did I take him there . . . to that place?'

'Darling, please don't upset yourself.' Joseph Ryan stood up and moved towards his beloved child. 'You know I can't bear it when you're unhappy.' He put his arms about her and she pressed her face against his shirt front.

'Then make me happy, Papa. Stop her. Get her out of town. Make her go away where he can't find her.' She tore herself from his arms and jerked to the window. 'Twice now she's humiliated me in front of all our friends.'

'Well, he was the one who went to her, sweetheart.'

She whirled about, her face ugly in its rage. 'Are you defending him, Papa?' she shrieked.

He stepped back hastily, for his daughter's temper was appalling and frightened every member of the household, which was why she had had her own way since she was a baby.

'No, of course not, dearest.'

'Then get rid of her. Do something to put her totally out of business, for I mean to have Lucas Barrie and while she's in Liverpool he will continue to . . . *Get rid of her, Papa!*'

28

The two men worked methodically, starting at the top of the building in the workroom, smashing sewing machines and the workbenches they stood on. Every length of material, lovely satins, velvets, muslins, semi-transparent barege, softest cashmeres, mohair, jaconet, a rich poult de soie, some in lovely, vivid shades, others muted and pale and soft, spilling in a destructive curtain, a rainbow of colours on which the men, big, burly men with brutish faces, stepped carelessly in their heavy, dirty boots. Feathers and ribbons were slashed, the feathers floating like snowflakes about the men's heads and landing on their shoulders. A bucket of tar was emptied in great splashes, up the walls and across the devastation of fabrics, black, sticky and reeking, and something else that smelled even worse. Paint was daubed wherever there was a flat surface, the men wielding brushes in what seemed to be frenzied madness but which was in reality calculated to create more havoc. Dummies on which half-finished gowns were draped were destroyed with blows from hammers and knives and the gowns themselves hacked to pieces. It was late at night and they had been told to be quiet for there might be someone in the premises adjoining, but nevertheless they smashed the windows in a great clatter and all without speaking a word to one another. One might have expected them to laugh perhaps, for the type of man who did this sort of thing took great pleasure in it, but they were totally silent.

They repeated the destruction on the next floor, tearing

down velvet curtains, pulverising dainty gilt chairs and fracturing mirrors into a dozen pieces. Again tar and paint was poured over the floor, this time on a carpet the colour of parchment, then dribbled down the stairs until they reached the salon. In ten minutes it was destroyed, day dresses with wide crinoline skirts, a ball dress meant for a dear friend of Miss Helen Moore, Miss Nora Ward's exquisite wedding gown which was ready for the final fitting, a ball dress of white tulle, once draped in velvet ribbons now decorated with thick black tar. Her lovely trousseau, the bridesmaids' pretty dresses of pale peach, fans, dainty reticules, shawls and bonnets were all given the same treatment and when they were satisfied that no more could be done the men stood back and studied their handiwork. Still not a word was spoken and as silently as they had got in, they left, shutting the door behind them. They had not touched the window display, for they did not wish to draw attention to their handiwork. They walked quietly along Bold Street, dodging into a shop doorway for a moment when they saw a constable saunter by on Hanover Street in the direction of the Lyceum. When he had gone, despite their great hobnail boots which were sticky on the soles with what they had spread across the floors, they moved on without noise, disappearing into the cobweb of courts and back alleys that made up the poor area of Liverpool.

As was her custom Gilly was the first to arrive the next morning. She stood for a moment in the already warm sunshine, for the summer continued to smile benevolently up and down the land, the farmers beginning to worry about their crops because if they did not get some rain soon they would be ruined.

She put her head on one side and looked into the window, deciding that today she would remove the black and white striped day dress and high crowned black straw hat and replace them with a cream silk gown and a bonnet with cream velvet ribbons. She would drape a shawl across a chair, the shawl in cream silk deeply fringed in a coffee colour which exactly matched the feathers curling round the brim of the bonnet. The reticule of cream silk decorated with pearl would look splendid with the outfit and perhaps the dainty lace fan pinned to the backcloth of velvet.

She took out her key, put it in the lock, opened the door, her mind filled with plans, designs, ideas, colours, and stepped into a nightmare. It must be a nightmare. She must still be asleep in her bed and on waking had found that her sleeping mind had created this horror that lay before her, a horror she could not comprehend. She had come into the wrong shop, this was not *her* lovely, smart, well-ordered salon, the one on which she had closed the door last night. There was some mistake and so sure was she that she had wandered into the wrong building she stepped back into the doorway, ready to apologise to . . . to . . . Oh, sweet God . . . and at that moment her mind emptied itself of all thought. A blankness took over and with a soft sigh she sank to her knees just inside the doorway.

She was still there five minutes later when Nell and Sadie arrived. They were laughing about something as they clattered up the wrought-iron steps to the arcade and for a moment, as Nell glanced back at Sadie they were not aware that anything was wrong.

'. . . and d'yer know wharr 'e said, the cheeky blighter,' Nell was saying, but as they turned at the top of the steps and reached the doorway they both froze, speechless, their young faces turning the colour of uncooked dough. They stood behind the crouched figure of their employer, their eyes wide and from Nell's mouth a thin trickle of sound came. Not a sigh, nor a murmur but a choking sound as though she might vomit.

'Oh my God . . . Oh my God . . . Oh my God,' Sadie started to babble. She put her hand to her mouth and backed away until she was against the railing that edged the arcade. It was as though there were some frightful thing in the shop which had left this trail of destruction and at any moment she expected it to leap out and do the same to her.

They all three came slowly to life almost at the same time.

'Miss Logan . . .' Nell moaned, leaning against the door frame. 'Wharris it?'

'Nell . . .' Gilly could manage no more.

'Who . . . who . . .?'

'I d . . . don't know . . .'

A man who had come up the steps excused himself politely as he tried to get past the three young women who for some reason were hovering in Miss Logan's doorway and he was bewildered to see Miss Logan herself squatting on the floor.

He stopped. He was a shop assistant who worked at Lafter's, a clothier and shirtmaker further along the arcade, a polite young man who had often wished he could become better acquainted with the glorious Miss Logan, but this was not the opportunity he had imagined. His face took on the same look of horror as was pasted on those of the three women and he was, like Sadie, ready to reel away from it.

'Jesus Christ!' he whispered. 'Who done this?' He stared into the havoc that really not one of them could make sense of. Four pair of eyes slithered from one obscenity to another, each one worse than the last until finally Gilly climbed painfully to her feet. She clutched at Nell and trembled so violently she and Nell looked as though they were caught in the grip of a hurricane. Sadie was crying now, great tearing sobs that shook her frame, while the young man from Lafter's at last came to himself.

'Have yer sent fer the bobbies?' he asked grimly. 'Bobbies should be fetched. An' I wouldn't go inside fer yer don't know who might still be about.' They stared at the sea of paint and tar and other easily identifiable substance on what yesterday had

been a lovely carpet, and all three wondered, almost hysterically, who in their right mind would venture to walk across it. It
was a mass of ripped fabrics, smashed chairs, broken glass,
several buckets in which presumably the paint and whatever
else had been deposited there had been brought. The stench
was appalling and it took Gilly back to Rose Alley and the
obscene privy which stood in the centre of the court. Whoever
had done this had emptied the contents of the privy bucket into
her lovely premises, casually shut the door and walked away!

It was Anne who put it to rights, or at least Lucas Barrie
when Anne informed him of it. A police constable had been
brought from the corner of Bold Street where he had been
enjoying the bit of sunshine on his back and though he was as
appalled as they, could not help in any way in the cleaning up,
he told them, but he would certainly report the break-in. Had
anything been stolen? he asked, licking the tip of his pencil as he
prepared to write down the details in his official notebook. How
could they tell unless they were prepared to venture across the
defilement of the salon? Nell asked bitingly, since Miss Logan
was still in a state of shock and seemed unable to answer. Could
she tell him exactly what damage had been—

'Bloody 'ell, lad,' Nell shouted, 'can yer not see it wi' yer own
two eyes?'

'Wharrabout upstairs?' he ventured, as unwilling as they to
step into the beastliness beyond the shop door.

'Well, seein' as 'ow you're the law why don't you go an' 'ave a
look?'

'Eeh, I'll 'ave ter get me sergeant on this. I've never seen the
like . . .'

The young man from Lafter's, seeing a chance to make
himself useful in Miss Logan's eyes, took her arm, and with a
nod at the other two young ladies, one of whom seemed about
to throw herself off the arcade, ushered them towards his own
place of employment.

'A cup of tea, I think,' he said importantly. Another gentle-man, obviously his superior, bustled along the arcade, the look of horror on his face telling them he had seen what had happened at Gillyflower's, elbowing aside the young man who looked most put out but the manager, for it was he, took over.

'Miss Logan, oh, my poor lady . . . Who can have done this to your lovely shop? Yes, Simpkins, I will see to this. You open the shop and then put the kettle on for these poor . . .'

Gilly barely remembered the next few hours. The kindly manager put them in a cab and directed the cabbie to take them to . . . where? Seymour Street, of course, and if there was anything further he could do Miss Logan had only to let him know. The police sergeant had arrived and the constable was . . . well . . . if Miss Goodwin, meaning Nell, would make sure Miss Logan was taken safely home, taking no particular interest in Sadie. Oh, there was another young lady expected . . . well, they were not to worry, Simpkins would see to it all and make sure she was informed.

Flo and Queenie were just about to set out on a visit to the market. They had on their sensible cotton dresses that Gilly had made for them, Queenie's the colour of sherry and Flo in pale grey. They wore bonnets to match, for with a dressmaker and milliner in the family they prided themselves on being as stylish as some of the ladies of quality. Flo had discarded her eye-patch some time ago but she still wore the steel-wire protective spectacles, slightly tinted with hinged lateral visors. They had a chain which she hung round her neck and as the horse-drawn cab drew up and deposited Gilly, Nell and Sadie, all wilting like flowers left too long in a vase, on the pavement outside the door they fell off her face and thumped against her generous bosom.

'Dear God . . . Dear God . . . Dear God,' she moaned, somewhat in the manner of poor Sadie, clutching at Flo's arm until she winced.

'What . . . what is it?' Jem, who had been seated at the table, his fingers busy on the pages of his book, stood up, knocking his chair backwards, and Flo's cat, who followed her faithfully from one house to another, jumped to a higher position of safety on the dresser. Jem felt round the table, bumping into the two women who were at the front door and at the same time another cab drew up behind the first and Anne alighted from it.

The six women and Jem crowded in the narrow passage and chaos reigned, for all except Gilly were jabbering quavering questions and equally quavering answers, none of them making any sense. Gilly leaned against the wall, her senses reeling and it was not until Jem, the Jem they had once known, found her and drew her from the mêlée into his arms that she steadied.

'What is it, Lovedy?' he asked quietly, holding her close and she shivered against him, thankful for his support.

'Yer never seen anythin' like it, 'onest ter God . . .'

'. . . the mess . . . an' the stink . . .'

'. . . 'ooever done it wants 'angin', an' that's the truth . . .'

'Gilly, love, wharrisit? Yer frightenin' me an' Flo, int she, Flo? Tell yer Mam, chuck.'

'. . . bobbies are there but they'll der nowt . . .'

'Gilly, dearest, please tell us what has happened. Is it something to do with the shop? Has there been a break-in?' Anne stammered, huddling up to Flo who put her arms about her, since the lass, who was not as strong as she might have been, seemed about to faint.

'. . . them bastards musta brought . . .'

'. . . don't know why nobody saw 'em . . .'

'*Will you all be quiet and let Gilly get inside.* She needs to sit down. Queenie, make a pot of tea and Flo, nip next door and fetch that brandy you keep for emergencies.' For all of them were aware Flo liked a nip or two before retiring.

He brought order from the chaos and when Gilly, Nell and Sadie, and, of course, Flo, for she was all of a doo-dah, she said, had had a sip and the brandy had calmed them, the tale was told in all its nasty details.

'Who would do such a thing?' Jem, with Gilly beside him, her hand still in his, had returned to his place at the table. She had been patted and hugged and kissed by her mam who was not prone to such demonstrations but her girl was still in a state of terrible shock and needed the ministrations of her family. Flo took her in her arms for a second and murmured something, for the girl was deeply loved by them all. They drank their tea and at last some colour returned to her cheeks and she straightened up, lifting her head in a vague semblance of the girl she once had been. Who had done this to her? Someone who hated her. Someone who wanted her to suffer. Someone with power, obviously, for it would take power to perform, or have performed this terrible act of vandalism. Way off in the far spaces of her mind she felt the first stirring of awareness. Awareness of what she hadn't quite grasped yet, but it was on the edges of her consciousness and she would find it. A vague memory of something . . . someone . . . a sense of foreboding . . . vindictiveness, for whoever was to blame for this crime against her carried an implacability that was re-morseless. She did her best to grasp it but she felt as if she were trying to catch smoke in her hands and she was too beaten at the moment to try.

Anne sat quietly while Nell and Sadie took themselves off home, for what a tale they would have to tell their families. It was not that they were unthinking, as they liked their work and Miss Logan was a good employer, but they were excited now. They were learning a trade under her tutelage and by the standards of the day, which were not good for seamstresses, they worked in decent conditions. Miss Logan had promised them they would be paid despite what had happened and as soon as the shop was cleaned up, her heart heaving at the thought of settling to the horrendous task, they would be back in business, she said. The brandy had lifted her, given her courage, but at the thought of the dreadful undertaking ahead of her she began to wilt again and then, in a way that distressed them all, making them swirl about the kitchen, not knowing what to do to console her, she began to weep brokenheartedly.

Anne watched her. She herself hadn't seen the destruction but to make Gilly, strong, determined, stubborn, headstrong Gilly act like this, it must be horrendous. No one noticed as she quietly left the room and let herself out of the kitchen. She found a cab at the bottom of the street and within an hour she was across the water and in her brother's office.

He studied the mayhem from the threshold of the shop, no expression on his face. The constable was still there, guarding the place, he said, though what good would it do for the damage was already done, didn't the gentleman agree. The lock had been picked and was still workable and all they need do, in his opinion, was shut the door and walk away until it could be cleaned up. No, he said, no one had been inside yet. At least not upstairs. He thought his sergeant had gone back to the station to fetch stout boots, for no one was game to walk across the shambles the intruders had left. He'd be back soon, no doubt, if the gentleman would like to wait. The gentleman wouldn't.

'Is there a bootmaker about here?' he asked abruptly.

'Yer wha'?'

'A bootmaker, man. I need a pair of stout boots. I can't go in in these,' indicating his fine leather ankle boots over which his grey striped trousers lay.

'Ah, 'old on. No one can go in until the sergeant ses so.'

'My name is Lucas Barrie. My father is Herbert Barrie of Barrie and Hughes, the shipbuilders. I have an interest in these premises and I mean to inspect the damage done.'

'D'yer mean yer own them, sir?'

'I do,' Lucas lied.

The constable scratched his head, wishing his sergeant was here. 'Well, in that case, sir, there's Jenson's in Bold Street. They sell a good . . .' but the gentleman was already running down the steps.

He was back in ten minutes clutching a heavy pair of boots which, when he had tucked his fine trousers into them, reached his knees. Taking a deep breath and holding his cambric handkerchief to his nose, Lucas Barrie crossed the threshold into the ravages of his love's salon.

When he came down the stairs, his face was ashen and the constable thought he might be trembling. He was a tall man with good shoulders on him, lean and athletic-looking, the constable would have said, but what he had seen upstairs had burdened him and he could barely stand up straight.

'Thank you, Constable,' he said politely, standing outside the door to remove his boots, which were coated with something the constable did not care to study too closely. He dragged great breaths of air into his lungs, leaning over the railing as though he might be sick, then he steadied himself. He dropped the boots into a bucket the constable had considerately provided with a promise to get rid of them, and pulled his own good boots on. Men and women from the various shops along the arcade were hovering and staring in appalled silence and one, a man from the clothier's, quietly asked him if he would care to make use of his shop to wash his hands. They had all heard who he was by this time and were eager to help the wealthy son of such a well-known businessman.

Lucas Barrie was acquainted, through his business affairs, with many people from all walks of life and they, in their turn, could lay their hands on others who were willing to take on any sort of work as long as the pay was good. Before the day was out and consulting no one, not even the owner of Gillyflower's, a squad of people moved in, working through the night, scrubbing, scouring, disinfecting, painting, all under Lucas's tireless supervision. Carpets were thrown out on to the balcony and hastily disposed of, broken furniture, mirrors, heavily soiled materials, bits of delicate gilt chairs, in fact every object that had once been part of Gilly Logan's dream. The premises were scrubbed again and again by an army of sturdy women who were not unaccustomed to nasty smells and filth, on their knees, their arms up to the elbow in buckets of soapy water. Workmen painted every inch of every wall and ceiling. White-wash only for the moment, for Gilly would want to choose her own colours but by noon the next day it stood empty and sterile, smelling of paint, disinfectant and the sharpness of carbolic soap.

'Will you come with me, Mam? I don't think I could go on my own. We'll have to wear something that we can throw away . . . afterwards. Dear God, I just feel as though I can't . . . well, to begin again . . . where'll we get the cash, Mam? Mr Field at the bank might help us but . . .'

'Chuck, first things first. Let you an' me an' Flo gerra cab ter't shop an' see what's what. Lord, me an' Flo've done some cleanin' in our time, an' still can so one step at a time, eeh, love.'

'I'd come myself, Gilly, but I can't see what good I can be to you,' Jem said forlornly, but Gilly interrupted him lovingly, for no matter what had happened between her and Jem, she knew that there was still a deep fondness between them.

'Besides, Anne will be here soon to take you to the school. You must keep up your reading.'

He sighed sadly. 'I suppose so.' There was something he must tell Gilly soon but just at the moment when she was in such despair he couldn't bring himself to spring it on her.

The constable was still there when the cab pulled up at the corner of Bold Street and Remington Place and as Gilly reluctantly mounted the wrought-iron steps to the arcade, Queenie and Flo at her heels, he was standing in the doorway, on his face an expression of total disbelief. The door was open, for the sergeant had confiscated a key and he leaned against the door jamb as though he might faint right away, which was not the custom of a policeman!

Gilly moved towards him, taking her place in the doorway and when he turned to look at her the amazement on his face was almost comical. As it was on hers! Her mam and Flo crowded behind her, looking over her shoulder and when she sagged they were there to catch her, since she would have fallen had they not been there.

'Dear Lord,' she whispered.

'What 'appened?'

'Someone's . . . cleaned it,' she managed to whisper.

'Cleaned it? 'Oo would do such a thing?' Queenie had not seen the horror of it but she knew from her daughter's manner yesterday how it must have been, for Gilly Logan had not been brought up softly. She had known filth and squalor and the odours of Rose Alley and it would take a lot to turn her squeamish. And she had been close to fainting at it yesterday. Now it was gone. It was as clean as Queenie's own kitchen and smelled as fragrant. Who loved her daughter well enough *and had the resources* to do this for her? It could only be that chap who had saved them once before when Queenie had been so brutally attacked. The one who had given them the shelter and protection of his home and whose feelings, since Queenie had known them once herself, she recognised. Jem had taken up with his sister, turning against Gilly whom he had loved all his life and it could only be because he too recognised what was in her and in Lucas Barrie.

'It must 'ave bin 'im,' she murmured, holding her daughter's arms as though she thought she might dash down to the Pier Head to go to him.

'Yes.' Gilly's voice was no more than a whisper, for she knew exactly who her mother meant.

'That chap . . .' the constable muttered.

'Chap?'

'He went in. Asked me where he could get boots. A gent, he were.'

'Lucas.'

'Aye, that were 'im.'

On the far side of Bold Street a smart carriage stood against the kerb. The hood was up but a girl's face was at the window and it wore an expression that boded ill for someone.

The coachman whipped the horses into a frenzy, nearly causing a serious accident when her voice cut through him, and he hoped to God it was not him that was in trouble, though he could think of nothing he had done to warrant it. But then you never knew with the master's daughter.

29

The door knocker sounded loudly and unexpectedly, making Jem jump. He stood up and felt his way to the door. As he did so he experienced that lightening of the darkness in which he dwelled and this time there was even a blurred shape where the small arched window over the door shone. It was the shape of the arch so he knew he wasn't imagining it and in his heart a small bud of hope warmed him. He didn't know what these changes meant, these unexpected but increasingly regular occurrences, but he could not help that leap of gladness which he kept to himself. And then there had been that wonderful moment when Gilly had turned to him, leaned against *him* in her distress just as she had done in the past. She had turned to *him* and what might that mean . . .

He opened the door, still smiling, a smile of great joy which fell over the figure of Anne who stood on Flo's achingly clean doorstep. His gaze drifted over her head, for until she spoke he had no idea who was there but when she stepped inside and lovingly touched his cheek, he knew and the smile slipped away.

'Has Gilly gone to the salon?' she asked, a lilt of excitement in her voice, turning to close the door behind her, then moving to kiss him on the cheek. Her expression was soft and glowing with her love for him and her eyes, the same silvery velvet as her brother's which had enchanted Gilly Logan, smiled up at him. Even though he couldn't see it, he could feel its warmth. She was sweet, gentle, kind, generous, trusting and she was carrying his child. Soon they must announce it, not only to his family but to hers and there was no doubt in his mind what the outcome of that would be. Herbert Barrie would be dangerous in his outrage at the wrong done his daughter, for he would blame the man who had got her into this predicament and her mother would go into a decline, for how could she hold up her head in her social circle with a pregnant, unmarried daughter in their midst? The scandal would strike her a blow from which she would never recover and she would never forgive her daughter. Anne would be rejected, thrown out on to the streets where every disgraced woman deserved to be and the only people she could turn to would be himself, Gilly, Queenie and Flo. The two older women would be just as distressed, though Queenie herself had once given birth to an illegitimate child.

Not that Anne's child would be a bastard, for Jem meant to marry her. What else could he do? He loved Gilly Logan with every fibre of his being, with every beat of his heart and pulse but he could not have her, he sadly accepted that. Yes, she had leaned against him earlier when she was frail and unsteady but it meant nothing really. She loved Lucas Barrie and it seemed Barrie loved her. Besides, hadn't Anne led him towards what might be his salvation? Did she not deserve his support? If he never regained his sight she had rekindled in him the pleasure of books and she would lovingly, willingly guide him through life, his hand in hers, if necessary. She was to give him a child. Though she had never washed a pot or boiled an egg in her life she would learn and both Flo and Queenie would be in their element teaching her. Somehow they must all fit into the houses on Seymour Street which would be a tight squeeze with a baby but they had no choice. Somehow he must earn his living, for with a wife and child to support he could not expect hand-outs from Gilly for ever.

Anne, unaware of Jem's antipathy towards her brother, at once and innocently created a situation that threatened to explode the very walls of the small house.

'I told Lucas what had happened though it's still a mystery who did it, or why.' She moved into the kitchen, picked up the purring cat and sat down with her in her lap, fondling her ear and making her purr even louder.

'What?'

'Well, I knew he could put it right since he knows so many people. I don't mean who did it or anything like that but get the frightful mess cleaned up and he will. He was so cross—'

'*Cross!*'

'Well, it's hard to describe because with Lucas you don't really know what he's thinking but he—'

'*What the hell are you babbling about?*'

Anne sat back, alarmed at his tone and the cat jumped from her knee and took up a position on the top shelf of the dresser. Her face paled and her eyes widened.

'Lucas is going to—'

'Bugger Lucas and what he's going to do. Why in hell's name does he have to be brought into this?' Jem crashed into the table in his fury and Anne recoiled. 'Every time there is trouble who should be there but that sod . . .'

'*Jem, please . . .*'

'I know he didn't cause it, but God help me if St Lucas isn't there to put it right, sticking his bloody nose in where it's not wanted.'

'He wants to help Gilly, Jem.'

'I bet he does and what does he get in return, tell me that, you little fool?'

Anne began to cry. 'Nothing . . . nothing. He expects no payment, Jem, really. He doesn't need money, you know that. My father—'

'Christ tonight! If your father knew . . .' Jem stopped himself before the words were out, for what was the point in hurting this child. His own frustration had burst out of him because it should be he who was down at the salon putting to rights whatever had been done there. Someone, for reasons unknown, had trashed Gilly's shop, not only that but defiled the elegance, the loveliness, the immaculacy of what was her pride and joy. The very heart of her which she alone had created. Dear God, if he had his sight he would make it his business to find out and exact the most brutal revenge. Had he not been in gaol his first thought would have been his pa but perhaps from the Borough Gaol itself Tommy Wilson had reached out through his network of cronies and done this thing. But whatever it was, bloody Lucas Barrie was putting it right and he, Jem Wilson, could do nothing about it.

He sat down heavily and held out his hand to the girl opposite.

'Sweetheart, I'm that sorry. Come here and sit on my lap and let me show you how sorry. I'm a brute but . . . well, you know how Gilly and I were brought up together. She is like a sister to me,' he lied, 'and a brother wants nothing more than to protect his family. See, kiss me,' which she did willingly, her tears drying as he held her fiercely, then, since he needed some outlet for his ineffectuality, his hand fell to her gently rounded belly and from there to her breasts which had grown fuller with her pregnancy. He opened her bodice and exposed them, small but ripe, the nipples hardening under his touch. She demurred at first, murmuring that the others would soon be back but he took no notice, standing up and then laying her on the table. She tried to sit up but he pushed her back, lifted her skirts, pulled down her drawers and his fingers were between her thighs feeling for what he needed. He took hold of her and pulled her legs fully apart then pushed himself hard inside her.

'The baby . . .' she gasped but again he ignored her. His pace quickened for seconds, minutes, hours then he gave a last powerful lunge, throwing back his head in a yell of triumph. He slumped forward on top of her and then came the part she liked best. She held his head against her bare breasts and crooned to him as though he were a child. When at last he came out of her and stood up he leaned over, his face flushed, and kissed her softly on the lips.

'Sweet . . . you're so sweet.'

'I love you, Jem,' wishing he would say the same.

Jem felt better, not that she loved him but that he had been able to release the strain, the bitterness, the frustration in the only way that was open to him these days and that was in the sweetness of Anne Barrie's body. 'We'll be married soon, sweetheart. I suppose we must go and see your father and tell him and find somewhere to live and if—'

They heard the sound of the key in the lock and instantly sprang apart. Anne managed to do up her bodice and though they were both flushed and breathing hard they were seated apart when the three women entered the room.

Jem stood up and reached out his hands in a silent supplication to be told what was happening and was bewildered when the three women began to laugh. Not loud bellowing laughter that denoted great amusement but soft, joyful, for what had happened was joyful. They could hardly believe it and the strange thing, at least to Queenie and Flo, was that Lucas Barrie had made it happen, according to the policeman who had witnessed what had been done. Overnight, Mr Barrie had performed the miracle of having it cleaned up for their girl. They had no idea why. Perhaps it was something to do with the fact that Jem had once worked for him, or that his sister was a friend of their Gilly but whatever it was it had certainly put the smile back on Gilly's face and a spring in her step.

'Anne, Anne, I don't know how you persuaded him . . . yes, I know it must have been you who told him so don't pretend.'

'I'm not pretending, Gilly. I admit I told him and well, you know how determined he is to help you.'

'Help me! Lord, do you know what this means? I can start again.'

'Will someone tell me what the devil's going on?' Jem's voice was truculent, for no matter what the goodness behind the deed it always seemed to come back to Lucas Barrie and despite the fact he was to marry Barrie's sister, he was still bitterly jealous.

Gilly turned to him and took his hands, then put her arms about him in a huge hug, clutching him to her. 'The shop, Jem. The shop has been cleaned. It's absolutely spotless and it seems that Lucas did it.'

'What, got down on his hands and knees and scrubbed?'

'No, of course not, but he must have summoned women to clean and then it was painted and all it needs is the furnishings: mirrors, materials.' Her face clouded over and she sat down abruptly. She had been so overcome with the rapture of finding her lovely shop clean and sweet-smelling that she had given no thought to the expense entailed to bring it back to life. To make it into a viable business again. To regain custom. To have Nell and Sadie working beside her with young Rosie as apprentice. To fill it with lovely garments designed and made by herself and her staff. She had some monies in her account, monies transferred long since from what had been her mother's and she had added to it when she could.

She stood up suddenly, once again upsetting the cat who had settled herself comfortably on Anne's knee.

'I must go and see Mr Field.'

'Nay, 'ave a cuppa tea first, my lamb,' Queenie protested, taking off her bonnet and bustling to the fire where the kettle was gently steaming.

'No, I can't waste a minute.' Gilly made for the door and they all looked at one another as she banged it to behind her.

Mr Field had received another visitor who was shown in to him almost before the good gentleman had had time to remove his top hat and sit down behind his enormous desk.

He stood up politely as the visitor entered, for this was an influential man whose considerable wealth, or at least that of his family, was safely ensconced in the Royal Bank of which Mr Fields was manager. He indicated for his visitor to be seated before he himself lowered his fleshy frame into his own comfortable leather chair. They chatted of this and that, the unusually hot weather which seemed determined to continue, the forthcoming visit of the Prince and Princess of Wales and the grand ball that was to be held in their honour, and at which both gentlemen, being prominent in the town, were to be guests. They talked of the state of business generally, until at last Mr Lucas Barrie, son of Herbert Barrie of Barrie and Hughes, came round to the reason for his visit.

'I believe you know a Miss Gilly Logan, Mr Field. Now I know you cannot reveal to me the extent of her account and if you did I should instantly remove mine, for a bank manager who discusses a client's account with another is not to be trusted.'

Mr Field shifted uncomfortably in his chair and inclined his head. 'Indeed.'

'Now you may or may not have heard of Miss Logan's misfortune . . . No, I thought not,' as Mr Field looked bewildered. 'Well, I will tell you. I am giving away no private matter because the whole of Bold Street and perhaps Liverpool knows of it.'

'Dear me . . .' Mr Field began but Mr Barrie held up an authoritative hand.

'Her salon was broken into and to put it bluntly totally destroyed, but not only that, the intruders, if you can call them by such an innocuous name, deliberately vandalised the place. In fact they desecrated it with the most unspeakable filth you could imagine. I have taken it upon myself to put it all back together.'

Mr Field's mind began to tick over, taking the most obvious route and on his face slid an expression that he quickly removed. It was a knowing expression that said, 'So that's the way of it, is it? A beautiful young girl, working class, of course, and a successful and rich young man from the upper class and what would they be to one another? But then it was nothing to do with him how Miss Logan disported herself, was it?'

'I have no notion of the size of Miss Logan's account, Mr Field, and I don't wish you to tell me. She will, no doubt, come here shortly and discuss her financial affairs with you. To be blunt, I wish you to make available to her anything she needs. You will take it from my own personal account and tell her it is a loan. From you! From the bank. At the lowest rate of interest, which she will not question. She is an intelligent woman and will expect to pay interest on a loan, of course, and if we could get away with it I would like you to lend it to her interest-free but I do not wish her to be suspicious. This could be arranged?'

'Naturally, sir, but am I to understand there is to be no limit on what you will "lend" her?'

'Mr Field, you know Miss Logan and her mother . . .'

'Indeed.' Mr Field cast his mind back to the stately, dignified woman who had first opened an account in his bank several years ago. Honest as the day is long and her daughter was the same.

'Miss Logan will borrow the very least she can manage on but if you are able encourage her to . . . to . . .'

'Splash out a bit?'

'Exactly. She will need to purchase materials apart from the furnishings for her shop and I do not want her to scrimp and—'

'Leave it to me, Mr Barrie. Miss Logan and I are old friends and I will persuade her not to cut corners.'

Lucas stood up and held out his hand which Mr Field wrung heartily.

'Thank you, Mr Field. I shall not forget this.'

*   *   *

Barely an hour later Gilly Logan entered the bank and asked if
Mr Field might be free and was told that if she would care to
wait the clerk would enquire. Within minutes she was shown
into Mr Field's office where he insisted she drank hot chocolate
with him and chatted about this and that as he had done with
Lucas Barrie.

But Gilly was eager to get on with the business of why she
was here, for if Mr Field could not help her she didn't know
where she would go. A money lender? God forbid, but if she
had to do it, she would. She needed to get her salon back in
business as soon as possible, since while it stood empty of
customers she was losing money. She had her mother and Jem
to support, not to mention the expensive lengths of materials,
silks, satins, velvets and a dozen other items that her customers
demanded, and of course the plainer and more reasonable
fabrics that her less fortunate ladies were able to afford. Dear
God, the list was endless and she thanked God for Nell who
had called at Seymour Street just before she set off with an offer
of her help.

'I'll come wi' yer, Miss Logan, when yer choose yer fabrics. I
know just what yer like an' I'll get the workroom set up ready fer
the machines. And the machines theirselves ter be chosen.
Lord, an' then there's carpets an' . . . well, owt I can do and
Sadie ses the same, fer we both want ter work for yer again.'

She had wanted to weep then, for even Anne had offered her
services in any capacity she could manage, the look that passed
between her and Jem unnoticed by Gilly though Queenie
caught it and wondered. No, she didn't wonder, for Queenie
was not daft and the jaunts Anne and Jem took together were a
bit odd!

'Now what can I do for you, Miss Logan?' Mr Field asked
innocently.

She told him the dreadful tale of what had happened to her
little business, with Mr Field shaking his head and tutting at the

appalling behaviour of the lower classes, forgetting that his client was just such a person.

'So you see, Mr Field, if I am to start again I must take out a loan. There is so much to replace . . . well, everything, actually, bar the shop itself. And I must do it soon, so if you cannot help me . . .'

'Now, now, Miss Logan, not so fast. Let us first discuss your requirements and see if something can be worked out. I know what a good business head you have and your propensity for hard work. You have proved in the past that you are worth a risk and I am inclined to help those who repay my confidence in them as you, and, may I say, your mother, have done. Now then, tell me what you need.'

She couldn't believe it was so easy, she told them later as they sat round the table and drank a reviving cup of Queenie's strong tea, though Gilly said she felt they should be opening a bottle of champagne, which was ridiculous really in view of what had happened. The interest was to be waived for the time being and any money she required was available at once. Mr Field had been so helpful, even walking to the door with her and insisting that she come and see him at any time, with any financial queries she might have. He would tell his wife and daughters, who had not as yet frequented Gillyflower's that she would be open for business within the week and beg them to come and see her. He had heard her fashions were . . . and on and on until she felt he believed he was dealing with royalty.

'So there it is. I shall send a message to Nell and Sadie and the three of us will put it all together again, starting this afternoon at Benson's. They have the best materials.' She shook her head in disbelief. 'Honestly, I can't get over Mr Field and his kindness.'

They all smiled and sipped their tea and when Jem stood up and reached for Anne's hand, which somehow he always knew where to find, the three ladies looked at him and Anne in surprise. He tucked her hand in the crook of his arm and smiled in her general direction, then turned to the others.

'Anne and I have some news which, in the circumstances, should be announced as soon as possible.' Anne looked down at the table, shy as a snowdrop and, with that instinctive gesture of a pregnant woman, her hand fell protectively to her belly. Three pairs of eyes followed it, then looked up at Jem.

'We are to be married, Anne and I, probably within the month. She is carrying my child, you see.'

There followed a silence in which the purring of the cat, curled up on the mat before the fire, could plainly be heard. From outside in the street the call of the rag and bone man echoed about the houses and someone walked past with a clatter of hobnailed boots. Anne chanced a small glance and on seeing the three open-mouthed faces looked as though she might cry but Jem was defiant, and even, in the way of a male creature, somewhat proud of this proof of his masculinity.

He cleared his throat nervously. 'We are to go to see . . . to see Anne's family tomorrow, which I don't suppose will be easy. They have given her a lot of freedom, thinking she is at the art gallery and learning to improve her painting so it will be a bit hard . . .'

Queenie had sensed that something was going on between Jem and Anne ever since the pair of them had taken to slipping off to the library and the School for the Blind where, she had been pleased to be told, Jem was learning to read one of them there strange books that were full of dots. Clever, she had thought it and good of Anne to be taking so much trouble. And she and Flo had often discussed Anne's devotion to Jem. They had thanked God for it, since Gilly was far too busy to do what Anne did. Although Flo had a small income from the savings her husband had left her and the rent from the house in which Queenie, Jem and Gilly lived, it wasn't enough, and if Gilly had not made a profit from her shop they would have been in 'queer street'. So it had been a boon to have Jem occupied and at the same time learning something that might, one day, make it possible for him to get a job. What at, she couldn't think, for surely a man needed his eyes for any kind of occupation. At the blind school those impaired were taught to make ropes and baskets and such like, but Jem, a qualified draughtsman, had so far refused even to consider it. Now there was to be a baby and who was to support all this lot but Gilly?

'Well, is nobody going to say anything?' Jem barked.

'What is there ter say, lad? Milk's spilt and can't be put back in't jug.' Which was a strange way to describe Anne's condition. Anne, who easily and sometimes irritatingly was reduced to tears, began to weep silently, the tears running down her cheeks and splashing on to the bodice of her pretty muslin gown. Jem turned to her and though he couldn't see the tears he knew they were there.

'Oh, for God's sake, Anne, don't cry.' His voice was sharp and all three women realised that Jem Wilson did not love his wife-to-be as a man should. He had made her pregnant and he was doing the right thing by marrying her but it was obviously something a decent man did and Jem was a decent man. His blindness was slowly corroding the man he had once been but the woman beside him was helping him out of the deep, black hole into which he had been swept. He was far from recovered, or even accepting, but perhaps the sweetness of Anne as his wife and the delight a child would bring might lift him over the rim of the hole and bring him some sort of peace and perhaps joy.

Gilly stood up and moved round the table. With a lovely gesture she put her arms about Jem and Anne, holding them to her, unaware of the pain it caused in Jem, but knowing at once that Anne was delighted.

'I'm so glad, for both of you, for I'm sure you'll be very happy. What you have told us here today could not have come at a better time. This house would be too small for us all, even with Flo's to spread out in. So, when the shop is renovated, which it will be in a week or two, I shall make myself a small apartment on the top floor. Mam, you and Flo can move in together and Anne, Jem and their baby can have this house. But, dear Lord, Jem, I don't envy you going to Bracken Hill and telling the Barries you are to marry their daughter and what's more they are to be grandparents!'

30

The cab drew up at the front steps of Bracken Hill just as the Barrie family were about to sit down to luncheon. As it was Sunday Rose Barrie had invited her married daughter and her son-in-law plus her elder son to eat with them and to her surprise Lucas had accepted the invitation. They made seven as they sat or stood about the drawing room drinking a pre-luncheon sherry, the gentlemen, Lucas, Angus and Herbert Barrie and Ernest, Emily's husband, discussing business as usual, standing by the open French windows that led on to the terrace where terracotta pots exploded in a multitude of colours. Geraniums were at their best and across the lawn that ran down to a strip of woodland, flowerbeds almost hurt the eye they were so bright-hued. Mrs Barrie always said she had no eye for colours, at least in her garden, and so her gardener was allowed to run riot and run riot he did. Antir-rhinums jostled with dianthus, petunias with delphiniums, a rainbow of colours from pale pink to the deepest blue and the roses in their circular rose bed, which were a particular fa-vourite of the gardener, were a picture, really they were, their fragrance reaching even into the drawing room.

Though the gentlemen stood, the ladies sat, straight-backed, in the velvet chairs arranged about the fireplace though no fire was lit, all except Anne who was restless and fidgety. She constantly rose to her feet, moving across the carpet which was the exact rose colour of the chairs, to peer out of the window, flitting backwards and forwards until her mother told her sharply to sit down and be quiet, just as though she were a naughty ten-year-old!

It was again, as it had been for weeks now, a hot and sunny day and the gentlemen wished they could remove their jackets but Rose was a stickler for the proprieties, even when there was only her family present. The ladies wore cooler, lighter muslins but they still wielded their fans quite vigorously, for not even the slightest of breezes came through the window to stir the air.

'Luncheon is served, madam,' Hetty, the head parlour-maid, announced from the doorway, and Rose got to her feet, heaving herself rather gracelessly from her chair, for she was putting on weight. The gentlemen turned and began to wander across the room and into the wide hallway, crossing it to the dining room. The dinner table looked splendid and Rose smiled in satisfaction. She had her complete family about her and as usual her servants had spared no effort, following her instructions to make the settings a work of art. The table was laid out with the best Barrie Crown Derby ware and silver cutlery, seven places flanked with an array of gleaming knives, forks and spoons, delicate crystal wine glasses and pristine napery. There were roses from her own garden in the centre of the table, arranged in an exquisite cut-glass bowl and Lucas was seen to raise his eyebrows at the trouble his mother had gone to for a family luncheon. She was still smiling as she seated herself and indicated that they should all do the same and at that precise moment the front doorbell rang and for some reason Anne, who had been hovering at her chair to the left of her father at the head of the table, sprang to attention and began to move towards the door.

Her mother sighed with exasperation at the sound of the bell then looked with bewilderment at her daughter.

'And where are you going?' she asked her daughter, her face pinched with disapproval. It was not often she had her complete family about her, particularly Lucas who often made excuses not to attend these family affairs.

'The door, Mama,' Anne stammered, but obediently she stopped.

'Since when was it your job to answer the door, may I ask?'

'Well . . .'

'Really, one would think anyone who knows anything would not expect to be received at this time of day, especially on a Sunday. Might it be for you, Herbert?'

'I'm not expecting anyone, my dear,' her husband replied mildly. He was eager to get to the splendid saddle of lamb which he knew was standing on the kitchen table ready to be brought in for him to carve.

Rose tutted irritably. 'Oh heavens, I suppose you had better go and see who it is, Hetty. If it's not urgent send whoever it is away and ask Janet to fetch in the soup.'

'Yes, madam.' Hetty bobbed a curtsey and hurried away while, for reasons known only to herself, Anne, who had seated herself in obedience to her mother's command, stood up again.

'Whatever is the matter with you, Anne? Please sit down.' But at that moment the door opened abruptly and Hetty's excited face appeared at the door and behind her could be seen the figure of a man. A man with a cane which he was carefully tapping in a circle about him as he stood hesitantly in the middle of the hallway. All the menfolk had risen to their feet, for it seemed there was something unusual here, not exactly dangerous, or at least they hoped not, but something that might need their intervention. But the strangest thing was Anne's behaviour. Ignoring her mother, who had not yet got to grips with what was happening and was sitting open-mouthed at the table, napkin in hand, Anne ran into the hall and took the man's arm. At once he became still, one could even say calm.

'What the devil's going on here?' Herbert blustered, his own napkin crumpled in his fist, then he stopped his inclination to rush into the hall and tear his daughter away from the intruder, as he recognised him. 'Why, it's Jem . . . Jem . . .' For the life of him he could not remember the surname of the man who had saved the life of his partner's son, the man who had been educated and brought into the firm at John Hughes's insistence, the man who had been blinded in some affray, the details of which slipped his mind. After all it had been John Hughes who had had the dealings with him.

Lucas stepped forward hastily, not that there was to be violence done, he hoped, but there was something here that might need a calming hand and since he knew Jem Wilson and had been involved in his tragedy and, more importantly, loved the woman who was part of this man's family, his words might be listened to. By Jem and by his father.

Anne began to babble words that none of them could understand. They had all risen slowly to their feet and an expression of horror crept on to Rose Barrie's face, for what was this common man doing in her house and, more importantly, why was her daughter clinging to the man's arm?

'Shall we go into the drawing room?' Lucas began calmly, leading the way out of the dining room and taking Jem's arm to guide him. Jem obediently turned but Anne still held his arm, dragging along behind him and her brother and in a silently stunned line the others followed.

'Sit down, Jem,' Lucas murmured politely, hoping to detach his sister from Jem Wilson, but Jem refused, equally politely. They stood about, the family of Anne Barrie, and waited dumbly, for surely something terrible was about to happen. Why was Anne holding the arm of this man from the lower orders, since despite his neat suit and well-brushed appearance he was not of their class?

'No, thank you, Mr Barrie. It was your father I came to see.' Jem was calm. He had dreaded this confrontation, for he knew very well how it would end, but now he was here, like all things that are anticipated, good or bad, it was not as terrible as he had expected. He would say his piece and, according to the reactions of her family, Anne would leave with him. Of that he was sure. But she had wanted this meeting, hoping for a happy outcome, because what young girl wants to part with her family?

'Well?' barked Herbert Barrie, his heart pounding with fear, with dread, with lost hopes and with anger, for he knew what was about to come, at least part of it.

'I wish to marry, Anne, sir, and she wishes to marry me. I have come to ask your permission to—'

With a great shriek Rose Barrie fell back on to the sofa which was conveniently handy. She had made sure of that. Her daughter Emily sprang towards her and wielded her fan vigorously then pressed the bell for a servant and when Hetty entered suspiciously quickly sent her scurrying for the smelling salts. Mrs Barrie continued to moan and the men stood about like frozen effigies, all except Lucas who moved towards Jem with what looked like a strong need to hit him. Of course, no gentleman could hit a blind man so he stood as indecisively as the others, clenching and unclenching his fists.

'Why, you blackguard, so that's it. You hope to get back into the firm by marrying my daughter, do you? Well, let me tell you—'

'No, sir. Your daughter and I are fond of one another and . . .'

'We love one another, Papa. That is why we wish to marry and . . . well, you see . . .'

The room became as silent as the grave and Hetty, who had just entered the room with the smelling salts, froze by the door. It was as though they knew what was coming.

'Anne is to have my child, Mr Barrie.'

Rose began to scream so loudly and piercingly that the

servants in the kitchen, who had been told a drama was unfolding, were paralysed with shock. Mrs Dobbs dropped the gravy boat she was holding, smashing it to smithereens on the tiled floor, gravy spattering over the hem of her Sunday, go to church dress. Janet fell against the dresser and knocked a plate to the floor and twelve-year-old Lizzie in the scullery began to cry.

For several long moments nobody in the drawing room moved. Now that he had said what he had come to say Jem longed to be away. He could, of course, see nothing, though there was a patch lighter than the rest in the left-hand corner of his vision and as soon as this was over and he and Anne were married he meant to consult with Mr Jenkins at the infirmary. He was conscious of the still figures all about him and of Anne's hand gripping his arm so tightly he thought she might stop the flow of blood to his hand.

'Get out of my house,' Herbert Barrie hissed, ready to do harm to this man whom they had all befriended, even put on the road to success before his accident, but who had disgraced his daughter and her family. The man was blind so no violence could be shown him, for how could a man strike another who could not see the blow coming. 'Get out and it might be as well if you left Liverpool for I can guarantee you will—'

'If Jem goes, so do I.' Anne's voice trembled but she lifted her chin and stared round at her family.

'Don't be ridiculous, Anne,' Lucas snorted. 'There is no need for that. These things can be arranged . . . you shall go to . . . just because you and this bastard have . . . have . . .'

'Lucas!' his mother shrieked, the horrific picture he was painting of her innocent young daughter and this oaf unbearable.

'No, I do not wish things to be arranged. I shall not be sent away. Jem and I wish to be married. I shall have my baby and we will—'

'Don't be ridiculous, Anne.' Lucas's voice was flat. 'You cannot marry this man. He is far beneath you.'

'As Gilly Logan is beneath you!'

'Stop it, you silly girl, stop it,' her father thundered, ignoring the reference to the Logan girl, for men must have their little indiscretions. He had one himself! 'Even if he was not unsuitable for a girl of your class, he is blind and cannot support you.'

'I care nothing for that. I love Jem and will have his child. We will find a way.'

Rose Barrie was in a real faint this time. Her daughter Emily and Hetty the maid frantically waved the smelling salts under her nose but when she came to, rising like a fish from the depths of the sea, they wished she was still in a state of unconsciousness.

'Never . . . never,' she screeched. None of them was quite sure what she meant but she was about to tell them. 'She is not my daughter, for no daughter of mine would cause such a scandal. I shall not be able to hold up my head in this city ever again. My friends will shun me and my sons will never find suitable wives, for who will want to ally themselves to a family with such disgrace hanging over it.' Her voice rose even higher with her hysteria. 'I don't care what you decide, Herbert Barrie, but I will not have her in this house ever again. She must go and take her misbegotten child with her. Dear God, I rue the day that stupid child of John and Marie Hughes fell into the river and this . . . this ruffian pulled him out.'

She drew herself up and her face was frozen in her hatred. 'You will leave my house, miss, and never come back for I shall not receive you. Marry this blackguard and be damned to you. Come, Emily, this woman is not fit to be in the same room as decent women.' She stood up and with great dignity took her elder daughter's arm, leaving the room with her head high.

The men watched them go then turned back to Jem and

Anne, Anne drooping against Jem's shoulder. She did not weep, for, really, had she expected anything else? Her hand fell to her belly and the men watched her, the significance of the movement lost on none of them. Herbert bent his head, for he had loved this pretty, docile child of his but she had brought great shame on his family. It might have been rectified by sending her away on the pretext of her health to somewhere out of the country where, when it was born, the child would have been adopted by some family. Jem Wilson would not have been hard to silence in some way but his wife's words and Anne's defiance made it all out of the question.

'Papa . . . ?' Anne quavered.

'Go, Anne, and take nothing with you. You have chosen to associate with this man who has taken advantage of your youth and innocence and so you must live with it. Your mother will never forgive you and neither will I, and any member of this family who . . . offers you help will incur my displeasure.'

'Sir, your daughter is not to blame for this. I wish to do the honourable thing and make her my wife and—' Jem began but Herbert Barrie cut across his words.

'Get out of my house, you bastard and take your . . . this woman with you.'

Owning nothing but the pretty summer gown she wore, Anne Barrie, clinging to Jem, at the same time guiding his footsteps, walked down the steps and along the drive of her home. The servants, who were all fond of her, crowded at the morning-room window to watch her go, most of them in tears and as she and Jem walked down the gravel drive and passed the gardener, Mr Sutton, who had watched her grow from a toddling child to the young woman she was, pressed a single white rose into her hand. If they sacked him for it he didn't care. She did not weep, for somehow Anne Barrie knew that she would be the mother of two children, the one in her womb and the one holding her arm!

*   *   *

They were married within the week and despite the words of his mother and father, Lucas Barrie attended the simple ceremony at St Luke's Church. It was the last day of the long, hot summer that had held Liverpool in its grip for so many weeks and Anne was glad it was still warm, for she had nothing to wear but the light dress in which she had left Bracken Hill. Gilly had offered to make her one for her marriage, since after all it was the most special day in a woman's life but she had refused.

'Jem and I have no money to pay you. No, no, I realise you will make it for nothing but we must get used to economising.' Gilly wondered if Anne had the remotest idea what true economy was! 'I shall wear this dress then when we are more . . . more – what's the word? – more established, I shall have a new winter dress. I am hoping that you will employ me in the shop. I don't care what kind of work, really I don't and Jem is to ask at the School for the Blind if there is something, a job of sorts that he can manage that will earn him a small wage. Don't worry, my love, we will manage.'

Anne was drifting in a sea of rapture that hid from her the difficulties that lay ahead. She had got through, as she thought, the worst of their hardships when Jem had informed her parents that they were to marry and on her wedding day she looked quite beautiful, as all brides do, carrying a small posy of pale pink rosebuds which Mr Sutton had sent over with Lucas. She had accepted a pale pink satin sash for her dress and as Lucas took her down the aisle her face was as serene as an angel. There was only Gilly, Queenie, Flo, Nell and Sadie there, though at the last minute, as if they were not sure they would be welcome in view of what Tommy had done to his son, Jess and Rosie Wilson slipped in and sat in the back pew.

They ate Flo's rich fruit cake and drank a glass of sherry, another gift from Lucas who did not attend the small ceremony in the parlour of number 19 which was to be Jem and Anne's home. They had spent the week moving the furniture about

from number 17 to 19 and back again, Anne in transports of
delight, like a little girl with her first doll's house. Queenie was
to live with Flo, and Gilly, with the help of Ginger from the
market, Nell's brother, and his handcart, took what she needed
from both houses to set up in her own small apartment at the
top of the shop. She had a parlour where, in the winter, she
would keep a good fire burning. There was a narrow bed in one
corner and a plush-covered armchair before the fire. There
were brightly coloured rugs on the bare floor and a small table
and chair where she would take her meals. Downstairs behind
the discreet curtains of the salon she had the facilities to make
tea or hot chocolate and a simple meal, and to bathe she visited
her mam and Flo at number 17. She had fitted out the shop
exactly as it had been before the destruction, soft pale-coloured
carpets, small gilt chairs, occasional tables on which magazines
were fanned out, models draped in the lovely fabrics of the
morning gowns she had hurriedly created during the week with
Nell and Sadie's help. There were beautiful silk fringed shawls
hanging on the walls and even flowers in a copper bowl, all
purchased at the market. She visited Mrs Fletcher who had
been so helpful when she first opened, buying the best of her
end of rolls and visited Benson's, the enormous fabric warehouse off Dale Street. Upstairs in the workroom she assembled
roll after roll of velvets, silks, satins, delicate muslins and
gossamer chiffons ready for the hoped-for return of her clients.
She had advertised in the *Mercury*, informing them that her
salon was to reopen the following Monday. She also had a
strong lock and bolt put on the shop door.

'I don't like yer bein' there on yer own,' Queenie told her
worriedly. 'Could yer not squeeze in wi' me an' Flo?'

'Aye,' Flo added. 'Yer could 'ave my bed and me an'
Queenie'd share, wouldn't we, lass?' She and Queenie were
like sisters now, in perfect accord, probably due to their passion
for cleanliness. They would scrub and scour most days and

had even taken it upon themselves to give Gilly's little upstairs apartment a good 'bottoming' before Ginger moved her stuff in.

'No, there really isn't enough room, Mam. Jem and Anne need their own place, especially when the baby comes.' And at once, as she knew they would be, the pair of them were distracted by the thought of the child who was to come. It would be related to neither of them but they were like a couple of grandmothers expecting their first grandchild, knitting and sewing on little garments, determined that this baby would be the best dressed in Liverpool. It was not due until early spring which is probably why no one had noticed Anne was pregnant and so, leaving Jem to make his way to the School for the Blind, which he could do on his own now, she would set off for the salon and do the small jobs that Gilly set her. At first it was playing hostess to the trickle of customers who began to return, some of them out of curiosity but who stayed when they saw the pleasant state of the place which was almost like that of their own drawing room. They knew, of course, that she had married beneath her, some working chap her family disapproved of, and that she was estranged from her parents, and as time went on and her waist thickened they drew in their breath in horror for it was obvious she and the man who was now her husband had anticipated the wedding ceremony.

To keep her in work and earning the wages she and Jem so desperately needed, Gilly found her tasks to do in the workroom, embroidering the dainty chemises and nightgowns that had been made by Nell or Sadie. She wanted nothing to upset the delicately smooth running of her business in the early weeks as her first tentative customers sat in her salon, drinking hot chocolate, coffee or her expensive Orange Pekoe tea, discussing gowns for the coming winter, since no one knew better than she that any scandal that touched Anne also affected her, and so slowly, day by day, she rebuilt the structure of her business.

Jem, swallowing his pride, was weaving baskets which were purchased from the school by stallholders at the market, from which he earned a small wage. It was like a pack of cards, built up with gentle, careful movements, scarcely daring to draw breath but rising slowly from disaster. Gilly had, of course, missed the chance of Miss Nora Ward's wedding outfit but the suffragist Miss Moore, who firmly believed that women should be given a chance in business as men were, had produced a cousin from West Derby who was prepared to allow Miss Logan to make her daughter's trousseau, on Miss Moore's recommendation, of course.

And then, at the end of September, when autumn was beginning to creep over the woodlands and parklands about the city, when leaves were turning to rich colour ranging from the palest gold to a vivid flame, and beech trees were becoming increasingly bare, when the days were mild but the nights turning cold, when mist crept about in the mornings and the blackberry hedges where Jem and Anne used to walk were laden with fruit, when Gilly was beginning to breathe more easily, Angela Ryan stormed into her father's study and threw an old copy of the *Mercury* on to his desk.

'How long has this been going on?' she demanded in a piercing voice, which reached even those in the kitchen, just as though whatever was in it was Joseph Ryan's fault. Had any of his business acquaintances or employers been there they would not have believed their ears or eyes, for there was no harder businessman in Liverpool.

He looked at the newspaper and his heart sank. He had read the advertisement some weeks ago and, as he always did with his daughter, chose to shield her from it, since he knew how much it meant to her. She never opened a newspaper or even a book and he had hoped it might go unnoticed, unmentioned by her friends and it had until, as she passed by a housemaid making up the paper firelighters, she had caught the name of

Gillyflower's. She had knocked the maid, who was on her knees by the breakfast-room fireplace, on to her bottom, snatching the sheet of newspaper from her, hardly able to believe what she read. Her father had put Gilly Logan out of business and next weekend she and her mama and papa were to dine with the Barries, the party including Lucas Barrie and this time she meant to get him to propose. *If she had to seduce him she would have him.*

'How has this come about, Papa?' she asked him dangerously.

Joseph Ryan sighed. 'She got the money to start again.'

'How?'

'She approached the manager at the Royal Bank in Dale Street. It so happens that the . . . the Barries bank there and it seems . . . I have some influence so I made it my business to find out: Lucas Barrie lent her the money. She is not aware of it. She thinks it's a loan from the bank but . . . well, does it matter, dear girl? Why do you fear this—'

'I do not fear her, Papa. I fear no one, you should know that, but she stands in the way of something I want. I wish to see her finished.'

Joseph Ryan stood up and moved round his desk, ready to put his arms about her, to soothe, to promise her some treat that would take her mind off this obsession she had with Lucas Barrie, but she knocked his tentative hand away.

'No, Papa, no. I shall handle this in my own way since you seem to have failed me.' She turned and made for the door.

'No, darling, let me . . .'

But she let herself out and banged the door violently behind her. The servants cowered in the kitchen praying she would not come near *them*!

31

He watched over her as he had watched over her since the day of the break-in at Remington Place. He was very discreet, receiving reports from the two men he had employed, both ex-police constables who worked in shifts so that she was under constant surveillance twenty-four hours a day. This was not to be permanent, of course, for once they were married – as one day they would be married – she would be under his protection, but until that day she, and her shop, were safe from further attack. She was not aware of it, for the two men were expert at their jobs, blending into the scenery wherever they were, or wherever she led them in her business dealings, the sort of men who could mingle in a crowd or if there was no crowd managed to look as though they had every right to be wherever they happened to be. He took a watch himself, whenever he could, for it was a joy to him to see her swinging along Bold Street with her graceful stride, her head held high in the bright sunshine which turned her head to a fiery golden copper. He had seen her at his sister's wedding but had not spoken to her and had made his polite refusal to attend the 'wedding breakfast' in Seymour Street, for the thought of making stilted conversation under the eye of her family had not appealed to him. He would wait a few weeks then call at the salon one evening, since he had learned from his detectives that she was now living there; all the more reason for him to have her protected!

On the night he called her heart bounded in her chest and thudded frantically when she heard the knock at the shop door, then her logic told her that an intruder, one who meant her harm, would hardly announce his presence in such a way. It could not be Jem or Anne for she had left them at Seymour Street earlier in the day where Anne had given what she grandly called a 'dinner party', most of the food being prepared by Queenie and Flo who were desperately trying to teach her to cook.

'We'll start wi' summat simple,' Queenie had declared, peering into Anne's larder and frowning at the odd selection of food on the shelves. She was convinced her Jem, who had lived for most of his life on good, nourishing meals, hence his health and strength, was not getting the right things to eat and probably not enough. She and Flo had accompanied her to the market and stocked her up on the basic foodstuffs, bacon, sugar, tea, butter, bread – since she was not able to make her own as they did – eggs, potatoes, stewing beef, carrots and onions, for a good 'scouse' was easy, cheap and filling. All you had to do was put the meat and vegetables in a pan and leave it to simmer on the fire.

The meal had been a surprising success and it was a delight to see the happiness shine in the new Mrs Wilson's eyes as she played hostess, though some of the 'tricks' she got up to, apparently learned from her mother who was a famed hostess, were, to their working-class minds, immensely comical. A tray of coffee, the fine bone china of the cups, saucers, coffee jug, sugar basin and cream jug given by her brother as a wedding present, placed on a small table at her side. She poured them each a cup of coffee, smilingly enquired if they took cream and sugar, and handed the cup and saucer to each of them as though they were in some grand drawing room. But you could not help but love her. Her sweetness, her goodness, her solicitude for Jem, her longing to be of help, her obvious joy over the baby and though they got the impression she was living in a dream world and would come plummeting to earth one day, they could not resist her. It was also obvious that to some extent she irritated Jem, who was no more than fond of her. His face constantly turned to Gilly's voice as she moved about the room but at least he had someone to love him and surely, when his child was born, he would be content. He was to go to the hospital in the next week for Mr Jenkins to check his eyes and Anne was ready to be convinced that it would not be long before he regained his sight.

Lucas stood on the step and waited. His face was stern, unsmiling, as though this were not a visit to be taken lightly. He had not come on a whim and though it was many months since he had made love to her in this very salon he did his best to convey to her that he was not here for the same purpose. They loved one another, that was not to be denied by either of them, and if he could have told her without embarrassment he would have admitted that he had not gone to other women since that day.

Her face was pale, strained, and her eyes wary, and the man who loitered behind the wall of St Luke's Church on the corner of Leece Street and Berry Street, where he had a good view of Remington Place but was himself out of sight, took out a notebook and wrote something in it. He was not one of Lucas's men!

'May I come in?' Lucas asked her, his voice no more than a soft murmur.

'Why?' She could barely speak, for there was nothing more she wanted than to take him round the neck and drag him over the doorstep. He set her on fire, as he had done in the church when Jem and Anne were married. She had felt ashamed of her feelings as she stood behind him at the altar, studying his broad shoulders, remembering the night they had been naked under her hands. The proud set of his head and the way his hair curled over his collar, his profile as he smiled down at Anne, the lift of his eyebrows and the curl of his lips. He had not looked

back at her and her heart had been heavy, for though she had
made it plain to him months ago that there could be nothing
between them, she had not bargained for the ache that had
persisted night and day ever since.

'I want to talk to you.'

Though their eyes said everything that was to be said in their
hearts, their words were mechanical monosyllables.

'Have we anything to talk about, Lucas?' Her voice caressed
his name.

'I think so. We – you and I – we cannot waste this . . . please,
can we not talk upstairs or at least inside?' For he was conscious
of his man who was well concealed somewhere across Bold
Street, watching this little scene. 'Please, Gilly.'

She was dressed in a wrapper of ivory silk. It was full, falling
in ripples about her feet, edged with coffee-coloured lace at the
cuffs, the hem and the neck, for she had locked up for the night
and was relaxing in front of the fire she had built up in her
pretty sitting room. It was perfectly modest, showing not an
inch of flesh except her face and hands but under it she was
naked. The lovely lift of her breasts was clearly outlined and
Lucas, who was a man of the world and well used to women's
bodies, noted that her nipples were erect.

'I'm not dressed for callers,' she said coldly and was about to
shut the door in his face but he put his foot between it and the
frame. Her heart leaped gladly, longing for him to overcome
her weakness and force his way in but he merely waited, for
Lucas Barrie wanted this woman to come to him of her own
volition. He was prepared to allow her more freedom than any
woman of his class had ever had if she would only marry him.
Her salon, her mad trips to the market and the various warehouses to buy her fabrics, her friends, her family, the risks she
took in her search for exactly the right commodity for her shop.
She went about boldly, his detective told him, even down to the
docks to meet the ships which brought in fans from China,

exotic shawls of glacé or figured silks from India, of embroidered organdie, fringed foulard, cashmere with printed designs, fancy gloves, beaded bags that could be got nowhere else,
moving about among rough men, and surely her beauty and
elegance was a great draw to any male creature.

'I promise I only need to talk to you, Gilly. We cannot go on
as we are.'

'Stop it, Lucas.' Her voice was high, ready to break but
astonishingly she drew back and allowed him to step inside.

The man in the churchyard made a note in his little book
and even as he did so Lucas Barrie swept Gilly Logan into
his arms and for five minutes they clung to one another,
trembling, both ready to weep at the beauty of this, to weep
at the waste, the emptiness of their lives without one another
in it.

'Sweet God, I cannot do this . . . I cannot . . . you must go
or . . .'

'I know, I know, my love . . . my love.' His voice was muffled
in the hollow beneath her ear.

'I love you so much,' she wept. 'What you did for me . . . the
shop . . . to clean it as you did . . .'

'Darling, my dearest, I won't say it but you know what I
want.'

'Yes.'

'Let me come up. Just to talk, to look at you. I must see you. I
promise I will do nothing that – you do not want. If you would
allow me to come, even once a week, just to sit with you and talk
. . .' He was humble before her, the proud and arrogant Lucas
Barrie who could have any woman he fancied, begging for
nothing but a few minutes of her time.

She led him upstairs but when they entered her cosy sitting
room where the kettle was wisping on the fire she kept well
away from him. He could smell her perfume, French, he
thought and his heart was glad that as her business prospered

she was able to buy herself expensive things such as the perfume and the lovely peignoir she wore.

He kept his word. Though his loins ached with his need and he was forced to keep his legs crossed as he sat opposite her lest she notice the bulge between them, he drank her tea and watched her, drank in her beauty, for it might be a while before he saw it again. They barely talked but seemed content simply to be in one another's company. When he left an hour later, the man in the churchyard wrote the time in his notebook which, tomorrow, he would show to the man who employed him.

The shop was full the next day. It would be Christmas soon and the ladies were engrossed with their need for afternoon gowns, evening gowns, new bonnets and all the little things that Miss Logan sold and which seemed to be unavailable anywhere else. Dainty lace caps, pearl powder which, discreetly used, gave the skin an interesting pallor, handkerchiefs of lace and lawn, made, though they were not aware of it, by the daughter of one of Liverpool's most influential hostesses, Mrs Rose Barrie, who sat upstairs with her swelling belly which it was not proper to display, sewing contentedly in a special chair ordered for her by Miss Logan. Miss Logan's glorious taffeta ball-gowns were on show, her gold brocade, her sheer pale silk stockings, her ropes of pearls, her gloves of kid, suede and silk, embroidered parasols, lace collars, dainty muffs, scent bottles and all manner of things, ideal for Christmas presents, set about the salon, all tempting to the lady of taste *and money*. Of course Gilly had not forgotten her less prosperous clients, the wives of tradesmen and clerks and to be had, though not so much on show, were cheaper versions of the lovely things displayed to the wealthy.

Miss Helen Moore was in the fitting room, the hem of her sensible walking outfit, which she was to wear to Sheffield next week to hear Mrs John Stuart Mill speak at the Sheffield

Female Political Association in the Democratic Temperance Hotel, being adjusted by Sadie, with the help of Rosie Wilson who was learning the trade. Miss Moore's mother, Lady Harriet Moore, had been persuaded to accompany her with a view to looking at Miss Logan's designs and she was in a pleasant conversation with Mrs Clarke and Mrs Braithwaite as they drank Miss Logan's excellent coffee. Mrs Raines had brought her second daughter, Laura, who had just become engaged to an up-and-coming young attorney and with the wedding planned for the spring might not Miss Logan, who had overcome such trials, be prepared to plan her wedding gown and trousseau? Mrs MacDonald was trying on one of Miss Logan's lovely winter bonnets, a wisp of a thing trimmed with swansdown and as the door opened on a drift of cold air and a curtain of mist all turned to see who had entered.

Gilly had been about to run up the stairs for the umpteenth time to ask Anne if she might work at home that evening, since they were so frantically busy, on the lovely lace-trimmed chemise just ordered by Laura Raines but even as her foot touched the bottom step she turned and looked across the shop floor into the pretty, smiling face of Angela Ryan. Miss Ryan was followed by her maid who carried a small lapdog which looked as though it had been drugged, so flaccid was it.

For some reason the hum of conversation stopped, then Miss Ryan spotted Miss Raines whose father was a business acquaintance of her father's and who had on occasion dined at Rosemount Lodge, the grand home of the Ryan family. Miss Ryan gave Gilly no more than the coolest nod, for she knew a nobody when she saw one and besides, one did not greet a servant except to give an order. She turned about so that everyone could see her expensive velvet gown and basque jacket and the magnificence of the grey chinchilla with which she was draped.

'Laura,' she exclaimed prettily, 'what a surprise to see you here,' sitting down beside her friend, 'and Mrs Raines. Good morning to you. I trust you are both well.' She smiled round the room at the other ladies who, again not knowing why, felt uneasy. 'I was just passing on my way to the bootmaker, for though Mama and I shop in Paris for our gowns we find that the English boot is the most comfortable and smart, of course.'

'Indeed,' fawned Mrs Raines, for she could not afford Paris gowns but admired those who could.

Angela smoothed down the lustrous velvet of her gown, her smile of self-satisfaction very evident, the diamonds on her fingers and about her throat as she threw back her furs sparkling even in the dim interior of the salon. A bright fire crackled in the grate and the lamps were lit, as the day was bleak. The salon was warm and the light from the lamps very flattering. The colours of the shawls, the draping of velvets and silk and the rich colour of the curtains that divided the salon from the fitting rooms were reflected on the white walls. The aroma of coffee and chocolate, mixed with French perfume was very pleasing and the ladies were comfortable as they chatted to one another, not at all eager to go out into the November streets.

Angela chatted for several minutes to Laura, glancing about her. If any woman in the room had happened to look deeply into her eyes she might have grown alarmed. There was something swimming in their depths which might have re-minded them of a shark circling in deep water, that is if any of them had ever seen a shark, which none of them had. But Gilly saw it, saw the shark, saw the malevolence, saw the paleness of Angela's face and the streak of red high on her cheekbones and her bones froze with her blood and muscle so that she felt she could not move. But she could hardly stand on the bottom step of the stairs for ever, could she, going neither up nor down. Should she greet her, go over and bid her a polite good morning as she would do with any other client? She felt a horrid premonition of approaching danger but somehow, with a smile that was more a grimace, moved across the salon to where Angela sat with Miss Raines.

'Good morning, Angela,' she said tremulously, at the same time annoyed with herself for the shake in her voice.

Angela looked up at her as though surprised. 'Good morning, *Miss Logan.*' The inflexion and meaning in her voice were very evident as she spoke Gilly's surname.

Gilly gritted her teeth, longing to slap Angela Ryan's face as she once had done at Miss Hunter's school but this was her business and she must be polite to those who gave her, or who *might* give her their custom. 'Might I offer you a hot chocolate or perhaps coffee?'

Angela looked her up and down as if she were some beggar who had had the temerity to accost her in the street. She smiled, showing her perfect teeth.

'I think not. I am not in the habit of drinking coffee with women such as you. I should not have come into this . . . this establishment' – making it sound as though Gillyflower's was a house of ill-repute – 'had I not seen Laura and her mother inside. I must say I am surprised, Mrs Raines,' turning her attention to the open-mouthed mother of Laura, 'that in view of its reputation you still frequent such a place.'

The ladies exchanged astonished glances and Angela's smile deepened. She would never forgive this woman who had insulted her at school when she struck her in defence of that silly nincompoop Anne Barrie, Anne who had married a man from the underclasses who, it was said and she liked to believe it, had been this woman's lover. But worst of all she had stolen the man Angela had earmarked for herself and though she still had hopes of getting him back, she meant to destroy this woman however she could. She had read the man's report, the man who worked for her father, and she knew of their clandestine meetings here in this very salon.

She stood up, smoothing down her wide skirt, taking great pleasure in the feel of the rich and expensive material beneath her hands. 'I really must go, for Mama and Papa would be greatly upset if they knew I was in this establishment.' She spun round as if in surprise. 'You know, of course, of Miss Logan's misfortune when her shop was broken into and smashed up. Not only that but I believe the intruders poured the . . . well, I hesitate to mention this in the presence of ladies, but they emptied the contents of a . . . a privy about the place, over carpets and . . . oh dear, I'm so sorry to have upset you.' For the ladies looked about them with horror as though they expected to see what Angela Ryan had just described lying about their feet. They stood up almost as one and for a moment Gilly felt the temptation to laugh hysterically because it looked as though they were about to leap on to their chairs. It was as though a mouse had skittered across the carpet, or even a rat.

'So,' Angela continued, 'I must continue on my way to the bootmaker. Mama will be wondering where I am.' She turned a terrible smile on Gilly. 'I'm so pleased you were able to put it all back together again, Miss Logan, for I know how difficult it must be for someone in your position to find the necessary funds to start again. How lucky you were to have a *male friend* to pay for it all. I won't mention his name though my papa, who does business with the Royal Bank in Dale Street, told me of it. From such a good family too, but then young men from good families are allowed their little indiscretions, are they not? I believe he was seen leaving your premises only last night and the weather so cold!'

She turned her brilliant smile on them all, on the ladies who were paralysed by her revelations and when she had left the shop, her maid trailing behind her, they turned as one and stared at Gilly in horrid fascination. They had never met a woman with a *reputation* before and here they were drinking her hot chocolate! They themselves had wondered how she had found the means to start again from scratch but had imagined that perhaps her mother who, it was said, had once had a business of her own, of what sort they didn't know, had savings. It was rumoured that Miss Logan had been seen entering the Royal Bank herself. Presumably her lover, for that was what Angela Ryan had intimated, had supplied what she needed and she, the hussy, had paid him back in the only way she knew how!

For several minutes there was a black silence interspersed with hissings and mutterings, for quite literally they were not sure what to do. Weeks ago they had been prepared to give her a second chance since she was an extremely clever dressmaker. Her designs were so original, her salon was so comfortable, her staff so polite, but even as they gathered up their belongings, still casting horrified glances at the floor, the walls, the very chairs upon which they had, not long before, been sitting, Miss Logan stood as though turned to stone in the middle of her salon. Her face had not a vestige of colour and her eyes had a haunted, almost one could say desperate expression. Her girl, the pretty one called Nell, still with the pins in her mouth which she had been using to pin up Miss Moore's hem, moved slowly across the carpet and put her hand on Miss Logan's arm just as though she knew that this was the end for them, or if it was not it would be a hard climb to get out of the pit Miss Ryan had just dug for them. She had pushed them in and with a few clever words had started the process of filling it with them inside.

Before five minutes were up the shop was empty, all the ladies suddenly murmuring about appointments that they had quite forgotten, errands to be run and how could they have not noticed the time. They did not speak to Gilly, just nodded in her general direction, not able, it seemed even to look at her. She was a fallen women. A woman who had paid for her lovely salon, *and their valued custom* in the worst way a woman could. Only Miss Moore stood before her for a moment then, shaking her head, moved sadly to the door, following the rest as they made their way to their carriages. She had expected better of Miss Moore, Nell was to say later, for she was not a woman like the rest who were reliant on each other and whose husbands were reliant on their husbands in the way of business. They could not afford to be tainted in any way, and certainly not those with young daughters with husbands to find. But Miss Moore had no husband, no daughter and was a free spirit, or so she would have them believe, with a firm belief in the independence of the modern woman for whom she was fighting for equality.

But Miss Moore was a realist and she was of that class that judges those among them who step out of line. She had managed it with her mad ideas about women's enfranchisement, for it was looked on as a harmless pastime for females of a certain disposition who had no man or children, and was of no harm to their class. But Miss Moore had a younger sister, Felicia, fourteen and just about to 'come out' and no scandal must be attached to the Moore family, since it might harm her chances of a good marriage.

They stood in the empty shop, Nell and Gilly, while upstairs they could hear the clatter of the sewing machine as Sadie got on with the job of finishing Miss Moore's smart jacket. Anne was singing a lullaby which she had taken to doing as she sewed on the scrap of material in her hands and now that the hubbub in the shop had ceased the words could be plainly heard.

> *Golden slumbers kiss your eyes,*
> *Smiles awake you when you rise . . .*

And downstairs as she stood in the wreckage of her dream, the one just blasted by Angela Ryan who had threatened years ago to bring her down, Gilly wondered desolately when she would ever smile again as she awoke.

32

She strode into his office like a warrior queen going into battle, her shield before her, brushing aside the clerk who tried to intercept her like an irritating fly. Her cloak flew round her, swinging with the weight of what looked like a raging anger and the ribbons of her bonnet, which she had tied securely before leaving, had somehow come loose and the bonnet flapped down her back to her shoulder blades. Her hair, freed from the bonnet, also flowed down her back in a tangle of damp coppery waves, the day being so dank it had made her waving hair spring into a curling mass. Her eyes snapped in a tawny blaze, the golden specks in them clearly visible and the clerk thought he had never seen such a glorious creature in his life, but at the same time he was relieved that her obvious temper was not aimed at him but at his employer.

'Sir,' he gasped, 'this lady insists . . .'

Lucas Barrie rose to his feet. He had been sitting at his desk studying some complicated plan of a new steamer the yard was to build, and as she stormed into the room, which was warm and comfortable in contrast to the weather outside, her face a blazing rosy pink, his expression of amazed delight at her appearance turned to one of bewilderment. He looked at his watch, for some reason registering that it was barely half past seven, he himself having arrived only ten minutes ago on what he had imagined would be the last ferry across the river due to the fog. He always started his day early and more often than not finished it late, especially since he had fallen in love with Gilly

Logan, for it gave him time during the day to attend to the obsession that had become his life, which was to keep her safe from harm.

He forgot discretion was needed in front of his clerk and spoke the first words that came into his head. 'My love, Gilly, what on earth are you doing here and on such a day?' glancing at the window. 'Not that it isn't a joy . . .' Then he remembered the man hovering in open-mouthed fascination at his door. Pulling himself together as he moved round the desk, he motioned to him that he might leave and, disappointed, the clerk did so.

'What brought you to . . . ?' he began again, putting out loving hands to take hers, the expression on his face a mixture of pleasure, concern and astonishment, but she flung away from him, unable to contain whatever it was that had brought her here and he was not to know that it had been simmering in her for the past fifteen hours, in fact ever since the last of her valued customers had sidled awkwardly from her shop and she had understood that it would be the last time they crossed her scandalous threshold, thanks to Angela Ryan and her long felt malice.

Since their schooldays Angela had taken against her, believing that it was beneath her to mix with a girl of a class much lower than Angela's own. She had blamed Mrs Hunter for taking Gilly in and had never missed a chance to belittle the girl from the 'slums', as she and her cronies termed Rose Alley, which was a true description. But she had also been a girl who never missed a chance to bully those who were vulnerable and Gilly's defence of Anne Barrie and that blow that Gilly had struck had hit not only Angela's face but her pride, and her enmity had hardened over the years.

Since they left school their paths had not crossed because Gilly did not move in Angela's society but Angela had set her sights on Lucas Barrie, and having been denied nothing in her life she had confidently expected to get him. But it had proved more difficult than she had thought. Through her father, who knew everyone in Liverpool and what they were up to from the lowest operative in his factories, the dockers who worked his goods from ship to shore, thugs who could be relied on to do a bit of dirty work should it be needed, which was often the case in Joseph Ryan's somewhat shady world, right up to the Lord Mayor himself, she had discovered Lucas's interest in Gilly Logan and her low-born family, the attack on her mother and the one following on the man who she believed was Gilly's lover. Lucas had been instrumental in rescuing Gilly Logan's mother, taking her, Gilly and the lover back to his own home in Duke Street where he had cared for them and given them his undivided attention until they were all back on their feet. He had been involved in the recovery of the shop which the common slut had built up and even arranged for monies to be available to her at the bank and it would not do. It did not suit Angela Ryan nor her plans, for she would have Lucas Barrie no matter what she had to do, what her papa had to do, to get him.

Which was why Gilly was here in Lucas Barrie's office!

Lucas watched her, his eyes wide with wonderment, the pale silvery greyness of them, which reminded Gilly of moonlight on water, almost black as the pupils distended. His jaw had dropped and his eyebrows rose almost to his hairline so that he looked quite foolish had either of them been disposed to notice. She marched backwards and forwards across the rich carpet, kicking aside her full skirt at each turn as though she did not know what she was to say or even where to begin. They had begged her not to come, Nell and Sadie and Rosie, who had turned up as usual this morning at seven o'clock though none of them expected any customers. After yesterday it was unlikely she would ever have any customers again, besides which the weather was enough to persuade any woman, or man for that matter, to stay snug at home.

'Don't go out, lass,' Nell begged her though she had no idea where Miss Logan could be going on a day such as today. She and Sadie and Rosie had blundered their way from Rose Alley along Great Charlotte Street, Ranelagh Street and into Bold Street, feeling for the walls of the buildings, taking a frantic gamble as they dashed across the road, listening for the sound of traffic, for noises were muffled, phantom-like, in the strange world to which they had woken. It had been foggy yesterday in wisps and swirls as the slight breeze moved it, but today it was solid and from the river came the clanging of bells, the hoot of fog-horns and even whistles as ships did their best to make their positions known.

'You shouldn't have come in,' she told them shortly as she tied the ribbons of her bonnet under her chin and wrapped about her the warm, lined cloak Nell and Sadie had made for her at the beginning of the winter. 'You know there will be . . . no one will come, even if the fog . . . there's nothing to be done.'

'We can finish what we were doin' yestidy, Miss Logan,' Sadie protested and Gilly wondered at the loyalty these young women had shown her. What were they to do now? Who would employ them? And if they did would it be at one of the sweat shops that crammed the back streets of Liverpool? Well, it was no good brooding about it. She would do something, find some way out of this hell-hole that bitch had flung her in and begin again. Dear Lord, wasn't that what she and her mam and Jem had been doing for years, knocked down, faces in the muck, then springing up to their feet and starting again? But first she had a task to do and she must be about it at once while she still had the courage.

'. . . I don't suppose Mrs Wilson'll be in,' Sadie went on and for a moment Gilly could not quite grasp who she meant. Anne Barrie who was now Anne Wilson. Anne Wilson who was his sister and whom she had come to love as her own.

'No, I don't suppose she will but I must . . . I have something to see to . . .'

'In this?' All three girls looked towards the shop window beyond which nothing could be seen but an almost solid wall of dirty white. 'Leave it 'til termorrer, miss.'

But she had eluded their concerned grip and stumbled her way down to the Pier Head, so wound up, tight like a clock that has been *overwound*, she scarcely noticed the condition in which folk were creeping along like snails, bumping into one another, cursing and clutching at anything solid. She caught what was to be the last ferry boat from the Liverpool side. She had stood by the rail staring into the almost solid curtain in which from time to time shapes loomed but she did not see them in her senselessness. Not really that, for she had her wits about her but she was insensible to the conditions that prevailed as the steamer crept through them.

And here she was prowling about in a seething rage that threatened to overcome them both.

'I've had enough of this,' Lucas protested suddenly, catching her arm as she made another pass across his carpet. 'Either you tell me what has brought you here in this appalling fog or I shall—'

She turned on him, snarling like a tiger caught in a net, shaking off his restraining hand with such violence he fell back across his desk and as her anger mounted his took shape. He loved her. He would willingly die for her but the arrogance and pride, the stubborn belief that he was right, which had been bred in him from boyhood, for a man needed these traits in business, erupted to the surface of his mind. He had been amazed to see her thunder into his office, pleased that she was here though he didn't know why, longing to put his arms about her and scold her for coming across the river in such appalling weather, to enfold her against his chest and kiss her. He also felt a great desire to laugh out loud at this ludicrous situation.

He leaned his buttocks against the edge of his desk, his arms crossed and watched her storm about the room, waiting for her to tell him why she was here. He didn't attempt to touch her again. He was more than shaken by her sudden appearance and even more by her explosive temper. She positively crackled about the room and to tell the truth he wasn't sure what to do for he was afraid he might make the situation worse. Somehow she had managed to get across the river in what they were saying was the worst fog the cities of Liverpool and Birkenhead had ever known, found her way up from the landing stage, across the yard where the strange, ghost-like shapes of workmen felt their way from place to place, cursing and swearing, and up the steps to his office. Perhaps if he stayed still and silent long enough she would give him a clue as to why she was so bloody mad and why she had come to direct that madness at him.

She stopped her twisting and twirling at last, standing with her back to him, her hands on her hips, her breathing deep and uneven. Then she turned and looked at him, her face expressionless.

'Aren't you at least going to ask me what I am doing here?' as though he hadn't already done so!

'I was hoping you'd stand still long enough to tell me.' He continued to lean casually against the desk, his face as blank as hers but in his eyes was a snap of something that said he was not as calm as he appeared.

She threw back her head and he was alarmed to see not only the rage she had managed to subdue somewhat but what looked like a mixture of contempt and was it anguish?

'Perhaps you'd better ask Angela Ryan,' she spat at him.

'*What?*' He unfolded his arms and his long, lean, handsome body rose to its full height. Gilly felt her heart contract with pain, and shudders of it seemed to flow into every part of her body. She loved him so, more than her own life, more than anything she had known since she had been old enough to reason, and yet she was never to see him again. This was the last time they were to meet, for in his desperate need to help her he was destroying her. Every time some disaster occurred he put it right and in the background of these events Angela Ryan, whose father was one of the most powerful men in Liverpool, lurked and plotted. Her malevolence reached out and suffocated Gilly Logan. Angela wanted Lucas, that was obvious and she would move heaven and earth, through her father, to get him. Gilly stood in her way and must be removed, hounded, her business ruined, her growing clientele destroyed, for the ladies of Liverpool would not care to be contaminated by scandal. It had taken Gilly many patient days, weeks, months to build her business and her reputation and with a few acid words Angela had knocked it all down. She had all the required components: the elegant premises Gilly had dreamed of, the clever designs she herself had created, the superb materials, silks, satins, velvets, and the staff who were devoted to her and her aspirations. Clever young women willing to work themselves to a standstill for her, but without customers, without any outlet for this enthusiasm she might as well put a match to it and burn it to the ground. Oh, this man, this beloved man would take it all on his shoulders, put his money, his resourceful skill, his unyielding will into an attempt to rebuild it once more for her, but he could not persuade, bully, tempt, influence, *charm* ladies like his mother, his married sister, Mrs Ernest Davidson, Lady Harriet Moore and her daughter Helen, and all those who had begun to patronise her salon. And if by some miracle he managed it, Angela would do her best to lay waste to it once more.

'May I ask what Angela Ryan has to do with this . . . this temper you are in?' he asked unwisely.

'Temper is it? *Temper!* Has it not occurred to you who is doing this to me? Who wants me out of this town and her life?

And yours! She ruined my reputation with a few words yesterday. In my salon she casually told my customers that it was
your money that had put me back on my feet when my salon
was fouled, and I shouldn't be surprised if she had something to
do with that, and everything in it destroyed. That, being my
lover, you had put your hand in your pocket to restore it and
naturally I repaid you in the only coin a loose woman like me
has at her disposal.' She laughed bitterly. 'And there was me,
simpleton that I am, thinking that Mr Field at the bank was
lending me funds, without interest, to begin again. Twice now I
have been knocked back and though I admit it was not, strictly
speaking, your fault . . .'

'Thank you for that,' he said, irony in his voice.

'. . . it is because of you that it has happened. Angela has a
fancy for you, that is the reason and she wants a clear field—'

'That's enough,' he snapped, striding across the deep carpet
to stand ominously in front of her. 'I can't understand your
damned foolish reasoning that Angela Ryan is at the bottom of
all this tangled skein you seem determined to weave, but it's a
load of nonsense. I don't give a straw about Angela Ryan. She is
nothing to me.'

'She doesn't think so. As far as she's concerned—'

'Bugger what she thinks. She can go to hell for all I care. I
only care about you. You know how I feel about you. Dear
Christ, I've told you often enough. I want to look after you. See
you come to no harm. Jesus, I want nothing more than to see
the back of that bloody business of yours and have you safe,
with me, in our own home. *As my wife!* And don't look at me
like that. God's teeth, you act as though I'd offered you some
insult and not an honourable proposal of marriage. Gilly, my
dearest love, you can keep your damned shop, even when we
are married, I promise, that is until the children arrive, then,
naturally . . .' He began to smile at the very thought and for a
moment she almost responded. He took her hands, thinking he

saw her weakening, but she slapped his away and brushed past him.

'Stop it, Lucas, stop it. I'm not one of your fine ladies who can sit at home and embroider from morning till night waiting for her lord and master to come home.'

'Why not?' he snarled, beginning to lose control again. 'Other women do. They are content to run a home, see to their children—'

'One of which would arrive every twelve months.' Her face was white now and her eyes seemed huge and almost black in their setting of long, narrowed lashes.

He turned furiously away from her, leaning the palms of both hands flat on the desk, his head bowed.

'Why do you fight me so?' he groaned. 'I love you, dammit.'

'And your love does me damage. Every time you try to repair what Angela in her jealous rage smashes, you make it worse. I can't afford you, Lucas.' She whirled away, her wide skirt dipping, her arms flung out in despair. 'I need to make my mark, be my own woman and I was doing it until you decided you loved me and since then—'

Savagely he turned to face her. *'Decided!* You make it sound as though I chose you as I might a decent hunter. You had a good figure, a lovely face, a sweet nature and would suit my purposes admirably. As a bedfellow, perhaps a brood mare for my children. Good God, woman, I love you. I didn't *choose you*. What man in his right mind would choose a woman whose acquisition creates nothing but problems?'

Even as he spoke his mind and senses were bemused by the way the firelight from the leaping coals in the grate tangled in her bright hair, streaking the copper with gold. It curled vigorously about her head and down her back, the clammy dampness of the fog beyond the window causing it, with a life of its own, to twist and tumble almost to her waist. It had been neatly coiled that morning into a chignon beneath her bonnet but the weather, her strenuous eddying about the room and the heat of her anger had loosened it into a maddened halo. It had also put a flush beneath the fine creamy smoothness of her skin. Her coppery eyebrows dipped and the tawny brown of her eyes blazed at him from across the room. He felt a sudden puzzlement as to why this should be happening, for surely the answer to it all was simple. They loved one another, they both admitted that with brutal honesty so why the bloody hell were they glaring at one another with what seemed to be hatred? They were both free and could do as they pleased so why was she making it so complicated? Who gave a damn about Angela Ryan, for God's sake? She meant nothing to either of them so why . . . ?

He sighed deeply and his shoulders slumped, but his face was ready to crease into a smile if only she would meet him halfway. He refused to believe that they could not sit down and talk quietly and put this stupid disagreement – for that was how it seemed to him – behind them. He was sorry she had hit another problem with her young business but it could be put right and if it proved to be impossible, since he knew the ladies of his own class and their sense of what was proper, he was here to look after her, to love her, to help her family if it was needed, to exert his own growing influence in any further adversity that might attack them.

His expression softened and in it was his desperate need to help this self-willed woman. He did not like this hunger of hers to be independent, to be her own mistress, to exclude him from her life, her working life which he was willing to accept but surely if they were to . . .

'Don't struggle like this, Gilly. Don't fight so. Can you not see I am not your enemy? I want nothing more than to help you.'

'That's the trouble, Lucas. That's how I got into this . . . this dilemma. Your help has cost me my reputation and my

business which will take a great deal of hard work and diplo-
macy to build up again and I can't do it with Angela Ryan
watching my every move – and yours. So leave me alone. Let
her see that you have no further interest in me.' Her head lifted
imperiously and her eyes were a vivid flashing gold in her
colour-flooded face.

'I find that impossible even to consider. Can you not—' he
began, but she did not want to hear any more for she could feel
her weak, woman's body straining towards him, yearning to
give in, to lean against his strong male body, to have him enfold
her in his strong, male arms.

'No, I can't. Whatever you have to offer I don't want it so
don't come near me again. Ever, d'you hear. Get on with your
life and allow me to get on with mine.'

'Dammit, woman.' He thrust his face, which had become
hard and uncompromising, into hers, his rage growing again,
his frustration at her unwillingness to listen boiling inside him.

'No . . . No . . .'

'Then you can go to hell in a handcart for all I care, carrying
that pride and bloody determination on your shoulders, with
your empty belly flapping against your backbone. Oh, Jesus,
go.'

He turned violently away, unable to face her for a moment
longer so great was his anger and – what was it? – this biting,
clawing thing that ate at his guts.

When he turned she had gone.

She was never to remember how she retraced her way down the
outside steps of his office through the dense white cloud that
had her in its clutches the moment she shut the door. It was like
stepping off a roof into space where there was no point of focus
so that even as she clung to the rail and put her foot to the
cobbled ground she had no idea in which direction she should
move to get out of the boatyard and on to the short road beyond

the gate to the landing stage from where the steamers crossed the river to the Liverpool side. She could hear muffled sound coming from every direction and she stood perfectly still doing her best to get her bearings. There were whistles, fog-horns, hooters off to her right, sounds that surely came from the river where ships, boats, ferry steamers were doing their best to warn other vessels of their presence, so if she moved in that direction she should find the gate out of the yard. There were other noises closer to the building where she hesitated at the foot of the steps, men's voices drifting eerily from every corner of the yard where they were presumably doing their best to continue to work in the appalling conditions.

'. . . give us a shout, Fred,' one cried hoarsely, 'or I'll never find me way back . . .'

'. . . over 'ere, Bert. I'm in't shed on't . . .'

'. . . know tha', yer daft sod, but where in 'ell . . .'

'. . . I'll be in't bloody river at this rate . . .'

'. . . blast this bloody . . .'

'. . . 'ow am I ter put bloody rivets in when I can't see buggers . . .'

The figure of a workman loomed up beside her carrying a length of wood over his shoulder, starting violently as he almost bumped into her.

'Jesus Christ, lass,' he gasped, for even on a clear and sunny day one did not expect to find a female hovering at the bottom of the steps that led to the owner's office. 'What the 'ell are yer doin' 'ere? Yer shouldn't be standin' about, chuck, an' in this lot,' indicating the white blanket that enveloped them. ' 'Ow did yer . . . ?' he continued but she smiled in the general direction of his face and lifted her hand as if to brush away the haze which felt like cobwebs clinging to her face.

'If you could just direct me to the gate,' she said politely.

'Chuck, I dunno where bloody gate is meself.'

His face creased and he lowered the length of wood to the

ground, wiping his hands down his trousers. 'Christ only knows 'ow we're ter work terday, lerr alone gerr 'ome. Master should lerrus go.' But even as he spoke he realised he was addressing a fog-filled nothing, for the strange female had gone.

She tripped over so many unseen objects on her way across the yard she felt as though she had been in an accident. Piles of wood struck her shins and even through the thickness of her cloak she felt the skin break. She fell across a great pile of logs which were as tall as herself and found to her consternation that as she tipped over once more she was in a small boat, a rowing boat that was being built for some purpose, but at last she realised she was at the gate and turned left, which she knew would lead her to the landing stage, hugging the wall until she reached it.

There was a crowd there already, waiting for the ferry, jostling one another with apprehension, for the sounds of the anchored ships in the river was alarming, businessmen who worked on the Liverpool side and even some women as the ferry drew up cautiously to the landing stage. The drawbridge clattered down and the ferry emptied, and with the other surging passengers she crossed it. She found a quiet corner forward and she sat down on the slatted seat, feeling nothing, her mind empty, her heart empty of all but the vicious pain of knowing that she would never see Lucas Barrie again.

33

The *Alexander*, a large sailing ship belonging to Messrs S. and M. Cassell of Liverpool, had arrived in the river from Calcutta early the previous day. She was in charge of the pilot and was brought to anchor at four thirty in the morning a little to the west of mid-stream between the entrance to Alfred Dock and the Seacombe landing stage. Besides the sailing ship a good many other vessels, steamships, tugs and river craft were anchored in the river as the fog became even more dense. The clanging of bells, the anxious hooting wail of horns and the shrill sound of frantic whistles, muffled by the fog, boomed and shrieked, one minute seeming close at hand and the next far away, so that those who boarded the boat were disorientated. These came from the boats anchored in the river, which were taking every precaution to warn the steam ferries under way of their vicinity.

Gilly was oblivious to everything but her pain which centred somewhere in her chest and spread over her whole body so that even her hair, stuffed carelessly beneath her bonnet, hurt her. She sank down on to the slatted wooden bench that lay along the rail on both sides of the boat and now that her anger was spent and what she had come to do had been accomplished, she felt that she could withdraw into the great emptiness that was the hole left by Lucas and in which she must hide from the world. When the misted blankness had evaporated from her mind she must start to plan her life again, build it up into a worthwhile existence – for it would be no more than that without Lucas, an existence – that would fill her empty days and nights. She felt a great yearning to have the weeks and months pass so that the pain would lessen, for it was said that time healed all wounds and she must force herself to believe it and yet there was in her a refusal to accept that she would never see him again. She was lost and frightened, shivering with what seemed to be the clammy cold of the fog but which she knew was nothing to do with the weather. She sat like a marble statue, her eyes fixed on the wall of white nothingness that surrounded the boat but seeing only Lucas's face, and when a voice loomed at her from the deck beside her she could not bring herself, for the moment, back to the present.

'Yer'd be best in't cabin, miss,' the male voice said, emanating from the indistinct figure of a crew member who hovered beside her. 'It'd not be ser cold for yer there. All the other ladies 'ave gone inside. Will I show yer? We'll be castin' off in a minnit.' His voice was polite.

She stood up obediently. She would have jumped over the rail and into the invisible water had he suggested it, and he put his face close to hers, for it seemed to him the young lady was not herself. But then could you blame her. Anyone with a bit of sense would be frightened in these conditions. He was himself and he was an experienced sailor. They shouldn't be on the bloody river, in his opinion, not in this, and was thankful to have learned from Jack Murphy, another member of the crew, that this was to be the last ferry to the Pier Head landing stage in Liverpool until the fog lifted.

There were shouts, phantom-like, as they cast off. The ferry's whistle sounded and with a slight shudder *Jewel*, as the ferry boat was called, edged her way from the landing stage and into the river. There were passengers, all men, on the deck, fidgeting about, wondering, it was obvious, if they had made a mistake in leaving the safety of their own homes in this terrible gloomy and frightening shadow that lay about them. They were men of business with concerns to run, merchants and commercial men, clerks, some of them, in busy offices and could not afford to miss a day's work. The *Jewel* was already half an hour late in leaving Seacombe and then when they reached Liverpool they had to find their way through this appalling invisibility to their place of work. They lined the rails, peering into the murkiness with great intensity as though the progress of the steamer depended on them.

Gilly allowed herself to be shown into the cabin, and sat down on a padded leather seat next to a matronly woman who clasped her umbrella in front of her with both hands, huddling in her warm cloak, and turned every few seconds to look out of the window at the backs of the men and the murk ahead of them.

'Eeh, I wish I 'adn't bothered,' she complained nervously, 'but our Bob sent across last night ter say our Lizzie 'ad started. It's 'er first and I couldn't not go, could I?' She turned again to look out of the window and then smiled tremulously at Gilly as though waiting for her to say something comforting.

'No, of course not. No, indeed,' Gilly answered in a lifeless voice so that the woman, forgetting her own troubles for a moment, peered at her from under the brim of her sensible black bonnet.

'Are yer all right, chuck?' she asked kindly.

'Yes, thank you.' But she wasn't, of course, for she wanted to moan and rock backwards and forwards in the age-old rhythm of grieving women.

The boat crept forward and in the bow the most experienced and watchful lookout squinted into the murk. The *Jewel* was registered to carry 500 passengers but, probably owing to the weather, there were only 300 on board, most of them travelling from New Brighton, Egremont, Liscard and Seacombe. Gilly's companion, who seemed inclined to talk since she was very evidently nervous, told her how difficult it had been to get from home to the landing stage. Her husband had begged her not to go and if it had not been for their Lizzie, it being her first, she would never have ventured forth.

The master of the vessel, Captain Rhodes, was an old, steady and most trustworthy servant of the company and he kept the *Jewel* at a slow pace across the river, picking his way through the craft that loomed ahead of him. The tide was nearly at flood and there was a strong current and it was not until the vessel was nearly at mid-stream that disaster struck. Suddenly from the fore part of the *Jewel* there came a shout of, 'Look out, there is a vessel ahead. Go back, go back.' As the voice rang out every woman in the cabin stood up and began to gabble as they made a rush for the entrance and the men on the deck also began to panic, blocking the deck and impeding the exit of the ladies. Some climbed the steps on to the bridge where Captain Rhodes yelled at them to go back to the deck and to stay calm, which it seemed no one was able to do. Others climbed on to the paddle box, the boards around the paddle wheel, hoping this vantage point would keep them from the terrible waters beneath. There was utter panic and Gilly found herself carried along with the rest who had no idea what they should do. She felt completely calm, which was strange in view of the pandemonium around her. It was as though the worst had already happened to her and what was taking place here could be nothing to be afraid of.

It was then that the first woman began to scream. She held a baby in her arms, a squirming bundle from which at one end poked a red face and joined its mother's cries. Other ladies made unintelligible sounds of distress, dragging at gentlemen's sleeves and begging to be told that they were safe, but when the ship loomed up in front of them even the most phlegmatic lost control. The bowsprit of the vessel with which they were about to collide hit the funnel of the *Jewel* and with a horrid and fascinating leisureliness it tipped sideways and downwards towards the prow. The whole space from brow to stern was thickly peopled with panic-stricken passengers, milling about like sheep harried by an excited dog and dozens of them, peering forward into the fog to get a glimpse of the ship they had collided with were in the path of its downward descent. It fell with a great crashing din, catching those who were in its merciless way and crushing them to the deck. As it went it knocked several passengers into the river. The sounds of their cries were pitiful as those who went overboard were carried away on the strong flood tide up the river. A second shock shook the *Jewel* as the *Alexander*, swinging round with the force of the collision, hit the starboard quarter, caving in the timber, causing such an ear-splitting burst of noise that those still on their feet became paralysed and silent with terror.

It was as though the tumult of the splintering wood had sounded a death knell to those who were now eddying about the deck and in the rush for the lifeboats men were knocking women aside. The woman with the baby, clinging to it with one arm, not realising that the mite was now upside down, climbed on to the rail and attempted to climb over it to the *Alexander* which had drawn up to the *Jewel* and where seamen were shouting to those aboard to jump. They threw ropes and lifebuoys and several men, unimpeded by the full skirts of the women, managed to catch either a rope or the hand of one of the *Alexander's* crew and get aboard, but the woman with the baby, stretching out her hand in desperate appeal, slithered between the two boats and, her face a mask of terror, her mouth a wide hole, threw her baby back to where where she had been standing on the deck and instinctively Gilly caught it.

'Holy Mother of God,' the prospective grandmother moaned, crossing herself feverishly, turning for a moment to look at Gilly who held the baby, now quiet, before she climbed the rail and did her best to reach the stretched-out hands of those on the *Alexander*. Like the infant's mother she slipped and fell between the two boats into the icy river. Both women disappeared, dragged down into the depths by the weight of their skirts.

Cries came from the front of the ship where someone was shrieking for a doctor, since there were injured there and probably some dead. One gentleman, more compassionate than the panic-stricken men who cared only to save themselves, moved forward and tied his muffler round the bleeding leg of a young man who lay still as death and from the bridge the captain's voice could be heard exhorting his passengers to stay calm. There was no danger, it seemed, for the *Jewel* was returning to the landing stage, he shouted, and would make it despite the damage to the hull if they would just stay calm.

Gilly placed the silent baby on the seat and removed her bulky skirt. She had seen two women dragged down and the survival instinct, which still was strong in her even in her anguished state, told her that should she find herself in the water she would have more of a chance without it. She had got hold of a lifebuoy, fighting off the man who did his best to get it from her, and had it about her, the baby in her arms, when the man, maddened with fear, crashed against her in his attempt to reach the other ship and with a low cry she and the child toppled over the rail and hit the icy waters of the river.

Lucas sat at his desk, elbows on the plans he had been studying, his head in his hands and groaned. He didn't believe it, of course, for he would get her back no matter what she said. It was so bloody ridiculous, this tale about Angela Ryan wanting him and because of it destroying Gilly's business. It would not have done her reputation much good, certainly, but when they were married, and he meant to marry her if he had to drag her to the church by her hair, she would be above reproach, as virtuous as the women who now blamed her. They had both lost their tempers, he admitted that, and had said things they should not have said but goddammit, he would make it right and there was no time like the present. He would—

He was startled when his clerk burst into his office, his expression one of great excitement with that strange vicarious emotion that strikes those who are not involved in a tragedy but are determined to enjoy it none the less.

'What the devil . . . ?' Lucas began but the clerk spoke over him.

'There's been an accident, sir, a dreadful collision.'

Lucas sprang to his feet. 'A collision? What sort of a collision?' imagining two of his wagons pulled by shire horses meeting head-on in the yard, but the clerk continued to tell a garbled tale.

'Two boats on't river. A ferry boat an' a . . . the fog, yer see, an' what . . .'

For a moment Lucas turned to stone, his face ashen, his mouth open and ready to wail that it could not be his love, not his love who had left here only minutes ago heading, he presumed, for the ferry but . . . what?

'. . . in't river, sir, they're sayin' the fog, yer couldn't see yer 'and in front o' yer face. Shouldn't 'ave sailed in my opinion an' fellow what just ran 'ere ter tell us ses there's some drowned.'

'Sweet Jesus Christ,' his master whispered then pushed past him and ran through the office where other clerks were clustered talking, aquiver with excitement, dashed for the door and down the steps into the unrecognisable obscurity of the once familiar yard. Without hesitation, as though some inward sense guided him, he ran through the impermeability towards the gate and out into the street where, to his surprise, others stumbled towards the landing stage, crashing into one another in their haste, picking themselves up and continuing their clumsy way. It was as though their blindness made them like animals in the dark, feeling their way to their goal and he realised that these people were on the same errand as himself.

There had probably been many travellers on the ferry boat and these who crashed along with him were on the same mission as himself, seeking news of the disaster.

There were flares on the landing stage to guide whoever sought news of the collision. A great crowd had gathered, all, he found, who had relatives who had left home that morning to sail across the water to Liverpool, the flares making a halo of strange light for those who gathered at the shipping office where a flustered official was doing his best to answer their frantic questions. Where was the ferry boat? What was her name? Had the boat sunk? Were there any survivors? And at the front of this babbling crowd stood Lucas Barrie who would have shoved the lot of them into the water to get the answers he needed from the bedevilled clerk. There was a constant noise of frantic voices as everyone tried to make theirs the loudest, then: 'She's landed!' someone cried from the back of the crowd and at once all those gabbling the names of their loved ones turned in the direction of the voice.

The number of lost was said to be sixty or seventy but it seemed the ferry boat had limped back to the Wallesey Cattle Stage further along the river and at once, with Lucas in the lead, the crowd turned, following the one who seemed to be able to penetrate the curtain of the fog as he ran, *ran*, mind you, along the road that led to the landing stage. They had a job to keep up with him, some holding on to the coat tails of others, anything that might guide them to where the tall, frantic fellow led.

The *Jewel* was tied up at the landing stage and even through the dense fog that blotted out the shape of the boat Lucas could see the damage to the hull and the smoke stack that lay across the deck. 'Oh, God, oh, God,' he was repeating though he was not aware of it. Passengers were slowly making their way down the gangway on to the cattle stage, most of them shaking, the women weeping, and he thrust his way to the front of the crowd, standing at the foot of the gangplank waiting for her to come down and, by God, straight into his waiting arms where she would stay for the rest of her life, and this time he would not listen to any bloody daft thing she had to say. He was terrified, his brain almost beyond reasoning, for all he could think of was that his dearest, his darling girl would soon come down to him. One after the other they came, dragged, most of them, into someone's arms.

'Oh Jesus God,' he moaned out loud as they came and she was not among them. The company did not, of course, know the names of those on board and until everyone had been accounted for by their frantic relatives they would not know who was missing.

The last faltering woman came down the gangway, her hat gone, her face as white as the fog around them and then there were no more. The captain stood at the top, looking down at the few who as yet had not found the person they were looking for and was surprised and offended when the tall chap pushed his way past the seaman posted at the foot of the gangway and began to mount it.

'Gilly, Gilly, for God's sake, woman, don't do this to me. Come out at once.'

'Sir, sir, there is no one left on board.'

'Don't talk daft, man. This was the last boat to Liverpool, I was told. She must be on it.'

The captain's face was compassionate as he did his best to grab the frantic man's arm but Lucas eluded him and began to run along the deck towards the fallen smoke stack. There medical men summoned from the hospital attended those who had been injured or, worse, crushed to death and when he insisted on studying the bodies, and the faces of those poor souls who were bleeding, moaning, or lying completely still on the stained deck, there was not one who could restrain him. The captain, who had followed him, signalled that they were to let him alone and was glad when the poor chap turned away, his face grey, sunken, his eyes like black holes, but indicating that the one he sought was not there.

'Where the bloody hell is she?' he roared as though the captain had her hidden somewhere.

'Sir . . .'

'Where is she?' Lucas snarled, ready to strike anyone who stood in his path.

'Sir, if you would allow me . . .'

'Where is she, goddammit?'

'Sir, there were—'

'What . . . what? Out with it, man.'

The captain was reluctant to say what he had to say but this man must be made to see that whoever he looked for was not on his damaged boat. His own face was gaunt with shock and grief, for he had a family of his own and how would he feel if . . .

'Say it, man.' Lucas's voice was dangerous.

'There were several who went . . .'

Lucas grabbed him by the lapels. 'Went where?'

'Overboard, sir. They tried to get on the ship we collided with and fell between. There was panic . . .'

'I won't believe she is . . .' But Lucas Barrie's resolve was weakening as the anguish that threatened to overwhelm him savaged his body.

'Search the boat if you will, sir, but it has already been done and—'

'By God, I will . . .' And for ten wasted minutes Lucas Barrie ran frantically from cabin to cabin, up to the bridge, down even into the engine room and they left him to it, devastated themselves by his suffering. He did not find her and without a word he leaped down the gangway and through the fog, which was lifting slightly, towards the small landing where the river gigs and flatboats were tied up. Some of them had already bravely volunteered to move out on to the river to search for the missing and when the demented man jumped on board a gig and without a word untied the rope and pushed off they had no choice but to go with him.

'Fifty guineas to the man who finds her,' he yelled. 'She's out there somewhere, for she's so bloody determined she'd not let a thing like this finish her off.'

'Who, sir?' one gig-man ventured to ask.

'The woman I'm to marry by the week's end, you fool.'

'Right, sir. Now don't worry, if she's out there we'll find her.'

'Gilly . . . Gilly . . . Gilly,' Lucas began to shout, his eyes doing their best to split the whiteness that rolled about them and so they began to shout too, her name echoing across the waters, sounding like some lament for those who are already gone.

She was so cold she could not feel the lower half of her body. It was November and the waters were at their winter's coldest. The lifebuoy, which was securely fastened around her body beneath her armpits, held her head and shoulders above the water and, perched like a limpet on a rock, the baby was tucked on the top of it under her chin, both her hands clutching its clothing. The mother had tied a shawl round its body, the ends, now wet, fastened so securely it kept the garment about the child. It made no sound and when she managed to get a glimpse of its face it appeared to be asleep.

'Don't let it be dead, please,' she whispered, then realised that whispering would do no good, not out here in this grey world. She must shout as loud as she could, for the river was teeming with boats and surely one would hear her and pick them up. The river was on the flood and the current was carrying her and her burden upstream where, unfortunately, there would be fewer vessels but it would be on the turn soon and she would be carried downstream towards the . . . the . . . mouth of the river, the bay and . . . Oh, dear sweet Christ, the open sea! If that was to happen she would simply float into the Irish Sea and never be seen again. Oh, Lucas, Lucas, please don't let me die. I will be just what you want me to be but please don't abandon me as I begged you to. I love you, I love the life you would have given me and I will not give it up. My own bloody independence, my stupid anger which was totally, woefully mistaken, has led me to this and I deserve to be abandoned but don't, please don't . . .

'Lucas,' she shrieked, the volume of her voice in its ear waking the baby, who added its voice to hers. 'Lucas . . . Lucas . . .'

For a second, no more, it seemed to her that he answered, for her own name floated through the white shroud about her but she continued to float mercilessly onward, her own voice the only one she could hear. She screamed in terror then, but every time she opened her mouth the water slopped into it and she felt that she would drown. But even though she was growing hoarse she continued to call his name. She even shook the baby, for its tiny wailing added to her feeling that surely someone would hear them.

Her strength was going and she became afraid that she would let go of her precious burden. The child was a symbol, an omen, a reason for her to live, for if she let go of it the poor creature would float away and then sink to the bottom of this vast river. As long as she held on, to life, to hope, and to the child, she would be saved and the infant with her. She could not let it drown, or its poor mother who had found, at the last moment, the strength and will to throw it to her, would have died in vain. She must live so that it could live and if the mother had died then something of her would live on again in her child.

She thought she had gone to sleep then and was surely dreaming, for the baby had suddenly gone from her arms. She began to scream, to beat round her in a circle looking for the child. It must not drown. *It must not drown.* The baby must save her because if she gave it life, so it would return hers.

Suddenly she began to feel warmth and wanted to cry as she must be already dead and gone to heaven where the sun shone, but the strong arms round her and the strong voice in her ear whispered that she was safe.

'The baby?' she murmured, then knew no more. She had been in the water just over three hours.

34

It was Jem who kept her with them, and though Lucas was devastated that it was not his name she called out in the night he was a big enough man to feel a great thankfulness to the individual whom she had loved as a child and who loved her, as a child and as a woman, for bringing her, even intermittently, from the deep well of silence in which she dwelled.

It was his gig that had found her. The men in it with him had begged him to give up, for no woman could survive this long in the icy waters of the winter river. She would have been driven upriver beyond Jericho Shore until the tide turned and then back towards the dock area of Liverpool where, as the fog slowly cleared, she would have passed dozens of river craft on the lookout, not only for her but other passengers who had gone overboard. He would not give up, he bellowed, and until he saw her body he would not believe she was dead and if it took the rest of his life he would find her.

One of the drowned passengers was found still clinging to the *Jewel*. A seaman belonging to another vessel observed a dark figure under the water attached to the sponson, a triangular platform abaft of the paddle box. A search had been made and a young man had been found with his arms firmly clenched round the iron stay. An elderly gentleman, still clutching his umbrella and with his pipe in his mouth, was found clutching a lifebuoy, floating unconscious in the Sloyne and was picked up by the steam launch of HMS *Resistance*.

She had got as far as the entrance to the river when they

found her and in another half an hour would have been in the Crosby Channel. It was the wail of the baby that alerted them and when he plucked her from the water her arms were still bent in the cradling position she had adopted when she and the baby fell into the water. The baby was taken from her but her arms remained in their curve as he ran with her across the sands at Bootle and up the steps to the promenade.

'Run on ahead, man, and get me a cab,' he gasped to one of the gig-men who had been with him from the moment he commandeered their boat. Her head fell back against his arm and her hair streamed like dank seaweed almost to the ground and behind him another of the men carried the weakly wailing baby. When they reached the cab he flung himself into it, holding her sodden, icy-cold body against his, which was equally wet, for it was he who had jumped into the water to lift her into the gig, and the gig-man followed him. They sat facing one another, one with the woman, the other with the baby. When they arrived at Duke Street Mrs Collins flung open the door with Bridie the kitchen maid beside her and as Lucas sank to his knees in the hallway with the seemingly lifeless body of Gilly Logan in his arms, she and Bridie took her from him without a word and somehow between them carried her upstairs.

'Drive like the devil for Mr Jenkins at the infirmary,' he managed to say to the fascinated cabbie, 'and on your way back go to Seymour Street, number 19, and fetch Mrs Logan. Tell her . . . tell her . . .'

'Aye, sir,' and the cabbie set off as though he were on the racecourse at Aintree.

'What shall I do wi't babby?' the gig-man asked diffidently and with an effort that was superhuman Lucas Barrie turned his attention to the man who held the child, whose name was Nick Murphy, he said respectfully, for he admired this man and his perseverance.

'Kitchen . . .' He got to his feet and the two men took the baby into the warmth of the heart of the house and between them managed to remove its little clothes. When they had done so it proved to be female but since they had gone through so much together, he and the man, they were not embarrassed. Without a word the sailor placed the baby on his knee and, taking one of Mrs Collins's rough kitchen towels began to rub the little girl vigorously with it until, with a weak cry of protest, she lifted her fist and opened her eyes. She was a plump baby, which had probably stood her in good stead the doctor said later. When the man, who told Lucas that he had six children of his own, two of them girls, remarked that they might try her with a drop of milk if he had such a thing, Lucas looked vaguely round him wondering where it was kept in Mrs Collins's shining kitchen.

At that moment the doorbell rang and when, falteringly, for he was beyond exhaustion, he opened it to reveal not only the doctor but Queenie, Flo, his sister Anne and Jem Wilson, the house was suddenly filled with the promise of hope and life for the two who had been so miraculously saved. The doctor and Queenie went at once up the stairs and Flo, with a great deal of tutting, as though to say what the devil were they doing with the poor child, whoever she was, took her from Nick's arms and began to instruct Anne on what she needed. A feeding bottle from the chemist on the corner and she was to ask what should be fed to a baby of – how old did Anne think the child was? – six months, seven? fresh milk and a warm shawl to wrap her in. And if Mr Barrie didn't go upstairs at once and get into a hot bath she would not be responsible for the outcome.

'Get this man's full name and address,' Lucas managed to mumble, indicating the gig-man, and with a nod of thanks he stumbled upstairs and within a few minutes was sound asleep in a tub full of hot water. Jem found him there and with Anne's help managed to get him into bed, all the while exhorting his wife to remember she was carrying a child and was not to lift her brother. Lucas did not notice that Jem was wearing spectacles.

For the next few days Gilly lay in Lucas's bed, unaware that she was there. She had been bathed, her hair washed and her legs, which it seemed would never carry her again, massaged gently with warm oil on Mr Jenkins's orders. They had been immersed in the icy waters of the river for just over three hours and the very blood in them appeared to have frozen. They were white, the skin shrivelled, the toes on her feet in a state that the doctor described – had they been subjected to snow and ice – as frost-bitten and might have to be amputated. She lay unseeing, uncaring, unknowing, even of her mother who sat by her bed and would only be persuaded to leave it by her loving friend Flo, the only one she would trust to watch over her child, beside Jem, of course.

Downstairs the baby thrived, a dear, plump little thing with dark glossy curls, bright blue eyes which blinked at everyone who came within her orbit, with long, silky lashes fanning her flushed satin cheeks. She had small, fat hands with questing fingers and two tiny teeth no bigger than pearls which shone in the pinkness of her gums. She seemed to have suffered no lasting harm, taking placidly to the bottle fetched hastily from the chemist in which were mixed milk and the Mellin's Food for Infants and Invalids the chemist recommended. She was happy to be nursed by whoever took her and they all waited sadly for someone to come and claim her. By the end of the week no one had and by then Gilly Logan's name was on everyone's lips and the flowers began to arrive.

The first were from Miss Helen Moore who expressed her admiration, indeed affection for Gilly and hoped she would soon be up and about as Miss Moore was sadly in need of a new outfit for Christmas. They came from Mrs Margaret Clarke, Mrs Lucinda Braithwaite, Mrs Atkinson, Mrs Lawley, Mrs

Edith Raines and her daughter Laura, all with the same message of goodwill and all indicating that the moment she was well enough they were hoping to patronise her salon again. Mr Field at the Royal Bank in Dale Street sent roses which had been grown in his own hothouse and even Perce and Ginger at the market had clubbed together to send her flowers, and a basket of fruit came from Mrs Fletcher who had provided her with her first materials.

It was perhaps those that came from the most unexpected quarter that touched them all, even Gilly when she was told of them, from the inhabitants of Rose Alley who scraped together farthings and halfpennies to purchase a bunch of wilting Michaelmas daisies from a stall in the market with an ill-spelled, ill-written message of good wishes.

'Rose Alley,' she whispered, 'why has this happened? What . . .'

'It is in all the newspapers, Lovedy,' Jem murmured, his face close to hers so that he could see the blurred outline of her pale face through the new spectacles Mr Jenkins had prescribed for him. They were thick and his eyes looked enormous behind them but he could see, his sight, which had been returning gradually over the last few months, now magnified so that he could get about on his own. The good doctor had told him that the nerves to his eyes, which had been damaged by the blow to his head, had healed and his sight would improve from now on, though he would probably always have to wear spectacles.

'You are described as a heroine and the whole of Liverpool is singing your praises.'

'But why, Jem? Why?'

'Don't you remember the baby?'

'The baby?'

'You saved the baby.' But she turned her head away and gazed out of the window of Lucas's room at the bare branches of the trees in the railed gardens that divided Duke Street. She

had lost interest. Jem sighed and turned to look helplessly at
Queenie who bowed her head and allowed her tears to slip
silently down her gaunt cheeks. The doctor had told them that
she had been through a harrowing experience and that her
mind could not cope with memories of it and so she lay in her
bed, her mind blank, and even Lucas who hung about outside
her door was not admitted.

'Leave her, Mr Barrie,' the doctor told him. 'You cannot
force her to remember you, to come back from that quiet,
peaceful place where her mind has put her.'

'But I love her and she loves me. We are to be married, tell
her, Jem.' He swung round to the quiet man who sat in the
warm kitchen drinking the broth Mrs Collins put in his hand.
His wife was sleeping on Bridie's bed, warned by the doctor
that if she didn't rest he would not guarantee her pregnancy a
happy outcome.

'Lucas . . .' Jem was sorry for the man who he had always
considered to be his rival for the affections of Gilly Logan. But
strangely, Jem had come to value the sweet, shy woman who
was his wife, the sister of this suffering man and the mother of
his unborn child. He had gone through the fires of hell, the
blindness, the helplessness, the frustration and had come out
the other side with his hand firmly held by his wife and he knew
that without her he might have faltered and fallen.

'Lucas, leave her for a bit. Let her ask for you when she is
ready.' But she asked for no one but Jem. Not even her mother.
It was as though the time she and Jem had shared when they
had lived in Rose Alley and he had been her sole companion,
her champion, her teacher, was all that was bearable to her and
they grew used to her cries in the night calling for Jem in a voice
that was not hers but the voice of a child.

Lucas grew old before their eyes and Queenie thought he
might go the way her daughter seemed to be heading. To
everyone's surprise, he seemed to have taken to the baby whom

they named Jewel after the ferry boat from which she had been rescued and when the authorities came round to enquire after her, for surely she belonged to some family, Lucas told them shortly that he and his family, intimating that the Barries were involved, would care for her until someone claimed her. And then he would want proof, he said coldly. No, she was not to go to the orphanage until that date. She would be looked after here where . . . where . . . He wanted to say, where she was already loved, but he knew the authorities might look on that as peculiar so he added that there were five women in the house who were perfectly capable of caring for the child until then.

'But, sir, she belongs to someone . . .' the tight-collared gentleman said.

'Then where are they? It is two weeks now and no one has come forward. Leave her where she is and if you need proof of our respectability then I suggest you apply to my father who is the head of Barrie and Hughes, the shipbuilders. You have heard of them, I trust?'

'Oh, indeed, sir. I am sure there will be no need for that but we will keep an eye on the situation.'

'Do that.'

He was shown out by the gaunt-faced son of Herbert Barrie, who was a man of influence in the city, wondering what had happened to the chap who had been described to him as the most eligible bachelor in Liverpool, handsome, charming, a great favourite with the ladies, which was why he had been sent round to check on him, for it seemed implausible that such a man would be interested in a young baby. He had found him to be none of these things. He had saved the 'heroine of Liverpool' from a watery death and the baby with her, and in a way was considered a hero himself but he looked like a man on the edge of an abyss to him.

On the northern outskirts of Liverpool at Rosemount Lodge a furious tempest was getting under way in the shape of Angela

Ryan who was in fierce contest with her father, and the subject was the very man who was at that moment sitting before his drawing-room fire cradling a sleepy baby in his arms.

'But, Papa, they are saying the woman is, if not dying, then out of her mind and surely if that is the case should we not do our best to help poor Lucas to recover from what he has suffered in rescuing her? The newspapers are making much of her.' A sneer lifted her lip and for a moment the pretty face of Joseph Ryan's daughter was distorted. 'Dear God, they seem determined to make a saint out of her as though what she did was in any way out of the ordinary. There were others who nearly drowned and some who *did* drown. There is a list of the missing on the board outside the shipping office and I cannot help but wonder why this woman should be singled out. We can do nothing about that but we can do something about Lucas. Let us have him and his family to dine. Celebrate his bravery with our friends and his and when—'

Joseph Ryan held up his hand wearily and his pretty daughter stopped speaking in surprise.

'Papa?'

'Enough, Angela, enough. I have done some things . . . things I should not have done because you are my daughter and I love you above all others—'

'Well, then, do this and I promise that by the year's end Lucas Barrie and I will be engaged.'

Angela's face was flushed with anticipated triumph. They were in her father's study where a good fire burned and the flames were reflected in the hunting prints on the walls though Joe Ryan, as he once had been, had never hunted. It turned her dainty white gown with its blue ribbons to peach and put a glow in her bright ringlets but her papa was acting very strangely and she did not like it.

'You can do no more, my dear, and neither can I. It is known all over Liverpool that Lucas Barrie is in love with this woman and is in fact fading away because she is not recovering.'

'Nonsense. I cannot believe it.'

'She lives in his house. Her family lives in his house and he has not been seen at the shipyard since the day of the collision. His father and John Hughes are hard pressed to manage without him and it has been rumoured that Herbert had threatened to cut him out of the business if he does not return. Do you want to marry a penniless man, should he consent to it?'

'Mr Barrie will not—'

'Stop it, Angela. Stop it.'

'No, no, Papa, I will not.'

'You will, my darling.'

She began to scream her temper then and in the drawing room her mother cowered and the servants clung together in the kitchen, for it seemed that their master was, for the first time in his life, denying his daughter something she coveted.

She was alone in Lucas's bed when it began to snow, the white flakes drifting like petals beyond the window and for the first time her attention was caught and her mind dragged from its depths by the wonder and loveliness of it. The room, a strictly masculine room, was plainly furnished with a washstand on which stood a matching set of jug and bowl and soap dish in white with no pattern of any sort to adorn it. There was a tall wardrobe, a comfortable leather chair, a cheval glass, long velvet curtains the colour of ox-blood at the window and a couple of rugs scattered on the polished wooden floor. On a stand beneath the window was a silver-backed clothes brush decorated with a simple border and a silver-backed glass box containing several tie-pins and a cologne bottle. That was all.

Gilly sat up and looked about her. Her mother was asleep in the deep leather chair. A fire blazed in the blackleaded grate and the room was warm. The snow whirling in big, fat flakes drew her attention to the window and slowly she slipped from the bed and moved towards it. Her legs felt weak but otherwise she thought she was on the mend. She had no idea what day it was, or what hour and it did not seem to matter. She just wanted to look out on the snow.

The square was deserted, the snow which was falling in thicker and thicker swirls stealthily deadening and muffling the progress of a cab that turned the corner from Hanover Street. The driver was up to his ears in an enormous cape and his horse had a blanket thrown over it, but nevertheless they were both coated in white. Its wheels made no sound in the deepening, dazzling whiteness and the trees in the gardens were exquisite in their mantle of silvered white. The cab stopped beneath the window and she was surprised and pleased to see Jem alight from it, surprised since she had not known he had left the house. She was not afraid without him as once she might have been, for the love she bore Lucas and which she knew was returned made her strong.

She sat down on a small stool set by the window and watched the curtain of white fly past the panes so that it blotted out the gardens and the trees and the slowly disappearing horse and cab. Putting her chin on her hand, she stared dreamily through the window where the snow slithered gracefully down the glass then, with a small smile at her mother, she threw a shawl that lay across the bed round her shoulders and opened the door, closing it behind her so as not to disturb Mam.

There was the sound of voices from downstairs and she heard someone say he was sleeping in the drawing room and another answer that he would not disturb him then but would go right up. A figure on the stairs, for some unexplained reason, made her step back behind the curtain at the long window at the head of the landing and she smiled when she saw it was Jem. Dear Jem who had got her through so much in her life, but he was not the one she was looking for. She felt well, rested, peaceful and wondered why that should be. Had she been somewhere? She couldn't remember and it didn't really matter, for she was home again now or would be in a very short time. It was as though she had been sleeping, like the person downstairs, the one she was looking for and had woken refreshed and ready to get on with her life, the life that lay ahead of her.

Her feet were bare and made no sound on the stair carpet. From the kitchen she could hear women's voices, one of whom was Flo and she wondered what Flo was doing here in Lucas's house but again it didn't seem to matter at this strange moment. Jem had gone up another flight of stairs and as he opened the door she heard him say, 'Have you had a good sleep, my love?' and a woman's voice answered sleepily, lovingly before the door closed.

The drawing-room door was closed and she was careful not to make a noise as she opened it. She wanted to look on him as he slept, as she had never looked on him before. When he had come to her at Remington Place he had never slept. They had never shared a night together and, in the true sense of the words, *slept* together in that perfect trust lovers put in one another during the dark night.

He was lying on the deep, low-backed leather chesterfield, his head on a cushion, his dark hair in an uncut tumble of dishevelled curls about his head. He had removed his jacket and tie and the top buttons of his shirt were undone to reveal a dark spring of chest curls at the base of his throat. His boots lay on the rug beside the sofa and his jacket was flung beside them.

She made a small sound in the back of her throat as she gazed on his sleeping face, for he looked so ill. He had obviously not shaved that day, which surprised her, as he was a meticulously tidy man, but the most surprising thing of all was the small, plump baby who was curled on his chest. One of his arms was round it protectively. It was a lovely baby dressed, though Gilly did not know it at the time, in a little gown that had been made by Anne for her coming child. It was too small and the infant's starfish hands and wrists stuck out of the sleeves which were halfway up its arms.

It was the baby. *The baby!* The one that Jem had talked of but in which at the time she had taken no interest. She had taken an interest in nothing, for her life had been over, finished from the moment she had struck out from Lucas's office to spend alone the lonely nights and days she had persuaded herself she wanted. Her salon. Her designs. Her customers. Her girls. *Her lonely life* without him in it. The waters of the Mersey had closed over her head in a merciful haze that day and she had rejoiced, but the baby, this baby, had kept her afloat and her confused mind had taken her away until this moment when she looked down on it and on him. Her love, her beloved, her future. It seemed complete to find them here together and though she didn't know the child, not yet, she felt that it . . . surely *she* would be part of it.

She bent her head and placed her lips on his but it was the baby who awoke, struggling to sit up to look at this interesting stranger whose hair was soft and tickling on her face. She grinned and a huge dimple was created in her rosy cheek, then reached out to grab a handful of this new person's hair. She chuckled and Lucas stirred. He opened his eyes and looked up at the two faces who had turned to smile into his and before their astonished gaze he began to weep. The baby's lip quivered and at once Lucas gathered her to him with one arm while the other went round Gilly.

'My love, oh, my love, my dearest love, you have come home.'

'Lucas . . .' burying her face in his neck, her glorious hair floating round him and the baby who fought her way out of it and chuckled.

'The baby . . .'

'Yes, my darling, meet Jewel.'

'Jewel! That was the name of the . . .' For a moment Gilly struggled to escape from his arm, and from the remembered feeling of horror the name of the ferry boat evoked, then she moved closer to him, her arm going about him and the child.

'We can't call her that, Lucas. It would forever bring back memories of . . .' She buried her head in his shoulder and the baby, who was held by his other arm, stared down at her with wide-eyed interest as though she were aware of the emotions that stirred in Gilly's heart.

Lucas pulled Gilly closer and though it was a bit of a tight fit, the three of them settled comfortably on the sofa. 'What do you suggest then, my love? I must say I have grown fond of her, as have we all. They can find no trace of anyone who lays claim to her and I thought we might . . .'

'Keep her?'

'If the authorities allow it, but she must have a name.'

'I believe Mam's mother, my grandmother who I never knew, was called Jacinth. God knows where *her* mother got it but I always liked it.'

'Jacinth, I like it too,' Lucas mused and neither of them seemed to think what a strange discussion this was after all that had happened to them. They were both aware that they had come to the end of the rock-strewn road they had walked for so long. That there was really no need even to talk about the future, for it was as fixed and certain as the child who had brought them together. The three of them, and the children they would have would go forward together and as if on cue, making the moment positive, the doorbell rang. They lay dreaming, scarcely aware of the commotion at the door and when the drawing-room door was thrust open aggressively all three sat up, startled, looking at the man who had entered.

'I've had enough of this, Lucas,' the gentleman at the door thundered, ignoring Mrs Collins who hovered at his back.

'That yard's going to pot without you there' – which was not strictly true though he was missed – 'and while your mother . . . well, I put my foot down and the sooner you wed this lass and get back to work the better. I see you've still got the baby so I suppose she must come too. There's a nice little house on the front near Jericho Beach and I told your mother . . .'

Lucas began to laugh and so did the baby who at first had been somewhat alarmed at the sight of the loud gentleman in the doorway.

'Father, I haven't even asked her yet, at least not recently, but when we do we'll choose our own house.'

'Lass, Gilly, isn't it, tell my lad you'll wed him and put us all out of our misery. I know you're over fond of that shop of yours but I reckon our Lucas won't say no to it if you say yes to *him*.'

Lucas looked down into the glowing face of the woman he had loved and fought with for so long, raising a questioning eyebrow. Gilly kissed him and nodded and the baby clapped her hands.

'Right, where's that woman?' Herbert Barrie roared, turning to find Mrs Collins at his back. 'Ah, there you are. Have you such a thing as a bottle of champagne in the house? You have. Good, then fetch it and we'll set a date for the wedding. I think your mother would fancy spring!'